suite
harmonic

suite
harmonic
A Civil War Novel of Rediscovery

EMILY MEIER

SKY SPINNER PRESS
SAINT PAUL, MINNESOTA

© 2011 by Sky Spinner Press
117 Mackubin Street
St. Paul, MN 55102
skyspinnerpress.com

Published in the United States of
America

Sky Spinner Press Books Distribution
through Itasca Books

itascabooks.com

ISBN 978-0-9836692-0-3

First Sky Spinner Press Printing, 2011

9 8 7 6 5 4 3 2 1

Library of Congress Catalog Control
Number: 2011909888

Cover and book design:
Jeenee Lee Design

Cover photograph:
"Eigner Cabin" © Historic New
Harmony/Southern Indiana University

Cover photograph modification:
Jeenee Lee

Civil War jacket:
Courtesy Minnesota Historical Society

For my grandchildren

CONTENTS

viii CHARACTERS
    viii *In the Field*
    ix *On the Homefront*
    xi *Miscellaneous Minor Characters*

   1 Northern Tennessee, February 1862
  39 New Harmony, Indiana, Late February and March 1862
103 Pittsburg Landing, Tennessee, Late March and Early April 1862
141 New Harmony, Indiana, April 1862
161 Camp near Monterey, Tennessee, May 7, 1862
177 Camp near Memphis, Tennessee, Late August and Early
     September 1862
195 New Harmony, Indiana, October 1862
213 Camp Davis Mills, Mississippi, Late November and
     December 1862
235 Memphis, Tennessee, June 1863
261 New Harmony, Indiana, July 1863
289 New Harmony, Indiana, November 1863
313 Southern Tennessee and Mississippi, December 1863
     and Early 1864
335 Decatur, Alabama, Spring and Summer 1864
357 The Siege of Atlanta, Late Summer 1864
375 New Harmony, Indiana, Fall 1864
391 Virginia, with the Eastern Army, Late March 1865
417 Virginia and Washington, D.C., Spring and Summer 1865
435 New Harmony, Indiana, Fall 1865 and Early Winter 1866
459 New Harmony, Indiana, February–September 1867
483 New Harmony, Indiana, 1868–1871
505 New Harmony, Indiana, February 2, 1880
521 New Harmony, Indiana, January 1, 1898

535 EPILOGUE
536 AUTHOR'S NOTE
537 ACKNOWLEDGMENTS

CHARACTERS
In the Field

Officers and Men of the 25th Indiana

Colonel James Veatch, regimental commander
Lieutenant Colonel William Morgan
Major John Foster
Major Jesse Walker, adjutant
Major John Walker, surgeon

Company A
Captain "Wash" Saltzman
Lieutenant Enoch Randolph, later captain
Lieutenant Absalom Boren, husband of Charlotte Sampson Boren and later captain
James P. Bennett, sergeant and later captain
Reverend John Heuring
Robert Clark
Felix Edmonds
JOHN GIVEN
George Ham, last captain Company A
Alex Hugo
John Hugo
Romeo Keister
Max Munte
Fred Perkey
Bill Reid, one of the band boys
Jacob Schaen
Henry Schafer
Bill Taylor
Levi Thrailkill, also on town list
George Tretheway
Dave Vint

Company B
Captain John Rheinlander, later lieutenant colonel of regiment
Captain Alexander Darling

Company F
Captain Victor Larkin
Robert Shannon, later captain
Albert Norcross

New Harmony Men in the 15th Indiana

Harry Beal (see Beal Family)
Godfrey Gundrum
Harry Husband
Vic Miller
Jim Rippeto

Officers and Men of the 208th Pennsylvania

Lieutenant Colonel William McCall

Company C
Captain Prosper Dalien
Lieutenant Albert Corl
Jimmy Cassady
Joshua Delancy
Patrick Feeney
Joe Feagan
Joe McAfee

Company D
Lieutenant F. W. Keller
John Gaugler

Company L
James O'Neal

On the Homefront

New Harmony Residents during the Civil War

Given Family
Emigrants from the townland of Drumboarty in County Donegal, Ireland
John Sr.
Margaret O'Donnell Given, his wife
JOHN JR.
CATHARINE (KATE)
Margaret
Denis
Mary
Charley
Absent Member: Bridget (Biddy), who died during the Potato Famine

Thrailkill Family
Jesse, Tennessee native and a member of one of the Owenite communities
Mary (Polly) Flora Thrailkill, his wife
Levi, one of John Given's two best friends
Caroline
Absent Members:
Mary Ellen Thrailkill Barton, resident of Galatia, Illinois, and mother of Mary Ann Barton and wife of Captain William Barton
Amaline, who died in the 1850s

Sampson Family
Employers of Margaret Mulhern, Margaret O'Donnell Given's niece

James, prominent New Harmony citizen and Feiba Peveli settler in Owenite period
Eliza Wheatcroft Sampson, his wife, Owenite, and daughter of Mary Maidlow, original Harmonist known for her home cures
Eliza Sampson Cox, wife of E. T. Cox, geologist
Charlotte Sampson Boren, wife of Absalom Boren
Mollie Sampson Owen, wife of Julian Dale Owen

Lichtenberger Family
Kate Given's employers
Adam, prominent town merchant
Caroline Beal Lichtenberger, his wife and daughter of John Beal
Alice
Mary
Eliza

Beal Family
John, Yorkshireman, carpenter, and builder of the Philanthropist, which brought Robert Owen and the "Boatload of Knowledge" from Philadelphia
Rose Ann Clark Beal, his wife
Mary, wife of Charles Slater, newspaperman
Caroline (see Lichtenberger Family)
Harry Beal, nephew of John Beal, and John Given's other best friend
Walter Beal, nephew of John Beal and cousin of Harry
Hectorina, Walter's wife

Fretageot Family

Achilles E. Fretageot, leading merchant in town, who was born in France to Madame Marie Duclos Fretageot, associate of Robert Owen's partner, William Maclure
Mary, his second wife
Alexander
Achilles H.
Ida and several other children

Other New Harmony Families

Armstrongs, Arnoldys, Blackburns, Boltons, Fauntleroys, Fords, Hugos, Marshals, McMunns, O'Neals, Owens, Perkeys, Smiths, Truscotts Wheatcrofts, Wiles, Wilseys

Other New Harmony Residents of Importance to the Story

Ann Bradley, woman John and half of New Harmony are in love with
Francis Cannon, childhood friend of John Given Sr., member of Owenite Preliminary Society and uncle to Ann Bradley
Michael McShane, John's cousin
Margaret Mulhern, niece who accompanied John Sr. and Catharine to America in 1855, and "help" for the Sampson family

New Harmony's First- and Second-Generation Descendants of Robert Owen

Children of Robert Dale and Mary Jane Robinson Owen: Florence Dale, Julian Dale, Rosamond Dale, and Ernest Dale Owen
Child of William and Mary Bolton Owen: Mary Frances Owen

Children of Robert Henry and Jane Dale Owen Fauntleroy: Constance, Ellinor, Arthur, and Edward Fauntleroy
Children of David Dale and Caroline Neef Owen: Alfred Dale, Anna Maclure, William Herschel, and Nina Dale Owen
Children of Richard and Anna Neef Owen: Nora Edgeworth, Eugene Fellenberg, and Horace Pestalozzi Owen

New Harmony's Minerva Society Charter Members

Charlotte Mejia Sampson Boren (see Sampson Family)
Florence Dale Owen Cooper
Constance Owen Fauntleroy
Lydia Hinckley
Anna Jane Burrows Mann
Della M. Mann
Sally Nettleton
Eliza Oetzmann
Anna Neef Owen
Virginia Fauntleroy Preaus
Mary W. Sampson (Mollie Owen— see Sampson Family)
Eliza Jane Twigg

Additional Members

Mary Elizabeth Chadwick
Harriet Mahitable Collins
Elizabeth Cooper
Ella Dietz
Miriam Elliott
Rachel Homer Fauntleroy
Ellen Hinckley
Natalie Burrows Mann
Kate Nobles
Rosamond Dale Owen
Angeline Reeder
Eliza Robson
Celia Rogers
Mary Isabelle Wheatcroft
Martha Deborah Wilsey

Miscellaneous Minor Characters

Captain John Batty, quartermaster
   in the Army of the Potomac

Rose Given Butler, Mary Given
   Gleason, Ellen Given McAuliffe,
   John's Chicago aunts

Charley Diver, Donegal man in the
   11th Missouri

Hamilton, black clerk with 25th in
   Decatur, Alabama

Mick Given, John's uncle lost in
   New York

Colonel William Grower, 17th
   New York

Dennis O'Donnell, cousin of John's
   who taught school in County
   Donegal

Menomen O'Donnell, John's hero
   cousin from the 11th Missouri

Denis Ward from Eglish in County
   Donegal, 11th Missouri

George Warren, leader of the
   Evansville band and son of the
   inventor Josiah Warren

Ulysses S. Grant

Abraham Lincoln (offstage)

Northern Tennessee
February 1862

1

Aggregate casualties: Lauman's Brigade, 2nd Division, Army of Brig. Gen. U.S. Grant: 357. Siege of Fort Donelson, Tennessee, February 12–16, 1862.

War of the Rebellion Official Records

John Given was chilled and damp. He was lying on the ground and thinking earnestly of times when he'd dried his gansey and trousers at a peat fire in Ireland, in Drumboarty, and then drunk his tea. He wanted to crawl into his blanket, but Lieutenant Randolph was ordering them up. He was ordering them to fall in, and John heard the long roll. He made his way into line and wished that he'd burned his letters when he'd had the chance. If he got shot, if he was killed today, he didn't want some Johnny Reb rifling through his pockets and reading his letters from his father or sisters or his friends. His skin grew hot just thinking of it. He would kill a man who did it. He would rouse himself right up from the dead and break the man's neck.

It was eleven charged days since the 25th Indiana, Volunteer Infantry, had left St. Louis on the *Continental* and traveled with the fleet down the Mississippi. The men had watched warily as flatboats edged between ice floes. They'd rushed to fill buckets to keep the deck wet beneath the boat's fiery chimneys. Steaming past canebrakes and turkeys perched on tree branches, they'd kept a lookout for guerrillas and spotted herons and red-tailed hawks flying at water's edge, eyed pignut hickories and saw Judas trees not yet in bud. A steamer suddenly crossed their bow, and the captain reversed engines just in time to avoid a collision.

At Cairo, its broad levee swarming with soldiers, they escorted angry mutineers to quarters. One of them, hearing the west of Ireland in John's voice, cursed him in Gaelic. At Paducah they saw an otherworldly boat, brightly lit: plumed officers and beautifully gowned women strolling its upper deck. Then, the *Iatan* had turned from the Ohio into the Tennessee. It had pushed down the western knob of Kentucky. It had steamed into Tennessee. It had entered the Confederacy itself where the citizens weren't just wavering but gone. When at last the boat came into view of the Stars and Stripes newly flying on Fort Henry after the navy's victory, a thunderous, foot-stomping yell erupted around John. The wood of the boat shuddered clear through him. He was cheering so loud his throat hurt. A big fight was coming. He knew it. They all did.

Now, after a night bivouacking at Fort Henry and the march to Fort Donelson and the long, sleepless hours in front of the Confederate rifle pits, the fight had arrived. Captain Saltzman was dressing the line. He talked to the men. "There's a hill. Then there's the enemy's breastworks. The hill first. Give us a cheer, boys."

John's hands were clammy on his gun. He swallowed and joined the sharp "hi! hi!" rising from man to man, and the deep roar that followed it. He was afraid he might break out of line. Then they were moving forward. They were clambering through the underbrush, the rifles glinting where the sun struck them through the trees. They were going uphill through the thickets, John's heart pounding in his ears. He strained to keep his step, to stay steady and not take the bandy leap forward he'd learned as a boy in Ireland walking on boggy ground.

When they reached the top of the hill, the line halted. John tried making out the enemy works through the heavy timber. The woods were as dense as thick fog, but now and again, in the way fog lifts over a mountain, there was a break in the timber. John could see something that looked man-made. He could spy places where the earth had been cut deeply to make breastworks or to place batteries. The gunboat was firing from the river and the thunder rolls from McClernand's troops kept up, but the very loudest thing was closest: the bugle call to fix bayonets. It sounded toward him and toward George Tretheway and Henry Schafer, who were the only men he could see on his right, though he could hear Jacob Schaen coughing. Then it sounded to the left, but quieter, as if it were going away like a moving train. John pulled his hand across his face and touched his ammo box. He locked the bayonet onto the muzzle of his gun. His heart was going even faster. It was banging in his chest.

The adjutant galloped by below them and then slowed to angle up the hill, his horse flicking up mud, a saber slapping at his side. Crows yammered from the smoky treetops. John ran a nervous hand across his neck and wiped it on his shirt. He wondered if the woods were on fire. It was either that, and they'd fry right here on this hilltop, or the smoke from the batteries on the right had drifted all the way to their lines. A moment later, the adjutant descended the hill, heading the other way and dodging tree branches, and the corporals were ordering men into single file, pacing them off five feet apart. With a flush of new excitement, John realized what was happening. They were the forward skirmishers. Or part of them. Captain Saltzman and Company A—Indiana men from New Harmony and Posey County—were starting the ball.

Since their wagons weren't with them, Levi Thrailkill, who was company wagoner, was in front of him in line. John focused on the stray bit of hair poking north from under Levi's cap and on the worn spot on the seat of his pants Levi had tried to mend with his housewife. Of his two best friends, Harry Beal was off in western Virginia with the 15th Indiana, and Levi was here. John couldn't say how good it was Levi was close. Still, he felt as if tiny shards of glass were pricking at his stomach. He couldn't get past it, though if he thought of this fight as just another drill, it wasn't as bad.

On command, they moved forward on the double quick. John scanned the trees, trying to pick out landmarks. Then he saw the

Rebel breastworks stretching far to the left. "Jesus, there're more of them!" somebody yelled, and the cry went up the line. Then the order came to wheel left. Blind as it was, the men and trees all mixed up, the pivot seemed to work. They were headed down a ravine, and soon they were scrambling up another hill that was farther west. Panicked, John looked for Levi, but he couldn't see him anymore. For as much as he could tell, the rest of the regiment and half of the company might be clear back in Indiana, but it was hot as the devil where he was. He gripped his rifle. He could see the enemy breastworks. He could see dove-colored caps and hear the yipping, wild yells. He thought there were swifts rushing by. Then he realized it was minié balls. They squealed and slid through the air, a thick rain of them, and John felt as though he were pushing into a headwind. There was a terrible scream overhead. It was louder than a train whistle. It was like a foghorn blown right in his ear. Then a shell landed behind them, spitting up earth.

John, and every soldier around him, hit the ground. They were under orders to return fire at this range. When he raised his head, he saw a Rebel taking aim behind the breastworks. He inhaled, locking his finger in the trigger of his rifle. At the last minute before he squeezed, he pulled a little left and took the recoil in his stomach. When he looked up, the soldier was gone, but he didn't think he'd hit him and he wasn't really sorry.

Other soldiers were firing as well. Firing and yelling. John let out his own yell. The first shot had calmed him. Wherever the regiment was, he knew it was the company's job to cover the flank. He rolled on his back and, using his teeth, pulled a new cartridge open. With the taste of gunpowder on his tongue, he jammed the charge in. He crept to his knees. More musket balls flew by from the rifle pits and far to the right he saw a man hit, his body jerking back and then forward, his head a horrible, pulpy mass when he fell. John swallowed. Another shell roared overhead. It crashed in the trees, but John had seen the flash and smoke from the big gun that launched it. He spotted the gun through the timber.

Others had, too, and Felix Edmonds, the corporal nearest to them, yelled in a squawky voice for them to fire. They peppered the gun with their rounds. The shots that reached it winged off the side, but John heard a crash and swearing. He thought the artillery crew had dived for cover. He loaded and aimed for the rifle pits behind the abatis: all those downed trees for defense with their trunks sharpened into points. He'd been eyeing them, and he realized he had pictures now for words that he'd heard. Not just abatis, but crossfire. Killed in action. Where was Levi? Who was the man he'd seen shot?

He ripped another cartridge open. Shots were still whizzing by but, with their return fire on the rifle pits and the field gun, the fire on them had quieted a little. John was drawing his sights on the gun when Dave Vint, another corporal on the line, touched his elbow with his bayonet. "Lieutenant Boren wants us forward. Fifty yards," he said, moving off in a half crouch.

A long moment later, the swimming images of a clean-furrowed Irish field and his sister Biddy's face, small and feverish before she died, and the shelf of schoolbooks in Kildare Place in Dublin that started with *Wonderful Escapes* and *Wonderful Fishes*, *Bligh's Dangerous Voyage*, and the *Adventure of Mungo* having flashed through his mind, the signal came.

John hunched into a run. His mind charged past other scenes: the alleyways and smoky rooms: *Dublin*. Navan where he'd descended the stairs of Power's Duck Egg at St. Finian's intent on becoming a priest. The journey to New Harmony. They were haunting visions, all of them, and in their way frightening and exhilarating, but they were nothing like this. He could see the men on either side of him quick-stretching forward and forward and then freezing stock-still, checking where they were like a bunch of jackrabbits. There were bullets zinging at their feet. All of them fired on command, half at the breastworks, half at the cannon. There was so much screeching of voices and bullets that John didn't know what he actually heard and what was the general bedlam in his head. Something that sounded like a bumblebee jarred his ear. When he reached for his cap, it was gone.

Another shell howled overhead. John ducked. This time the shell got more than earth. There were screams behind him and cheers from the rifle pits. When he turned to look, he saw men who'd been thrown to the ground, and one man twisted and reaching for his arm that was flying away. John stood up, hardly able to believe his eyes. The man had crumpled to the ground, blood gushing from his side. John thought he should get the arm back, that he should put it in the empty socket. He took a step toward the man and the men writhing next to him, but Henry Schafer hooked him with his leg and knocked him to his knees.

"Easy, Jack. Get the big gun," he said, his voice perfectly steady.

John pulled away. He was thirsty. He saw a puddle near him and, taking a swallow of muddy water, he watched the puddle turn black from the gunpowder on his mouth. He was dizzy from the noise, but Henry was right. He needed to get hold of himself. They needed to shoot at the cannon so its men were pinned down and couldn't load another shell. And the fire was heavier again from the rifle pits. The men there were rowdy and jubilant from the shell's hit, and bullets were whirring by once more. There was a barrage of fire followed by a commotion down the line. Someone else was hit and John heard Alex Hugo screaming that the Secesh kill him if they could.

John blinked the sweat from his eyes. He jammed a charge home. A flock of mallards flew up, flushed from a thicket and, with all the popping from the line, he thought men were shooting at the sky. He shook his head, trying to clear it. Then he took aim at the field gun. He was ready to fire once more when he heard the bugle call to retreat. It startled him. Clearly, it had surprised everyone, for they were all stumbling awkwardly, dodging trees, and shooting on the move. They scrambled down a smoky, blind ravine and into a brutal fire. Men took cover wherever they could.

John was in the loudest place he'd ever been in his life. The shells had a piercing sound like a struck anvil, though a hundred times louder. There were so many cries of wounded men and so much swearing that it seemed like a whole new language. A bullet pinged off the downed tree he was lying behind, and he buried his head under his arms. He wondered if it was the ground that was shaking or just him. More bullets spattered the tree wood and lodged in it.

Finally—John had no idea how much later—the racket dimmed. When it dimmed some more, he waited longer. Then, very carefully, he raised his head and stared through the smoke that drifted in the air. He'd lost his landmarks. He couldn't find his company either. He saw some of Captain Rheinlander's men and more men he didn't even recognize. Still, when he heard the order to fall in, he joined the line and started the charge on the abatis, struggling to make his way through the brush and around the logs. Halfway up a hill, with the Rebel breastworks in sudden full sight and flames of gunfire blazing all the way across them, the line halted on command. John smelled the sweaty stench of the men and heard them panting and coughing. They were so near, so alive. It was all he could think of, but they were straightening the line. They were advancing again and into a hail of bullets. John could see men shot, men falling, and officers on horseback yelling and riding back and forth, trying to close up the line.

It wasn't just musket fire now. There was grapeshot and canister. Two field guns on the right opened up on them. Shells screamed in once more, and the whole line of men threw themselves to the ground. John hugged the earth. When the shells landed, he felt the vibrations slamming his stomach, even the small bones of his ears. There was nowhere to go.

The fire kept coming. Now and then a man on the hill got off a shot, but there was really no point. As far as John could tell, there was no fighting anywhere else, and here they were cannon fodder if they moved an inch. If they twitched a muscle. Maybe if they didn't move at all. Yet the longer he lay still, the more he began to feel that he was not going to be shot. Not here. Not now. His leg fell asleep. His side cramped. His belly ached from hunger and from just plain aching, but he thought it was less likely he would die on this hillside than it was that he was simply in a dangerous waiting game. He had an urge to draw figures—to inch his hand forward in the mud and busy himself in that familiar way. He forced himself to stay still.

The minié balls were buzzing again. John ducked his head close to the log. The bark cut into his cheek. Beyond him, a man started humming. John knew the song: "Yes, Let Me Like a Soldier Fall."

"Keep your damned balls," somebody yelled, and there were agreeing, angry voices and men who made their protests with shots they got off toward the rifle pits. The return fire was heavy, the heaviest it had been in, what? Half an hour? An hour? Two? At this rate, John thought, this battle, if it was a battle, was a Union success. The whole Confederate Army would run out of bullets.

In a while, the word spread man to man that, fire or not, they should prepare to withdraw. They would break for the bottom of the hill. John checked his rifle to make sure there was no mud in the barrel, and that was it. The order came from Captain Rheinlander. It was nothing like half right or guide center or forward. It was, "Run, boys. Stay low and *run*."

John took off. It was every man for himself. They fell and scrambled in wild disorder. They plunged down the hillside, the undergrowth tugging and ripping at their legs. They stumbled over bodies and downed trees, Rebel sharpshooters firing and firing as they fled.

2

Michael Given 27—clerk, Margaret Given 54, Margaret Given 15, Mary Given 10, Rose Given 22, Denis Given 12, Charles Given 7, John Given 21.

Entry on the Manifest of the *Fidelia*, Liverpool to New York, Debarkation, November 14, 1857

When John Given first explained to his little brother the geography of where their family came from, he fudged and spoke of concentric circles on a map. Charley looked puzzled, so John drew a set of nesting ellipses, which was certainly more accurate. "Here, Charley," he said, roughing the pencil across the page. He drew in Drumboarty, the townland where they'd both been born. He rolled off its list of familiar names and made them sound like barristers' offices: *Deermood and McDermott. Thomas, McGivin, and Given. O'Donnell and Donnell. McKelvey, Griffith and Griffin. Moghan, Keevnoaghth* (with all the letters, Charley couldn't pronounce it), *Kevin, and Ward.* Then John added Drimarone and scrawled its cluster of townlands on the Blue Stacks and in their valleys. Since Drimarone was the Catholic, top half of Inver Parish, with its Protestant lands to the south, he added Inver, too. Then, making a large swoop, he drew in County Donegal, which bordered the Atlantic on both the north and the west, and agreed with Charley: this new egg meant the others looked like an eyeball that was missing its mate.

Finally, John drew all of Ireland. "There it is," he told Charley. "The country England keeps in its pocket to spend like loose change."

The description was their father's—John Sr.'s—and their Grandpa Given's. John didn't know if it preceded or was born with the potato famine. It could have been either. It was certainly the famine that meant the family left for America, though it had not been immediately. Distrustful, and bitter that the government had sold Irish grain abroad and let people starve, John Sr. was determined to leave as soon as he'd saved enough money.

It took seven years. When he, and his daughter Kate and his wife's niece Margaret Mulhern, arrived in New Harmony, it meant a hard two years more to earn passage for the others who were coming. For the whole two years, Givens on both sides of the Atlantic wondered if John, the oldest son, would stay in Ireland. While his father trusted he wouldn't, his mother prayed that he would. She hoped he would become the priest she'd always wanted him to be. She prayed, too, that she could bear to leave him behind when the family set out for Indiana.

In the end, John had made his own difficult decision. With the ship's din still roaring in his memory and the morning still vivid when they'd spilled out into New York—the clattering clip-clop, the steaming horse dung, and the laundry waving on rooftops—John and the family had come up the Wabash to New Harmony. It was a town that even his Grandpa Given had talked about and that John himself had found in *Don Juan*. The reunion was joyous. Their news, though, was sobering. As planned, Rose, his father's youngest sister, had headed to Chicago, which was where two of their sisters lived. John had made the arrangements himself. But earlier, his father's brother Michael had disappeared in New York. While John huddled his mother and Rose and the children in a doorway, his Uncle Mick left with a man to find lodgings and never came back.

John knew he might have gone with the man himself, and it was hard for him telling his father what happened. "Are you sure he's vanished?" his father asked. "Did you hunt for him? John, did you wait long enough? And who was this man? Mick would know how to get here himself?"

"He would," John answered, holding out hope, though he had little himself. None, really. None at all. Too late, he'd learned of the gangs who preyed on immigrants straight off the ships.

In his first days in New Harmony, John had watched his father waiting for Mick. He saw him shouldering his work tools and then detouring to the landing to see who got off the boats; he heard him ask about telegrams and letters. Later, he noticed that part of the family earnings was sent to buy missing person notices in the eastern papers. But as the weeks passed into months, his father became resigned. Mick wasn't coming. Mick was lost. For John, what remained was his own guilt. Though his father never blamed him, John felt responsible. It had come down to this: while his parents had often warred about his own future and his mother had often won, for the moment, his father's feelings held the greater weight with him.

Kate, who was second oldest, and two and a half years younger than John, had already shouldered a very large share of the family's burdens, but she was easier on him than he was on himself. "It wasn't your fault," she said. "When Father and Margaret Mulhern and I arrived in New York, I doubted we'd ever find our way to New Harmony. I've no idea how Father managed it. But you like it here, don't you, John? And John"—Kate paused—"I know it sounds selfish and terrible, and I liked Mick ever so much, but if someone had to be lost this time, I'm grateful it wasn't you or Mother or one of the children."

"It shouldn't have been anyone," John said, and he set himself the task of working as hard as Kate. Harder. He farmed long hours with his father so they could earn enough to buy a house. He let it be known he was educated and, when chances came, he did businessmen's books, along with more menial tasks such as bagging wheat. He convinced his parents to keep his sister Margaret from becoming a maid so she could finish school and help their mother at home; he saw to it that Mary and Charley, who were the youngest children, had shoes from the cobbler and new slates. And he pleaded his brother Denis's case, saying he was better off farming, a thing he knew, than trying to write English in a school where the other older boys would harass him.

But it wasn't until rumors of war became actual war that John felt the keenest sense of accountability. He had his political ideas. As an Irishman, America seemed far too much the promised land to let anything imperil it. He believed it was worth a fight if that's what it took to keep and better the life in New Harmony he and his father had started to build. It also hadn't slipped past him that the simple fact of enlisting seemed to add luster to a man. Nobody said it in so many words, but when it came to Harmony girls like Ann Bradley—and, for John, this was a vital consideration, though his mother's wishes and his own thoughts about becoming a priest still plagued him—a man who stayed behind was generally considered a coward. But the main thing was that it was clear what his father expected.

"It'll help the family," he said. "Younger, I'd go. But if a man's to be accepted somewhere, John, he needs to make other men's fights his own."

John was aware of his own uncertainty. He could farm or do books, but he didn't know if he'd make a soldier, and he didn't know if the younger children, or even headlong Kate, could avoid the wounding slights of New Harmony's privileged set on their own. But he'd seen the look in his father's eyes. He'd heard the emotion in his father's voice and understood what the words had cost him. In the end, it was that, and the war fever, that settled it for him.

———

At nightfall on his first day of combat, his father's words were far from John's mind. Making his way back to the company bivouac where, hours ago, dawn had broken to the racket from a battery, and rifle fire had made him wonder if McClernand's men on the right had gotten into it, John was amazed he'd survived the whole day. It had not seemed a likely thing. By the time he'd gotten down the tangled and bloody hillside and out of the range of Rebel guns, he'd found himself in a mass of deranged-looking strangers. They were grimy-faced with gunpowder and covered with mud. They were gasping and spitting on the ground. One was coughing up blood and another trembling violently. Some men were milling aimlessly about, while others wasted no time taking off through the woods. John himself was ravenous, yet as he opened his haversack, his stomach rose in his throat and eating seemed out of the question. When Colonel Morgan, the regiment's commander, rode up and ordered everyone back into line, John thought with horror that he meant for them to assault the hill once more.

Instead, they waited where they were. The sky clouded over. A cold wind kicked up. When dark came, they were ordered back to their morning's positions in a heavy rain that was quickly turning to snow. Hunting down a ridge for Company A's bivouac, John made his way past huddles of dripping soldiers. There were no campfires, but he finally spotted Jake Schaen and George Tretheway shivering along the line. John unrolled his blanket and shared it with them, glad they were both short. He wasn't about to admit he'd been lost with a part of the regiment he hardly knew, and he wouldn't say the words that were churning in his mind. *Chaos. Exhaustion. Futility.* He finally asked if they'd seen Levi, but they hadn't.

He thought of the men the night before when they all were still safe, when they were wakeful under the trees and stars and a brief shower of meteors. It was hours before he'd fallen asleep. When he awoke, for a shadowy moment, it was the first time he'd left home. He was a boy off at school in Dublin again. He was trying to cash in merit tickets for a pair of socks. Then his mind cleared. He'd pulled up his braces and joined the men as they moved and grumbled through the dark. By the time strips of clouds had colored the dawn—thin strips like the meat for pemmican—the company and regiment, the brigade and division were lined up to march. From their vantage point, John could see the stacks and flags of boats on the river and watch them turning to head back downstream. Transports with more men for

General Grant's army. Men to reinforce the divisions under Smith and McClernand. Men who would take the river route of the Tennessee to the Ohio to the Cumberland and Fort Donelson.

They'd marched over wet ground, and for once the air was clear of column dust. The breeze lightened and, to John, it felt for all the world like one of those rare childhood days in Donegal—in Drimarone—when it didn't rain, and he and his grandfather walked through the Blue Stacks and up to the graveyard and on to Carn Lough. They took their clothes off to swim. Or his grandfather swam. John had done what he could, paddling until his grandfather dove under him and towed him, both of them bellowing like dolphins.

Marching in the perfect day, John had felt the shock of foot after foot. Beneath him, the earth seemed fragile like river ice waving when boys skated out after an early freeze. As the column snaked forward, squirrels scuttled through oak leaves. The Hugo boys tossed their caps in a tree, and Alex climbed up to get them. Then he landed with a thud at John's feet.

"Trample him," Levi said, and John laughed and lifted his foot obligingly, but Alex, holding his rifle to his chest, laughed too, and rolled out of the way. He scrambled back into line.

It was all like a lark. It was like going to a picnic where you met up with the girls or like going to the fair with a coin in your pocket to bet on a horse. Men shed their overcoats. They tossed their blankets beside the road and emptied their knapsacks of excess baggage until they were down to their absolute fighting weight. John didn't have a long coat. He hadn't brought anything he could spare, but otherwise he was like the rest of the fellows—wiping the sweat off his neck and walking around the column's debris. They were marching up and down and up and down the hillsides of the land between the Tennessee and the Cumberland where the ravines were soggy with river backwater. John remembered the sudden flash of the Cumberland between the trees and the booming of a gunboat on the river and the sound of sniper fire coming from the direction of their forward skirmishers. For him, the moment was indelible. The glimpse of the river. The noisy shock of the gunboat's cannon. The popping of muskets that turned a brisk hike into a rapid march and a rapid march into an intent deployment to a position not a half mile from the enemy rifle pits.

It all seemed a precious lifetime ago.

"I saw a man cut in half. Shot," Jake said from under the blanket. "Where *was* everybody?" His voice was so guttural and hoarse that it sounded like a bigger man's. He was shaking more, and his hair was turning white with the snow. "Where were you, Jack?"

John didn't answer. He leaned down and pushed his trouser cuffs into his socks and wondered if there were other soldiers who'd been as useless as he was—other men who'd been just as confused and outright lost and couldn't keep track of their best friend.

"And Mike Chancy and John Hugo," George Tretheway said.

"What about them?" John asked.

"Dead. Killed. And it's a wonder they didn't get Alex Hugo, too, screaming and shooting off ammo. Yelling they could kill him since they'd killed his brother. He was crazy."

John felt a moment of stunned recognition. He tracked back to the morning's fight and Alex's voice and the gunshots that came as fast as a man could load when the mallards flew into the sky.

The snow was growing heavier. It was actually part snow and part sleet, part drizzly rain, but the ground was getting covered. George knocked ridges of ice off his shoes. "I thought it was warm in the South. Sunny," he said. "It's a worse damp than in Yorkshire. When was yesterday? I ditched my coat and my God! Just to have it back. Cough the other way, Jake."

John felt the weariness that had settled in his legs and back. For a while, he tried to sleep in the line. He couldn't. If he began to doze off, picket fire would start and Colonel Morgan would order them to fall in, and then they'd be up on their feet. When the firing stopped, they could lie down once more, but it was too cold to sleep, and there was less heat from George and Jake than he'd felt from even the newest calf. Snow struck him like pinpricks. When he pushed his hands into his pockets, they froze anyway and, when he rubbed them together, they were fiery with pain. He thought he might freeze entirely, that the cold would creep up from his feet until it froze the blood in his veins, until it actually cracked his heart.

But he must have slept, for Lieutenant Boren and Felix Edmonds appeared so suddenly, standing over him, he thought they were specters. He grabbed his gun and sat upright. "Where's your cap, John?" Lieutenant Boren asked quietly, and John shook his head. "You can get one from a man who's died. We need you on detail."

John struggled his way out of the blanket. His feet felt blocky. When he touched his hair, it was crusted with snow. Felix held a canteen out in his bony fingers. "Coffee," he said. "Go ahead. Some boys went down the ravine to build a fire. They brought up a camp kettle."

John took the canteen with both hands, afraid that his stiff fingers wouldn't hold on and afraid, too, that his hands would make the coffee cold. He took a swallow. The coffee was bitter, but it warmed his mouth and insides and, really, he hadn't tasted a thing in his life even half as good. "What kind of detail?" he asked. He handed the canteen back since he had to, but he could have emptied it himself.

"Wounded men. Bodies. Maybe bodies," Lieutenant Boren said, looking at George Tretheway sleeping with his mouth open and Jake shivering and coughing in a drowsy half sleep. "If they're close to our lines, we have to get them. And I hope to God these Rebels tend to the others."

John checked his gun and touched his belt to make sure he still had his ammunition box. With the snow, he'd lost his sense of time, and he wondered how late it was, how close it was to morning. Together, he and Felix Edmonds walked along the ridge. Lieutenant Boren was picking up more men, and Felix gave out coffee until his canteen was empty. The lieutenant gave them their orders—no talking to draw the fire of Rebel sharpshooters; take the wounded men first—and then they stacked the litters that Captain Saltzman and Max Munte had managed to find for them.

As they walked, snow fell from the tree branches in wet, heavy thunks. It was still sleeting, and there was thunder but no lightning.

Except that it wasn't thunder. It was a single shell far off to the right. John heard the dim, answering skirmishers' fire, its sound muffled by distance and snow. He pushed up the collar of the hickory shirt he'd pulled over his uniform and clenched it tight to keep snow from beating down his neck. Underfoot, it was slippery and treacherous. They needed a scout, he thought. They needed a scout like the wild men who lived downriver from New Harmony and knew every inch of the woods by heart, men who could find the way in even the false light of a snowy midnight.

In the end, their guide was the cries of the wounded. Felix Edmonds stopped and lifted his hand. John heard a mewling sound like a baby's whimpering. The other men were listening, too, and Lieutenant Boren ordered them half right and then, in single file, they moved forward. They could hear more sounds. There were shrieks that seemed to cut through the snow. There were moans John had first thought were the whine of the wind, though not anymore. As the sounds grew louder, they were more distinct. Finally, they were not just screams of pain filling the night but the broken litany of curses and prayers from actual men. In the snow-lit darkness, John saw that the voices had brought them to a scene of nightmarish carnage.

"Jesus," Felix said. John gazed at the icy hillside where earlier in the day he'd lain with bullets whizzing over and past him, though actually it must have been earlier yesterday, he decided, for surely it was past midnight and the fourteenth by now. Valentine's Day. It was St. Valentine's Day. With a rush of emotion, John wondered if he would ever see the valentines the Harmony girls had made. There would be valentines from his sisters and friends; there would be valentines from every Harmony girl he knew. He was eager for all of them, though he knew it was Ann Bradley's he looked forward to the most. It seemed such a trivial thing after all that had happened, but he'd wanted so much to prize open those girlish riddles. He wanted it even now.

Here, though, were the men who had not gotten away. There were bodies half drifted with snow. Bodies tossed on the ground like dolls. Bodies thrown across other bodies, or among branches. Bodies that moved.

Lieutenant Boren signaled a halt. He blinked snow from his eyes as he spoke to them. The surgeons had taken the men who needed immediate help. They had left men who would die anyway and men who could wait. And they were here now for the men who had waited, and they should know, as well, that if it was their turn, their fellow soldiers would come for them, too. And they should still keep it down, though no civilized man would shoot at them while they were getting their wounded under a flag.

John took a litter with Felix Edmonds. Felix looked at him down the length of it. "I thought you were getting a cap. Your brain might freeze."

"It's Valentine's Day."

"The lad there got shot in the heart. Go on, Jack. Take his cap. I'm the corporal. Do what I say."

John shifted the litter to one hand and leaned down. The man that Felix had pointed to was stiff with death, stiff with cold. His eyes were glassed open. With his thumb, John tried pushing them closed, but the eyelids were frozen. The man's gaze stayed locked on the sky, though his eyes seemed to be looking inward, too, as though he were still holding his very last thought. John took the cap and put it on. He brushed off the crystals of blood that had thawed enough to stick to his sleeve when it touched the man's chest. Then he stood up. He and Felix moved on through the snow. Men were crying out for help, and begging for them to take them or to shoot them out of their misery. John felt like God, having to decide which man to listen to, and then he thought, suddenly angry at all that had happened, Why not? Somebody needed to do the job. There was clearly a vacancy.

"We should do what the surgeons did," Felix said. "You know, check for the goners and the ones that can make it till morning. Lieutenant has a crew moving trees off people. Maybe some of these fellows can walk. Wait. This boy." Felix had stopped at the sparsest cry.

It seemed like a bush that was talking. They set the litter down, and John went forward on his knees, scraping snow and brush aside. The boy they had found looked about Denis's age, sixteen or seventeen, and he was very fair with black hair under the wet snow, and blue eyes. He didn't look fragile exactly but so handsome he was almost pretty.

"It's good that you've come," he said, his voice oddly clear, oddly precise. "My mother needs me to work on the farm. My father died, and I'd better go home. Did you bring water? I drank what I could of rain. And the snow. I've a terrible thirst."

"You're hit?" Felix asked, and it was John's question, too, because the boy looked untouched. "We'll get you water. Whoa. Jack, take out your knife. His hair's froze right to the ground."

John felt the slippery, cold hair in his fingers. He held it close to the roots so it wouldn't pull while he cut at it with his knife. When it was free, Felix raised the boy's head and gave him some water, and then he pulled the litter toward his feet. "There you are. Heave ho. Pick him up, Jack," he said, and the two of them tried, and then started rocking him gently from side to side since his clothes were stuck, too. "Try now," Felix said and, on a count of three, both of them lifted him, and there was an instant rush of blood from his back. It was like a cataract and John was juggling. He was trying not to drop the boy, and trying to plug the hole with his hand. But it wasn't a hole. It was an abyss. The air whooshed out of the boy with the blood. He was dead in their arms.

"Holy Christ," Felix said.

John felt his head jerk in an involuntary recoil. He looked at the boy's staring, blinkless eyes. "Felix—my God, we killed him," he said.

"Lay him down, lay him down." Felix said and, when they had, Felix slumped into a crouch. Then he pitched himself onto the ground and rolled in the snow, trying to get the blood off his shirt. "Holy Jesus. But you're wrong, Jack. He would've pegged off with that hole. We were just here when he died. Find something we can send to his ma. Oh Jesus, holy crap."

John nodded, but he was desperate to get his hand clean. He scraped it against the snow and then scraped it again. The snow stuck. It was crusty on his fingers, and he shook it away and then dried his hand against his shirt. Only then did he reach into the boy's breast pocket. There was a letter there and, thin as the light was, John thought he could make out the writing. It was dated the thirteenth and it started, "Dear mother, brother and sisters." It was the letter like most of the men had written, and John put it in his own pocket. Then he reached down and trimmed off a lock of the hair he'd cut, and he took that, too.

"He would've pegged off. He would've," Felix said once more. "But Jesus, Jack. Check where the next one got shot."

For the rest of the night, as the hours crept toward dawn, there was a numbing rhythm to their work. With the other soldiers of the detail, they made trip after trip down the snowy hill, carrying men onto the bloody path that led to the two-room house that was serving as a hospital. Each time someone directed them where to put the man they had brought, John tried to avert his eyes. He did not want to look at the soiled rags and amputated legs on the pile in the corner or see the bandaged men who were tossing and delirious on the floor. He wanted to plug his ears to the cries. On one trip, there was a man smoking on a camp stool on the porch and, when Felix told the man to mind the litter, he gave them a blank, drunken look. John took in his scraggly beard and leather apron and realized he was the surgeon who'd gone to work on the first man they'd taken in.

By their last trip, there was scarcely room for a man more. They waited by the door until a man with bloodied clothes scooped up the pile of rags and limbs and tossed them into the fireplace. "Put him there," he said, and John and Felix eased the man off the litter and onto the cleared floor space.

Felix squatted on the floorboards. He tilted his head toward his shoulder and cracked his neck. "I'm dead," he said. "I mean dead tired. Maybe I mean dead."

John heard the clicking sleet on the roof. He smelled the flesh beginning to burn in the fireplace. He wanted out and he turned on his heel toward the door and then in spite of the din of screams and moans, he heard his name as clear as anything. He looked at Felix, but it wasn't Felix who had called him. He stood scanning the room.

"John. Hey, Given." The voice was weak, but the drawl was familiar. "Over here, Jack."

John edged his way around the wounded men and skirted a table where a surgeon was cutting a screaming man's shoulder. He made his way past the sprawl of men to the far wall. "Levi," he said. He tried to compose himself. He leaned over a face so pale that he saw freckles he hadn't known it had and saw the bandaged arm immobile on Levi Thrailkill's chest.

"Are you all right?" John asked.

"What do you think?" Levi grasped at his sleeve. "In my pocket," he said, his voice hacky and thin.

John drew back. "You're not dying," he said, but Levi shook his head impatiently. "My pocket," he said again, and John, though he didn't want to, slid his finger inside Levi's jacket, being cautious he didn't jar his arm. Levi felt hot. He was pale and feverish at the same time, and John didn't know what that meant.

There was an envelope in the pocket—John could feel it—and he slipped it out. For a moment he was confused. It was a large envelope from home. In the light from a lantern and the fire, he could see it was postmarked from Mount Vernon. It was addressed to Levi and hadn't been opened.

"It's the valentines our sisters sent," Levi said, his eyes closed. "Caroline addressed them to me. Kate thought you'd open them early."

John pushed his fingers into his hair so the cap rode up. He was laughing quietly. When he looked at Levi again, Levi was watching him. "Son of gun, but you scared me," John said. He reached for his knife. "Caroline wrote they sent valentines?"

Levi nodded. John pressed the knife blade under the envelope flap and slit the end open. Carefully, he removed the contents. There was one thick packet for Levi and one for him. He stared at his, suddenly uncertain that it held a heart from Ann Bradley. "Should I read yours to you? Or should I hold them up so you can read them yourself?"

"Is there one that's signed Margret?"

John put his own packet under his arm and began looking through Levi's. The top valentine was a heart cut from a cigar box picture. There was a tiny gash in one corner where the knife had sliced too thin in getting the paper off. Though the valentine was unsigned and someone else had copied it, he knew it was his sister Kate's because hurrying Kate would count the picture more than the flaw. And, too, this valentine's creator had made her riddle from Shakespeare and he'd left his Shakespeare for Kate to read.

"Here's Kate's," he said to Levi. " 'What looks with mind and not the eyes / and therefore paints winged Cupid blind?' "

"Love," Levi said. "Did Margret send one?"

"My mother Margaret? My sister Margaret? Just what Margret is it you're speaking of? My cousin Margaret Mulhern?"

Levi was reaching for the valentines, and John turned away with them. "There's one with dashes for a signature. Seven dashes and a space and five dashes more. So maybe you have one from say. . . let's say Margret Smith. Miss Smith, you think? It has lovebirds that look like they were embossed from ironing it on a mold and there's a green ribbon between them. Very fancy."

"Give it over. No, read it first."

" 'Wind is to _____ as distance is to love. / It blows out the small and ignites the great.' "

John held the valentine so Levi could see it, and Levi answered "fire" for the blank and then he took the valentine with his free hand. He put it on his chest and let his arm fall. His eyes drifted closed again.

"You all right, Levi?" John registered Levi's pale face once more. He felt punchy and tired from getting shot at and, with the valentines, for a moment it had almost seemed he wasn't even here in this sour-smelling house with its wailing men and Levi being hurt. It was like he was back in New Harmony where pious Father Rapp half a century ago and pie-in-the-sky Robert Owen a decade later had tried making utopias, and where girls now made excellent valentines. "You want water, Levi?" he asked.

Levi shook his head, his eyes still closed, and John slipped Margret Smith's valentine out from under his hand. He folded it into the envelope with the rest of Levi's valentines and put it back in his pocket. A faint trace of light was coming through the window, and he knew that they had to get back to the lines—that he and Felix did—but he turned to his own valentines anyway. He opened the packet. He looked at the valentine that was a sugared heart from his sister Mary and at the fluted paper one from his cousin Margaret Mulhern, its verse drawn from Colossians. Then he slipped out the valentine with the gray silk window that was shaped like a heart and read the verse from Victor Hugo: "Life is the flower for which love is the honey."

John touched the silk. He was certain it was the same gray silk of the gown Ann Bradley had worn to the farewell ball the night before he and Levi and George Tretheway and all the other Harmony boys who were part of Company A had left for the fairgrounds and then for Evansville and Camp Baker. "Miss Bradley, we can take a glass of lemonade outside," he had said, aware of her perfect face and her breasts just arced above the silk of her dress as she fanned herself. She'd shaken her head. She would not go outside. She would flirt with him (and with every other man), her gown just brushing his trouser leg, but she would not go outside.

"Mr. Given, you'd have me trade the company of your friends for the company of mosquitoes?" she'd said. "I've told you I'll write you, John. I'll start a letter this very night before I blow out the lamp. But I'm promised to dance for the whole evening."

John had wanted to argue with her. He had had the sudden impulse to grip her shoulders and steer her outside. He hadn't done it, of course. With a laugh, she'd curtsied to a soldier and stepped onto the dance floor, and John had caught only glimpses of her for the rest of the evening. She had written, however. Not frequently but, as good as her word, she had written to him. And he'd thought of her at Paducah when he saw the beautiful gowns of the women on the starlit boat. With the luminous boat, luminous Ann had come back to him.

Now, even as his heart raced when he fingered the silk, he knew he didn't really grasp what Ann had meant to say about love with her card. Whoever could know what Ann meant anyway? And how many others had gotten a valentine like this one made from leftover scraps from her gray silk gown? Yet the flower part was right. John understood that tonight in a way he never had before. Life was remarkable and fragile. Above all, it was terribly, terribly mortal.

"Be well, Levi. And safe," he said, reaching down to touch the cuff of Levi's sleeve. He was sleeping and John, looking around, thought he should ask about him, make inquiries, but the choices of doctor were a surgeon who was operating and the drunk doctor he'd seen on the porch. Squeezing around the men, John went back to Felix. He was asleep in the corner where he'd left him, and John picked up the litter and prodded him awake. His left cheek was creased and red from lying on it and he was gimpy legged, trying to stretch out, but he followed John outside. He shivered in the cold.

"I've seen enough of Tennessee. Damn, this is a cold country," Felix said.

To John, even in the frigid air there was something of phantasm in the early dawn. An inch of new snow covered the bloody tracks that he and Felix and the other men had left, and the trees on the ridges were frozen in a clear, pockless ice. Light rose in the hills. Each branch had the sudden, dazzling shimmer of crystal.

As he and Felix did their quickstep over the uncertain ground, John saw a snow-dusted squirrel try to scamper up a tree only to slide backward and land with a thump at its base. Crows, frozen to their perches, complained overhead, and tatters of minutely snow-flocked spiderwebs shadowed him at knee height as they headed toward the lines.

Their bivouac, when they reached it, was full of rumors. The brigade loss was heavy, but it was nothing compared to the beating taken by the Illinois men on the right in McClernand's division. Somebody said they'd gone forward three times, running heedless into a terrible fire from artillery and muskets. Colonel Morgan, who was regular army, looked grim, which didn't surprise John. If it had happened as men said, green troops had been massacred, and all for no purpose.

The other news was that more troops were here or on the way. Some had marched overland; some had arrived with the gunboat fleet that had come up the Cumberland overnight. It meant the ranks were closing up and, if they fought today, the line would not be as thin. But lying on the ridge next to George Tretheway, John watched the men who'd spent the whole freezing night shuffling in line. They looked miserable, and he was sure that they'd all fared worse than he had. He wondered how they could possibly fight.

"It looks like you stuck a pig. Where were you, Jack?" George asked.

John took a pilot biscuit from his haversack. He didn't have a response he wanted to give, but George was waiting and so he said, "Hospital detail," and turned away.

"You hear Levi got shot? Somebody said it was his arm but it was bad and he passed out. He would've bled to death if Dr. Walker hadn't got it stanched."

"He's in a house down the ridge," John said, putting the biscuit back, which was so rock hard, and frozen besides, it had cut his gums. "A hospital house. He'll be all right."

George was crouched on the snow, leaning against his rifle, and Jacob Schaen was hacking away in John's blanket farther up the line. "Did you see any more Harmony boys?" George asked, staring across at the rifle pits. John shook his head, though he couldn't swear that he hadn't. It was a bitter thought but, for all he knew, the bodies they'd left frozen in the snow were Posey County boys—friends, even, that he'd fished with or that he'd walked with, heading up cemetery hill so they could meet some girls. But a soldier looked different splayed dead on the battlefield or, for that matter, with his mouth black from gunpowder or his head wrapped in bandages while he lay on a floor.

"I don't think they had the morphine they needed," he said, looking away from George. He stared at the ground, remembering the moans in the hospital house that made a background dirge he'd tried to ignore while he opened the valentines. He blinked. He yawned in spite of himself. His rifle needed cleaning, and he thought he should pound on his shoes to thaw his toes, but the burst of energy he'd felt walking through the strangely radiant dawn had died away. All he wanted was to sleep. He yawned so wide that his jaw nearly locked. Then he yawned again.

"Wake me if there's coffee, or for report. Or if there's a battle to fight," he told George. Then he went past him to Jacob Schaen and crawled in under a corner of his blanket. It was full morning. Yet in only an instant, he'd fallen asleep.

3

Headquarters Army in the Field
Camp near Fort Donelson, February 16, 1862

*Sir: Yours of this date, proposing armistice and appointment of commissioners
to settle terms of capitulation, is just received. No terms except unconditional
and immediate surrender can be accepted. I propose to move immediately
upon your works.*

I am, sir, very respectfully, your obedient servant,

> *U.S. Grant, Brigadier-General*
> *Commanding*

[To] General S. B. Buckner, Confederate Army

There were some things John thought later he'd done in his
sleep. Or he thought he'd wound them into his dreams.
He felt the melting ice on Jake's cap roll down his own
cheek. He was present for roll call. He counted the members of the body detail that left carrying spades. He rubbed his fingers on the silk in his pocket, remembering the winter he'd arrived
in New Harmony and the first time that he saw Ann Bradley. She'd
been wearing a blue coat and bonnet, and he'd thought, Oh God. She
was the prettiest girl he'd ever seen. She looked Irish to him, though
she didn't sound it or even American, which he understood later when
he learned that her parents were Irish who'd gone to New York and
then Canada. Most provocative, she and her sister had come to New
Harmony because of their uncle, the very same Francis Cannon who
was a reason the Givens had come. Mr. Cannon was his father's boyhood friend. If he'd believed in Fate, John would have thought there
was a sort of destiny about it. And, believing or not, he still felt it.

Yet wherever his thoughts or dreams wandered, they were marked with an insistent *rat-a-tat-tat* fire. There were skirmishers. There were sharpshooters on the highest points of the ridges—Birge's hotshot boys who were part of their brigade now. When he slept, it was an odd and fitful doze in which he couldn't get warm and in which he'd start suddenly, thinking he'd heard the bugle call. Sometime after midday, Jake's coughing shook him fully awake and the skirmishers' fire picked up. There was no order, but John wondered if they might be going to attack soon. Instead, Lieutenant Randolph sent a detail of men to make coffee, and John, seeing them leave, quickly asked permission to go.

He was halfway down the ravine when he spotted a column of Union troops tromping through the snow. They were well behind the lines, moving toward the right, and John thought they'd come the long way around from where they had landed. It puzzled him. Then he decided they didn't have a choice, that they'd had to skirt the backwater from the swollen creek. There were two seasons here, he thought— a flooded spring and a serious winter—and if he'd had to bet on it, he'd take his chances that the delays they'd caused—all these men still not in position—meant they wouldn't be fighting today.

When he'd caught up to the coffee detail, the men had scraped a clear spot on the ground and started a skimpy fire, which was all that was allowed. It started to smoke since the tinder was wet.

Henry Schafer stomped it out. "So signal their sharpshooters," Henry said when Bill New protested.

John didn't get into it but let the others argue about what to do. Bill and Henry. Romeo Keister, whose name he'd grown used to, though he and his friend Harry Beal had had their fun with it in New Harmony, Harry telling him, "A nice fellow though, as you might imagine, the butt of all jokes and most of them mine." They were getting nowhere until Robert Clarke, who was younger than John and a sergeant, came down the ravine and told Bill to try another company for a splitting maul.

When Bill returned, he had the maul, and he chopped into a downed log until he had enough dry chips and slivers of wood to make a tidy fire that didn't smoke. John thought there was hardly heat enough for the pot, let alone for them to warm themselves, but the coffee was what mattered. It would brace them, and it would warm them from the inside. Their feet were frozen anyway.

"Esculupeous Bilbelly," he said, drawing an arc in the snow with his heel.

"Jack, you getting the duck shits like me?" Bill spat into the woods behind the fire.

"It's just a name." John kept his eyes trained away from Romeo Keister. He had the strongest impulse, but not the slightest desire to laugh, and he had no real idea why he'd remembered the name and said it out loud. "Just a soldier I met in St. Louis," he said. "An Indiana boy. Just somebody's name."

"I am so frigging cold," Bill said. "Hurry up and heat up, damn you."

It was three kettles of coffee later (and a sniper's shot that knocked the fourth one into the fire) before John was back in the line. He'd softened some biscuit in his coffee, and on a scale of feeling well, he wasn't, but he'd thawed out some. He was thinking seriously of taking out his valentines. He wanted to study Ann's handwriting. He wanted to see the silk as well as touch it. He wanted to look at the valentines he hadn't read. As strong as the impulse was, he knew the razzing would be merciless and the kind that was fun only if you could give as good as you got, which he couldn't since nobody else had their valentines to read.

He was still considering it, and thinking about Ann (and her graceful manner with Mrs. David Dale Owen, Robert Owen's daughter-in-law she was maid to), when he heard a series of booms from the river. Smoke rose into the sky. Quickly it swelled to the size of giant thunderclouds. In a moment, there was return fire from the fort, and John saw the shrieking shells and the flames tracking them from the batteries.

Henry Schafer had moved into the open space beside him. "Are they fighting without us?" he asked, shouting over the racket, which was loud enough that even a half-deaf man like Henry could hear it. "Is it Fort Henry again where the fleet wins and the infantry never fires a shot? I'm ready to fight, Jack. This Secesh rabble has killed our friends."

John thought of what Levi had told him when they'd crossed into Tennessee—that he might have gone either way fighting. He had cousins all over the state.

"Duck," John said. A shell flew over the Rebel breastworks and headed straight toward them. At the last moment, it blew up in the air.

"Our boats must be close," Henry said. "I tell you, Jack, I'm ready to fight."

Instead, they held the line while the gun battle raged between the river and the fort. Men stuffed what they had into their ears. Bits of paper. Dried oak leaves. They pulled their caps down and covered their ears with their hands or arms. John could still hear cheers from the fort every time the Rebels launched their shells. When shots from the river landed, dirt kicked up. He saw what he thought was a sandbag shoot through the air.

After a long while, the Confederate fire seemed to grow quieter. Then it picked up again and the racket from the river lessened. John could hear a metallic noise—a thin, odd ringing—and he wondered if it was shells hitting battleship armor. There was another flurry of shots from the river and, suddenly, a huge cheer went up from the fort. Then there was no firing at all, but only a raucous celebration from the water batteries and the breastworks across the ridge.

Their own line, reading the sounds, had grown very still. Finally, John couldn't stand it anymore. "You get your wish, Henry," he said. "If the navy can't do it, we'll get them on the ground. We'll get our chance, and we'll take it right to them."

Yet at sundown, they were still in line and the Rebels still noisily celebrating their victory over the fleet. When the company was relieved by another unit, John started a letter to Kate, intending to thank her for sending the valentines. It was an easier thing to do than writing to Ann Bradley (with Ann, he always felt he had to strike the right note), but he couldn't bring himself to tell Kate about Levi or about what else had happened—not here in the middle of it all. The only things he really wanted to write were good-bye and how cold it was, so he put his paper away and settled in for another bitter night.

The men huddled together, trying to get warm. It didn't work, but they all had their fantasies of what they thought would. Bill New wanted to burrow under a mound of hay with his wife or any other available woman. Jake Schaen said that, small as he was, he could shrink further and tunnel underground with the field mice and moles. Some of the men thought fondly of St. Louis, and not for the fun they'd had when Colonel Veatch's watch was stolen or for the sight of men jumping saddleless over vaulting bars. Not even for the opportunity to smuggle in whiskey or have their pictures made when the machine wasn't broken. The only thing at all from St. Louis that any of them wanted was another chance at burning their backsides on the barracks stoves.

Max Munte, who'd just been made quartermaster sergeant, said they'd all have to freeze. Pressed, he told them he'd see about their tents and about blankets and coats to replace the ones they'd left on the road. John kept his dream to himself. It was two dreams actually, the one merely theoretical of the kind of warmth he might find bundling under a blanket with Ann Bradley, the other of the long-ago scene in Drimarone with the sheepskin stretched yellow across the window and peat burning in the fireplace and, by the far wall past the bed where he'd slept with his sisters and Denis, the cow and her warm breath. John knew the Harmony house was tighter but, for thinking of the warmth he'd experienced, there was nothing to equal the memory of crawling into that bed of sleep-flushed children while his mother rocked Charley and sang her low song.

It was endless hours later, when men had grown quiet in their misery and the effort to keep their feet moving, that dawn came. Teeth chattering, John relieved himself behind the lines. Afterward he soaked his hardtack in the tepid coffee sent up from the ravine. He scraped a bit of sugar from Mary's valentine and stirred it in. A biscuit weevil was floating on the surface, and he pinched it out and flicked it away.

He was halfway through the coffee when he heard gunfire on the right. It was a lot of gunfire, and he quickly downed the rest of the coffee and, still chewing at the biscuit, hurried with the other men to fall in. In very short order, they formed a battle line along the ridge. Every man was ready with his rifle, and Colonel Morgan, who knew his soldiering inside and out, gave them his stern, perpetually sad-eyed look and reminded them discipline was all, that soldiers who followed commands were soldiers in armies that win.

The firing grew heavier. Men were wary, looking toward the right, but there was still no command given to move there or to move forward or to move anywhere at all. The bugle was silent. The men simply waited under the lowering sky, the ground trammeled from snow to mud and rutted beneath their shoes. Some squatted. Some marched in place. Some lay on top of their guns.

An hour went by. Then another. John thought there would be fire from the Rebel breastworks to their front or from the skirmishers, but there wasn't. A flock of panicked-looking geese flew overhead, their wings beating through tendrils of smoke. John wanted to shoot one and cook it. He wanted to eat the whole thing so he felt full and warm.

He looked around for Henry Schafer. He thought Henry would be impatient and angry, but spotting him next to a tree, John saw he was just waiting, too.

Sometime around one, when word had spread that McClernand's men were attacked and running and that General Grant had ridden off before dawn and left behind nothing for his commanders but an order to keep their positions, John heard Romeo Keister muttering, "Lordy Lordy. There's himself. There he is again, General Grant."

John looked where Romeo was pointing with his gun. There were men on horseback, and one of them was a familiar, squattish figure riding behind the lines as fast as a horse would carry a man over icy ground. The men along the ridge gave a cheer. John watched until the figure was only a blur and a flying, last flick of horse hoof.

"Something'll happen now," Bill New said beside him. He raised his voice. "Henry, you're getting your fight."

John thought so, too. They were not waiting so much as anticipating. In a way, it was as if Thursday's chaotic action had not even
happened and that this was the actual battle coming. He felt his own
blood rising. Their whole army—General Grant's army—would storm
the fort and show their mettle. They'd show all these Rebels. They'd
force them to see that the Union wasn't a thing to be broken over
Kansas bloody Kansas, or over an election, or over a feud about whatever things it was that men had thought and argued about to get them
to this place. It wasn't a thing to be broken at all. John had a whole
polemic throbbing with his blood. It was the fiery, thwarted politics
he'd learned from his father and grandfather, growing up in Ireland. It
was about the consent of the governed to be governed and the impera-
tive of keeping compacts to ward off anarchy and despotism and, even
if it put both North and South in oddly straddled positions, the entire
brief was still in his head as they formed their battle line, answering the bugle calls. The skirmishers went forward. John could feel the
vibration of the ground from their double-quick through the trees,
and his mind focused on practical things, on the things that had been
drilled into him again and again.

General Smith rode up. His horse was gigantically tall and his
long mustache flying. It was as white, John thought, as his eyes were
blue. He was ordering men into position and telling them to hold
their fire until they cleared the abatis. Then he was ahead of them,
leading the charge, waving them on with his sword as they cheered
and screamed. They went over the downed trees. They went through
muddy, creek bottomland. There were houses scattered here and there,
and John thought they must be full of men with guns. They halted
near one of them anyway.

Captain Saltzman was leading them now. They waited for their
right to come up, and it did, hurtling down rows of corn stubble. Then
they were in battle line again and all on the run. John saw General
Smith once more, his mustache still blowing. He saw the frozen preci-
pice he was taking them to.

They were near it. Then they were going up. They were running with fixed bayonets, though it was all but impossible.

Steep.

Slippery.

Still, they clawed up the snow. Rebel screams shrilled down on them through a tangle of branches. Sharpshooters' bullets banged off the trees. Their artillery was firing in cover, but men were falling in spite of it, crumpling, it seemed, body part by body part in the smoky air.

The lines put up a hellish fire. John thought he saw blue uniforms in the ravine beyond them. There was a sudden order to cease fire, and he wondered what had happened, if something horrible had happened, but soon they were on the move again. The Rebels were yowling like a pack of cornered animals, and it was hand to hand finally, men fighting fiercely in the thickets with their bayonets. John charged at a Rebel who was charging toward him. They were so close he could see the tobacco stains on his teeth, but the man veered to the side, struck by a bullet, and John's bayonet plunged into a different man's chest. He could hardly believe it. He'd run the man through. In a terrible instant, he'd felt the flesh give.

When he pulled his bayonet out, blood spurted into his face. He swiped his arm across his eyes and, half-blind from blood—and from sweat or tears, he couldn't tell which—he kept on fighting. They all did. There wasn't a choice. They were making headway. They were crossing ground, going farther and farther until at last they were clear inside the enemy works that other Union men had already breached. They were past the rifle pits. They were advancing in spite of shots that smashed the earthworks with such force that the air stunned men backward. Pushing on toward heavier fire, they ran through a field. John didn't know at all how long they'd been fighting, he was so thirsty and panting like the oldest dog, yet he felt oddly exhilarated. He hadn't known this would happen. *Blood lust.* Was that what it was? Something overwhelming and atavistic from deep inside his brain that he thought could worry him, though it didn't yet. His body was tight like the coil of a watch spring that would either keep working or explode.

They halted in a low hollow to form a new line, men gasping, some retching in the snow, but John was ready to move. He wished he had the bugle now. He wished he could sound the forward or that he had the colors and was leading them all on the charge. There were men in front of them he was wild to join.

Then suddenly, in one blurred instant, the forward forces were retreating, firing as they came. "What's going on? What happened?" John yelled, as if the men backing toward them could hear or heed him—as if they could answer so that a man would know what they'd said over the rifle fire and the scream and boom of riverboat shells that were sounding once more, Johnny-come-latelies to the day.

Captain Saltzman was moving among them, checking the line. "Steady," he said. "Give them cover as they come. Steady, boys, steady."

And it happened that quickly. With John still eager to surge ahead, and Henry Schafer loading and firing so fast it seemed a mirage-like flicker, a bullet shot past George Tretheway as he jammed his charge home, and arrived with John's name on it.

He saw it come. In all his life, he never doubted that he had. He turned his head to the right at the very instant another man was grazed in the act of speech, and the bullet whistled on, coming straight down the battle line, and lodged in his own flesh and blood.

He crumpled, the sky going cockeyed with tree branches.

New Harmony, Indiana
Late February and March 1862

4

Dwelling 635, Absolem Boren 28, Charlotte M., 27, William S. 3
Dwelling 638, James Sampson 53, Eliza 49, Mary 25, Mary Maidlow, 72,
    M. Mulhern, Help
Dwelling 744, Adam Lichtenberger 41, Caroline 35, Alice 12, Mary 10,
    Eliza 6, Catharine Given [21], Help

1860 Census, New Harmony in the County of Posey in the State
of Indiana

Kate Given was hurrying up Church Street in New Harmony, a chilly wind whipping at her skirts. It wasn't her day off. She was supposed to be scrubbing floors at the Lichtenbergers', and it worried her that she wasn't, for she knew how lucky she was. Of the Irish girls in New Harmony—and they were all of them serving girls—she had one of the very best jobs. Adam Lichtenberger was a leading merchant in town. Mrs. Lichtenberger was the daughter of John Beal, who was famous here. He'd built the ship that brought Robert Owen and his followers from Philadelphia, and he still had a wonderful orchard outside of town. Kate was proud of her position, and she was careful to guard it.

Since the report in the Mount Vernon paper that the 25th was fighting at Fort Donelson, she'd been anxious, and today it had shown. On Monday, she'd been all right for the old Harmonist bell had rung and the whole town—wild with excitement—had turned out to celebrate the Union's victory with a bonfire and torchlight procession. Kate had been as thrilled as everyone else. Yet two days had gone by, and there still wasn't word about the men she knew. Or about John.

40

The whole afternoon she'd kept remembering October when Captain Highman of the 1st Cavalry was killed at Fredericktown. Mr. Hugo had gone for the body. The home guards had come from Mount Vernon and Farmersville. When the funeral prayers and eulogies were finished, the Harmony and Mount Vernon bands played the "Portuguese Hymn" and the hearse and Mrs. Highman and her children left for the cemetery, a six-pound artillery piece and more than a hundred wagons and buggies accompanying them. Kate had been living it all again, understanding it, she thought, for the very first time, but it had made her so distracted that Mrs. Lichtenberger had finally sent her home.

"Go see about your mother, Catharine," she'd said when Kate spilled a bucket on the kitchen floor. "At this rate, you'll burn yourself with the lye."

Mrs. Lichtenberger had not spoken unkindly, but Kate had still been embarrassed. She felt like a shirker. Going home meant not only that the floors were unscrubbed but also that she wouldn't be at the Lichtenbergers' to serve supper or to see to Eliza while her mother helped the older girls with their schoolwork.

At home, going in the squeaky door, Kate found her mother alone. She was knitting, and the yarn ball fell as she rose from her chair.

"Nothing yet," Kate said quickly. She took off her cloak and went to retrieve the yarn from the cat. Her mother sat back down, and Kate gave her the yarn. "Mrs. Lichtenberger sent me to sit with you."

"Then do. Sit, Kate." Her mother looked out the window at a sound in the street, and Kate pulled a chair around, and her mother starting knitting again. "Your father's gone out to see if there's news."

"I hope there is, though I hope, too, there's not." Kate made a throat-clearing sound to cover the small tremor in her voice, but her mother had noticed it anyway. She nodded toward the crooked basket that Kate had helped Charley make.

"You can work on the sock Margaret's started."

Kate stared at the basket but didn't get up. She looked at the shawl that her mother was knitting and tried to follow the stitch. The yarn moved behind one needle. The other needle caught two stitches. Then her mother's finger circled the yarn around the second needle until, finally, that needle pulled the loops through, and two stitches were pushed loose and two new stitches settled in place.

"I'd like to learn that stitch. And the pattern," Kate said. "I'm tired of knitting socks. I know the boys need them for marching and the cold. But I'm still tired of it."

Her mother didn't look at her. She didn't slow down her knitting. "It's a stitch that takes patience, Catharine. And patience isn't a thing that you have."

"Is that why you learned it? For patience? But you've always been patient."

"It's a stitch you can work if it's loose. It's an easier tension. It was to learn that," her mother said, and Kate added things up for herself. Her mother the worrier. The two years that Kate and her father and her cousin, Margaret Mulhern, had been here in New Harmony earning the money for the others to come, while John was at Trinity College in Dublin, and for a reason Kate had not understood, reading with Protestants. Her mother had learned this pattern then—the big looping stitch that could make her relax. Waiting with the younger children, she had wanted something to make her easy, which was what she wanted once more, waiting to hear about John.

Her mother stopped to stretch her fingers and wrists, and Kate looked at the shawl in her lap—at its lacy stitch and the slaty blue of the yarn. It was new wool, and the shawl meant for a baby at the poor farm. Kate knew that both of these things astonished her mother. That she should be knitting for charity. That she should have new yarn when in Drimarone the new yarn had always been sold, and knitting was from scraps of pulled-out ganseys, the ones grown too ragged to mend.

This was America to her mother, Kate felt: a place where, even in wartime, the yarn would always be new. But the stinginess, the care would never really disappear. Kate thought of the army socks her mother had made, all of them short at the top. Constance Fauntleroy, who was one of Robert Owen's granddaughters and, in Kate's opinion even more superior-acting now she was Mrs. Reverend Runcie, had been clearly disdainful when Kate deposited them in the basket at Union Hall.

"Irish socks," she'd muttered, and even the apologetic smile from Mollie Owen, who was a Sampson by birth and Robert Dale Owen's new daughter-in-law, couldn't take the sting from the words. The worst of it was Kate knew they were true. Nothing she did would nudge her mother to add an inch for a soldier's boot. And as far as the baby at the poor farm was concerned, his blanket, too, would be shorted. To be warm, the child himself would do well to be small.

Kate watched a moment longer. Then she picked up the army sock she could do in her sleep.

Her mother had fixed tea and Kate had finished the heel when the latch pulled and the door opened, squeaking loudly once more on the hinges. This time her mother didn't get up, but Kate felt her sudden, poised stillness as Denis and her father came in.

"Is there news?" Kate asked, and her father was nothing like the spirited fellow, well into his cups, who sat at the supper table while she and her sisters laughed until they choked, and then put his glass down and happily roared, "Where did your man get such plump-faced girls? Could they be any finer? Or louder?" At the moment, her father looked totally grim.

"No word about John or the other boys. The papers say the victory's been celebrated all through the North, but it's what we feared. The losses are heavy."

Denis spoke up. "We can go find John, Michael McShane and me. We can take Michael's horses," he said, but their father shook his head.

"You can't find a man when you've no idea where he is. Margaret, get out your rosary."

~

Since the day when she and her father and Margaret Mulhern had arrived in New Harmony, Kate had considered it an essentially happy place. To her, its main quality was optimism. As she'd come to understand her adopted town better, she'd decided it was because the founders—the Rappites—and their successors—the Owenites—had intended to make a perfect society. They hadn't succeeded, of course, but they'd left a real legacy. The town's German landscape and architecture came from the Rappites. The Owenites had sparked a tradition of intellectual fever. And though there were many people like her own family who were simpler sorts, many of the townspeople had been utopians themselves. Or they were descendants of them. Or they were the writers and artists and scientists who'd been drawn here later. The result was that New Harmony had a unique sort of energy.

Kate loved it. Though it could feel oppressive being an Irish working girl in a world that had better-regarded girls, and though there was the occasional unpleasantness with someone like Constance Fauntleroy, to Kate, New Harmony's real face was the eager and sociable one it had shown in sending off Company A. In August there'd been flags and hurrahs and a huge, cheering turnout with all the girls in their Sunday best (Kate had seriously coveted the pale green lawn that Ann Bradley had worn—a castoff from Mrs. David Dale Owen, who now wore nothing but widow's weeds). But now, after that first enthusiasm for the win at Fort Donelson, Kate saw nothing but somber-looking people.

It wasn't that the war had not been a concern earlier. It had been—and not just when Captain Highman died. In a town where nearly every family had a son or husband in uniform, nothing was anticipated more than the mail packet, and everyone did something to help with the war effort. Not only had the women knitted an army's worth of socks, but they'd also made quilts and countless bandages and everything else that a soldier might need. Not a steamer left the landing without cigars or a barrel of ale that men were sending to the boys in their camps.

Yet the war's early months had held much less urgency. In letters home (and in letters to her), Jim Rippeto and Harry Beal might brag about skirmishes and chasing Rebels, but the 15th Indiana had seen only minor action in West Virginia. The 60th, under Colonel Richard Owen, Robert Owen's youngest son, was only newly formed. And though the letters Kate got from John in the 25th were full of soldiering, it was all drilling or guard duty. Their first foray from St. Louis was to patrol the railroad between Jefferson City and Sedalia, and they hadn't been in the fighting to their north. All John could write was that they'd camped near Georgetown on a plot of soggy grassland not half the size of Owen's pasture next to the Gullett house.

The 25th had missed combat at Lexington and arrived too late at Springfield to support General Frémont, with the battle over and the general already relieved of command. Kate had heard stories that the Missouri Irish dragoons, who'd fought so well at Lexington, had also done well at Springfield, and it made her feel proud. But from what she could tell, it was nearly Christmas before the 25th had even seen a Confederate, and then it was only as guards for the thirteen hundred soldiers who'd surrendered on the Blackwater. They took them by rail from Sedalia to St. Louis where John wrote that they'd moved back into barracks and their lives were drilling and more drilling—the 25th, to a man, hacking from colds when they did the battalion double-step. To Kate, it had all seemed very much like a practice war, and it was an idea she'd gotten used to. It was what she expected.

Now, though, it all felt quite different. The war seemed far more real because of Fort Donelson. It was on everyone's mind for every minute of every single day, and it was why Kate rose with alarm when she saw her father tapping on the window at the Lichtenbergers' the week after the town's raucous victory celebration. She'd been helping Eliza wash her hair and drying it backward in front of the fire so it covered her face. It made Eliza giggle, but Kate's laughter had frozen in her throat.

"Is it John?" she said, hurrying to open the door.

Her father seemed unsteady on the porch, and Kate wondered if he'd been drinking. It was only morning, but she thought that he had. She watched as he tugged a folded newspaper from inside his coat.

"It's got the dispatches. They marched from good weather into a snow-storm. Our Indiana regiments were outnumbered, but here it is: 'they fought with the coolness of veterans and the desperation of devils.' They're fine boys. They were full of bravery."

"But what about John?" Kate was trying to read upside down and trying to read her father's voice, seriously doubtful that he and her mother could stand it if the worst happened, and uncertain whether she herself could bear it if it did. It was the two of them really, she and John. They were the oldest, with the large gap after them where Biddy had fit ahead of the younger children. For all the years and months of years they'd spent apart since John had first left as a schoolboy going off to Dublin with Father O'Gallagher and Father's half-blind mule, he was still her best friend.

"The officers are all right. Two of the men from Company A were killed. Mike Chancy— I don't know him. And John Hugo Jr., Kate. Levi Thraillkill and George Tretheway and Robert Clarke are wounded, and this, too—so is John. He's here on the list. Catharine, I need you to come home with me to tell your mother."

Kate swallowed hard. She gripped her wrist to keep herself from trembling. "I'll run up to Mrs. Lichtenberger, and I'll get my cloak," she said when she could. Then turning around, she saw Eliza's big saucer eyes.

"He's wounded," Kate said, "my brother. Wounded is all. He's going to be fine."

It was the same thing she said to her father as they went down the street. It was also what she said when her mother went pale and her sisters both started to cry and Charlie raced into the yard shooting an imaginary gun at imaginary Rebels. And it was the thing she said under her breath again and again in the days that followed with no further word. He was wounded—John, the best brother a person could have. He was wounded, but he was certain to be all right.

Yet when she met Caroline Thrailkill in the street, Kate knew exactly what any passersby would think: they were looking at the sisters of men who'd been shot.

It was several days later when Kate found herself standing in the Sampsons' kitchen and waiting impatiently for Margaret Mulhern. Her father had heard in the tavern that Levi was on a boat home and Kate, certain Levi would know about John or that John would actually be with him, had vowed to meet every boat that she could. She was glad when Margaret agreed to go with her, but now she was holding onto the blankets she'd brought while Margaret stoked the parlor fire. Margaret nudged the cat from the settee. Margaret put the last bit of crocheting back into Mrs. Sampson's hamper.

Kate was exasperated. This was so like Margaret. A month ago, she'd waited for her in the bitter cold for a long quarter hour. When she'd finally knocked on the door, Mr. Sampson in his night-shirt opened the upstairs window and jokingly asked her up. For days, Margaret had been icy with Kate, vexed that she'd "unsettled" the household she ran like a ship.

Kate, trying to calm herself, looked at the perfect bowl of apples on the kitchen table. "Are you ready?" she asked as Margaret came in. "Mr. Cannon's taking us. He's probably waiting."

Margaret tasted the stew. She seasoned it before pushing it back on the stove. Then at last she got her shawl from the hook by the brooms and wrapped it around herself. Kate, who was still annoyed even when they'd left the house, thought for the thousandth time that style was lost on Margaret. She could have a bonnet and cape. For all the money she'd saved, she could have a fur collar to set off her face. And she had a good face. From her looks, no one would ever guess she was past thirty. Thirty-three, in fact, which was ten years older than Kate. But Margaret was so set in her ways. Her shawl was the same one she'd had in Donegal Town where they were both in service, the one she wore wherever she walked in Drimarone, the exact one she'd shivered in belowdecks in the dismal hold when they'd crossed the sea.

"I knew you'd be early," Margaret said taking one of the blankets to carry. Then she laughed, and that was Margaret. She was stern about her work and mean with herself, but Margaret did have the love-liest laugh. And when she set off at her quick pace, Kate thought that that was Margaret, too. There was something iron about her. In fact, it was family gospel: the Mulherns from the Glen. They were agile. They were tough and smart, and they kept on living forever, though Kate's mother always added that Margaret, as she was, was half an O'Donnell.

Kate heard Mr. Cannon calling to them. "Over here, girls. Whoa, here we are." He wasn't in his room in the hotel where they'd have summoned him with a pebble thrown against his window. He was straight across Main Street with his wagon.

"Have you heard anything?" Kate asked. "Father thinks it's likely they'll come on the mail packet." She followed Margaret's lead, putting her blanket in the wagon and then planting her hands on the open wagon bed to swing herself up.

Mr. Cannon started the horse. "Not a word," he said.

"Are you sure?" Kate called to him, but Mr. Cannon, who was her father's friend from long before any of them had come to New Harmony, was sunk into his collar. Kate realized he hadn't heard over the horse snorting.

The wagon wheels bumped over the street, and Kate and Margaret rode like children with their feet sticking out. The day was masked gray. There'd been no sun to strike the hotel sundial, but as the wagon lurched down Church Street toward the river, and Kate looked over her shoulder, she saw a bright spot that made bands of clouds in the middle sky. A lone chicken crossed the road in front of the wagon. Two dogs nipped at the horse's tail until Mr. Cannon flicked their noses with his whip and they ran off yelping.

"John will be thinner, of course," Kate said. "If he's here. If he's on the packet. All the soldiers are thinner when they come home."

"Not Irish thin," Margaret said.

Kate thought there wasn't any point in comparing. There was war in America now. And often there was fever, too. But there wasn't real hunger. Not hunger of the kind that they'd known.

They were nearing the landing, and Kate scanned the river for the boat. There were flatboats upstream and the ferry was waiting, but she didn't see any packet.

"Are we still early?" she asked Margaret. "Or has it gone?" She got down from the wagon when Mr. Cannon stopped. She went to stand by the horse and rub his nose. He nibbled her hand for a root or some sugar, but she'd hadn't brought anything.

"It's there. On the horizon." Margaret had come up beside her and Kate thought she saw it now, the dark shape and the puff of steam where Margaret, with her sharp eyes, was pointing. Margaret was whispering a prayer to herself, but Kate wouldn't. It was too small a thing to pray for, that a person would be on one boat or the next.

The boat was nudging its long "V" in the water as it came closer, and Kate picked up the blankets so she was ready, and then nervously put them down again. The men on board waited as the boat slowed. Then they sent the long loop of rope out and one of them jumped ashore to tie up. Mr. Miller's boy had come for the mail, and Kate watched as he traded Harmony mail sacks with the mail sacks on board.

"Have you someone with you? Have you got John Given?" she called, and the pilot leaned over the wheel, cupping his ear.

"John Given—is he on board? Or Levi Thrailkill?" she asked, wondering why Caroline wasn't here.

"We've got mail, miss."

"They were wounded at Fort Donelson. You say you've got nobody?"

"Nobody but the working bums here. Step away, miss." Kate saw the deckhand pitching wood into the boiler as they fired up. She felt like throwing a stone at the pilot or maybe at the boat or at the crows that had landed to peck at the thawing ground.

"There'll be another boat," Margaret was saying. "If not the mail packet, then another steamer. Tomorrow. He's sure to be here soon, Kate."

"But what if he's not?"

Mr. Cannon was turning the wagon around. "We'll know when we know. Climb in, Kate," he said, and she sighed and stopped herself from finishing her thought.

She was glum for the rest of the afternoon and the evening. She was glum the next morning, and glummer yet in the afternoon when she left Eliza with friends and walked down to the mail packet and didn't find John. She'd started back when she saw Mr. Cannon coming down the hill with his wagon. Margaret was in the back.

Kate waited as the horse stopped, and Margaret got out. Kate shook her head. "If you're looking for the mail packet, it's already gone."

Mr. Cannon was holding the horse and pointing out at the river. When Kate looked back, she saw an eagle swooping over the ice floes. She squinted and saw a darkening gray blotch on the horizon.

"There you are," Mr. Cannon said, settling the horse. "Maybe Denis is on board. And your cousin Michael McShane. They went to Mount Vernon this morning."

Kate was startled. "They did? But why? Did John send a telegram?"

"Not that they said." Mr. Cannon's horse whinnied. "Margaret, do you know anything?"

"I think it's a boat for Fretageots' store. Mr. Sampson says they're expecting a shipment."

"But it could be Denis and Michael McShane. It could be John, couldn't it?" Kate said, growing excited. She looked at the ferry, bumping on the swell. She wanted to climb on board and order the ferryman to take her straight out to the boat.

"We'll wait," Mr. Cannon said. "Take the load off, girls? The two of you want to sit up here?"

It was the last thing Kate wanted to do—to sit still waiting—but it occurred to her that Mr. Cannon was cold and that he wouldn't take a blanket for a lap robe unless she or Margaret did. And, of course, Margaret wouldn't think it was proper to sit next to him in spite of the fact that his wife was dead. Or because of it. Margaret, Kate suspected, was afraid Mr. Cannon wanted to marry her.

"All right," Kate said. She climbed up on the seat and asked Margaret for a blanket and spread it out. Mr. Cannon smelled old to her. He smelled old and like his horse.

The boat was drawing closer now, cutting toward them across the river. Kate was suddenly dubious about its course. She wasn't sure—she couldn't really tell—but it seemed it had come from the Cut-off Island side of the channel, and she wondered why. Did it mean it wasn't coming from Mount Vernon? And did that mean it was another boat without John or Levi or anybody else? Considering the possibility, Kate felt worse than glum. She was fizzled out. Worn out. Her eagerness was gone. Her mouth tasted like metal. Beneath her, the wagon seat was very hard.

"Margaret, he's not going to be here," she said. "Mother and Father will be disappointed again and she'll be sharp with him for drinking, which is how it will show."

"Kate." Margaret gave her a look, and Kate felt her face burn, though she hadn't said anything that wasn't true. And they were *her* parents. She could say what she chose. But Margaret was right, of course. She shouldn't have.

Kate pushed the blanket aside and got down from the wagon. Her eyes had flushed with tears. She prided herself that she never cried, but all this waiting and uncertainty had made her a wreck. She was spoiled, she thought. In Ireland, you expected the worst and lived with what happened. Here in America, you expected the best, and the not-so-bad seemed a great deal harder to take.

The crew was readying to tie the boat up now, but they were making a bigger job of it than the mail packet had. Kate saw they had things to unload. If it was something for Mr. Fretageot, she hoped it was more Tell City furniture. She had her plans. Someday, when she had money to keep, she would walk into his store and point at a rocking chair and say, "Have that sent to my mother, please, to Mrs. Given from her daughter Kate."

She was thinking about furniture and silverware of her very own when Charley came running down the bank. "Is John here?" he asked.

"Is he coming?"

"I don't think so. I don't know." Kate brushed Charley's hair from his eyes. "We none of us know. He wasn't on the mail packet. Did Mother send you?"

"I was done with my chores."

Kate laughed. "It's all right," she said, and she felt calmer with him here. Or at least she felt a need to seem calm, and it worked the same way.

"Is that Denis?" she said quickly. She thought she'd seen Denis come out on the deck. She thought he'd put down a knapsack.

"There's Michael McShane," Margaret said. "And there's a knapsack." Margaret was standing on her tiptoes. "Is it John's? I think it is. It is! And there's John!" Margaret gave a little a squeal, and it surprised Kate for its oddness, coming from Margaret, but she was right again. John was here. He had four crutches—two wooden ones and Denis and Michael. He had a beard and a dirty, ill-fitting uniform, and they were easing him onto the deck, practically carrying him. Kate ran toward the boat with Charley. Charley got there first, and Kate nearly fell, but she caught herself and hurried to clamber on board. When she reached John, she tried to hug him and hold him up all at the same time. She squeezed his hand and felt how warm he was. Hot really. Charley had his shoulder, holding it tight. "You're alive, John," Kate said. "Thank God, John. You actually are."

"And the two of you—you'll knock me over." John made a short sound that was part laugh but more cough.

"Mr. Cannon is here. He's got his wagon." Kate looked around, and Margaret, who'd come up behind her, grasped John's sleeve. Tears streamed from her face to her shawl.

"Margaret," he said, and Kate could hear the effort in his voice, the fatigue, but there was still the faint trace of his teasing. He kissed their cousin's cheek.

Kate and Charley spread the blankets in the wagon. Very carefully, Denis and Michael lifted John in. He went white, wincing, and he held them off when they tried to shift his leg. "I'll sing to you,

John," Kate said and, as Mr. Cannon started the wagon, she sang the first song that came to her mind. It started, *There's not in the wide world a valley so sweet* and, when she switched to Gaelic, which was how she and John had first learned it, the horse put his ears back.

"You trained an Irish horse, Francis," Michael McShane said.

Darkness was growing as they made their way home. Lamps were being lit in parlors. All the town smelled of wood smoke. Kate kept on singing. Michael McShane and Charley were walking next to her, while Mr. Cannon drove the wagon, and Denis held on to the bridle. Some time after Margaret had left for the Sampsons' and they'd neared their own house, Kate motioned for Charley and Denis to run on ahead. Still she kept singing. The wagon jerked, and John started from his doze with a moan, but Kate didn't stop.

Then Mr. Cannon pulled the wagon up in front of their house. "We've a knapsack," Kate heard Charley calling at the door.

"And we brought Michael," Denis said. "And, Mother, the knapsack is John's. We've got John."

Kate pictured the yarn basket spilling and the slaty blue ball rolling across the floor. A second passed. Another. Then their mother was in the doorway, and their father was there, pulling his boots on as he came behind her, and Margaret and Mary were down from the loft, squeezing past Charley and Denis.

John was awake and moving in the wagon. "Battered, but present," he managed, and their mother was crying, "John, John," and hugging him over the wagon side. Their father, though he wasn't a big man, simply picked John up and carried him inside.

A loud bang, a short explosion of dried sap went off like a gunshot in the fireplace, and Kate saw John flinch. "Just the fire," she said quickly as her mother sent Margaret and Mary to fix the tea and hurried ahead to turn the trundle bed down.

Kate watched her father ease John onto the bed. Then he took out the whiskey and poured John a dram. He held the glass while John drank. His own mouth was open, and he didn't close it until John had finished.

Kate got the lamp and carried it into her parents' room. Her mother had begun cutting the threads in the seam of John's trousers and, when the leg was opened, their father and Denis eased the trousers off. There was dried blood and fresh blood on a bandage on John's knee.

Swiftly, Kate leaned down and kissed his forehead. "Mary's here with your tea," she said, but already John's eyes were closing. Kate shooed Mary out and Denis, too. She wanted to stay. "He liked me to sing," she started, but her mother shook her head. Kate backed toward the door. She waited a moment and then she pulled it to, leaving her parents to watch John as he slept. "Call me," she whispered into the crack.

Michael McShane was sitting at the table, drinking the tea that Margaret had brought him. Kate put her mother's knitting away. "Did you know that he'd be there?" she asked Michael. "I met the mail boat."

"Denis found him. I heard a hospital boat would lay in at Mount Vernon. And the Tell City boat was in with her stock for Fretageots'."

"What luck."

"He was cold on the boat. There're more boys coming in the morning."

"Is Levi?"

Michael shook his head. "I didn't see him. John didn't say. He's been asking after Ann Bradley."

"I heard she's in Evansville." Kate rolled the edge of the tablecloth under her thumb. She was seeing the bloody bandage, and seeing John wince again. She turned to listen for a sound from the bedroom. When she looked back, Denis was coming in from outside.

"Kate, if you're going back to Lichtenbergers', Mr. Cannon is waiting."

Michael McShane stood up. "I'll hitch a ride." He put his tea down on the table, and Kate reached over and pressed his hand. She was thinking that she'd never fancied Michael McShane, that even if he'd not still had a wife in Donegal, he was old for her taste and, too, he was a cousin. Yet the spring before she'd come to America, she and John had taken a cart to Meenacahan and then all the way to Ballinreavy Strand. Michael had raced his horse for them. Far, far out on the tidal flats he'd gone, the horse's feet splashing as he galloped. The sun shone through the streaky clouds and lit the water off in the distance. Kate had found it incredibly thrilling. Now, Michael had moved her again.

"Mother will need me. Michael, could you tell Mrs. Lichtenberger I won't be back tonight, please? And thank you, Michael. We're all of us very grateful."

He took his coat and got his cap from the pocket. "I'll walk out with you," Kate said, and she listened while he and Denis made plans for retrieving his horses.

Outside, the evening was chill and black. Kate thanked Mr. Cannon, too. She watched Michael McShane swing up beside him. He wasn't bowlegged. He wasn't at all. But Kate always thought he looked as if he should be.

She heard the horse clip-clopping into motion, and she thought of the smoke rising from the chimney behind her. She stepped back into the shadows. For that one instant when the fire had issued its retort, John had been afraid. She had known that he was. *The sound has frightened him*, she'd thought. For an instant her brother had been afraid, and that fact told Kate much more than the blood on his leg.

She nudged at the soggy leaves beneath her shoes. She watched Mr. Cannon and Michael McShane thicken into silhouettes in the distance and dark, all the while thinking that that single moment of seeing John's fear had given her her first real sense—nothing more specific than a feeling—of what the war really was.

5

Children of Robert Dale and Mary Jane Robinson Owen: Florence Dale,
Julian Dale, Rosamond Dale, and Ernest Dale Owen;
Child of William and Mary Bolton Owen: Mary Frances Owen;
Children of Robert Henry and Jane Dale Owen Fauntleroy: Constance,
Ellinor, Arthur, and Edward Fauntleroy;
Children of David Dale and Caroline Neef Owen: Alfred Dale, Anna
Maclure, William Herschel, and Nina Dale Owen;
Children of Richard and Anna Neef Owen: Nora Edgeworth, Eugene
Fellenberg, and Horace Pestalozzi Owen.

New Harmony's First- and Second-Generation Descendants of
Robert Owen

This was the way John began his recovery. In the days, he slept fitfully. At dusk, or later at rushlight or when the candles had guttered, his nerves came alive and he felt like one, gigantic, fiery knee. He could not sleep at all then but tossed and gritted his teeth and, if he thought no one could hear, moaned softly into the bed linen.

His mother, who in Drimarone had known every plant and leaf that could possibly treat an illness, trusted nothing in New Harmony she'd not fixed herself. When Mrs. Maidlow came with her bag of herbs, she was turned politely away. Later, Mollie Owen and Charlotte Boren, her granddaughters, arrived and the tea they brought was put aside on a shelf. Though Mrs. Boren had wanted to ask John for word of her husband, both women were sent away, too.

A chagrined Kate, who admired Mollie Owen most of all the young women in New Harmony who came from important families

(Mollie was a Sampson by birth, and her husband Julian Dale Owen, who was Robert Dale's son), told John all this with a worried look. Then she slipped him the laudanum she'd brought from the doctor, and his pain jumped to a little box in his head. There were beautiful angels like tiny statues, perched on its top.

The next day John heard Kate, who did not get angry with their mother ever, get angry and say she was bringing the doctor to the house. When he arrived, he listened and poked and prodded, and said the wound was suppurating nicely. Then he gave John more laudanum, and the angels on the box (one of them very like Ann Bradley) began battling. It was a terrific battle over heaven and hell, and John, raging with them, could hear his mother ushering the doctor out and closing the door with a bang. Finally, the angels collapsed on the box, exhausted and disheveled, and John slept for hours, though the mixture of fever and laudanum gave him a horrible nightmare. He was in close combat again. He was in a fury, and he'd killed another man, but the man came back to life, his face bloody and hideous, and drew on him point-blank. John woke with a scream that brought his parents stumbling in their nightclothes to his bed.

In the morning, his mother ordered Charley to get Margaret Mulhern and to dig up every kind of root they could find. Later she gave John the new medicine she'd made and broth that caused him to boil inside and out. He said he was burning up and was there snow to roll in, and she rubbed him with alcohol until his teeth chattered. To get him warm again, his father and Denis pushed the bed out by the fire, and his father poured whiskey into him that made the box open and more angels spill out.

In spite of such help—or because of it—as the week passed, John began to grow better. It did not happen smoothly. He still had his days and nights as turned around as a baby's. There were times when he wanted to cut off his leg or when the fever made him nearly insensible. He would forget where he was, and it was only with the greatest effort he could convince himself that his mother was actually in the room, and not an apparition. He would startle to awaken in such familiar surroundings and think he was hallucinating, that he was really in a soldier's bunk or still lying cold and immobile on the shattered ground while the blood seeped out of him. There were other times when all he felt was a diffuse sense of terror.

The good moments came mostly in the mornings when his fever was down. His mind wandered restlessly over books and events. At times, he daydreamed himself a boy again. Often, he was riding with Father O'Gallagher in his cart behind the mule that was blind in one eye, the socket layered permanently fleshy and pink. They'd turned off of the Carbragh Road and started their way into the heart of Dublin, John gazing at gull-perched buildings as tall as a cliff, at pubs named Cassidy's and Sweet Mollie's, the Stag's Head and Paddy O'Reilly's, though he was looking for Mick O'Gallagher's, which belonged to Father's brother. He was taking it all in when a band of roaming boys, armed with apples, ran into the street and landed one of them square on Father's forehead.

Father's eyes had glazed like a stunned sheep's. He tumbled backward, and John thought he was killed. He was bloody himself. An apple had hit him in the chin, opening him up like a freshet. He was yelling for help. He was a gusher and a priest dying against his leg.

At least once, when he had this daydream, it was an actual dream and Kate had been home. He'd wakened with her soothing his head with a damp cloth.

"Shhh. The rowdies again?" she said and, when his heart had slowed down, she helped him to change his soaked nightshirt and, while she did, she picked up the story.

"Margaret and Mary were afraid of the mule. It was the one Father O'Gallagher took into the Blue Stacks when he gave the Last Sacraments. They always hid when they saw it."

"But you were fond of it."

"I was. The morning you left home for Dublin, I rubbed his ears. I put my nose next to his, and I told him to take care of you the whole way to Dublin. Then you ran back to kiss Charley in the cradle and to leave Denis your slingshot on the bed. When you left, Mother was crying and Father gave you a coin."

"He did. He told me that I'd be in real poverty, that it was a holy thing for the priest Mother wanted me to be, but to keep the coin just in case."

"And he told Father O'Gallagher you'd better be off, that if the wind on the sea road didn't die down, you'd both be eating ocean salt half of the way to Sligo. You never said where the mule slept or if Father O'Gallagher did, but each night traveling you slept in a different parish house. You had a bench or a pile of rags at the end of a hall, and Father giving a verse in the kitchen to go with the drink. In Dublin, you woke in a pub with wadding on your chin. You thought Father O'Gallagher was dead until his brother told you, 'Look over there. He's wearing a goose egg is all. It's him that's ahead with the drinks.' And he gave you a coin for the coin the gang took."

Kate had finished with a laugh, and John made an effort to smile, though his strongest memory was of the pub's darkness, of the narrow, smoke-smudged window and of the dust pushed into the corner. He'd thought of home without him, Denis helping with the cow.

John grew quiet then as the harsher, nearer memory came crowding back.

Kate's expression registered the change in his mood. "What happened, John," she said in her softest voice, "when you were shot?"

He shook his head. He closed his eyes and, even if he wouldn't speak of it, he could see the sky of branches that had fallen on top of him. He was less clear about what had happened afterward. He didn't know if Dr. Walker had cut the ball out of his knee there on the field, or if he'd done it the next day in the hospital, putting a rag of chloroform over his mouth and rubbing morphine into his wound. John knew that he'd lain outside for a very long time, that he was pinned under a tree with sparrows flying frantically over their nests and, around him, men weeping and gunfire dying away.

He had not been cold while the fighting raged but, lying there, the sweat soaked his hair and lay in the small of his back and chilled him clear through. Yet it seemed a distant cold, almost abstract, and he'd considered it as though it were an extra part of himself. A new organ. A new set of fingers.

An owl was perched on his tree, staring, and John stared back at eyes like the sparking lights that came in the fall—will-o'-the-wisp flashes that skipped over the moorish Drimarone landscape when a cloud shaded the moon and poteen drinkers up in the hills sat by their fires. On nights like those, the younger girls had hidden behind their father's legs for fear of the little people and ghosts, though Kate never hid, nor Biddy before she grew so sick.

There were other fires, lanterns bouncing in the distance and coming slowly nearer. John heard voices and muffled laughter and, for a time, he thought it was the poteen drinkers themselves coming to steal the coin he had from his father although, when he'd roused himself more, he knew he wasn't in an Irish field. The noise in his ear wasn't the lapping sound of the Eany Beag when it flooded, making a lake, but his own heartbeat.

They were after his money once more. The light settled on the ground and they were at him, strong-smelling fellows reaching roughly into his pockets and, if he'd had his arms free, he would have struck at them, struck them hard for him and Father O'Gallagher both.

"Bloody, dumb Yank," he heard. "This one's got nothing but valentines."

If you'd turned out a priest, John, then we'd have one in New Harmony," Charley said on an afternoon when he'd come in from school. John's leg was fierce, but he was still determined to help Charley with his figures.

"You'd rather have me a priest than a soldier?" he asked from the bed. He did not tell Charley what was true, that if he'd been a priest it would mean he was a lonely curate in Ireland whose closest family had all gone to America. Englishmen like George Tretheway and Harry Beal would be his enemies instead of the Rebels. He would have never met Ann Bradley. He would never have shot or bayoneted a man who meant to shoot or bayonet him. He wouldn't kill a man in every one of his nightmares.

John reached over and wiped Charley's slate clean. "Try this one," he said, writing out a problem from James Mulhern—Margaret Mulhern's brother who knew all of math. While Charley worked, John told him the game they'd had in Drimarone when their father and uncles, thatching a roof, would promise him a farthing if he could do a sum or a puzzle faster than James. As furiously as he'd scribbled and as idly as James proceeded—taking out time to cut a scraw or talk to the dogs—James had always had the answer ready before him.

"I thought you were smarter than anybody," Charley said.

"Not smarter than James. Not at figures," John said. "And James was older," he added, remembering the men drinking and each one louder on the fineness of the hedge schools he and James had gone to before either of them left for Dublin. Then they grew misty-eyed about the schools of their own day that were still hidden behind bushes. A boy stood lookout so the Catholic master didn't get hauled away.

John considered asking Charley about his own teacher, though he hadn't asked about anyone else in New Harmony. He'd overheard Kate say that Ann Bradley, who was the person he most cared to hear about, was in Evansville, but he hadn't inquired if anyone had sent her a message to say he was home. He hadn't asked about Levi either, though he wanted to. For the moment, feverish as he was, he really couldn't muster the energy for any of it.

The next afternoon brought a small remedy. His mother told Mary to sit with him while she went to the store, and John felt well enough to tempt her to say what she knew. She sat cross-legged on the trunk, and leaned forward against their parents' bed, clearly bursting with things to tell. John thought how pretty she looked, how lively, and how much more grown up she'd gotten in just the months he'd been gone. She was hardly a little sister anymore.

He tried shifting his leg to lie on his side, and Mary got up quickly to help him. "Caroline's making a sling for Levi for when he can walk," she said, "except he's way too sick for now. But he'll certainly get better." She stopped and looked up at John, and the look on her face told him she wondered if she'd said too much.

"But he's home?" he asked. "Levi is?"

"Yes, but he was longer than you. For a whole day, he was on General Grant's headquarters boat, and he almost got sent to St. Louis. He's got proud flesh and the doctor burned it out. Twice. But it's not like the Hugos."

"And what about them?" John asked, and Mary looked at him uncertainly. "I already know John died," he said.

"They thought it was William at first. Mr. Hugo got a letter saying William was dead, and they all felt dreadful, and then the news came that it was John instead. They felt relieved and horrible all at once. I heard that Alex saw him when he got killed and that he shot at the Rebels twenty-nine times and dared them to come out and to kill him, too."

"I believe you're right." For an instant, John could hear the gun pop-popping down the line once more and, in all the din, Alex Hugo's voice. "But Levi's all right?" he asked, circling back.

"He will be. Are you cold? I can get you my comforter." Mary stood waiting, and he thought about shaking his head, but he was slipping back into sleep. He let it go.

As the days passed, John realized, with a first hint of boredom, that he was staying awake for longer periods. He'd also begun to read again, and he thought seriously of writing a letter to Ann Bradley. His sister Margaret told him Ann was in Evansville to accompany Nina Owen on a visit since Mrs. Owen was still in mourning and thought their house too oppressive for a child. John considered what Margaret had said and, instead of writing to Ann, he wrote to Harry Beal with the 15th in Kentucky. He was generally feeling better. Even if his knee was like a watermelon and his leg wouldn't go straight, it was no longer an acute source of pain. His father made him a sound walking stick, polishing it smooth, and the whole time complaining he didn't have bog oak to carve it from. John tried hobbling around the house, his father or Denis steadying him on one side. He could tell that his arms and his good leg were still strong, but he got lightheaded easily and often found himself digging his fingers into Denis's arm.

He still had no appetite. He had to force himself to eat the things his mother and the girls brought. But suddenly, as if a part of him that was basically comatose had reawakened, he was starving. He ate ham and eggs for breakfast and a whole loaf of bread with his mother's gooseberry jam. He ate half a chicken at dinner. He accused his sisters of posting word of his appetite on the doors of Union Hall since well-wishers, finally allowed by his mother, had started arriving in full force. A steady stream of women appeared with baskets covered in linen napkins. Margaret, rolling her eyes at him, ushered them into their parents' room and John would make his thanks and feel like a freakish display, though he'd shaved himself and wore a clean shirt, and Kate had trimmed his hair. There were married women coming to call that he thought had never in their lives walked over an Irish doorstep, let alone into a sick man's room when he wasn't kin. John felt squeamish with the celebrity of it all and puzzled at the little flags, decked out with home-painted stars and stripes, which festooned so many jars of canned meats or pear halves. He felt he was supposed to be some kind of symbol, that because he'd gotten himself shot, women felt like patriots if they brought food to him. Even Mrs. Owen, David Dale Owen's widow, came to call, and his mother received her with such calm and dignity that John thought, for a moment, she really was the royalty his father teased her about being, descended as she was from O'Donnell chieftains. John wondered how Mrs. Owen was getting along without Ann Bradley and, for that matter, how he was. She had brought her niece Constance Fauntleroy (with difficulty, John remembered she was Mrs. Runcie now), but Constance, who was just out of mourning for her mother, stayed at the front door, a fact that gave Kate endless reasons for commentary afterward.

John found Mrs. Owen, in her brief stay, very kind. He liked it best, though, when Mr. Cannon or Michael McShane came to visit so they could have a round of cards. He wanted to see his other friends, but the only ones he knew were in Harmony were Fred Perkey, who'd been in the hospital in St. Louis and was furloughed home on sick leave, and the men who'd been wounded. This included Levi (Kate said he was getting better) and Robert Clarke, though if John had heard right, Robert hadn't stayed home but had gone to the hospital in Paducah. George Tretheway had been hurt, but not badly enough to be sent home.

He was starting to wonder in earnest why none of the girls in town came to call. It was not just Ann Bradley who was missing. He'd not seen anything of the Smith girls, nor of Annie Perkey or of Susan Arnoldy or Martha Wilsey. Except for his sisters and Margaret Mulhern, who came most evenings to say a rosary with his mother, that disembodied, arch hello from Constance Fauntleroy had been the sum of it for girlish voices.

He asked Kate about it one day when she was home from the Lichtenbergers'. She seemed reluctant to answer. Finally, sheepish and laughing, she told him that their mother thought it improper for girls to visit while he was still in bed.

That did it for John. "Then I'm not in bed any longer," he said, lifting his leg onto the floor and pushing himself upright with the walking stick. "Kate, you and I are going walking."

They managed a half block and a little more. John felt exhilarated at the pure freedom of being outside, but by the time they managed their way back to the house and Kate had hung her cape on the door hook, he was panting and his leg hurt like blazes. He hit his good leg in frustration.

"John, it's all right," Kate said. "Your knee's been on furlough. Your whole body has. We'll try again tomorrow. I'll bring Eliza. She's been wanting to see you."

"Can't you bring anyone older?" he said, knowing he sounded curt.

Kate smiled at him anyway. "All the girls are just waiting."

They started now on what Kate called the "perambulating part" of his recovery. Each day they walked a little farther, and every day there was someone to join them. At first, John thought the girls Kate had planted along their route, which he was sure she had done, saw nothing except his limp. But after a while, he stopped really thinking about it. He found he could make a joke or flirt as well with one good leg as with two. And there was nothing like a Harmony girl. He hadn't realized how much he had missed them. They were fresh faced and quick witted, and he would measure them against any girls in that regard, although it wasn't every Harmony girl he held in such high esteem but only the ones he knew best—girls like his sisters, and Lizzie and Kate Marshal, and Susan Arnoldy and all of the Anns. Annie Perkey. Ann Armstrong. Ann Wilsey. And Ann Bradley if she'd ever get back from Evansville He'd kept an eye out for her everywhere they went, until Kate told him she wouldn't be home for another week. Then he'd simply felt gloomy.

It was from Susan Arnoldy and the Marshals that he learned just how immense the victory at Fort Donelson had seemed at home. "To think you were in General Grant's army," Susan said, the excitement plain in her voice.

"Unconditional Surrender Grant's army," the Marshals chimed in, and Lizzie asked when he'd realized they'd won.

John was feeling tired, dozy in his eyes and forehead, and he leaned a bit more against Kate. "I know where I was when I believed that we'd lost," he said. He was thinking again of the tree lying on him when the scavengers came through, and of how he'd believed that the Federal lines had been run back to Fort Henry and that he himself was heading straight for a Rebel prison camp. "I was looking at an owl," he said, aware of how much more he could tell them that he wouldn't, things like being lifted into the air and hearing the chaplain's voice and then bumping along on horseback, hoisted and draped there with another man. His head had been near stirrup level, and what he saw was the bloodied bodies of other men as the horse clopped through the snow. There was the stench, too, of the field hospital where he lay among the dying and mangled and asked for water. And at daybreak of some day, he was put on board a hospital boat, but it was a hellish thing, the wounded men crowded together and no one to fix their dressings if they jostled loose as the boat churned through the water. Men bled to death and stayed there until they reeked like the corpses they were.

"Sunday morning. That's when the fort surrendered and the boys ran up our flag," he said to Lizzie.

At supper that night, his mother told him he was looking stronger, and his father asked if it was the fresh air or all the girls.

Francis Cannon was eating with them, and he looked at John across the table. "It's the girls, of course," he answered for him, taking a drink from his glass, and John could see he was tipsy. "Those wounds are—what's the word?—like an aphrodisiac. For the girls. Levi Thrailkill's holding court at home. Emma West is ready to head for Paducah ever since Robert Clarke went on to the hospital there and wrote her that his wrist is stiff from the surgery. And he told her his finger is stiff."

"Francis," John's mother said, but his father, who was drinking whiskey, too—more whiskey really than Mr. Cannon—laughed and leaned back in his chair. He rubbed Charley's neck.

"I should go and see Levi," John said. "Kate, why didn't you tell me he was well enough?"

"I didn't know that he was." Kate put her cup down and got up from the table. "You can have Mr. Cannon take you since he's the authority on all subjects tonight," she said, and she started clearing the dishes.

"Well he is much better, John. Caroline told me, and I actually saw him," Mary said, and John noticed his mother give her a quick but measuring glance.

He touched Kate's skirt as she went by. "I didn't mean anything," he said. He watched her carry the soup to the stove, and then he looked back at Mary. "You have more reports on my comrades?"

"Fred Perkey's still at home sick, but he's getting better and Annie thinks he'll be back with the regiment soon. She says Mr. Hugo saved his life getting him furloughed from the hospital in St. Louis. Of course that was before Mr. Hugo's son got killed. I bet he wishes he'd gotten John sent home so he wasn't dead."

"And that would be an idle wish, Mary Given," their mother said, crossing herself. "Help your sister," she added. She stood up from the table and took a candle to the chair where her knitting was.

John's father poured another glass for himself and another for Mr. Cannon. Margaret, who had been quiet all through supper, rested her head on the table. A strand of her hair came loose as she scratched her finger across the cloth. "At home, the young men are marrying instead of fighting a war," she said.

"Hush," their mother said, but it was too late. It was as if a bell had been rung. Their father was up, unsturdy as he was, the whiskey in his glass splashing up the sides as he waved his arm. "*This* is home," he said. "And Margaret Given—you, miss—don't you forget it. It's what they quote from Mr. Webster. *Liberty and union!* We'd no freedom in Ireland and if it's union it takes to save it here, then they'll have our sons, and no daughter in my house will say a word otherwise." He turned to John, his eyes bloodshot and teary. "As long as they don't kill you, John. I couldn't bear it if they did."

"Nor I," John said. He looked at the shiny bit of gutta percha in Margaret's hair. "That's a pretty comb, Margaret. Is it a comb?" he asked, and he glanced at Denis for him to get their father to bed since he couldn't do it himself.

When Kate came from the Lichtenbergers' to walk with him the next day, John thought she seemed distant. "I asked Caroline," she said. "We can go to see Levi. Mr. Cannon was wrong. He's hardly had visitors, but we can go. If you're strong enough. If you don't think you'd end up both collapsed in the bed."

"Kate, are you angry with me?" he asked, and they walked on a moment with both of them quiet.

"I don't think so," she said finally. "I don't see how I could be, John. I just thought you were short with me—as if I hadn't done my part or told you enough or helped you enough. And I never like it when Father's drunk, and Margaret's right. All over Donegal, the lads and girls will be marrying now, and here all the boys are off at the war, including ones that I like. I can write letters but it's not the same as having them here. I'm in two places, John. I'm needed at home and at Mrs. Lichtenberger's. And it would go very hard on us all if I lost my job."

"That's a lot not to be angry about."

"Well I'm not angry. But you got shot, John. Every boy is getting sick or shot. The Highman children are orphans. Half orphans. And is there reason enough for any of it? I think Father's wrong. It really is like home again. It's politics and people fighting and, when people get hurt, what good can there possibly be that comes of it?"

John didn't say anything. He knew what Kate meant, but he thought, too, it was one of her moods. She'd been so incredibly proud. When he'd left for the war, Company A marching through town to board the steamboat for Evansville, Kate had run alongside and cheered the loudest of anyone. Her cheeks were so flaming with excitement that John was embarrassed, thinking if he was to be made over in front of everyone he would rather it was by Ann Bradley, not his sister. But Kate was like the weather. If it rained, she stormed. If the sun shone, she was full of happiness. And if the weather was uncertain—well, Kate was as changeable as the mercury.

"I thought of Biddy when I was shot," he said.

Kate kept walking. In a moment, she slowed her pace and looked at him. "Anymore, I don't remember her often, which makes me feel guilty—that I've forgotten—and so then I think of her even less, which makes me feel worse."

John felt the weight of the tree branches once more. "It seemed I had to warm her legs," he said. "The way that we did. And I saw her as red as she was, and the skin around her mouth so pale. I always see that. And how deeply hollowed her eyes were."

Kate nodded. "I thought when I gave her my vest she wouldn't die." She shook her head and gave a forced little laugh. "What a silly child to think that. But it's still as if our family's this tall bureau with the middle drawer missing. Did I ever tell you that before we left for the ship, Father and I went up to her grave? We stood there the longest time."

"I wrote 'Bridget' in the snow the way I carved it on her stone," John said. "I drew it with my fingers. It was something that, even with the cold and my arms pinned down, I could feel to do."

They'd stopped at a corner. "Should we go out to Levi's?" Kate asked. Her bonnet strings had come loose, and she fiddled at them and tied them again.

John's leg was throbbing, and the talk of cold had made him cold. He shook his head. "Not today. Let's just walk home. What you were asking, Kate? I have it all thought out and then I have to think it out again, but it comes out in the same place. It's what Father was saying. If states leave, they break the Constitution, and without the Constitution, there's no point. It's basically that. We wouldn't be free."

"But am I free? I'm not so sure. There're women who've gone to nurse the troops, and I don't know that even they're really free. And the states aren't free if you think about it."

"But men are. You've been reading Frances Wright," he said, remembering his own trips through the Harmony library shelves and finding Fanny Wright, advocate for women and friend to Robert Dale Owen, Robert Owen's eldest son.

"Free if they're not slaves. And the war's about that, too, isn't it? Yes, I have been reading Frances Wright."

"And so you'll band up with the other girls and wear bloomers?" John saw Kate catch a glimpse of herself in a storefront window, and he saw that she'd noticed him notice.

She gave him a squinty-eyed look with her mouth screwed up. "Mother would say I'm too vain to give up my dresses. And she wouldn't approve anyway. But for things like scrubbing a floor, bloomers would certainly be practical. Do you think, John, that we'd have a war if men all were in skirts?"

He laughed. "If the men were in kilts or on sidesaddles?" He paused a moment, considering various pictures in his mind. Then he took Kate's arm and turned to start home. "No, Kate. Probably not."

6

Marx and Engels commended [Robert] Owen and the other utopian socialists for their attack upon "every principle of existing society," but condemned them for failure to realize the significance of class antagonisms. The "utopian" element in Owenite socialism was that which prevented it from supporting revolutionary class action.

J. F. C. Harrison, *Quest for the New Moral World*

March 9th: Late snow today. Mr. Cannon reports river rising. March 10th: Snow melted and river higher. John wrote down both headings and then rubbed the feather end of his pen across his nose until he sneezed. His mother was at the neighbors'. Everyone else had something to do: Mary and Charley at school, Margaret helping Kate get ready for a dinner party at the Lichtenbergers', his father and Denis off mending a fence with Mr. Cannon. He had the house to himself, and he was writing in the book that Margaret Mulhern had given him. She'd bound it herself and it was more cover than paper, but he was intent on filling it so he could tell her he'd used it, and not feel guilty leaving it behind when he went back to the regiment. He dipped the pen again, trying to think what else he could write. Finally he made an entry under the weather notation for March 10th: *Denis earned a half dollar taking cattle to the Cut-off Island on the ferry boat and came home looking like he swam the river.* Then he sat back in the chair. He stared out the window and up the street with its canopy of bare rain trees.

The town he'd come back to after Fort Donelson was a place that felt entirely like home, yet John still remembered what a curious choice it had seemed when his father had settled on it. He might have gone to Chicago where his sisters were. He might have followed the O'Donnell relatives to Bridgeport in Illinois where John's cousin Menomen had already made a fortune. John remembered the letter his father had sent him in Dublin: *You heard about the Rappites, John—how the men don't take a wife but look to the Kingdom. Francis Cannon I knew as a boy lives in the village they built that Mr. Robert Owen bought for his new moral world, though it didn't turn out. Francis says he left smart folk and family behind. I thought your mother, Lady Margaret O'Donnell Royalty Given, might just find it good enough.*

What his father had not written, and John had learned later, was that Mr. Cannon had standing in New Harmony since some of his family had been part of the Owen experiment. His brother had joined its Preliminary Society. When the Community of Equality was formed, his sister had been married to a Randolph by Mr. Owen himself. But the continuingly remarkable thing to John was that dusty-looking Mr. Cannon had, at some point, brought two young nieces to live with him and his wife, and one of them was Ann Bradley.

John heard himself sigh a deep sigh. He turned back to his notebook, but he didn't pick up his pen. His knee was twingeing, and he pulled his trouser leg up to look at it. The wound had formed a floating scab that was circled with red. He had no desire to write that down. He had no desire to include a medical report of any kind, although if he'd wanted to, he thought he could write about Levi, who was still very sick.

"You'd make a fine suitor. Arm shot to hell. Oozing blisters. Shakes from the fever," he'd said when he visited in the morning and heard Levi badgering his father to take him to Smiths' so he could call on Margret. Levi had lobbed a pillow at him in reply and then fallen back against the headboard.

When Levi's sister Caroline showed John out, she'd asked him to come again soon. "You're a tonic for him," she said. "Father's off working most days. It's been mostly my mother and me, or my sister when she came with her girls. I think he needs a man he can swear with."

John thought of writing that down. *March 11th: Went to Levi's and heard him pining for Margret Smith. Should practice swearing so I can visit again.* Instead, he put his pen in the well and looked out the window again. He would rather write about Caroline, he thought idly. She'd grown tall and graceful and, though she could be quite serious, she had a definite talent for banter. Or at least for the right, slightly pointed phrase.

His pen was still in the inkwell when Michael McShane walked past the window and then came in the door and sat down.

"You're dressed up. Did you steal the jacket?" John said.

Michael didn't say anything, but he started whistling. He shooed the cat away from his trouser cuffs.

"Don't tell me the widow's in town."

Michael whistled louder. He looked at one corner of the ceiling and then at another.

"Let me guess. You left your crew to finish their work. You've had a bath and got a shorter haircut to show off that bull neck. You're hoping the Wilseys will ask you to supper so you can charm the widow, though Mother rails at you you've a wife back in Drimarone. And you've time on your hands, which is where I fit in."

Michael stretched his legs out. "You're looking better, John," he said. "Not good enough for Ann Bradley to look at, but better."

"Ann Bradley's back?" John leapt up from his chair, forgetting his knee so it buckled under him. He caught himself on the writing table.

"There were two extremely fine-looking women who blew in on the Evansville stage. And, yes, I do believe the younger one was Miss Bradley with an Owen child in tow."

"Ann! Ann and your widow? Did you talk to her? Did she ask about me?"

"I did. She didn't. I gave her my greetings. She said if she'd had her hoop on, she'd sail up the street. And then she crossed the street with the little girl, and I paid my respects to her traveling companion."

John grabbed his walking stick and hobbled as fast as he could to the commode in the corner. He reached for a comb and, ducking down to look in the mirror that was hung for his sisters, he worked on his hair. He was wondering if it was the mirror and the light or if his eyes had actually changed from blue to green when he got shot. "Does my hair need cutting? Where's Kate? Do you see her coming up the street? Blast it! She'll be at the Lichtenbergers' tonight. Can you cut this off?" he said to Michael, and he yanked at the side of his hair. Then he poured water in the bowl and scrubbed at his face and beard, thinking that at least with his mother's soap, his hair had turned back to brown from its greasy dark. "Should I shave off the beard?"

"If I didn't know you were done with your fever, I'd think you had one," Michael said. He laughed. "What's the plan, John? You think you can limp over to the Owen house and say, 'Excuse me, Mrs. Dr. David Dale, but you've a parlor maid I'd like to speak to and marry before I go back to the war and get shot at again. Could you please send her out?'"

"Who said anything about getting married?" John splashed more water on his face. He tried plastering down the stray bits of hair that wanted to curl. "But she's here, Michael? You're not pulling my leg."

"She's here, and maybe she'll give you the time of day with so many lads gone. I wouldn't expect more."

John splashed water across at Michael, aiming for his jacket and hitting his mother's yarn instead. "So you don't think I can just call in to see her?"

Michael wiped at the water with his handkerchief. "I believe it was you who said Mrs. Owen doesn't allow Ann male callers at the house. Or that Ann told you that. But go on and get ready. We can stand out in front of Fretageots' and smoke. You can look wounded and hope Ann spots you across the street and comes out. Or you can try to calm down and wait here for your sisters to bring her to visit. And you're right. I'm eating at Wilseys'."

"I need my uniform. Not the pants. They're cut up. But the jacket and cap."

"So now you'd like a valet?"

By the time his mother came in, John was ready to go. Her face whitened when she saw him in his uniform. "I'm not leaving," he said. "Michael and I are off for a walk. There was something in my pocket," he added, and his mother nodded and went to her drawer. He saw his own letters tied with a string, the flag on the top envelope flying under the cancel mark. His mother searched in the drawer for a moment. Then she brought him the valentines.

"There was something else. A letter," he said, looking at the valentines and noticing that the top one was Mary's. He could see the faint imprint of the sugared heart he'd licked clean on the hospital boat and, with a start of excitement, he felt the silk on the bottom card.

"Is this it?" his mother asked. "John?"

With an effort, he turned his attention to the envelope his mother was holding up. He nodded and made his way across the room. He took the letter from her and, light as it was, it felt like the weight of a live shell in his hand. He knew he needed to read the whole thing. He knew he had to find out where to send it. And, too, he had to write his own letter that would tell a mother not that her son had bled to death freakishly in his arms and was a beautiful boy, but that he'd been a soldier who spoke of her in his last words.

John felt himself wavering. He was drawn in two different ways, but the one felt more immediate. He put the letter and valentines back in the drawer. "I'll take care of it later," he said. "Come on, Michael. You can't be late for your widow. Mother, Michael's widow is back. Not his widow. It seems he's alive. But somebody's widow."

"Michael," his mother said, and then: "John, you won't be gone long?"

John kissed the worry lines on her forehead. "Just if I'm lucky."

When they went out, it was to the bright light of late afternoon and to dogs barking. It occurred to John he needed a plan. On a normal New Harmony day, a man could ask a girl to walk out to Maple Hill, but he was no particular specimen of either walker or manhood right now. It didn't count that before he'd left home he could run backward up the whole steep pitch of the hill faster than anyone. It didn't matter that three weeks ago he'd scaled his way over underbrush and straight up to a ridge while people shot at him. And if to some girls just the fact of his uniform would make his case, he knew Ann Bradley wasn't one of them.

"Let's stop at the hotel," he said. "If the McMunn girls and Fanny Wiles are working, we can get one of them to take Ann a message."

"They'll be fixing tea—fixing supper," Michael said, and John shook his head impatiently.

"We can ask them anyway," he said.

At the hotel, they found Mrs. McMunn at the top of the stairs. She was carrying linens, while Mrs. O'Neal, who was running things while her husband was off with the 60th, was headed up to the third floor with a crying child.

John took his cap off. "Excuse me, but is Jane here? Or Fanny Wiles?" he asked.

"The answer's yes."

Mrs. McMunn went into a room and John glanced back over his shoulder at Michael and spoke in a low voice. "Your field. She's a widow."

A moment later, Mrs. McMunn called down to them. John made a careful trip up the stairs with Michael behind him. Inside the room, Mrs. McMunn had set the clean linens on a nightstand by a pitcher, and she was pulling sheets off a bed. John couldn't tell whose room they were in. There were books on a shelf and a small drawing of an old couple and two young girls, but he knew the room wasn't Mr. Cannon's.

Mrs. McMunn piled the dirty sheets on the floor and looked across at him while she put on the pillowcases. "I'm not one of them, but there's people in this county who'd find it all right another Irishman got shot. Jane says you had a birthday."

John was taken aback. "More than a month ago," he said, realizing the date had come and gone without his even remembering it. He was twenty-six.

"Jane thinks it's a waste of a marriageable man for you to stay in the army, and I told her it's better for an Irishman to marry late. McMunn told me that, and he was right. Of course, McMunn is dead." Mrs. McMunn fluffed a pillow up in the air and plunked it down on the bed. "Jane's likely in the kitchen if you want her. You won't find her in here or Fanny either. And neither will your fancy-looking friend."

They were headed downstairs before John looked at Michael. "I told you she's got her eye on you," he said, and he was laughing when they turned toward the kitchen.

Fanny was the only one there. She had a big apron on, and her face was hot from the stove. She was stirring a kettle. "If you've come for Mr. Cannon, he's not back yet, but he'll be here for supper," she said. "John, you're looking fit. Fitter. Did you know Ann Bradley's home?"

"It's why I'm here," he said, and he wanted to lean against the counter, but he made himself stand up straight. "Could you go across the street and ask her if she'd meet me?"

"Meet you where?"

John was quiet. He was thinking it was too cold to sit in the back garden at Mrs. David Dale's even if Ann agreed to it, and it was certainly too cold to offer her an ice cream, which he didn't even know if Julius Miller was still selling.

"What about Union Hall?" Michael asked.

"It's open?"

"You could sit in the back row. They're rehearsing the play."

"If you'd ask her that," John said to Fanny, and she looked doubtful, but she pulled her apron off, and gave him the spoon to stir the beans. She said she'd be right back.

She wasn't. John thought she was gone longer than it was possible to be gone anywhere in New Harmony. He kept asking Michael the time. He was afraid the beans would scorch. The heat from the stove made his knee ache. "The hell with you and your fancy jacket. You stir," he said to Michael, and then Fanny came rushing in, all out of breath. She put her apron on and took the spoon back.

"She's not home, John. I talked to Kate Marshal and Ann's gone off with Mrs. Owen. Kate didn't know where. They didn't go in the buggy. I went to the Fauntleroys' and four stores. I didn't tell Kate you'd meet Ann because, frankly John, you look too done in to wait someplace for somebody who doesn't even know she's supposed to be there."

"Then we'll do that smokers thing, Michael. By God, we'll stand out front smoking and ask the whole town if they know where she is." John hit his fist on the counter. He wished he could pace. He wished he could kick something. He'd been patient since he'd gotten home, but this was the end of it.

"She won't like you if you hunt her, John." Fanny pushed the kettle back from the flame and wiped her face with her apron. "You know how she is. She'll like the attention, but she won't like you."

"So a man comes back from the war and he can't even see a girl?"

"If Francis is back, he can drive you home," Michael said, starting for the doorway. "John, she's not here."

John looked intently at Fanny. "You're sure Kate Marshal didn't say when she'd be back?"

Fanny shook her head, and then she put her hands up. "Stop, John. She didn't. There's tomorrow. Do like he says and let Mr. Cannon take you home. Go. Leave. I've a meal to fix."

Later, when he thought about it, John felt he'd totally given his hand away. He thought, too, that he'd been rude to Fanny. When Mary mentioned at supper that Ann had arrived from Evansville, and quite in style, he made a point of seeming uninterested. In a way, disinterest was actually what he felt. He'd been back more than two weeks and, if a girl wrote to a fellow and didn't at least want to see him when he was home wounded, well, that man might be indifferent himself.

Mary leaned around Charley to speak to him. "John, are you going to the play Saturday? And there're at least three parties and a ball."

"I'm not." John felt his jaw clench tight. He pushed himself back from the table.

Lying on his cot while Denis wrestled Charley in front of the fire and his father wrote a letter, John tried to read. He couldn't concentrate. He was thinking of valentines and Ann and of what he might write to the dead boy's mother. Finally he blew the lamp out and, closing his book, he simply lay there, his eyes closed. He listened to the occasional sound of a horse or cart in the street, or to the rarer muffled conversations of passersby. Sometime around midnight, long after everyone else had gone to bed, Margaret came in, back from helping Kate at the Lichtenbergers'. She tiptoed past him and climbed up to the loft. If she'd been Kate, he might have called to her quietly and talked to her, but she wasn't Kate. Kate was staying at the Lichtenbergers' tonight, and John was by himself with his sleeplessness, which was a form of homesickness, he thought, odd as it was he could feel such a thing lying in his own house with his sleeping family. But he missed something in the way that he'd missed home on the first nights in Dublin when he'd made it through the harsh school day and crept into the lineup of beds in the boys' unheated dormitory, the stench of waste from the back alley just out the door. And he missed that same ineffable thing in the way that in the later time at the minor seminary in Navan—and even when he'd gone to study with Bishop McGettigan in Letterkenny and was long used to being gone from home—he'd sometimes ached for what was familiar: plowed ground, cut turf, the rhythms of stories and tin whistle tunes. Each day at Navan, he'd felt himself more unanchored. It was as though he whirled in some vast space that was meant to claim and transform him with its hard demands. A space meant to seduce him with spiritual ecstasies. With ghostliness.

John rolled over into the pillow. He missed the lads, too—the camaraderie of camp. He missed even the terrifying moments like the one when they'd followed General Smith and clawed their way up the snowy hillside toward the Rebel screams. And something more. He missed a thing he'd never had that Ann Bradley both represented and didn't represent—that chance for a solid life of his own fashioning and, one day, children but, most particularly—most most ardently and disturbingly—a woman whose body would decipher his own.

Finally, after the first bird had sung at the far end of night, he slept.

For the whole time that he'd lived in New Harmony, John had known that stories of its utopian past were part of the ether. Often, they were colorful. The Rappites, its founders, were clearly hard workers, yet John felt that Father Rapp and his sect of German pietists were essentially comic. It amused him that in the millennial throes of the Second Awakening they'd renounced both tobacco and sexual unions. When they left Pennsylvania and came to the Wabash for more land and a climate for vineyards and orchards, they'd all dressed alike. The men wore frock coats, and the women checked aprons with plain gowns and caps. John imagined them as orderly as figures in a Swiss clock who step out at the hour. In a perverse sort of way, it delighted him that, in spite of their piety and hymn writing, they'd grown so prosperous making everything from flannel to beer that they could loan enough funds—at interest—to keep the whole state of Indiana afloat. He wished he could tell his Grandpa Given how they'd awakened to French horns and then worked in the fields with a band playing.

John didn't know of anyone in New Harmony who hadn't had fun with the tale of celibate Father Rapp taking up with Hildegard Mutschler in his old age. Nor was there a child or man who hadn't tried to match a foot to the Angel's Rock. Rumor had it that Father Rapp believed it held the imprint of Gabriel's feet, though David Dale Owen (who'd acquired the rock with Father Rapp's home) said the marks were an aboriginal carving. At one time or another, everyone in New Harmony had wished for the secret stash of money Father

Rapp had kept so he could head to Jerusalem at the very first word of the Second Coming. John also had a genuine fondness for the inscription a Harmonist had left when they returned to Pennsylvania. It was beneath a stairway in Dormitory No. 2, which was now the hotel and Fretageots' store: "On the twenty-fourth of May, 1824, we have departed. Lord, with Thy great help and goodness, in body and soul protect us."

It was an unsettled question why the Rappites had sold the town to Robert Owen. Some stories said it was fear of Indians. Others mentioned problems with envious neighbors and concerns about the malaria that had left the Rappite burial field with scores of graves. Still others said they'd left out of greed. Whatever their motives, they'd sold out lock, stock, and barrel. For $100,000, farmlands and houses and orchards and community buildings had been transferred from one set of utopians to the next.

It was clear to John that the impulses behind the two attempts at utopia were very different. While the Rappites had worked to prepare for Christ's Second Coming, Robert Owen's millennial hopes were decidedly more secular. It was a bit murky to John but, as he understood it, Mr. Owen wanted to create an ideal society right here on earth. People were to achieve not only an elevated moral sense but also material gain. And while New Harmony was intended to be the model for other communities it, too, had a precursor. In his Scottish days, Mr. Owen had acquired the New Lanark spinning mills from his father-in-law, David Dale, and made them such a showpiece of productivity and happy labor that observers came from all over to watch workers mill cotton and see their children dance and do military drills. Even the crown prince of Russia had visited.

That was one story. The somewhat darker view was that, in return for education, medical care, communal gardens, and recreational spaces, Mr. Owen expected a reliable source of docile and extremely pliable labor. Whatever his intent, it was clear to John that New Lanark had been the impetus and New Harmony the broader canvas for Mr. Owen's goals. The shaping of children was key. Mr. Owen, believing they would learn cooperation through his particular brand of firmness and gentleness, insisted they be separated from their parents at an early age to escape bad influences. To encourage curiosity, he had their classrooms hung with colorful paintings of large animals and charts that illustrated the Stream of Time.

It was all part of a grandiose ambition. Robert Owen believed his idea for communities would spread from New Harmony to the rest of America and the rest of the world. Yet from early 1825, when he'd purchased New Harmony, there was one fortune spent (his), innumerable proselytizing trips and infamous speeches (his), at least a dozen society reorganizations (some of them his), but scarcely more than two years elapsed before his oldest sons, Robert Dale and William, wrote in the *Gazette* that the experiment had failed. There had been a hornet's nest of activity in New Harmony, barely any of it docile and, after a pair of farewell talks, Robert Owen, who'd actually spent precious little actual time in New Harmony, had folded up his Indiana tent and left.

Of the utopian stories, John preferred the Rappite ones, while Kate was far more interested in knowing about the Owenites, which John assumed was because there were many more of them and their descendants still living in New Harmony. Whatever the reason, she sometimes started rattling off names from the Owenite past as they walked, announcing them like some monitor reading a school roster: *William Maclure, educator and partner to Robert Owen. Madame Marie Duclos Fretageot, teacher and friend and collaborator of William Maclure. Thomas Say, entomologist. Gerard Troost, geologist. Charles-Alexandre Lesueur, artist and naturalist. Joseph Neef, Pestalozzian teacher.*

"Why did they come here, John?" she asked. "I don't mean about the Boatload of Knowledge and Mr. Owen traipsing brilliant scholars from Philadelphia to New Harmony when he'd left his son William in charge. And poor William Owen—all those hundreds of ordinary people, who'd heeded Mr. Owen's call, descending here, and men like Caroline Thrailkill's father not even able to find a place to sleep. Did you know that William Owen was younger then than I am now? I mean why New Harmony, which was nowhere and is still nowhere? Why would M. Phiquepal d'Arusmont even be here for Fanny Wright to marry? Why wouldn't he have stayed in France?"

John had laughed. "You might as well ask why we're here."

Kate had taken him literally. "Of course we had hopes, and Mr. Cannon was here before us, and Father talked Mother into it. And you said even Grandpa Given knew about Mr. Owen and his place in the working-class movement and his interest in poor law reform."

"Yes, he did know," John said, remembering his favorite Irish story about Robert Owen and Ralahine, the cooperative community he'd inspired in County Clare. It had started out well, but ended in what John considered perfect Owenite fashion: the owner gambled away the entire estate and then fled the country.

"I really don't understand why they all ended up here," Kate said looking up at him. "I'm really curious. John, why?"

It was this lingering question of Kate's that had brought John to the library two days after his trip to the hotel with Michael McShane. He owed Kate—he always owed Kate—and he'd done the math. It was twenty-four days since he'd left the field hospital. He had six weeks of furlough, and Frank Bolton, the Harmony man who understood the most about rivers, had told him he'd need a week to get back to the regiment. Calculating on the safe side since he'd absolutely no desire to be reported or hung as a deserter, even though being one tempted him otherwise, John added another two travel days. He hated the thought, but what it meant was he had just nine more days before he had to leave home. He had nine days to get well enough to travel, or to pretend that he was. Nine days to spend with Ann Bradley, when he had yet to spend one. Nine days to do everything.

John looked at the stack of books he'd piled beside him. *Characteristics of Goethe. Don Quixote. Dodd's Cattle Doctor. Sidereal Heavens. Diary of Life on a Georgia Plantation.* All of them interested him or had a use, which amounted to the same thing, but they weren't about New Harmony and he needed something from the library's cache of old ledgers and diaries he could recommend to Kate. There was a whole repository of material on what had gone on in New Harmony from the time Mr. Owen had left New Lanark until he'd abandoned New Harmony, and John thought he could find what Kate was after if he kept himself from poking into explications of Goethe or reading about cures for cattle diseases.

At the moment, though, his leg was bothering him. He squirmed his foot in his boot and tugged his trouser leg away from his knee. He shifted in the chair trying to ease the pain, wishing he felt better. It wasn't just Kate's question that needed his attention. There were things he knew he should do with Charley—Charley who was having trouble with math and was still so ignorant of geography that he'd put London in Ireland. There was nothing to teach Denis, for Denis was Denis, and Margaret had always been good at school. But he wanted to spend time with them. And with his parents. And with Mary. He needed to convince Mary she couldn't force her friendship on anyone, that New Harmony had lines she shouldn't try to cross.

And all he had was nine days. John ran his fingers through his hair. Already his mother and sisters were at work on his clothes, and Margaret Mulhern had begun a tin with things that would keep: smoked meat, strips of peach leather, various remedies for chest colds and coughs. He needed to spend more time with her, too. Especially with her. From the very first cannon shot, he'd known he didn't have it in him to pray that havoc be visited on one set of men over another, yet he still found Margaret's simple faith oddly assuring. It was her voice, he thought, with its even murmur of familiar prayers. Margaret Mulhern could ask for things that he wouldn't but that he somehow still wanted her to.

"You should have been the family priest," he'd said to her the last evening she'd been at their house, and she'd laughed at that, and he'd thought he could have told her brother James, but not Margaret, that he believed the gods of antiquity—the ones who defied the laws of nature to help warriors—were really the only sort for a battle. Given the dreadful weather and brutal fighting he'd seen, he didn't know how a god hampered by causality could be of use in an actual war.

John yawned. He rested his head on the books. In a moment, he'd started to drift off through the dull pain. With an effort, he caught himself. He shook himself awake and started a brief side trip into *Owen's Meetings in Dublin*, which had a plate saying it was a gift from Robert Dale Owen. He had moved on to the astrology book when the library door opened and Achilles Fretageot came in.

John took in the slight figure in the long coat. Then he looked back at his book in case Achilles wasn't inclined to speak. Not that he expected an outright snub. But they moved in different circles in New Harmony. Merchant class vs. farmer. Native vs. Irishman. And beyond that, Achilles was one of the town's young people who carried its historic mantle—a grandson of the Madame Fretageot who'd come on the Boatload of Knowledge and taught in Maclure's school. John didn't expect or want to be sought out.

Yet a few moments later, as he was half reading an explanation of sidereal time, the darkness that came between him and the light was Achilles offering him the *Harper's Weekly* he'd been hunting for earlier. "It has the story about Fort Donelson," Achilles said. "A great victory, but it sounds fearful. I'm glad to see you looking well."

John thanked him. "And your brother?" he asked.

"In Missouri. Pa thinks they're headed to Arkansas. Fredericktown was the worst of it."

John nodded, and that was the conversation. The two of them shook hands and, as he watched Achilles go out, John remembered Michael McShane saying that when Alexander Fretageot rode off with the 1st Cav on his horse, Dove, he'd groomed her himself, and it was the very first time that he'd done it.

John looked briefly at the *Harper's Weekly*. Then he pushed it aside and got up and went back to the shelves. Except for Mr. White, the librarian, and Achilles, he'd been alone for the hour that he'd been here, but there were voices now, the sound of children coming in after school, and men and women stopping in, too. John wandered farther back through the shelves. He was aware of the voices, but he quit listening to them as he made his way through a dusty group of pamphlets. He read for a time and then his eye caught a letter just sticking up from the cover of one of them.

He slipped it out. It was yellowed and fragile. Carefully, he opened it, glancing down the page and back up again. He couldn't make out the month. The year, though, was 1825, and the letter was addressed to a Thomas and Sarah. The Pears, he thought. There'd been a Thomas and Sarah Pears in Robert Owen's settlement, and here was a letter written to them from Pennsylvania. Reading it, John thought it was from someone who was himself part of another Owenite settlement. The letter was full of queries and a lament that Thomas had not told the writer—a man named Bakewell—how best to deal with community discord. There was one line that struck John particularly: "You wrote me that Mr. Owen's 'heart ran away with his head here,' and what, Thomas, am I to make of that?"

John backed up slowly, still reading. He had sat down to rest his knee and to study the letter more intently when he heard the light tap of a parasol and a familiar voice. "Mr. Given, have you hidden yourself so well to avoid me?"

He looked up. He had just learned that Sarah Pears of New Harmony, 1825, had thought the town concerts good but felt like a desperate, caged bird, and here now was Ann Bradley of New Harmony, 1862, in full regalia before him. "Don't get up, John," she said, looking down at his knee.

"Ann," he managed. He pushed himself up, slipping the letter back into the pamphlet where he'd found it. He made space on the table for her reticule and the book she was holding, but she didn't sit down. "I heard you were back," he said, trying to sound a good deal calmer than he felt.

"I had your messages from your sisters. And I've gotten a letter from you today that I think came by way of Antarctica. You were in St. Louis and planning to have your picture made." Ann was all sparkle and flashing green eyes as she smiled at John in her flirtatious way. He took in her brown dress and cloak and the bit of lace at her throat and the beaver hat that he assumed was a hand-me-down from Mrs. David Dale Owen. Then, to his great surprise, Ann grew serious and reached down a gloved hand and carefully touched his knee.

"Is it this leg?" she asked, and he thought he had felt every sensation in his knee it was possible to feel until he had felt this one. "It was such a shock seeing your name listed with the wounded. And poor John Hugo. I'm very glad you weren't killed."

"I am as well," he said, trying to cover his confusion by straightening the pamphlet against the table edge. He had managed a day and part of another without looking for Ann and, at the moment, he had no idea why.

"I won't ask if you're coming to the ball tomorrow, but you'll be at the play Saturday, won't you? I saw you just sitting here and, as much as I have to hurry, I knew I must ask."

So she hadn't been hunting for him. That was what registered, but John heard himself agreeing anyway. He would be at the play. And he could go to the ball, he told her. He was hobbled, yes, but he would be delighted to watch the whole night's sets. And, even if he didn't say it, he did think it, as she nodded a quick good-bye and went up to Mr. White to check out her book: he could go anywhere at all—anywhere Ann Bradley would be that he might be as well.

7

However to show you the heat is not so great and inconvenient to every one as it is to me, I must inform you that our balls have never been put off for the most sultry night of the season.

Sarah Pears, New Harmony, September 1825

Short as it was on young men and in spite of the war, New Harmony, John realized with a new curiosity, was still itself with its visiting; sociable ways. It was not just the balls and the theater. There was not an evening that went by without a musical gathering or Panorama show, a scientific exhibition or the discussion of a Brontë book. Not a week passed without a boat stopping on the river to sell wares to streams of clamorous shoppers, not a late morning without a gathering of knitters or quilters, or a late afternoon without an expedition to find early blossoms or to make rubbings from cemetery stones or to watch the old men of the home guard still drilling at E. I. Rogers's warehouse. It was not that John took part in all these things. He didn't. But he became aware of them, just as he was aware of the lingering traces of Ann Bradley's presence in everything that he did. They were like the trailing threads of sugar that spun from his mother's spoon when she was cooking sweets.

He went to the ball. Since he couldn't dance, he sat near the door and watched as Ann frolicked through the sets. Now and again she came to sit by him, her face flushed and her eyes full of laughter. It occurred to him she was paying him more attention than she ever had at a ball, and he was pleased until the thought crossed his mind that she was simply taking her cue from the other girls. They were treating him as a hero. There was always at least one girl at his side to fan herself and him and to ask if he was having a good time and to say he looked well. Ann, he thought, wanted to show her dominion.

"I must say, John," she told him from behind her fan, "of every man who writes to me, your wit is the keenest." John was flattered, as he knew he was meant to be. He wanted to answer that, of all the letters girls wrote to him, hers were the shortest. He also wanted to ask what other men she wrote to and if there was a man she fancied more than she fancied him. He was wary of the answers, so he asked nothing of the kind. Nor did he ask what might have been a wounding question—if she had had her cap set for Colonel Julian Dale Owen, Robert Dale's son, and found it a bitter pill when he'd married Mollie Sampson as the town gossips said. Instead, he complimented her skill with the new dance steps. He told her how amusing her letter was that arrived the month before he was shot and informed him she'd applied to the celebrated "Doctor" Maidlow when she was ill, and gotten "pretty near steamed to death" in trying to obtain a cure.

"Are you done experimenting?" he asked, and it was the right question for it brought out her throaty laugh, which stirred him as much as anything could.

"I believe not," she said. "You can see when you come to the play and make a study of the costumes. I'm in charge of them." She closed her fan, taking the arm of a new soldier who came for her, and went back out on the dance floor for another set.

Margaret Mulhern brought him cider, and she sat down, tapping her foot. "Where's Charles Ward?" John asked. He was remembering his last ball on the Fourth of July and the day's celebrations when John Preaus had read the Declaration of Independence and William Twigg had given a speech. Martha Wilsey and Mary Mumford had commanded a squad of thirty-four girls, one for each state and all dressed in white with blue banners studded with glimmery stars. At the parade, Henry

Fitton had led the Harmony band and the Zouaves marched in their exotic uniforms. The dance had been that evening and when John had left Ann, his temper at boiling point because she wouldn't go outside with him, he'd seen Margaret dancing with Charles, her eyes down and her face in full blush.

"Where is he?" he asked again, and it was enough to make Margaret turn red once more though it was months later.

"He's gone to Colonel Owen and the 60th," she said softly. "He left just as you got home."

John wanted to tease her, to talk about Charles's smooth hands, as snow white as new gloves, but he sensed something exposed and breakable in Margaret's expression, and so he didn't say anything.

As he'd promised, he went to the play. Ann came out briefly at the intermission to receive his compliments on the costumes. Before she could leave, he asked if she was going to the party afterward, and she told him she wasn't. She had a headache, she said. She was far too tired. And, too, she'd repaired so many costumes for careless actors that she wanted a vacation from the whole lot of them—in fact, from everybody she knew.

"But when will I see you?" John said. "I've written you, Ann. You've written me. I'd like to consider what you say when you're actually present."

She had already started up the aisle, but she stopped to look back at him. "You've been an excellent correspondent. I won't argue that. If you like, come and entertain me on Tuesday. I'll be dusting the bottles in David Dale's laboratory."

John swallowed. "Fine. And what time?" he asked, glad he was able to speak.

Ann turned to wave at someone who'd called to her. "One o'clock," she said and, before John could say more, she'd headed back to the stage.

He watched the last act of the play without registering a single minute of it. The only thing he could think of was that Ann was so unchanged, so perfectly, physically whole, that just seeing her made him feel well. He was following in her wake, of course. He knew that he was. He was like a small dog trained on a leash and the leash still attached. But she had asked him to visit her and, if it had taken getting shot to make it happen, he thought it was worth it.

By Tuesday noon he could hardly eat, and his mother fussed over him, wondering if his fever had taken hold again.

"He has butterflies. He's going to see Ann Bradley," Mary said, and his mother looked at John, and he looked at Mary, wondering how it was she'd found out. To save himself the fatigue of the walk, he'd asked Denis to pick him up in the wagon, but he hadn't told him where he was going.

"Excuse me," he said, getting up from the table. He licked his finger and pasted down the hair Kate had cut too short at his cowlick. He took a look at himself in the mirror—he'd shaved off his beard for the ball—and all he was certain of was that his eyes were both blue once more and that if he wasn't the handsomest man in town, he wasn't the ugliest either.

When Denis dropped him off in front of the laboratory, John paused and gazed up at the turret with the carp and shell on its weathervane. He had watched the laboratory being built. He had even seen the equipment being moved into it from the old Harmonist granary after David Dale Owen died, which had happened before the laboratory could actually become his new workplace or the gathering place for other well-known geologists. But John had never been inside. Had anyone else offered him a look, his interest would have been keen. As it was, all he could think about was Ann. Among the fossils and the apparatuses of geological measurement, Ann Bradley was waiting for him.

Denis was dawdling with the wagon, and John frowned and motioned with the back of his hand for him to leave. He didn't want to make a spectacle and he certainly didn't want to look unsure of himself. But he didn't know which door to try. He hesitated a moment longer and then went around back and knocked. He wasn't sure what he was expecting—Ann in a big apron with her head covered? Ann wrapped in a shawl to ward off the chill if there was no fire in the stove? Ann with a bucket of ashes for him to dump so they could build a fire? He knocked once more, hoping he didn't sound impatient. Then the door opened abruptly, and it wasn't Ann who greeted him—not Ann in any guise at all—but young Nina Owen, Ann's charge.

John was surprised. "I was expecting Miss Bradley," he said.

Nina looked him quickly up and down, but not really rudely. "I'll get her," she said, and John wondered if Ann was intent on outsmarting him. Had she really provided herself with a child chaperone?

"Here you are, Mr. Given." Ann appeared at the door, a canvas apron tied over her dress. She was laughing. "You've met Nina? She's her father's daughter. If she could, I believe Nina would live in the laboratory, wouldn't you, Nina?"

"If Mama allowed it. Everything Papa did was interesting."

"And you'll be ready for interesting things if you go back to school right now and learn your afternoon lesson."

"I was leaving," Nina said, and she got her coat on and went out.

John watched her go. Then he turned back to the room. He wondered if he and Ann were alone now. Listening and glancing around, he decided they were. She had started a fire, which meant the room was growing warm. But it had clearly been cold. There was a green bottle on a shelf in front of him, and the condensation still shrinking away.

"Hold this, please?" Ann tossed him her feather duster. She knotted her skirts at the hem and climbed up on a stool. John hurried as he could to help her, but she was already upright and reaching out for the duster.

"You must tell me about Fort Donelson," she said. "I hear from boys in the 15th, but I believe you 25th lads have had the more exciting time."

John considered this and, at the same time, studied both Ann's neck (where she'd let two wisps of dark curl come free) and the curve her arm made as she began dusting. "I could hand you the bottles," he said, glad of his height, though it was not Jim Rippeto's who, as Margaret had said (making Kate blush), was a veritable Mr. Darcy: tall, dark, and handsome.

"I invited you to entertain me, not to work," Ann answered, and John wondered if he should let that stand. It seemed to him that even the sight of Ann on the stool could not trump the possibilities inherent in their working side by side. "Just tell me what it was like," Ann commanded, and she motioned at a chair, but John, knee or not, wouldn't sit down.

"*Harper's Weekly* tells it better than I do," he said, certain he didn't want to talk to Ann about the war any more than he'd wanted to talk about it to the Marshals and Susan Arnoldy or to Kate. "I got your valentine. Caroline Thrailkill and Kate sent all the valentines to Levi. I got it from him."

Ann was rubbing at a spot on a bottle. "I'm glad you did," she said. "But I'm certain you're too modest. Surely a man who has your way with words could give a very lively account of the war."

John considered. He supposed he could talk about General Grant. He could talk about the river trips going south or the march from Fort Henry when the boys were all still in high spirits. He could talk about the meteor shower the night they were waiting for battle and ask if Ann had seen it, too. But all these things were so much a part of the bigger piece that he didn't want to talk about at all. "I thought about you," he said. "Before I was in battle. In the lulls between fights. Even after I was shot, I thought about you."

"Then I shall feel responsible," Ann said, stretching and reaching the duster up to the highest shelf. "I won't write you more if it puts you in mind of me and takes your thoughts off your soldiering. Is it my fault you were wounded? I don't care to have a man shot on my account. But you're teasing, I know. With a whole army to watch, I don't believe you'd be thinking of me. Not of me or of any girl."

"It's not all fighting. Not even in battle."

"Even so," Ann said, and she started to get down, sunlight reflecting through the bottle glass and giving the floor a greenish tinge, and the light from the window adding the faintest red sheen to her hair. John reached quickly for her elbow, but she'd already slipped past him.

"I was very happy to see the gray silk of the gown you wore at the farewell ball," he said, moving the stool for her—"very glad to find it in the valentine you sent."

"There was gray silk?"

"Stretched to make the window. There was a heart-shaped window."

"I do have a gray gown," she said, musing, and then mounting the stool again. "Perhaps I wore it to that ball, though I don't remember Nina and her friends using the scraps for valentines."

John was quiet. He thought of the heart that had burned in his pocket, and of the silk that had been so smooth beneath his fingers.

"Perhaps Nina did use them," Ann went on. "Maybe she did."

"But you signed it. And the verse. You certainly copied the verse."

"Did I? I scarcely remember."

"But you must have." John was fierce to quote the verse to her, to give her the bit of Victor Hugo. Then he stopped himself, for he was sure he couldn't stand to hear her deny that she knew it.

"I have the valentine still," he said quietly.

Ann laughed. "I'll tell Nina you saved it. I'm sure she'll be flattered."

"Ann," John said, and he knew he'd not kept the distress from his voice. She looked at him, an expression passing over her face that he couldn't quite read. It wasn't inviting, but it wasn't hostile either. It was calculating perhaps, though John had no idea what the calculus might be, unless she was regarding his interest in a new way and trying to decide if it could bring her advantage. He knew what people said about Ann, that she would marry well, that she would marry for love if it meant position, but she would never marry for love alone.

Not that marriage had anything to do with the two of them here in David Dale's laboratory. Ann had a singular effect on him, but he had never been confident that he had any effect upon her at all. Yet couldn't he hope? She might change in her feelings. She might come to think that a man with education had prospects. And she might, even now, feel drawn to him in some way. After all, she'd invited him here.

She'd finished with the bottles on the high shelf and this time, when she got down, she pushed the stool into the corner and started dusting her way along the bottom shelves. John wandered after her, picking up a piece of riverbed coral that she'd flicked with her duster. He'd thought about her question, and there was one thing he felt he might tell her. He could say that he was alive and that it was a remarkable thing, that he'd killed men like a savage, and dying on a battlefield or hospital boat had seemed the likeliest thing to do. And if he told her that, it would be a thing he'd not told anyone else. It would be something private between the two of them.

"Oh, don't drop it," Ann said looking at the coral and, as she reached to take it from him, it seemed the simplest thing in the world to John to lean down and catch her free hand and to kiss each finger. He had moved on to her wrist before she pulled away.

"Mr. Given, you've taken unfair advantage." She turned to put the specimen back on the shelf. "And, anyway, I'm not an ear of corn for you to nibble on. And I've finished here. I'm expecting Mrs. Owen very soon. She'll want me in the house."

"I like Mrs. Owen," John said, trying to make light of things, but Ann went to the fire, poking the log apart so it would burn out, and then started quite purposefully toward the door.

"But I'll see you again, won't I?" he asked, desperate, and following after her. He found himself grasping for the right thing to say. For anything. "If you'd come to supper with my family . . ."

Ann shook her head. "I can't. I've too much to do for Mrs. Owen. It's possible, of course, that I'll see you. We live in a very small town. But if I don't, I wish you a safe return. And since you've not told me the story of Fort Donelson as I asked you to do, you owe it to me in a letter."

John nodded, though he meant only that he would write. Ann had started to open the door, and it was clear she was serious about showing him out. It was also clear that she'd allowed all the liberties she intended to. If there'd been a chance to embrace her—duster and all— and give her a proper kiss, it certainly had passed. Still, this was a start. For one long moment, Ann hadn't resisted him and, to him—her lavender scent like some rare infusion to the very core of his being— the moment seemed wildly significant, important beyond all of his hopes. He went outside and, in spite of himself, might have turned back to kiss her but only the scent remained. Ann had already started up the path.

At the end of the week, John had put off packing for as long as he could. When his mother brought him his hickory shirt with the blood-stains scrubbed out so the stripes had faded, he was feeling uncertain. He did not regret the time he'd spent with Ann Bradley, or in hunting for her. He didn't even mind that he'd spent most of each day hoping he would see her again, for the more he remembered the fleeting hour in the Owen laboratory, the more momentous it seemed to him.

Yet in looking at his mother, John regretted the things he had meant to do and hadn't. He had thought he would spend more time with her, that he might have helped unroll her yarn while they talked, though it hadn't happened. He'd not drawn a map for Charley or gone with his father for a pint so they could get into the hot politi-cal talk that his father loved and that, to John's surprise, he always learned from. On one occasion, he'd made it back to the library, but the pamphlet with the letter he'd read was nowhere in sight. Since Mr. White couldn't find it either, John hadn't even told Kate it existed. And, though he had written the note to accompany the dead boy's let-ter and settled on a headquarters address that he felt meant the letter might eventually reach the boy's family, he'd not written any letters to the family in Chicago. He hadn't sent letters back to Drumboarty and Tullynaha in Drimarone—not even to Denis O'Donnell about his teaching exams, though he'd planned to send praise and commiseration together in case the exams didn't go well. And Denis—his own brother Denis, John had scarcely seen.

"Do you have time for another party?" his mother asked, smoothing the hickory shirt and tugging at the buttons to check them. "The Wilseys want you tomorrow before you leave. We can all go."

John nodded. He eyed the things he'd laid out for his knapsack. Just the sight of them, he thought with a certain dread, was turning him into a soldier again, though the prospect of a party had switched his focus back to Ann Bradley. Surely, Ann would be there.

The next afternoon when Michael McShane arrived, they were all ready to head to Wilseys', though Mary had to dart back inside to get the sheet she'd mended to use for a shadow play. They walked up the street together. Charley ran in the lead, and then he circled back to walk next to John.

"Go on and do it," John told him. "Walk funny-legged," and Charley tried a hobbling imitation of John's walk until he grew tired of it and raced ahead once more.

It was almost warm out. It was as warm, John thought with a shiver, as it had been on the march to Fort Donelson. The rain trees were finally coming into bud and, looking at them, John wished that they'd fanned into leaf or had already covered the streets with their golden petals.

It was a full house at the Wilseys'. Ann Wilsey was carrying a tray of cider and fresh oysters from Fretageots', and two little girls in long dresses climbed on the balustrade, a small dog nipping at their bows. John looked through the crowd for Ann Bradley and then waited until his sisters came down from leaving their bonnets and wraps upstairs to see if she was with them. Kate was last, talking with Margaret Mulhern, who'd added a lace collar to her dress to be her Sunday best. To John's keen disappointment, Ann didn't appear. He crossed the room. Charley was already in a game of marbles on the parlor rug, and Michael McShane was headed for the piano, where a pretty woman of uncertain age was just sitting down.

"There she is," Kate said in a whisper, coming up to John, and he looked around quickly for Ann before Kate added, "Michael's widow lady."

John took the drink that Mr. Wilsey offered him and found a chair in a corner. With Michael ready to turn pages, the woman at the piano had started playing Bach, playing it beautifully, and the clarity of that sound threading its way through all the voices and laughter, the clicking of marbles and the clang of pans in the kitchen, made John feel a sudden, acute sense of melancholy. He listened quietly until Susan Arnoldy came and sat on his chair arm.

"Mrs. Owen's sickly today, so Ann has stayed with her. Will you play charades later? You always guess first."

"I could if you flatter me more. Is Ann staying all evening?"

Susan nodded. "You know, John, that it's not like her to make good-byes."

"Apparently not." John sat for a moment longer, briefly reliving the hour in David Dale's laboratory. Then he stood up, ready to have his glass filled again. Waiting while Mr. Wilsey stirred the fire, he overheard Michael McShane inviting the pianist to go riding with him in the morning if the weather was good. John didn't hear her answer, unless it meant yes that she'd switched to a lighter air. When she'd played it through, Michael asked John's mother to sing "Annie Laurie." Then, just as the light began to fail and the lamps were lit, the Thrailkills came in, Levi braced on his father's arm and on Caroline's, and his mother hovering.

"He insisted on coming," Caroline told John in a low voice when Levi, with his sling-bound arm, was settled in a chair and everyone had gotten a plate of the food that had been set out on the table. "And Mother will worry," she added. Then she smiled a little ruefully. "Tomorrow she'll be worse because Father has promised to drive him to see Margret Smith."

John thought of sitting by Caroline, but it somehow seemed inappropriate when his thoughts were all on Ann. Instead, he sat next to Levi, and they talked about New Harmony and how different it was with so many boys gone, and how high the river was this spring. What they kept in a separate place from the room—and from the house and the town—was talk about fighting or about anyone being killed or hurt. Finally, though, a thin note of defiance crept into Levi's voice and it made John wonder suddenly if Levi had experienced the same battle thrill that he had. "Keep my team ready, Jack," Levi said. "Tell the captain to do that."

When they'd all eaten, Susan Arnoldy clapped her hands long enough to get everyone's attention to start charades. They played until the grand finale, which was Mr. Cannon's much perfected parody of Samuel Bolton's demonstration of a thinned turkey crop, helium-filled and set loose to sail to the ceiling. As familiar as both the demonstration and imitation were to everybody in New Harmony, Mr. Cannon's turkey performance was still so uncanny that gales of laughter swept the room, and there was more laughter when John's father said it looked as if, this time, the turkey had gotten goosed. Afterward, Mary and her friends did their shadow play, and there was more eating and more singing, and Mr. Cannon, still flushed from his charades success, played the fiddle with John's father. The little girls danced and whirled until they fell in a sleepy heap on the rug. The boys went outside to climb trees in the dark. John, listening to their shouts, knew the party would go on much longer. There would be popcorn and apple bobbing and ghost stories, but he was leaving early in the morning, and so he got up and went around the room to make his thanks and farewells. When he hugged Margaret Mulhern, he held her an extra moment and pretended not to see the tears in her eyes.

He was almost at the door with his parents and Kate when Levi's father stopped him. "If you can wait a second, I've got something to show you," he said. He went to the coat tree and fished in his pocket. Then, with Mr. Wilsey's help, he moved a lamp down to the table and opened a homemade map. "I've been there often, John," he said pointing, "here where you're going to General Grant's army. It's just Tennessee land and a few houses near the riverbank. There's a log church over here that's small and not marked. I've been there, too. I'll be damned, though, if I can remember the name. It means something like peace. Something like the place of peace."

John nodded his thanks. He took the folded-up map Mr. Thrailkill pressed on him, and he'd gone out the door behind his mother, whose thick hair sheened glinty-gray and lovely no matter what the light, and he was gazing up at the wide band of stars that stretched clear across the sky and all the way to Tennessee when he heard Mr. Thrailkill calling after him.

"I've got it, John," he said. "The name of that church is Shiloh."

Pittsburg Landing, Tennessee
Late March and Early April 1862

8

These volumes are dedicated to the American soldier and sailor.

Personal Memoirs of U. S. Grant
New York City, May 23d, 1885

Banking and lightening its wings over the river ports, an eagle flying the deep-river country south and east of St. Louis would circle its way along a broadened ellipse. To Cairo and Memphis. To Nashville and Knoxville. Then on to Louisville.

For John, who was heading south on the Tennessee to Savannah and so was not on the border of the ellipse but near its center, the water was not maplike but immediate. He had brought out a book to read on the deck of the *Gladiator* and, as it pounded the northward-flowing current, he was reminded of a childhood trip he'd made with his father and his uncles to an island off Dawros Head. He had no idea why they had gone or what they had done there, but he'd not forgotten trying to sleep at night as the water lapped and lapped against the shore. It had seemed like a drowning thing, a dark and eelish thing that would lash him to the deepest rock and hold him there. Now, although the day was warm and springlike and far removed from the gales and cold of the North Atlantic, as he headed back to war, the rising Tennessee felt just as relentless.

John put his book away in his knapsack. He poked at his leg and wondered how well he would drill on it, if he would be called out for the laggard he was. He wondered if he had it in him to get shot at again and to kill once more if he had to. He wondered if his leg would make him vengeful and if killing would stir him again, if it was something terrible actually bred into him from some O'Donnell chieftain that would turn him into a person that he didn't even recognize. In Ireland he'd never once shot at a Protestant or an Englishman, and here he was in America shooting at Southern boys that, for all he knew, would have been his friends in Donegal. He'd give a lot to be in Drimarone right now. Or just not to have had to leave New Harmony. He thought of what his mother had said, polishing a last button before he left—that he should not think darkly or spoil a fine day with borrowed trouble.

He had teased her then. "Excellent advice," he'd said, "from Margaret the Worrier."

"Listen to your mother, John," his father had told him.

It had been odd setting out for his regiment by himself. Alarming really. On the packet he'd caught at Mount Vernon, there were other soldiers who were recovered or recovering from wounds and heading back to their units. He'd made acquaintances enough for a card game, though the talk had grown heated when the conversation turned to politics and the war. Two of the soldiers were Democrats who thought the South had pushed things too far in seceding so that the whole Union was threatened, but who still believed the Confederates would be whipped soon and turning to Washington, tails between their legs. One man, who was an ardent Republican and an outright abolition-ist, had drawn John's particular attention. John listened to him and tried to decide if his arguments were reasonable or if he was another John Brown, wild-eyed and fanatical. When the man turned to him and asked him outright if he, an Irishman, wasn't here in America to escape slavery himself, John had so many thoughts in sudden pro-fusion that he couldn't say anything. He mumbled something about never having seen a black man before he got to New York. Then the soldier won the card hand and John's money with it so that two hours out of Mount Vernon, his purse was already lighter—money gone that he might have left with Kate or his mother.

On this trip, he'd changed boats at Paducah. He'd seen Fort Anderson from the water when the boat docked and, after making inquiries, he'd headed out Jefferson Street to the Union hospital and found Robert Clarke, paper thin and worried about the nasty-looking incisions in his wrist. He was sitting on a cot and eager for the mail that John had brought. John thought his hand looked worse than his wrist. He didn't say it, but he thought Robert's fingers were very close to a lost cause.

"I need a favor," Robert said. "My letters from Emma? Find all of them in the company and burn them when you get back. It's weighed on me having them there. I wouldn't ask, but I trust you, John."

"They'll make a bonfire. Maybe two bonfires," John had answered him, hoping to make Robert laugh, which was what Emma West did. The mirthful Emma, he thought. The lovely Emma and all of her labor lost.

Later, when he'd boarded the *Gladiator* for the journey to Savannah, John found it full of returning soldiers. Some of them, seeing there were officers' wives on board heading to visit their husbands, had rushed away and then hurried back onto the boat carrying wild-flowers for the cabins. John thought it was foppish, a foolish bit of gallantry, but the ladies seemed pleased, and it occurred to him with a certain feeling of annoyance that Ann would like exactly this sort of thing—young soldiers she didn't even know paying her court and bringing her favors.

He'd taken his book out and tried to read—tried to memorize actually, for what he'd brought along was a volume of poetry and he'd set himself the task of learning Pope's "Essay on Man." But the insistent water had filled him with somber thoughts, and he'd put the book away. By the time he knew a dime novel was what he really wanted (the kind that flew through camp and got read by almost every man who could read at all), he'd decided what he was feeling was a sense of unfinished business at home and of apprehension at returning to the field. Then a band started to play on the foredeck—a scratched together, bandaged foursome from three different regiments—and his mood began to lighten. He was a soldier, after all. He was a soldier going off to his soldiering job. It was fine that a band was playing.

It was the next night when they got to Savannah. There were other boats tied up at the wharf. John tried to size things up before setting about the business of finding how much farther upstream he had to go to rejoin the 25th and how he would get there. He'd kept to himself on this part of the trip, or as much as he could with the crowd of people on board and a man with a peg leg he thought had termites sleeping next to him on the deck at night. Watching the ladies being escorted onto land, he assumed it was the end of the line for the *Gladiator*. Just up the hill, there was a big, gleaming house looking down on the water. John heard the captain telling people it was Cherry Mansion and that General Grant had his headquarters there, that General Smith, who'd led his division up the ravines at Fort Donelson, was sick in bed upstairs with a dangerously swollen leg. "And that's General Grant's steamer," the captain added, pointing just upriver.

John tried to absorb all this and to settle it from his own perspective. They were together again, it seemed. Once more, they were a threesome—he and General Grant, who had raced behind the Donelson lines on horseback, and General Smith, who'd led the charge with the tips of his mustache flying. It was the three of them out here, and all the hundreds of thousands of other men around the country, who'd set off from home in order to make war. John stared up at the house and then followed the soldiers and passengers getting off the *Gladiator*. Since he knew he wouldn't get a boat until morning, and because he was tired and uncertain about what else to do, he made his bed beneath a tree beyond the wharf road and ate what was left of the food his mother and sisters had packed for him. Then he fell asleep in the warm night under the flickering lamplight of Cherry Mansion, where maps were being studied and plans made. He dreamed that they were.

Noon. The sun high and hot, and the boat slowing toward the shore amidst a whole host of other boats, mainly supply boats from what John could tell. The bank was crowded with men, but his first impression of Pittsburg Landing was that there was nothing there. An encampment yes. From the river, he could see wagons near the water, busy with their teams and drivers, and the lines of tents and tent peaks scattered away to the south and west on the flat lands among the ravines. But take the army away—subtract every trace of it—and the landing itself looked like nothing more than a couple of cabins and a pigpen flanked by bluffs. There wasn't a fort. There wasn't even a breastwork in sight.

John shouldered his knapsack as he got off the boat. He was in the sunny South all right. Coming up the river, he'd seen that the wheat was already six inches high. Yet warm as the sun was, the ground of the landing was still churned mud from the traffic of an army's worth of boots and hooves. Starting up the bank, John could feel it in his knee as the mud sucked at his boot.

A driver was trying to harness an untamed mule next to the rutted road that led from the river. John called out to him to watch the front hooves just as the mule turned. The driver jerked sideways and the mule kicked right past his head. In spite of his knee, John dropped his pack and went running to help. Other soldiers did, too. The air was noisy with shouts and the mule's cries until the men had it roped and harnessed to a wagon and then steadied in its traces.

John wiped sweat from his neck. He picked up his hat, which had gone flying when he'd ducked a mule kick. "I'm looking for the 25th Indiana," he said to the driver, wondering if he had a long hike through the woods past a whole sprawl of regiments. From what he had heard, camp had at least five divisions, and that could mean as many as 50,000 men.

The driver shook his head. "I've never heard of it," he said, but a corporal directed John to follow the road they were on for a half mile and then to go north at the branch.

"You got lucky, soldier. It's the first regiment south of the road."

John nodded his thanks. He started up the muddy track, which was lined with stacks of boxes and barrels and filled with drivers bawling at their teams. He could hear the drums in the distance and smell bread baking in the field ovens. Mice scooted through piles of unhusked corn. He watched as a flock of goats romped on a hillock. He'd taken the branch that the soldier had told him to, but in a while he started to wonder about the directions. Then he passed a thicket of trees, and the first thing he saw was Captain Rheinlander's company. The men were eating. John was starved, and he wanted to head straight for his own company while there was food left, but he made his way to the officers' tents to report for duty to Captain Saltzman. He found him drinking coffee in front of a tent and leaning intently over a paper-strewn table with Lieutenant Randolph and Sergeant Bennett.

John waited. In New Harmony, Captain Saltzman was a boss blacksmith descended from a Rappite follower and as well acquainted and well regarded as any man. He'd been the marshal for the Fourth of July parade before Company A left for Evansville, and he'd formed Company A himself, training the men for weeks. On a warm and dusty May day, he'd called them to meet in the Methodist church, where he lectured on the manual of arms and where John felt strange and heretical simply by being there. He was "Wash" to his good friends (George *Washington* Saltzman) and Mr. Saltzman to other people, but in the company, his role was clear. He was Captain Saltzman, an absolute rock who meant that Company A had come into the field not only well drilled but with its share of rifled muskets that could shoot straight.

John saw that the captain, looking up, had noticed him. He straightened and saluted. "Private Given reporting for duty, sir," he said.

There were salutes back from the officers and handshakes and then Captain Saltzman put down his coffee and, in an impulse that totally surprised John, hoisted him up in a bear hug. "Eat something, John," he said, putting him back down. "How's the leg? You got Levi with you? I thought you were worse off than Levi. I thought he'd come with you."

"Levi was worse," John said quickly. "You wouldn't find him at all fit for service, sir, although he's much better."

He did eat something then. He found his friends in the company and they swarmed him for letters. George Tretheway, who was brother to worrying Mrs. Cawthorne in New Harmony, looked as fat and healthy as if he'd never been wounded. The rest of the boys wanted to know about Harmony and about their folks and about the girls. Particularly the girls. John made up stories as fast as he could, marrying off as many girls as he could think of to wealthy widowers or old bachelors from Mount Vernon and Kentucky until the boys started pummeling him and grabbing at his knapsack for more mail. Laughing, John held his arms up to fend them off. He was glad to be back. He was in a world familiar all of itself—a world tricked out with ranks and insignia and tent villages as though it were all pretend, as if the real Secesh didn't shoot at them and maim and kill them, and where nobody came down with the camp quickstep and the best food anywhere was beans cooked for an entire day over hot coals in a hole in the ground.

In the evening, when the drills and review on the parade ground were over (he had carried his weight; he had not done well but all right), John sat smoking with Henry Schafer and Max Munte. Max was commissary sergeant now, but he still came back to the tents. John listened to the German lingering in Max's and Henry's voices the way the Irish stayed in his. He sometimes wondered what the cutoff point was. He and Kate still had their accents, and Margaret did a little, while Denis and Mary, and particularly Charley, sounded as if they'd been born in America.

The sky was darkening. John could hear marches that overlapped from at least three regimental bands. For the first time since he'd been in the army he realized that, though they got in your blood in a way, he didn't really like march tunes. They reminded him of marching season in Donegal when the boys and men all gathered in the fields waiting to bash in Protestant heads.

"Was there dancing?" Henry said. "And was there singing in Harmony? Did they know what a fight we'd been in?"

"Yes and yes. Dancing. Singing. They thought it was a great victory." John was quiet while the memory of the bullet, and his personal picture of home and of Ann Bradley in David Dale's laboratory, and the reports of the Confederates massing a huge force less than seventeen miles away all swirled together as one odd feeling in the pit of his stomach. He flicked away an acorn he'd picked up. "My Aunt Ellen's husband, Mr. McAuliffe, wrote from Chicago that the Merchants' Exchange stopped altogether when they heard the news. The whole North was wild. And *Harper's Weekly* said the terrain the 25th took was the toughest along the whole line. We're heroes, boys, if you care to believe it."

Max smiled and rolled another cigarette. "You think those Rebs down the road know who they're facing?" he asked, and then he repeated himself toward Henry's good ear, the one that hadn't gone deaf on the march in Missouri when the bad one had drained until Felix Edmonds swore Henry stunk like a polecat.

John lay against the tent flap and listened to all the stories that he'd missed—about the occupation of Fort Donelson and the march back to Fort Henry and about the transports that had brought the regiment to Pittsburg Landing just ten days before he'd arrived. The troops had lived soldier time, which was the slowed-down time of waiting for orders and doing the same thing over and over, while John had been his own man so that, for him, time had flown. It had blown away like dandelion fuzz.

Yet it had all come to the same point. From the papers at home and from what he'd heard on his journey south and from the men talking, John knew everyone was expecting a decisive battle, that once Grant and General Buell, who was coming here with the Army of the Ohio, had joined forces, they would smash Sidney Johnston's army at Corinth. They would sever the Confederates' rail lines the way they'd cut off their river routes; and before long the war would be only a bitter taste in the mouth. They would have arrived at the condition described by Mr. Webster's words that his father loved to quote: "Liberty and Union, now and forever, one and inseparable."

It sounded grand, and John believed it most of the time, though the quote from Daniel Webster that cut deeper for him was the one he'd discovered and remembered for himself and had never heard at all from his father: "When my eyes shall be turned to behold for the last time the sun in heaven, may I not see him shining on the broken and dishonored fragments of a once glorious Union; on States dissevered, discordant, belligerent; on a land rent with civil feuds, or drenched, it may be, in fraternal blood."

Henry Schafer offered him a plug of tobacco, and John took it and scratched at the ears of a dog who was asleep by the tent. He was back with his friends once more and trying to put himself into the big picture of where the army actually was. He had parts of it. Tennessee was the land of Nashoba, Frances Wright's foundered experiment that Kate was so intrigued by and that John saw as an utter contradiction: the plan to free slaves by working them as slaves. It was the home of the Hermitage, which John could only surmise was Andrew Jackson's effort, serious or not, to evoke something like civilized St. Petersburg in a country where half of the backwoods boys were named after him. As far as the smaller picture went, he was just trying to fit in once again, this time as an Irish private with a hole in his leg whose time on kitchen detail or a picket line would mean he was really here.

"There's a lot of men sick in camp," Henry said. "Lieutenant Randolph's been bad since Fort Donelson, but there're men sick with everything. I think it's the water."

"Some are more sick from the women. Missouri women," Max said, and Henry told him he could shut up and then they both laughed and so did John, but he wondered about Henry.

He thought he should look for Robert Clarke's letters. He thought more that he should wait. He was tired. Listening to the drawing down sounds of the day—men who'd been relieved coming in from picket duty, men reading letters to each other as the last light waned, and songs passing from company to company until a tenor sang a bawdy final verse—the only thing John wanted to do was sleep. He crawled into the tent and lay down with his feet sticking toward the flap.

The next thing he knew, it was sunup. At breakfast, he got caught up with more of the regiment, and he told the story of the Hugos and how they'd thought one son had died when it actually had been the other. The story seemed to fascinate the men who heard it, as it had John. Yet it made them uneasy, too, even though he'd made sure Alex Hugo wasn't around to hear him. He didn't tell it again. In fact, he wished he hadn't told it in the first place.

He was quick to learn the extent of the encampment, which was really a vast tent city. The land had been picked for its stretch of flat space between the ridges and bluffs. All the green troops, which were in Sherman's and McClernand's divisions particularly, had plenty of room for every kind of drill. Other soldiers could drill but have some conveniences, their camps laid out close to the creeks, though the handiness of the location was increasingly diminished by backwater from the swollen Tennessee. John thought the camp felt essentially like other camps. Yet every single thing about it—from the constant unloading of supplies from the riverboats to the frequency of drills and the strictness of the officers—was more confirmation that they were getting ready for a big battle. The army, with all its men and animals and its full complement of support wagons and artillery caissons and heavy guns, was preparing for a major advance on the enemy.

John had changed his mind about one thing. Before Fort Donelson, he'd thought the whole ritual of parade and review was basically theatrical and something better suited to the old men of the home guard in New Harmony. Now he didn't think so. Every day, when General Grant arrived from Cherry Mansion, the word that he'd come would spread through the camps and, after the last drill, men worked quickly and intently to ready themselves for inspection. Everything that was leather or metal was buffed or shined. At the parade ground, the band played and the units executed their exercises in arms. The officers, swords sheathed, marched up to General Grant for their instructions. The men, who'd obeyed the "parade rest" order, stood motionless, their rifle butts on the ground, their right hands gripping their rifle muzzles, their left hands behind their backs. The whole precision of it felt reassuring to John. He felt safe as if, in spite of the gloom that had accompanied him up the Tennessee, and in spite of the nightmares that still woke him at night, he could go into battle once more. He could go with these men. He could go with this general, who was so short and unprepossessing, but who looked comfortable in his saddle. He believed he could trust them.

9

Elias Keister, at the county infirmary, has a letter from his brother Romeo, a soldier of the Civil War from New Harmony, written after the Battle of Shiloh. It was written under date of 4-12-1862, on paper provided the army by the government, and the ink writing remains very legible after over 67 years.

New Harmony Times, April 1929

John had been keeping track. "Nine days or ten. It's my tenth day in Tennessee and my ninth day in camp. You'd think something would have happened by now," he said to Felix Edmonds on Saturday night.

"You looking to get shot again?" Felix asked. He pulled a picture out of his bedroll that John knew he'd gotten in the mail for fifty cents.

"Not shot," he answered. "Look at her all you want, but she's not getting her clothes back on so she can take them off again. Not shot, but it just seems as if something ought to happen," he said, and it was true that he felt that way. He thought every man did. For all the routine of camp life, so familiar now along the tent-lined roads, there was a general sense of nervous anticipation, of just wanting to get on with it. It had rained hard on Friday morning and rained more into the night, and the men had grown more and more irritable. When the rain had finally stopped in the afternoon, they'd emerged from their mud-spattered tents grumbling that it wasn't the sunny South, but the soggy South. Henry Schafer said if they didn't fight soon, they'd every one of them be drowned.

"I don't know I'm that eager to look at more Rebels," Felix said, still fingering his picture. "You turning in, Jack?"

John didn't answer, but stretched out on his bedroll and reminded himself to wake up early.

When his eyes flickered open before Sunday reveille, the tent air was muggy and stale. It took John a moment to know why he was awake, but that was all. Easing through the sleeping men, he slipped outside to the light of stars and a moon that was approaching its first quarter. He paused to be sure that the skittering sound he heard was night animals. Then he set off to find a place beyond the tents but well within the picket lines. On Sundays, which in camp meant cleaning and inspection of quarters, he liked to get up early this way and find his own quiet spot. Sometimes he knelt. Always he prayed. Often he said words from the ordinary of the Mass, which he knew as well as if he'd been finally ordained. He'd decided he did it for the ritual comfort, or even as a talisman against fear. Or he did it when he felt a resurgence of faith—that simple belief in Christ incarnate that was a tenet of his earliest creed: what his mother taught him. What the curate had said. What the St. Finian's priests in Navan and Bishop McGettigan in Letterkenny had echoed when he'd grown older. Mostly, he did it because it reminded him of the early Sunday mornings in New Harmony when the weather was good and he could borrow a buggy and drive his mother the long, bumpy miles to the German church at St. Wendel's. He listened with her to the murmuring Latin that put her deeply into the Mass, and all the way back to Ireland. He knew that it did, for it was the same thing that happened to him.

It was all mixed up, he thought as he scraped mud off a log to sit down on. His mother had feared coming to America, feared that it would rob them all of their faith—that, unoppressed, their faith might wither away. When the battle had started at home, John was in Navan trying to set his own confusing course, but Kate confided later that their parents had argued endlessly, that it went on day after day, and month after month. Their mother told their father that for him it was all political, that in Ireland he'd stay Catholic until the day he died because it meant he could stick a finger in an English eye, but that he didn't believe in the faith as she did. He didn't believe to the core, which had long been the source of the greatest pain for her.

"She was very troubled," Kate had told John. She stopped for a moment, brooding at the memory. And then she went on more slowly, telling John how their father's lips grew paler than pale as he listened and that he'd proclaimed finally, his voice rising, that he wouldn't lose another child where they weren't free to make their own children sturdy on their own crop. That he'd save every farthing he got in order to take them to America and that Kate could work, too. She could go to work in Donegal Town. And if the ship sank when they'd saved the fare, if a gale smashed it entirely to bits, so be it. They were not risking starvation again on their own land—on land that *should* be theirs. He was no man at all if he let them.

"And he was never drunk when he said it," Kate added.

John had his own variants of his mother's fixations to deal with and he knew just how powerful they could be. In her mind, he was still a priest in the making, one whose training had merely been interrupted, but he'd still been surprised at the nature of her opposition when he'd told her he was drilling with the regiment Captain Saltzman was raising. "There won't be a priest or Mass, John. For as long as there's a war, you won't have that. Of all my children, for you to turn away from the church."

He had told her that he wasn't, that if anything he would fight for the Union because the Constitution meant that the church was protected. The argument sounded awkward even to him, and the context wrong, for she'd been right in what she'd said to his father. The family actually had started drifting away from the faith. New Harmony was spirited and sociable, but it wasn't much for church-going. And the fact of the matter was that Kate was always working, and Margaret and the younger children resented the interminable wagon rides back and forth to St. Wendel's with Latin and German sandwiched in between. No matter what their mother said, Denis generally disappeared entirely.

"We should have gone to your sisters in Chicago," John had heard her tell his father, and when his father responded that when he'd wanted to she didn't, she'd repeated what she'd said and then added, "at least in Chicago they've got churches in the neighborhoods and Irish priests. All of them do, even if Chicago's full of dirt and sickness. Even if it's full of sin."

To his credit, his father had resisted saying what he'd told John more than once—that he hadn't so much needed to convince Margaret Given to go to America as he'd needed to find a place that would suit her. "If you've noticed, John, your mother has a bit of the snob about her. I dropped a few fancy names on her—Mr. Owen and Mr. Thomas Jefferson that Mr. Owen visited. That did the trick."

It was his mother's worry, John thought, that earnest look on her face that was the real reason he crept out of the tent these Sunday mornings, though he wasn't kneeling now. He was still sitting on a log, and he hadn't gotten through half of the Gloria before his mind had wandered far afield—down and up the rivers, and over the ocean—and he'd never trained it back. It was time to head for reveille, but he was listening now. He was listening to what he'd first thought was the familiar pop-popping from a picket line that happened when an enemy scout got too near but then, thin and distant as it was, increasingly seemed to him like something more. Somewhere near Shiloh Church, which Levi's father had shown him on a map and where General Sherman was quartered—crazy as a loon or crazy smart, the men couldn't decide— somewhere to the south of Shiloh Church, there was a steady, faint rhythm that sounded like muskets. Listening, John stood up and headed back toward the regiment. He was walking away from the sound and, though he couldn't be certain, he was almost sure it had stopped.

It was first light when he reached the 25th. The bugle trilled out reveille. The camp began to stir, men emerging from the tents, some with their clothes on, many with blankets around their shoulders. They straggled into rank. After roll call, some of them headed back to their beds until the call came for breakfast.

John poured a cup of coffee from the pot and ate some bacon and bread. He looked at the sky. It was a perfectly glorious morning. He heard a bluebird nearby—a little farm bird. The sun had risen with a sudden brilliance and, in the early light, the young foliage blurred the air a new-apple green. The breeze smelled of peach blossoms.

John walked back to his tent. Officers in their dress uniforms were getting ready to start inspection, though some men were still eating and some still cleaning their muskets.

"Did you hear anything?" John said to Felix Edmonds, who was getting a haircut from Henry Schafer. John checked his musket, which he'd cleaned the night before. He beat at the drying mud he'd gotten on his trousers. As the breeze shifted, he thought he heard the sound again. "Do you hear something, Felix? Do you think somebody's getting into it?"

"Probably just green troops shooting off rounds. Maybe clearing wet cartridges. Actually, I don't hear anything," Felix said. "Henry, can you clean out my ears?"

John rubbed at his shoes. He spit on them and rubbed at them again but, all the while, he was feeling more and more uneasy. There were other men starting to notice something, too. Heads were turning toward the sound that he heard. It wasn't steady anymore, but erratic and louder. He thought maybe he should report something, though what he'd be reporting he didn't know. Instead, he got his ammo box and his gear together. Then he heard the long roll from the 46th Illinois. Men ditched their food. They leapt to the tents to grab their guns and jam them back together.

"Fall in, men," Captain Saltzman shouted, "*fall in*," and as they started to, the word swept through the line they were forming that Sherman was under attack, that the enemy was on him in force, and that the whole brigade, with Colonel Veatch as acting brigadier, had been ordered in to support him.

"You get shot," George Tretheway said to Felix Edmonds, "they'll think you got one side of your hair shot off."

For once in a soldier's life, there was no waiting. The line had barely formed when they started to march. And now there wasn't any question. There was a regular din of musketry coming from the southwest. There was a constant chatter of guns and Colonel Veatch's regiments, including the 25th with Lieutenant Colonel Morgan firm and unruffled in the lead, were headed toward them.

John was fully alert. He was also stunned. At Fort Donelson, when the battle had started with the Confederates attacking at dawn and trying to break out and make an escape, General Grant was nowhere in sight. He hadn't even arrived in the field until the afternoon. This time, though, it was supposed to be different. The whole Army of the Tennessee was massed and prepared for an advance on the enemy and instead, from the sounds of it, the enemy had advanced on them. Clearly, the Rebels had marched all the way from Corinth, and John could only imagine what a morass of mud and rain they'd come through en route. And apparently—apparently, not a single Union scout or cavalry patrol had even noticed them.

John wanted to talk to somebody about it. What he wanted was to talk to Harry Beal in the 15th Indiana (and where *was* the Army of the Ohio?). Wasn't a soldier's life surprise enough without a surprise attack on a perfect Sunday morning? He could use a little more order than this. Maybe a lot more. Maybe they needed a German general. He'd written to Kate to tell Mr. Wilsey he believed they were about to have some fun here, and just what kind of bravado had that been? He wondered if he was going to get shot again.

John thought all these things in a single instant—one sharp flare-up of anger or of fear (he didn't care anymore if he was afraid). And then he stopped thinking about all of it—the whats and the what-ifs—and just concentrated on staying up with the line and keeping his pack shifted as much as he could so the weight didn't fall on his bad leg.

They were moving on the Corinth Road. They'd marched past General Hurlbut's headquarters and stopped just forward of the flag tent where General McClernand was headquartered. Soon they were ordered into position behind another regiment at the edge of the review field. For a moment, John thought that it was all just a different kind of Sunday drill, that it was actually practice for a surprise attack and not the real thing. He wondered if they'd be parading any minute before General Grant and his horse and that, later in the day after all the inspections and reviews, they'd be out hunting wild onions in the muddy woods where the Johnny-jump-ups were in bloom and the cockleburs stuck to everybody's sleeves.

Then he scanned the wider scene and knew he was wrong. On their left, a battery of artillery had started firing across the field. Below the middle distance of amazing blue sky, the woods flashed with the splintery light from musket barrels. Lines of men in gray and brown—guns at right-shoulder shift—pushed out into the open. A relentless mass of them moved steadily and quickly toward the field. John saw them fragmented between the shoulders of the regiment in front of the 25th. Parts of torsos. Caps. A feathered hat. Marching legs. He saw the silk banners of regiments lifting and falling against the blue of the sky, and the raised heads of officers' horses. And most of all, he saw guns. Men with their guns. To him, it was an astonishing sight. It was like a perfect tableau on a vast stage that rolled silently and unstoppably toward them.

Henry Schafer was next to him. "When do they start yelling? That bloody scream,"

Max Munte, who'd come from headquarters, was in line with them and sighting down his own gun. "A little spectral, yes?" asked the man who was so fair that he often seemed spectral himself. "It's as if they'd march through us like air."

John didn't say anything. Nobody else did either. Shells howled and flew from the battery. As they landed across the field and pitted up deep chunks of earth, the Rebel troops kept coming. It startled John, but he thought there was something beautiful in the approaching columns. It was like the 25th marching on Fort Donelson—all those companies of hopeful, perfect young men before they were broken and victorious.

Their own line was shifting again. The orders were to lengthen the line to their right and to stay in support. A racket of gunfire from the southwest was increasing in volume, but as they swung farther west along the Corinth Road, the noise shifted with them. It came more from the south now. Or John thought that it did. He wasn't sure anymore. It seemed there was gunfire or the echo of it nearly everywhere.

Their battery was getting the range now. A shell landed so near the Confederate front that the mere concussion of it sent men sprawling. Still, the Rebels kept approaching. Finally they were close enough to open fire on the Illinois boys in McClernand's command who were right in front of the 25th. It was louder than loud. John heard horses screaming up the line. There was an ungodly mixture of angry whinny and fierce explosion of air when the bullets struck. Men were hit, too. An Illinois regimental flag went down and was hoisted back up full of bullet holes. Then it went down again.

"What are we waiting for?" Henry Schafer muttered beside him. He raised his voice louder above the clamor. "Those are green boys and we're not. What're we waiting for?"

John was more than eager himself. Once in a real play he'd waited in the wings like this. He'd been ready to deliver the two lines needed of an Irishman in New Harmony, a foot poised and prepared to step forward. But here there was no script. Nothing explained why the firing was growing louder. Nothing said why the Union men in front of them were suddenly being driven back. They'd turned tail. They were fleeing. They were stumbling straight into the 25th. John was hit by a flagpole as men came pouring through. Some of them were wounded. Some had faces blackened from powder. More had clean faces from not firing a shot, and all were in a terrible panic. They were bleeding and crying. The horses carrying officers were rearing up, out of control. Line officers were shouting for men to halt, to stop and regroup, but the stampede kept on. It was a whirlwind rushing through. Men shed haversacks and canteens and even their guns so they could run faster. Their battery was still booming, fire streaking into the sky, and John knew the 25th was holding, too, though the line had been staggered by the routed men.

Then the battery went still. Before John knew what was happening, there were mules and battery horses crashing wildly through the regiment, some dragging harnesses, one with a man in tow. Men were knocked over and the line broken. Animals charged. Animals screamed. Battle smoke drifted everywhere. John could feel the regiment keep mending the line and trying to make a steady front, though now they were being shot at in earnest. Rebels dodged from tree to tree, stopping just long enough to reload and to pop out firing as they came. They were on the Union front and on the left where the battery was quiet, and the crossfire was absolutely merciless. Aiming his own gun, John was sure he saw two bullets collide in midair.

The firing had picked up from the Union lines. It slowed the Rebel advance, but the forward enemy was right on the 25th and shooting at point-blank range. Men were dropping. Men were dying. It was happening once more so that it wasn't a dream that had awakened John but an actual, conscious moment that seemed like a dream. In it, he shot a man in the temple and saw him fall dead.

For a moment, the fire lessened. Colonel Veatch, round jawed and square goateed, rode down the line and ordered them to fall back a full hundred yards and change their front to the rear where a new force of Rebels was trying to flank them. Somehow, they managed it. They moved back in reasonably good order, though fire was pouring in from the left. John's lungs felt full of smoke. He was two men behind George Tretheway. The sun had caught George's hair, and it was as bright a red as Biddy's had been.

They were struggling their way through the blackjack. John tripped on a horse's leg that was buried in oak leaves. For a second, the pain was so excruciating he thought he'd been shot in the knee again. He managed to catch himself and stumble on, not stopping to see if there was more to the horse than the leg. Lieutenant Boren was shouting and urging them on—*Hurry men, hurry!*—and no sooner had they gotten into their new position than it seemed every single tree had turned into a man. They were in front of a regular Dunsinane Wood. There were thousands of men, huge double columns of them, and they were all coming out from the timber and the scrubby underbrush. Even without the shouted order to lie down, the men of the whole regiment would have, but it wasn't a second too soon when they flattened themselves against the earth, for the real fire started then: bullets like hail. Bullets like pebbles caught in the waves and hurled up on a strand. Bullets flying over them like swarming locusts.

John thought he was lying beneath a hive of riled-up bees. There was a buzzy, frenetic-sounding racket, which should have been deadly but instead seemed to do no harm. Peering out along the ground, he saw three rabbits. They were crazy from the noise and bounding wildly through the rattly leaves. One nudged inside John's sleeve. He could feel its sudden warmth and the tock-tocking of its heart. He waited until they both grew calmer. Then he eased it away.

He was ready for the order to get up and return fire. Still, when it came, it was the most brutal thing he'd ever experienced. They were a killing machine. In repeated volleys, they struck the tight ranks of Rebel soldiers, staggering them in their tracks as they tried to keep coming. John wished he'd prayed more before dawn. He'd killed one man and it had hardly registered. Now he'd shot more—at least two. He was sure every man they faced was going to die.

He reloaded and fired. Reloaded and fired. From the corner of his eye, he thought he saw George Tretheway pitch forward in the line, but he wasn't sure. He felt a jolting, stuttered ping and saw the water rush from a hole in his canteen, from two holes where a ball had passed clear through. He fired again. He had the rhythm of it—his hand reaching into his ammo box and holding the cartridge while he bit the end off, his gun held tight against his leg while he rammed the charge home and then stuck the ramrod in the ground while he raised the gun and fired again. He could keep this up a long time, he thought. It was like swinging a scythe in a steady tempo down a field.

But the feel of the battle had changed. For all the enemy dead on the ground, John had the strong sense they were being surrounded. He was desperate for the bugle to tell them to fall back. Finally it did, and every man of them was rushing as fast as he could to get away.

Undergrowth snagged at John's feet and legs until it was all he could do to lift them. The whiz and scatter of minié balls went past him.

Somebody yelled that Colonel Morgan was shot. John kept going, though he felt the words like a sharp inhalation of freezing air. If Colonel Morgan was shot, they'd all be dead soon. They'd be a whole regiment of dead men.

John thought he didn't entirely care. Other men had died. Men were supposed to die. It was the point, wasn't it? You died so that somebody else could live and be vindicated. You died so somebody else could be safe. At some point, wasn't it bullets and fighting that decided how men actually lived together? Unless they were dead, of course. Unless they weren't even living at all.

John felt numb. He tried snapping his fingers. He clenched and unclenched his hands as he ran. Around him, men seemed uncertain whether to run or shoot, but the noise of gunfire was constant, and the belching artillery meant a growing clog of acrid smoke above the trees. A horse went by with its saddle under its belly. John watched a man leap onto it and then roll off as the horse's knee buckled. The horse went down in a patch of yellow wildflowers.

Four knees. *A horse has four knees.* It was a sharp revelation to John, and it brought him the clarity of a single question: what would it feel like to have four knees that hurt in four different ways? He was so terribly, terribly thirsty.

"Jack. John, help me." He heard the voice calling him, and he scanned trees and bushes that had leafed out just since the sun came up. He searched the blackened faces of dazed and panting men who'd stopped in the same ravine that he had.

Beyond a tree to his left, he found the glittery black eyes that were looking at him. "Romeo," he said, and he made his way through branches to Romeo Keister. "Are you hurt?" he asked. He crouched down, and he was wondering if, for the rest of his life, clear eyes and a clear voice would seem to him like a warning of imminent death.

"Maybe. Just a little. Grazed. But I'm caught." Romeo was on his side, and John could see that his leg was in a trap and that he was lying downhill so he couldn't get at it. He was mostly just dangling, and that was really the worst of it, John realized, glad that he wouldn't have to send a bad news letter to Romeo's family or to Lizzy Gauth, the girl in New Harmony Romeo wrote to.

John examined the trap. It wasn't like any he'd seen. More than a trap, it was like the horsehair *dol* his grandfather had used to catch salmon around the gills. "They thought you were a fish," John said.

He was working at the trap when Max Munte slid down the embankment, sneezing as he came. Max caught at a root and pulled himself upright. Then he leaned against a tree and wiped his sleeve across his face, holding his breath for the next sneeze. "They're not chasing us anymore," he said when he could talk, "but Lieutenant Boren is rounding up men. He wants everybody he can find to re-form the line. Romey, are you ready?"

"Where's Captain Saltzman?" John asked. He pulled the trap off and hoisted it up into a tree. "Wait," he said. He ran his hand carefully under Romeo's side. "Good," he said, and good was what he meant. No real blood. No broken bones. No man dying in his arms, though this one was a little wobbly getting to his feet.

"I can fight," Romeo said, answering Max's question, and then Max answered John's.

"I don't know," he said. "Nobody knows where he is."

The sounds of the battle were still a thunderous roar that shook the full circle of the horizon as Max led the way. Soldiers came out from behind trees. More of them crawled out from the underbrush. When they'd all gone down the next ravine and joined Lieutenant Boren and the men who'd already gathered around him, John made a quick head count. He could see maybe half of the company men who'd been present for the morning report, plus strays from other companies. There were ominous absences. No George Tretheway. No Dave Vint or George Ham or Felix Edmonds in the corporal ranks. No Sergeant Smith. No report yet on Colonel Morgan. It was as if the army was being lopped off from the top. Still, they were forming the line again, ready to link up with whatever was left of the regiment.

John looked up at the sky. There were tent tops poking into it, but the tree crowns were gone, shattered by cannon balls. "I'm glad I burned those letters," he said half aloud. Max gave him a questioning look, but he shook his head. "Just something for Robert Clarke."

Max eyed the holes in his canteen. "Here, Jack," he said, offering him his, and John took a swallow of water and thought how much he liked Max. He liked all of the Germans in the company. They were a decent sort and you could count on them to do things right, the way the Rappites in New Harmony had built things absolutely true. But where was Jake Schaen, he wondered, the good little fellow who came from Switzerland but spoke German and got called Dutch like all the real Germans. Was Jake missing, too?

John turned around, scanning the men once more. To his surprise, he spotted Jake right in the middle of them, filthy as they all were, and drinking from his own canteen. John went over to him. "Where were you?" he asked, and Jake finished his drink and pulled out his handkerchief.

He blew his nose. "When there's shooting, I'm too short to see. Where were *you*?" he said.

When he considered it later, John thought it was reassuring men could joke in the midst of such ruinous events. It was something unexpected that he'd learned from the war. He'd also discovered that the grapevine was indestructible. It was working fine as Lieutenant Boren led the company back through the underbrush. The last anyone had seen of Captain Saltzman was when his horse bolted during the general stampede and, while it was true Colonel Morgan had been badly wounded in the leg and been carried off the field by the band, it was also true he wasn't dead. Or not yet. Somebody had seen Lieutenant Brickett of Company C die on the battlefield just moments after he was shot. Nobody knew about George Tretheway. For that matter, nobody knew about Felix Edmonds; nobody had even seen Felix Edmonds since the firing had started.

The new order from the adjutant was to join Major Foster's battalion on the left. As they moved, the men grew more wary. They made their way out of the thickest woods, guns at the ready. Ahead of them, on a low place that was more or less sheltered from gunfire, John saw a downed tree and next to it, sooty and spotted with bullet holes but planted firmly, their regimental flag. The ranks went quiet. John, who liked a flag for the color and variety it added to a scene and for how it told him where he was, but who wasn't really one for patriotic displays and had, in fact, laughed at his sisters when they clamored to read the newspaper's description of this very flag ("It's a substantial and brilliant silk," Margaret said; "and the field is blue and it's covered with sparkling silver stars," Kate added; and Mary, fascinated by the description of the tassels, exclaimed over their being so many colors)—for all his very real cynicism on the subject, John felt ready to kiss this flag.

"Three cheers, boys," somebody said and the shout went up the line. John saw Major Foster waving his hat and rallying the troops, and he wondered if he'd placed the flag there, and if he had, what had happened to the bearer. For himself, he felt the first real rush of excitement that he'd had all day. He was ready to fight again if it meant protecting these men who were his friends, and the folks at home and the Stars and Stripes the Rebels had shot on at Fort Sumter when everybody knew it really would be war, that there were men who actually meant to dismantle the Union. He was ready to go.

The guns were chattery once more. They were in it again, with Rebels right in their front. The fire was heavy, and John didn't know if the columns of Confederates were the same ones they'd sent a blistering fire into earlier, or if they were new troops that had come up the Corinth Road. There was also fire on their flanks. The men held their positions. Howitzers opened from their own lines. A real din of rifles and cannons kicked up. John was wondering what Major Foster would do in Colonel Morgan's stead, wondering what any man would do with the command of a regiment thrust on him in midbattle. Then the order came to withdraw.

They did it against intense fire. When they were out of range, Henry Schafer banged his canteen against the ground and spit in an impressive arc down the line. "What's the point of all this?" he demanded. "We fight and withdraw. We watch, we withdraw. We might not get shot, but we'll get chafed just going back and forth. There's your battle wounds, boys. Raw balls."

Colonel Veatch's aide rode up. The drum rolled, and the next thing John knew, they were quickstepping over acorns to a high ridge to join General McClernand's troops. The pickets were ordered forward to reconnoiter and that meant a detail of Captain Rheinlander's men from Company B and men from Company A Sergeant Bennett had already picked. It meant John, wretched knee and all. He fell in behind Henry.

When he reached the top of the opposite hill, John took in what he could of the sight before him. The eastern theater had hot-air balloons that sailed over a battlefield, and he wished he had that view from aloft. He would have liked to sort it all out and see where the action was heaviest. He wondered where the lines had faltered or broken and how many Confederates were still marching into the field and if some of them were rifling through the Union tents. He wanted to know if Lew Wallace's division at Crump's Landing was marching to reinforce them and if Buell's Army of the Ohio was on the way. He wanted to look for the opposing commanders and see if General Grant was astride his horse and Albert Sidney Johnston on his.

Instead he saw the near view: cratered earth. Shattered trees in winding ropes of smoke. So many bodies of men and animals—even a baby goat with its head shot off—that it was hard to comprehend he was looking for upright men who might be moving on their positions.

John caught up to Henry. They refilled their ammunition boxes with rounds—forty apiece brought up by the quartermaster's man. John ate part of a cracker. There was gunfire to the left and occasionally to the right, but it was quiet in front of their lines except for occasional skirmish fire. It felt as if they'd found a storm's lulled center. The time simply passed and, sucking on his cracker, John thought about Levi at home, and remembered the tranquil way in which his sister had handled him and her mother, and how that serene manner contrasted with her sly wit. It was all very different from Ann Bradley's flair, her high spirit that rivaled the head-tossing eagerness of the Owens' finest racehorses. John tried remembering Ann's face just as she'd looked at him in the library with her "Mr. Given, have you hidden yourself?" He thought of her in David Dale's laboratory holding up a specimen glass and then stroking the duster down its long neck. He remembered kissing each finger of her hand.

Then an order came to fall back to the regimental lines. They moved to another hill and across Tilghman Branch clear to the woods near the review field where scouts had spotted a force of Rebels trying to flank the army's left. The field itself felt eerie. There was rough timber beyond it but, in the foreground, the tents of a whole battalion of cavalry stood silent and empty except for the wild hogs that were rooting among the dead.

The men were forming ranks in the new position, but John and Henry weren't. They were in the picket line Captain Rheinlander was leading forward. John felt a twist in his stomach to go with the permanent twist in his knee, but he was determined to ignore it. To ignore them both. He wasn't thirsty anymore. He was beyond thirst. He was chewing on the fatty part of one thumb, and he didn't know why he was doing it, but he didn't stop until a tooth broke through his skin and he tasted blood. More blood welled up in little dots, and he rubbed it onto his sleeve.

For the life of him, he couldn't think how to track where they'd been in the hours since sunrise. He knew where he was, and yet really he didn't, although he was aware of their purpose here. They were to draw fire. John thought of what Harry Beal had written him, of how, on a skirmish line in West Virginia with the 15th, he'd watched a man hold his cap on the bayonet point of his rifle, but aslant so the shot it drew wouldn't hit him, and how it had anyway, how a Johnny Reb had read the trick and shot him in the head.

The Rebel columns were approaching. The men with John were ready to start a commotion and decoy them so they wouldn't know a brigade was waiting undercover in their front though, when it came to it, John didn't know how much brigade they still had. He'd heard that the 15th Illinois had been decimated and the 46th Illinois had gone to the rear. If it was true, their whole brigade was only what was left of the 25th, and the men of the 14th Illinois who were still within shooting distance of the review field. John had his rifle steady, waiting for Captain Rheinlander to give the signal to fire. He could see the driblet of blood on his thumb.

The column came closer, and it seemed to John that the Confederates had an unlimited supply of men, for with all the fire still heavy on the right and left of the battlefield, they were coming straight at them from the front. It was as if they'd just moved out into a perfect morning and were high-stepping once more in complete order, oblivious to the carnage all around them. John stared. He wondered if there was such a thing as battle mirage, if you could see soldiers marching where there weren't any or if he'd conjured up the glorious lines from the morning's blue sky and reassembled them in his mind's eye now in the late afternoon: men with their body parts reattached, officers with plumes in their hats again, men with their souls returned once more to their bodies.

He shook his head, trying to clear it. For a second, he thought his ramrod was gone, that he'd left it in the ground when they'd retreated. Panicked, he ran a hand over his pockets and over his legs and down his sides and his back until he touched metal where the ramrod had swung around on his belt. He took a deep breath and exhaled. He took another breath. The columns were in firing range. Henry Schafer was yelling all at once that their uniforms were blue and John flashed on the uncertain memory of blue shirts in their front at Fort Donelson. Then a battle flag came over the hill and Max Munte said it was all right, that they were Louisiana infantry, that some Frenchman had just dressed his men up for style.

Captain Rheinlander gave the signal, and they opened up with a blaze of fire. John thought if there was ever a time to keep shooting, this was it, and that he'd get off every shot he could until he got shot himself. He kept loading and jamming home the charge, matching Henry Schafer's pace, volley for volley. He could see the 14th Illinois moving on the enemy flank, and he thought that the Rebel boys had a surprise coming, and he was right. The 14th started firing, catching them in a cross fire. The cannon fire was heavy and John could feel something else in the ground, something small but seismic. He thought that the rest of the 25th was slipping quietly from the front to flank the Rebels, too, and he knew that he and Henry Schafer and every other man on the picket line had to keep up the fire. They had to keep the pressure on until these Rebels—they were green boys, green as green—started to fall back.

And they were starting to, starting to right face and following orders to such a fault of perfection that—John could hardly believe it, he really couldn't—a cannon ball had sliced through a file of four men and cut the same raised thigh off each one. He swallowed hard. It was all he could do to ram a charge home and fire again but he had to and he did. Even if it seemed like slaughter, John knew they had to keep the advantage. All day they'd given up ground and if they didn't push forward, it would be their army that ran up the flag and was sent off as prisoners. It would be their families that wound up with Rebel soldiers in their fields and in their homes.

Except everything was changing again. The sounds of the battle had moved from the left, and it was suddenly bedlam. There were boys in Union blue on the run. Drivers flogged their mules as a stream of wagons bumped and rattled by. On the road beyond the flanking companies, officers cursed their horses, trying to rein them in and to turn them toward the rear. Men were fleeing everywhere. They were racing in the direction of the landing, and Rebels were after them in hot pursuit.

Captain Rheinlander ordered their line back into the regiment, which meant falling right. Or just falling, though John didn't. He wasn't shot. He was still on his feet and the whole regiment withdrawing in a rough semblance of order. Major Foster had wheeled his horse. He was dashing up and down the lines, urging the men to stay steady and to cover the retreating troops. John thought there was fire from everywhere—left and right and center—flying minié balls and Rebel screams that all banged together. They ricocheted. They echoed and echoed, a terrible melee of sound as the army retreated.

<hr>

Midnight and rain pouring down, cold and relentless. John lay shivering on his gun in a battle line that had been formed of pieced-together regiments. His clothes were soaked through. He'd swabbed his gun clean, and he was protecting it with his body and a bit of oilcloth he kept in his ammo box, but he was still afraid it wouldn't fire when he needed it. When Nelson's lead columns from Buell's Army of the Ohio had finally arrived and passed through the line and taken the front, John had gone out on picket duty and had seen the eerie moonlight that lit the details hunting for wounded. It unnerved him, but the lightning flashes that shocked the line were just as bad. Now, every few minutes a Union gunboat threw a shell over their lines, and it howled as it went and shook the ground when it landed in the distance in its own burst of light.

Once, when the line went white with lightning, John saw horses to the south and he thought that the Rebels were waiting to attack at first light, cavalry and all. He wondered what he would do if their own shrunken army was driven clear off the landing and into the Tennessee. He'd seen the astonishing numbers of shirkers and stragglers and men who'd fled from their units—hundreds, thousands maybe. Some had tried to swim the river. Most had crowded under the landing bluff. He doubted that many of those men would fight again—they were too sullen or scared—but the army was still being reinforced with more troops. Nelson's advance had arrived before nightfall, but the other units of Buell's army were still coming off steamers that had ferried them from their transports. Even now, they were slogging through the mud to bivouac.

John doubted that a single Union soldier had a tent for the night. A sergeant who'd been caught and then escaped said the Rebels were raising havoc and carrying on in the captured encampments, drinking up the medicinal whiskey and helping themselves to hams and over-coats and to whatever private things a man might have left in his bed-roll. They were celebrating, though what they were doing didn't sound so different from what had gone on at the landing. All night, Union boys had milled around in the rain, and some had found their own whiskey in the sutler stores. They'd brawled like hooligans until their officers put them under guard. A group of the stragglers had built a huge fire a hundred feet from the river and it had flamed up, sending sparks high into the night sky before the rain tamped it down. Max Munte had slipped away, hoping to get close enough to get warm, but he came back more soaked than when he left and said it was impossible, that it was solid men—hundreds of them—the whole way around.

"When we retreated, those first boys charging through?" he said in a while. "You ever see such gray-faced bastards? They were fight-ing all day. They held the center." Max lowered his voice. "There's a cart over there with nothing but arms and legs in it. And peach blossoms."

The night wore on, part utter misery, part dread. It was impos-sible to sleep. Once, when he'd almost dozed off, John jerked up like a yippy dog trying to run in its dreams. Henry Schafer was humming a low tune. Max asked if he was crazy or whistling past the graveyard and then told him if he had lullabies in him to save them for the men who were moaning and dying in the fields. Or maybe for the wounded men who'd been loaded onto steamboats and were screaming bloody hell.

John's legs moved without his wanting them to. He was jittery with all the images and noise from the day's last retreat. All those relentless columns. The Confederates had been like an unending tide. Shells had kept shearing off tree branches and entire trees so that all the world felt and sounded as if the sky had fallen. Wagons and retreating artillery had been jammed together on the road, and swarms of infantry and cavalry had hightailed it off solo into the woods, scared by the rumor, which turned out to be false, that the landing was taken, that the retreating forces were heading into a trap.

Will Jones, who was sergeant major and who'd been all over the field the whole day, had been shot ten feet in front of John, a terrible wound to the leg. The men struggled to carry him, hurrying and sliding over bloody ground. Will screamed for water, and when they got to a stream and cupped their hands to his mouth and were ready to drink themselves, a body bobbed up right next to John. Bodies were everywhere. The tents the men passed were shredded with bullet holes. Some of the hospital tents had caught fire from shells and had burned with the wounded inside so that charred skeletons lay scattered in blackened masses.

It had seemed an endless day. A whole city of men in sheer murderous force had tried to kill each other and mostly succeeded. At least twenty men who'd been with Company A when the battle started in the morning were simply gone. John still didn't know what had happened to George Tretheway. Felix Edmonds hadn't turned up. The regiments had been thrown apart in the retreat, with Colonel Veatch losing his horse and separated from the command. Major Foster had given orders to the entire brigade. Before that, Lieutenant Boren was hit by a shell, and the men who saw it said he'd put his hand to his side and, with his knees buckling, slid slowly onto the field. John didn't know if he was dead. There was no more word about Colonel Morgan. It was certain, however, that Captain Saltzman had died. A soldier who was with him had told Romeo Keister they'd been cut off on the far right when the forward regiments crashed through the lines in the morning and that, lost and wandering, they'd ended up clear on the left with a Wisconsin unit in the thick of things. Captain Saltzman had been killed fighting. He'd been shot straight through the heart.

What puzzled John was why they weren't all dead. Dead or captured. The battle had seemed simply to stop. He had no idea why—exhaustion maybe—but it was as if a wand had been waved and the Confederates had ceased being a pursuing army, though they were surely gathering again out there, intent on finishing them off. He could read about it at home, he thought. If he ever got home. He could sit in the library and hope for Ann Bradley to appear again—to pop up in real life from that place where her shimmery self stayed at the back of his mind—and he could wait for Achilles Fretageot to finish reading *Harper's Weekly*, and then read it himself and find out what had happened.

A shell flew over, chased by a lightning bolt, and John could see the men down the line. They looked pale but not the ghostly blue they'd seemed in the moonlight. As the shell shrieked into land, thunder boomed and the rain, which had slackened, picked up once again into a heavy downpour. John's leg ached so much that he wanted to pull it off. He was full of regret. He wished he'd given Charley a book to write in and that he'd urged his father more strongly to make sure Denis stayed at home—to do anything to keep Denis away from all this. Water streamed down his face and he realized he was glad of it, that it felt like crying but without the effort. Once again, he'd killed men. Today he'd even killed boys who weren't old enough to shave. He was still circling the idea of himself as a killer—*thou shalt not kill*—and still wondering if he was better off staying curled up against the rain or stretching out now and again so his legs didn't cramp as much (although it hardly mattered; he felt so wretched he didn't think anything could make him feel better or worse), and still wondering if eating the last two crackers in his haversack would mean he'd eaten his last meal (and better not to waste them), when the rain stopped.

A long or short while later—John didn't know—dawn arced the faintest pink over the river, and they were ordered into ranks. Men were spitting as they stood up and trying to crack their necks loose. Romeo Keister was wringing his cap out. "When all this water drips off me, that river'll be a whole inch higher," he said, and Henry Schafer, who was pulling the wet plug out of his rifle, looked over the barrel at him.

"I thought you were pissing down your leg," he said.

Then they were all at attention. Lieutenant Randolph, hacking and coughing the way he'd done ever since Fort Donelson, dressed the line. John didn't know whether they were getting ready to receive an attack or make one. With their gunboats on the river and at least fifty of their big guns massed to protect the landing, it could go either way. There was firing to the south. A picture went through John's mind of all those columns of Rebel soldiers marching through the woods and across streams and into open fields as though not a single one had an idea he was mortal. He wondered if they were out there once more— all those ghostly regiments getting ready to die again and to take the rest of the 25th along with them.

"Let's go, let's go," Henry said. "If we can't eat, we might as well fight."

Soon they were actually advancing. They'd gotten food as well— a few more crackers that had been forwarded through the line. They were moving out with their brigade, all four regiments, or what was left of them, which was more like two—less really—and John, looking around him as they marched and as the sun burned off the morning fog, saw again what a terrible thing yesterday's battle had been. It was as if a giant had stomped and flailed through the woods, smashing the trees and chopping away at their branches and knocking down tents as if they were so many rags, leaving rows of dead men and animals stretching far across the fields.

John flinched in surprise. Was the ruddy-necked officer at the far end of the line Lieutenant Boren? He squinted his eyes. He couldn't tell. He couldn't see at all clearly, but he felt a second of reckless hope. If it was—if Lieutenant Boren wasn't dead and was back in the company, John wouldn't have to write to Margaret Mulhern and tell her the Sampsons had lost their son-in-law, that delicate Mrs. Boren, turned away by his mother when she'd come to call on him after Fort Donelson, was a widow. And if Lieutenant Boren wasn't dead, then maybe George Tretheway and Colonel Morgan weren't either. Maybe nobody was dead except Captain Saltzman, though even Captain

Saltzman might have lived for as long as a deer could live, shot and staggering on until the arterial blood returned to its heart and it fell in its tracks.

John was still craning to see as they were ordered into position on the right in support of the attacking forces. It seemed their role here—to start the day slowly and lulled into an idea of safety. The morning dragged on, and all they'd done was dry along with their uniforms and move forward to stay close to the fighting units. John began to think they wouldn't fight at all, that they they might stay in the lee of this particular day's battle and listen in, which was unavoidable anyway for he hadn't gone deaf, though he'd been sure that he would. He'd thought he'd be at least as deaf as Captain Saltzman was from working in his blacksmith shop, except that Captain Saltzman wasn't deaf now but dead. There'd been that final change of consonant.

By noon, when they marched left to a gap in the line just west of the upper "V" where the Corinth Road and the Hamburg-Savannah Road crossed and split away from each other, John realized he was wrong. They were going to fight, and very soon. The new order arrived in the person of General Grant himself. "Oh, it's him, it's him," Romeo Keister said in a muffled voice, and the words had a familiar ring to John, which so much of this battle did, though so much of it didn't. General Grant, who the men in line said had sat his horse like a statue during the Rebels' advance on the landing, and who had hurt his ankle badly when his horse fell in the mud on Friday night and needed help getting into his saddle, had ridden straight up to Colonel Veatch. John thought one of his boots was cut because of his swollen leg but he wasn't sure.

The two men spoke briefly. General Grant gestured once. Then he rode off again with his aide, and the brigade wasn't waiting any longer. Colonel Veatch and the line officers, the familiar ones and the ones who'd been breveted due to casualties, were ordering the troops into battalion columns. They were heading on the double-quick toward the center of the Union front, which John guessed was wavering, and the freakish thing was that they were headed right back to the review field. They were crossing it and trying not to step on dead men, and they were going through deserted camps that had been plundered and strewn with abandoned bedrolls and mess pans, and with crumpled pictures and letters, everything squashed into the mud by horses' hooves except for one clean spill of grain that was dotted with feathers.

They didn't stop. They were headed on toward the woods. When they passed the left of another brigade and had charged a hill ready to strike the Confederate right, that right had mostly disappeared. The Rebels had left the field. They were withdrawing and, amazed as John was, he knew their own blood was up. The men were yelling—*don't let them off, boys, don't let the bloody devils go.* They followed as fast as the enemy retreated, still double-quicking until their brigade made up the forward troops of the entire army. They were ready to go the whole way to Corinth, to just keep on charging and charging, except that General Buell, who was in command in this part of the field, had sent a new order. Once more—one more unbelievable time, they'd been told to fall back.

John was incredulous. He couldn't absorb it. Was this how a battle ended when you were there for the finish? Was this how it all happened? They'd been stopped so suddenly it was as if they were horses and somebody had yanked hard on their reins. The men were swearing and shouting, sweat streaking down their faces and through the mud on their shirts. It was an astonishing, empty, empty moment. And yet they were turning back now. There was no more pursuit, no army captured. With men dead in numbers too high even to think of, nothing was settled except that both sides could fight, and fight unbelievably.

John took a long look over his shoulder at the last of the fleeing Rebels. He set his jaw. With all this slaughter and seesawing, he felt an ominous new certainty. He'd believed the war would end quickly, but now he didn't. This whole bloody thing would go on.

New Harmony, Indiana
April 1862

10

A storm has passed over our little town.

April 12, 1862, entry in the diary of Achilles H. Fretageot

Wait. You shouldn't do that," Kate said quickly, but she was too late. Eliza, who'd wheedled her sisters' necklaces from Kate for her dolls, had pulled a vest over a doll's head without taking the necklaces off first. Two of the strings had broken. The beads, which were rain tree pod seeds Mr. Beal had lacquered for his granddaughters in the summer, were pinging and skidding across the floor. They were shiny and hard and black, with tiny holes the girls had made with a needle. Now they were bouncing and rolling under the counterpane on the bed where Alice and Mary always slept.

Kate and Eliza both watched them, Kate considering her mistake. Earlier, Eliza had been in charge. She was home from school with a sniffly cold that got worse when she remembered it and all but disappeared when she didn't. She'd been the schoolmistress to Kate, first drilling her on spelling and then trying to teach her to play Feiba Peveli, a game based on a plan for naming towns by latitude and longitude that was also the name of the splinter Owen society where people like the Elliotts still lived. Kate's friends played it with lightning speed, challenging each other's answers, and Kate wanted to learn it, but she'd quickly grown exasperated.

"Since Feiba Peveli, which it seems to me should be Feiba *Paveli*, has the same latitude as New Harmony, why shouldn't we be Feiba Veinul?" she asked, looking at the atlas that Eliza had gotten from her father's shelves. "Are you sure Ipba Veinul is right?"

"It's because of the rules. You have to learn all the rules Mr. Whitwell made."

"And how do you decide where the *v*'s go to show that the longitude's west? If New York is Otke Notive, why did he make London Lafa Vovutu? It's a ridiculous name by the way. And why does the *v* come first? For that matter, why are there two?"

"It's the rules," Eliza answered again, and she held up the sheet she'd made that said *Stedman Whitwell, London Architect* at the top and had a long list of directions written below.

"They hardly make sense," Kate insisted, and she thought—not for the first time—that New Harmony, for all its learning and for everything that drew her to it, had an undeniable silliness in its past and present that her Grandpa Given in Drumboarty (Eifla Piever, of course) would have found quite preposterous. She'd left the atlas on the table and gotten out Eliza's dolls and, in a moment of weakness, the necklaces.

Eliza was still cross-legged on the daybed, the doll she'd been playing with facedown in her lap as she watched the last of the necklace beads roll away. "You'll be in trouble for letting me use them," she said. "We should have blown Easter eggs."

"You're a smart one," Kate answered. "If I'm in trouble, you are as well. Right here, and under you go, miss," she said. She held up the counterpane and waited while Eliza put the doll aside and came padding across the floor. "I'll help you, though," Kate said. "Careful not to rip your stockings." She got down next to Eliza, who'd stretched out on her stomach, and the two of them peered under the bed.

It was dark but once her eyes had adjusted to the dim light, Kate started pinching the beads up from between the floorboards and rolled them toward the middle of the room. Eliza did the same thing. In a while, Kate thought they had all the beads from under the bed plus enough dust on their dresses to call her cleaning skills into serious question. Eliza, who'd backed out from under the bed first, sat on the rug counting each bead into the little basket Kate had taken from the dresser. She sneezed from the dust. "Good. It's made my nose itchier, and Mama will keep me home from school again tomorrow," she said.

Kate would have laughed, and she would have told Eliza that she'd take the beads home for Margaret to restring and to make new clasps, that they'd both tell Alice and Mary how sorry they were, but she was listening now. There was a dim commotion started somewhere. It wasn't in the street outside, but from farther uptown.

"What's that?" Eliza asked.

Kate went to the window, and Eliza was right behind her. She was standing on the bed peering out past Kate's shoulder when her mother came into the room,

"Those rude men. Have those country men gotten drunk and are they fighting again?" Mrs. Lichtenberger asked, coming to the window, too, though there was nothing to see.

"I don't think so," Kate said. "Should I find out what's happening?"

"It could be war news. Yes, go ahead out and check, Catharine," Mrs. Lichtenberger answered. "But fetch the girls at school when it's time. I don't want them caught in a crowd."

Kate nodded and said that she would.

Downstairs, she got her bonnet and put her shawl around her shoulders. She thought she needed something to make herself look more purposeful, and so she got the market basket from the kitchen. Then she checked the butter in the icebox to make sure it hadn't separated. It hadn't, of course, but it was a thing to do to calm her nerves before she went out. And she *was* nervous. If it was about the war— well, she was nervous was all.

The noise was louder as she opened the door. There were other people headed in the same direction that she was, and there were dogs running and hens squawking in the street. Kate counted days in her head. John had left three weeks ago, which felt like no time at all. Levi Thrailkill was still at home, and it hardly seemed much more than yesterday that they'd all been at the Wilseys' for John's farewell party. Though she knew it wasn't particularly logical, Kate thought it was too soon for anything to have happened that John could be part of. If there was war news, it was about McClellan, she decided. It would be about McClellan and the army in the East.

When she reached the corner of Church and Main, she could see that the biggest part of the crowd was in front of Fretageots' store and that there were people leaning out of the hotel windows upstairs. Kate made her way closer, nudging with her basket when she had to. She could hear bits and pieces of what people were saying and, with increasing alarm, she realized that it wasn't McClellan they were talking about but General Grant. From what she could gather, there was news from the wires that his army had fought an even more terrible battle in Tennessee.

"How many casualties?" she asked, raising her voice so that the man in front of her could hear her above the din, but he shook his head. She turned with the same question to a boy about Denis's age, but neither he nor anyone else seemed to know anything. Everything was a jumble of rumor and speculation, with the name Pittsburg Landing repeated on every side. Kate took it all in. Then suddenly she felt her eyes opening wide. What had she heard? Had somebody said Lieutenant Boren was dead?

"Kate, come away. You shouldn't be here. Not in this crowd." It was Michael McShane with his hand on her elbow, and Kate, feeling the press of rough strangers around her, was glad to see him but annoyed at the peremptory tone of his voice.

"I'm here like anybody. I'm here for news of the war," she answered, keeping her eyes straight ahead, but when Michael didn't answer, she looked at him. "Do you know anything? Anything for certain? I've heard such rumors, that the Rebels attacked and General Johnston was killed and General Grant let him catch our army by surprise, that there was a frightful battle. Have you heard that, too? And, Michael, did you hear anything about Lieutenant Boren?"

"Come away, Kate. We'll hear as soon as anyone." Michael was steering her out of the crowd and away from a particularly scabrous fellow with yellow eyes and foul breath who'd pushed up against her.

"But Michael. Wait, Michael. Michael, stop," Kate said. "Mrs. Lichtenberger told me to get the girls. And we should certainly go to the Sampsons' and warn Margaret Mulhern in case something has happened to Lieutenant Boren. And, Michael—Michael, let go of me! I've a father already. If you need a daughter to order about, you'd best be in Donegal where you have your own. I can wait here and learn what's happened as well as anyone." Kate pointed at George Tretheway's sister, who was a maid to Colonel Richard Owen's wife. "See? Mrs. Cawthorne is here. It's a perfectly respectable place for a woman."

Kate stopped. She held her shoulder tightly under her shawl in an effort to calm herself. She knew that she'd spoken too sharply. From Michael's silence, she knew, too, that she'd wounded him, and she regretted it, though not, she realized, all that keenly. She reached down and picked at a loose bit of reed on the edge of her basket. She studied the ground with its crowded shadows, trying unsuccessfully to think what the latitude and longitude might be for Pittsburg Landing. "Eliza tried to teach me Feiba Peveli," she said, looking up at Michael again. "I'm not very good at it. Michael, I'm sorry for what I said. It's that I can't bear to think of the boys in another dreadful battle. John was just getting well. He was far from well if you want the real truth, but he would go back. He's so dutiful. Why, Michael? He has the spirit in him to be rebellious, but he always ends up so responsible."

"It's the priest in him. The almost priest. And Kate, I suspect you're rebel enough for two." Michael gave her a long look. "Now will you come away?"

Kate shook her head. "I can't," she said. "No." She looked over her shoulder at the Sampsons' house. She didn't mind being called rebellious. Maybe it even made her proud. It was what her father had implied when they came to New Harmony with Margaret Mulhern, and people were signing up for the agricultural society. It had been all men paying their dollars to join and, when she stepped up to sign her name below her father's, he'd told Richard Owen that in Ireland women did field work as well as the men and that Kate was the best of them, which was a very large fib.

"Why such a story, Father?" she'd asked him. "What's in an ag society that makes it just for men? I would have signed anyway," and her father had answered that he knew she would have, that she had his spunk, but he could have his fun, couldn't he?

"I'm going in to Margaret Mulhern to see what they know," she said. "And then I'm waiting with the crowd for more news until I go get the girls. Wait with me or not, Michael, but that's what I'm doing."

She straightened her bonnet, which had been knocked askew by a stray elbow. A few short strides later, she reached up and pounded on the Sampsons' door loudly enough that they could hear her over the crowd. In a moment she saw Margaret Mulhern peering through the parlor window, Mrs. Boren's baby sleeping against her shoulder. Margaret opened the door.

"Have you had any news?" Kate asked quietly before Margaret could frown at her for making a racket. Kate glanced at the stairs. She heard voices in the upper hall, and she thought one of them was Mrs. Boren's. "Is there news about Lieutenant Boren?" she asked.

Margaret put a hand over the baby's exposed ear. "Mrs. Boren doesn't believe it," she said. "She says it's all rumor and she knows he's well. She had a letter from him in the post today. Kate, there's no word of John?"

Kate shook her head. "There's never word about the men at first. Just the officers. But Mrs. Boren doesn't—" Kate stopped for Mrs. Boren herself was coming down the stairs with her older son. She sat down and leaned against the banister, drawing the child into her lap.

"Should we have let them go, Catharine?" she said, her eyes oddly glittery the way John's had been when Kate had given him the laudanum. "Should we have let those Rebels confederate all they wanted to? My husband's a Lincoln man and a Union man and I say all for the Union, but if Confederate women could have heard the poem Lydia Hinckley read at the Minerva Club, I don't think there'd be a war at all—'An Appeal to Kentucky!' And don't my boys need their papa at home, which he will be soon. William, show how old you are on your birthday."

"Five, Mama," the boy said, without putting up his fingers. The baby, who was maybe a year and a half—Kate wasn't sure—woke up then. Margaret helped him climb the stairs to his mother. He pushed at his brother to make his own place on his mother's lap, and Kate feared that one or both of them might tumble down the steps, but Mrs. Boren balanced them both. And, anyway, Margaret was blocking the stairs.

"Yes, Ralphie. Papa will be home soon for his baby boy. But where is my sister? Where's Mollie?" Mrs. Boren asked, and Kate glanced quickly at the picture on the foyer table: Mollie Owen—Julian Dale's wife and the youngest Sampson sister—calm and gently elegant in stripes. "I thought it was Mollie when you came, Catharine," Mrs. Boren went on. "Can someone go to the mansion for her? I've Mother and Father and my grandmother to be long-faced and worrying, but Mollie will know, as I do, that Absalom is fine. He told me that in his letter and in words so very full of love."

Kate looked at Margaret. "I could go for her," she said, but Margaret shook her head and whispered that Mollie had already been sent for.

"I'll tell Mother you won't come tonight for the rosary," Kate said in a low voice, and then, to her own surprise and because it seemed the thing to do, she made a quick curtsey to Mrs. Boren before she went out the door.

Outside, instinctively she looked for Michael McShane. He was nowhere around. The crowd seemed noisier and Kate, feeling uneasy, waited a moment tapping at her basket, and then decided Michael had either been convinced by her fine show of independence or had assumed she was staying at Sampsons' with Margaret Mulhern. She heard a carriage in the street and looked up to see Mollie Owen climbing out of it in her purple cloak and then hurrying into the Sampson house. Kate was tempted to go back, but she thought better of it. She tucked her shawl tight and made her way into the crowd. It was larger and more rambunctious, but nobody seemed to have more news—at least not anything definite. There had been a battle; that was all that was certain.

A horse went by, flicking up mud, and Kate felt a clot of it hit her knee through her skirt. There was a lot of jostling, and she was practically pushed off her feet. A fistfight broke out just a few feet away from her, one man yelling for the Union and another for the Confederacy. A lot of men were fighting and, to her surprise, not one of them was Denis. For that matter, her father wasn't here either. There wasn't another Given in the crowd. Kate didn't know a single one of the brawling men, though she was sure they were men who lived in the woods or in settlements on the river. Some of them would have relatives in Kentucky or Tennessee and they'd be fighting the men who didn't, though it seemed most people did. Some of the staunchest Union men she knew—men like Mr. Thrailkill—had actually been born in the South.

There was a man stepping on the hem of her dress, tugging it from the waist, and she pushed at him with her basket to make him move. He didn't, and before she knew what was happening, the whole crowd had surged backward and the fight was practically on top of her. She decided Michael was right. There were better places for her to be. She was trapped, and a man with a bloodied nose fell right into her, knocked out cold. Kate felt the air go out of her. She was trying to catch her breath and to get away from the blood that had smeared all over her hand. She was getting nowhere, and then the crowd parted. For an instant, it was as if the Red Sea had opened. Kate didn't know what had happened until she saw Mr. Cannon shouting from his window and throwing buckets of water down. She pulled at her skirt. The hem came free and, ducking her head down, she edged her way backward until, finally, she was clear of the whole crowd and the insults they were tossing at Mr. Cannon. She could go back to Margaret but, of course Mrs. Boren might be on the stairs still, and she did have this bloody hand . . .

It was Ann Bradley who rescued her, calling to her from Mrs. David Dale's yard. Ann got a dipper of water from the well, and told Kate to stick her hand out. When it was clean, which took three full dippers of water splashing bloody onto the ground, Ann took her into the kitchen and helped her tack up her hem. "Are you all right?" she asked. "I wouldn't want to write your brother that you perished in the battle of New Harmony."

"I'm fine." Kate shook her hem out. "I feel stupid is all. And I have to get Alice and Mary. Have you heard anything, Ann?"

"Just that a lot of men died. A whole lot. But I haven't heard your brother's name and that's good news. There's not a more entertaining letter writer in the 25th—or the 15th, for that matter," Ann said, and Kate, feeling protective of John, asked herself if that was all Ann saw in him—a man who could please her with a letter. She wondered, too, what men of the 15th Ann was referring to. Then she interrupted her own thoughts and decided that Ann was being kind and trying to tease her out of her worry. Still, when Ann offered to go with her for the girls, Kate told her no.

"I'm all right," she said. She left the house and, skirting the crowd, made her way straight to the school and waited while Alice and Mary gathered their things. Walking back with her, they were both full of questions and excitement that there was war news and a crowd downtown. Kate felt a momentary rush of anger but reminded herself they were really too young to know better. If the men who'd marched from New Harmony with the 25th in July had been so full of fervor for the war, why should children be any less naive? And it hadn't come home to them for no one in their family had been hurt. Still, though, she felt cross with them. She told Mary not to scuff her shoes. She told Alice that it was unseemly for a girl who was thirteen to wear her hat hanging like a sunbonnet.

When they got back to the house, Kate hurried to fix supper.

Mr. Lichtenberger had come home early from the store, and Mrs. Lichtenberger sent the girls upstairs and asked questions of him instead of Kate, which both irritated and relieved her. She wasn't usually one to eavesdrop, but she did now. She pushed the chopping board closer to the doorway and leaned back so she could catch the voices from the drawing room.

It didn't take long for her to learn that Mr. Lichtenberger knew more than she did. Or at least that he'd heard more. If early reports were right, the casualty numbers were terrible, and they needed to brace themselves for a long list of dead men. He said something Kate couldn't quite hear about Lieutenant Boren, and he added that there were worrying rumors about Captain Saltzman. Then he stopped talking and she heard the oddest sound. She didn't know what it was. She went into the passageway and stole a quick glance into the parlor. Mr. Lichtenberger was standing next to the clock and, though Mrs. Lichtenberger was pressing her face against his chest, he was the one who was crying. It was a dry and rough kind of crying, and it was clearly being done by somebody who didn't really know how. In a moment, though, he'd gathered himself, and Kate pushed her back against the wall to make sure he didn't see her.

"These good men," he said. "These friends. Two battles and they rip the heart out of our little town. What ungodly horror is it that we've brought on ourselves?"

Kate tried to stop herself, but finally she couldn't. She burst into the parlor. "Please—excuse me, sir, but Mr. Lichtenberger, is there any word of my brother? Of John?"

She'd startled them both. Mrs. Lichtenberger moved away from her husband's arms, and he himself made a self-conscious gesture of pulling out his watch. Kate thought Mrs. Lichtenberger was going to chide her, but she didn't. When Mr. Lichtenberger answered her, it was in a measured tone. "No, nothing, Catharine. I wish I could say he's well, but all we can do is wait."

"And, ma'am, your cousin," Kate went on, turning to Mrs. Lichtenberger. "Was Harry Beal in the fighting? I heard a man say that the Army of the Ohio was in the fight on Sunday. Isn't the 15th with General Buell?"

"Not a word of that to the girls, Catharine. But the answer is we don't know."

"I hope he's well, ma'am. For your sake," Kate said, "and for John's since they're the best of friends." Kate had started backing toward the kitchen. "And for his own sake, too," she added, and then she turned around quickly and went out of the room.

When supper was done and Kate had finished washing up, Mrs. Lichtenberger told her without her asking that she could go home for the night. Kate collected the sewing she had to do and picked up her shawl. The older girls were at the table doing schoolwork with their mother, but Eliza pressed a small bag into Kate's hands.

"What?" Kate asked, and Eliza put a quick finger to her lips.

"The beads," she whispered, and Kate thought back into the afternoon and to the dark space under the bed.

"I'll take them to my sister," she said, slipping the bag under her shawl and thinking how strange it was that the smallest concerns of life could be so very palpable while the largest ones hovered invisibly in the air.

—

The news in the next days arrived in incremental doses. Everyone knew that the Union had won and that the Confederates had retreated toward their base at Corinth. Everyone knew that the carnage had been terrible. But so many questions were unanswered. Kate felt the whole town was living in dread once more, and it all seemed hideously familiar. Her mother didn't let go of her rosary beads and, though Kate half expected her father to get drunk and stay drunk until he had word of John, he didn't touch a drop, which for him, she believed, was a form of prayer. It was certainly the closest he got to a Lenten observation.

Margaret Mulhern brought them the first news of any significance, which came from a wire from Mr. Sampson, who'd encountered an officer en route from Pittsburg Landing to General Halleck's headquarters in St. Louis. Mr. Sampson had gone as far as Cairo intending to get Lieutenant Boren's body, but the officer told him he'd seen Lieutenant Boren alive after the fight, and that he'd talked to him. Margaret said that Mrs. Boren, who had been certain all along that her husband was alive, was immediately struck with doubt and had crumpled into a chair, sobbing and sobbing. Her mother and her grandmother, Mrs. Maidlow, had finally put her to bed with one of Mrs. Maidlow's remedies.

A family or two had received letters that had made it through. There weren't any from the 25th, and the sole one Kate knew of that referred to the 25th's casualties said only that Lieutenant Colonel Morgan had been wounded in the leg. Finally, the day before Easter, papers arrived from Evansville, and the late dispatches were bursting with detail. Her father was in Mount Vernon working with Michael McShane, so it was Kate who hurried from the boat landing, reading the paper as she went and absolutely riveted by the words.

The horrible news was that it was true about Captain Saltzman. He was dead, and Kate, as she went up the street with the other people coming from the landing, didn't know when she'd seen so many grief-stricken faces. She wondered if many of the people, as she was, were remembering the Fourth of July parade when he'd been grand marshal and sat so erect in his saddle that he looked like a general.

The most relieving and best news was that John wasn't on the list of casualties, but Company A had taken a terrible toll. She counted the names on the list and found twenty-three which, given what John had told them about the company being understrength (and what she knew herself just from Levi Thrailkill and Fred Perkey still being at home) meant at least a quarter of the company was missing or killed or wounded. Mr. Lichtenberger was right. Their little town was getting butchered. They were losing men who were husbands and fathers, while men who should have become husbands and fathers were being crippled or killed. A lot of the men were ones she didn't know, or barely knew, but she certainly did know George Tretheway and Felix

Edmonds, and they were both listed as wounded. And Lieutenant Boren's name was on the list. For a second, Kate stopped, horrified, the word "mortally" floating before her eyes. Then she read the lines once more and saw the description had been applied to a private named Henry Boothe. Second Lieutenant A. Boren, as the paper identified him, had been wounded, but only slightly.

Kate shuddered with relief. Remembering Mrs. Boren seated with her children on the stairs, Kate thought she had seemed not only precariously fragile but like a woman totally separated from reality. Kate knew that she herself had been convinced, standing in the Sampsons' hallway, that Absalom Boren was dead. Even now, she wondered if the paper was right. How had the story begun that Lieutenant Boren was dead if he wasn't? She wondered if it was like the Hugos. If the official army word had been wrong for the Hugos, perhaps this paper was wrong in its report. Though if it was, it could be wrong about anything, and she didn't even want to consider that.

Kate shook her head and told herself sternly she had to stop being so morbid and distrustful. Things were bad enough as they were. As her mother often told her, she had no business conjuring something worse than there was. Thinking of her mother, she really wanted to see her. She headed home even though Mrs. Lichtenberger was waiting for the paper. The day had a vague warmness about it, and Kate wondered if she would find her mother in the garden starting to work the ground and reflecting, as her mother would since it was Holy Saturday, on the earthen tomb where Christ had awaited his resurrection.

She found her in the kitchen instead. "You've got a cobweb," she said, reaching to touch her mother's hair, which smoothed away from the part and swept to the top of her head where it was pinned. "Oh," Kate said, catching her hand in midair. "Nothing," she added, quickly, lowering her eyes. She spread the paper out on the table, still startled at the fine spin of white that seemed to have threaded through her mother's hair overnight. "Look," she said. "John's not on the list. It's all the men from Company A and he's not on it." She drew her finger across the page so her mother, who could make out Given though her reading was poor, could see that it wasn't. "George Tretheway's hurt," she said. "And it's true about Captain Saltzman. He was killed. Lieutenant Boren was only wounded, and just slightly. There's a whole description of the battleground after the fight. Shall I read it to you?"

"Your father will. Are you supposed to be at work, Catharine?" her mother said, and then she hugged Kate, holding her tight and pressing her face against her hair as she'd done when Kate was a little girl. "Is it sure then that John's all right?" she said softly, and Kate nodded and said that it was.

At the Lichtenbergers', she made Easter dinner as she always did, but it didn't escape her that the children did not get the silver dollars their father usually tucked into their napkins or that Mrs. Lichtenberger made a menu for the week's meals that required all the eggs Kate and the girls had dyed with none of them going to the poorhouse. To her, the Lichtenbergers had always seemed made of money, and she didn't know if this sudden streak of thriftiness meant that the war had somehow come to Adam Lichtenberger's pocketbook, or if it meant simply that he and Mrs. Lichtenberger had chosen to honor the gravity of what had happened in Tennessee by a small sacrifice.

She didn't ask. She wouldn't have. And she didn't say anything to anyone. Particularly she didn't say anything to her parents because she knew the alarm that would register in their eyes. They both would be concerned about her job. She might write to John. She could ask John if a certain carefulness with boiled eggs was a sign that a merchant was feeling the pinch.

He would laugh when he read it, and so she should write it, she thought. She would like to make him laugh. She would like to distract him for a moment from all that had happened in Tennessee—the horror of it that she couldn't really imagine, though there were things the papers said that stuck in her mind. It had surprised her that not just men had died, but horses, too. Their carcasses had been covered with brush. Then they'd been burned, but the stench remained when the sun came out. Far more than sun, there had been rain, and a reporter had written that men had struggled through the mire, packing their rations on their backs. Kate remembered exactly the way he'd put it: that a man would have to be hungry indeed to earn his bread at such an expense of wind and muscle.

Wind and muscle. Wind and muscle. It made war sound hard as well as bloody. It made it seem that war was real labor.

Later, there was a letter that Major Foster of the 25th had written to his father. It had been printed in a New York paper and then reprinted in the *Evansville Journal* that arrived right after Mr. Sampson got back from his trip and told Kate's father and the other men at the tavern that even though he'd been struck in the chest by a spent shell and carried from the field with a bruise over his heart, Absalom Boren was all right. He was most certainly alive, which was news that Kate finally trusted and which made her feel considerably better. She read Major Foster's letter carefully, and what interested her most was the part that told of the retreat of the Union forces. Major Foster had held his men in a wash on the roadside to keep them from being trampled to death. It had left them in the crossfire of the enemy, and he'd written that that was better than having their own army crush them. Kate's head swam just thinking of such choices. What a murderous pandemonium it had to have been.

In town, there was a great deal of talk of the thousands of ill and wounded soldiers who'd been shipped north after the battle, and Kate kept thinking of them. The Evansville hospital was swarmed. New Harmony's Minerva Club girls like Lydia Hinckley and Florence Dale Owen, who was Robert Dale Owen's daughter and Mrs. James Cooper now that she'd married, had gone off to nurse them. Kate wondered just what kind of help they would be, young women who couldn't do their own buttons. Certainly none of the girls she knew well had the freedom to be such gallivanting humanitarians, as her father called them. She wondered why the Sampsons hadn't sent Margaret Mulhern, who would be of real use. Or the Lichtenbergers might have sent her, though of course she lacked Margaret's experience. Yet it might as well have been Catharine Given saving lives and having boys pulling at her wrists to thank her for her all of her kindnesses. It might have been

Catharine Given as the young woman they begged to write their letters home. She could do it, too, if they weren't so particular as John about spelling.

She was being petty, she thought. She didn't doubt the good intentions of Lydia and of Florence Dale—particularly Florence Dale, who had a sweet face, although it sometimes annoyed Kate that so many Owens, including the women, had the Dale stuck in their name to show off their other notable lineage. She was still feeling piqued. When Captain Saltzman's body came home, she'd been left at the Lichtenbergers' to fix food for mourners while the whole rest of the town went out to Maple Hill. Even Charley was there. He told her afterward that the captain's horse had stood close by the grave, its head down and its reins trailing, and Kate wished she had seen it. Of course, she knew she'd been lucky in one regard. She hadn't missed what was far more important and personal to her: she'd been at the landing to say good-bye when Fred Perkey and Levi Thrailkill went back to the war within days of each other.

Her father had looked truly alarmed when Fred left. "A paler-faced wretch I've never seen," he told Kate, and Kate had shushed him. She didn't know if Annie Perkey had heard him since she was crying so hard that her bonnet strings were soaked. When it was Levi's turn to go, Caroline's mother had wept, but Caroline didn't. Kate thought she had found a way to be calm and steady for her parents, though Kate knew she felt Levi's leaving as much as anyone could. It was odd, Kate thought. Caroline was younger than she was, younger by several years, yet she had a sort of poise that made Kate feel coltish beside her. Not that Caroline couldn't be witty and fun. But there was something unruffled about her that seemed almost regal. Not imperious, though. She was natural, too.

Kate had stood with the families and friends as Fred's boat left and, later in the week, when Levi's boat pulled out. Both times, Denis and Charley were there helping to load baskets of delicacies on other boats that were headed for Evansville. The baskets were destined for the hospital and Kate, when she first saw them, had said how silly.

What would a man with a hole in his side do with preserves and cakes? What wounded men needed was soup. They needed beef tea and medicine for their pain.

She hadn't commented, however, when baskets were put on a boat near the one Levi boarded. As his boat moved out onto the water, its plume of steam bent backward in the moving current of air, what she'd felt was sorrow for the Thrailkills and the Perkeys, and for her own family and every other family that had sent a boy to the front. The war made her feel strange. It made her feel lonely. She had a sense not so much of loss but of being lost, of not knowing where she was any longer. The earth seemed tilted too far on its axis.

Still, there was one thing she'd known she could do. When she left the landing, she went straight home and made scones the way their Grandma O'Donnell had made them and took the plate of them, still warm, to Michael McShane.

She could not make peace, of course. It was possible, though, to make a peace offering, even if small.

Camp near Monterey Tennessee
May 7, 1862

11

I saw the applicant, Fred Perkey, on or about the 20th of April, 1862 on the field at Shiloh.

Henry B. Beal, affiant to the Board of Pensioners, August 8,1882

Dear Sister,

I received your welcome letter which you sent by Levi Thrailkill but as we were about to move forward I had not time to write to you and even now I have hardly time as it is half past eight o'clock and we have to march at 10 A.M. so that when I bundle up, receive my rations and so forth I have not got much time to spare.

On Sunday we marched out here from Shiloh and as soon as we commenced to march it commenced to rain so hard that we had to march in mud ankle deep from morning till night and then lie out on the wet ground in wet clothes for two days as the road became so muddy that it was next to impossible to move our baggage. We managed to get something to eat though we had to carry it through the mud (the wagons were stuck fast), but our tents have not reached us yet and I am afraid that it will be some time before they do as we move still further forward today and the roads are impassable. If dry weather does not set in pretty soon I am afraid that we shall have to suffer for something to eat before long. As regards the time when the battle of Corinth is about to come off it is more than I can tell nor even conjecture, but it is thought that our regiment will not be in the fight. That is they will not be in front, but kept back as part of the reserve corps. If the regiments in front should have to retreat then we must take their place. You inquired if I was well of my cold yet. I was getting well but lying out in wet clothes on the wet ground on Sunday night gave my cold a fresh start so that I am worse now than I was when I wrote to you before but cold is nothing or considered nothing in the Army though it makes a fellow feel bad sometimes. Levi Thrailkill and Fred Perkey got a pretty hard introduction to soldiering after being so long at home. I thought it would have gone harder with Perkey than it did. Levi's arm is not well yet though he is doing duty. I am glad to hear that Capt. Saltzman was interred with military honors and that his remains received the respect which he himself deserved and which his memory should always receive at the hands of every person from Harmony and every true soldier of Indiana.

The camp is dull and as we are out here so far in the woods it is doubtful whether this will ever reach you so I think it is useless to write any more, my object being just to let you know that I am still alive and comparatively well. I do not know where the 15th Regiment are at present. I have not seen any of them for some time.

Give my respects to father, Mother, brothers and sisters, and to all the girls particularly those with whom you have most intimacy.

I remain, dear Sister,

Your ever affectionate brother,

John Given Jr

John put his pen down after he'd made the final flourish on his name. His scalp itched. He itched all over. He thought of the man in camp in Missouri who'd poured kerosene on his head to kill the lice, and then gone too near the fire and set his hair aflame. John sneezed once. Then he went into a regular sneezing and scratching fit that made him wish for kerosene himself.

When he'd finally stopped sneezing and the itching was less, he looked once more at the letter he'd written to Kate. It was right in the particulars, and it was right in telling her how dull he felt, but what had seemed most important to him in recent days was simply not in the letter. He hadn't put it there any more than he'd put it in the last letter he'd written to her. It was between the lines again, like the empty ground between opposing forces on the battlefield. He hadn't said at all how much it mattered to him that the 15th had left. They'd arrived with General Buell on the second day of the fighting at Shiloh and, sometime between the moment the 25th was halted in hot pursuit of the enemy in their rush for Corinth and the following endless hours and days of burying the dead and hunting for wounded—unpacking them at times like sardines from piles and piles of bodies—he'd found himself face to face with Harry Beal. John could scarcely believe it. There he was, blond and blue-eyed Harry and as fit looking as he was at home, Harry who could carry more sacks of grain for his weight than any other man in New Harmony. He hadn't a scratch on him that John could see and, as soldiers went, he was hardly even dirty. John had registered all this in the second it took for Harry to recognize him with his matted hair and muddy uniform caked with the blood of so many unnamed soldiers.

"I've been hunting you. My God, Jack," Harry had said, grabbing him around the neck, and John couldn't hug him hard enough. When they let go of each other, John punched Harry in the chest.

"About time you boys got here," he said, and what he was really thinking was that it was the most amazing thing in the world—that he was standing here on this battlefield with his best friend he hadn't seen in months and they were both actually alive.

The other Harmony lads from the 15th had been there, too, and with so many men of the 25th missing or wounded, John couldn't even say what it had meant for morale to see them. But they were gone now. They'd been gone at least two weeks, and it was partly that that made camp dull (there was nobody like Harry for a joke or cards), and it was certainly what made home seem so much farther away.

But at least Levi was back. Understrength as he was, he was still Levi, and that meant a good deal. John had tried to analyze it once— the way he was friends with Harry, and the way he was friends with Levi. He'd found more ways of getting a handle on it with Levi. For one thing, he and Levi both liked to read, though they'd come to it from a different place, Levi having grown up in New Harmony with a library practically at his doorstep. There was also the fact that Levi had the plainness of the workingman about him and none of the fancy-gloved manners of some of the Harmony young men. There were family matters as well. Levi lived with his family, as John did with his, and Levi was close to his family, as John was to his. And, too, their families knew one another. From circumstances, it seemed a natural thing for them to be friends, though John was well aware it took something more than happenstance and similarities to make a real friendship.

The something in this case had taken awhile for John to size up and to understand. There was a quality Levi had—Caroline, his sister, had it, too—a certain self-possession that had acted like a lure to John. If Levi didn't share Harry's antic sense, he did have a dry, pitch-perfect wit that sprang from that particular manner and always appeared at just the right moment. He had presence, John thought, which was just what Caroline had, and it was uncertain where it came from as their parents, good people that they were, seemed to lack it altogether. It was the thing, though, that John found to be the key to Levi and his appeal.

Harry was a different sort entirely. With Harry, it was all about charm and animal spirits. In spite of having uncles to draw him from Yorkshire to New Harmony—and one of them no less a personage than John Beal, boatmaker and carpenter for the Owenites—Harry was very much his own man. He liked doing what he wanted to, well considered or not, and he had a readiness to explore that John had seen in so many other immigrant men who'd made their way to America alone. When it came to women, while Levi looked at a girl like Margret Smith, with her sweet domesticity, Harry had an eye for high-spirited girls, including, John knew, Ann Bradley.

John folded the letter for Kate and addressed the envelope. He took a stamp from his pack. His mess plate had been drying on a branch—or what passed for drying in this weather—and he put it and his pen away and went down his mental checklist to see that he had everything. He didn't, of course. He'd burned his letter from Kate and one from his father in the coals of the breakfast fire and, though he'd read them often enough that he had them by heart, he wanted them back. Yet he'd carried them longer than he'd meant to already. On a march, a man didn't need even the slightest extra weight in his pack. And even if he was crazy and willing to carry a whole bundle of letters on a march, what man didn't flinch at the memory of all those letters scattered through their army's tents when the Rebels had camped in them at Shiloh? Still, John had saved the slight letter Levi had brought from Ann Bradley, though she'd not made even a hinted reference to the afternoon in David Dale's laboratory. John thought she'd written just enough to claim that she'd written. The letter had kept its faint perfume after days in his knapsack. He could detect the scent even with his cold.

When he got his rations, it was time to fall in, though falling in had a different meaning these days with the men sucked into the mud up to their boot tops and as leery of the roads as if they were quicksand. The drum roll sounded, and the bugle, and the men started off through the steamy, heavy-leaved woods where breathing the air was very much like breathing water. John kicked at a soggy branch that had fallen across the road and watched it collapse into a dozen rotten pieces. The air was so dank and misty that moving through it seemed almost like swimming. Or swimming beneath the waves with a hollowed-out reed the way he'd done with his cousins in Inver

Bay. There it had meant a certain, panicky thrill. Here everything was pure slog.

He was marching with Fred Perkey, whose breathing sounded so labored that John half expected him to pitch over in the mud unconscious. They were all wrecks. John didn't know a man in the company he could honestly consider well. Half of the men had diarrhea that was so bad it was a relief to change camps just to flee from the stench of the sinks. Most of the men had colds or worse. A lot of them—he and Levi for starters—weren't fully recovered from wounds and, though they didn't talk about it, it wasn't a sure thing that they ever would be. Enoch Randolph, who was captain now that Captain Saltzman was dead, had never stopped hacking since Fort Donelson. John hadn't heard him give an order yet that didn't sound like his last gasp.

Marching—mucking was more like it—John was still thinking about his mail, and to think about the mail anymore was to feel resentful. Except for the letters Levi had brought from Kate and from his father and from John Smith and Ann Bradley, he hadn't had a word from anybody since the Battle of Shiloh, though he always answered every letter he got. He had his theories about where his mail went. He believed that what he wrote left camp in a mail pouch and then went straight into the river. Or it got stuck among the grain bags on the wagons that the birds pecked at so that the only chance for his letters to get to their destination was if a bird snatched one up in its beak and flew off with it, dropping it somewhere outside of Tennessee where a charitable woman or lad might find it and send it on via post.

As far as the letters he received from home were concerned, he thought all of his correspondents weighed their words like gold and so sent as few as possible. If a man wanted to find out about a picnic at the river or a frolic at somebody's house, or what men had stayed out of the army and were cutting in with the girls, he might as well make up the answer for himself. And for that matter, here in the company and the regiment, it was all but impossible to find out what was going on in the war. They didn't know what was happening in the East. They didn't know whether Washington or Richmond was more threatened.

The fact was that if you were in a war, you hadn't had an idea of what was going on in it. On sick leave in New Harmony, he knew he'd learned more about what was happening from *Harper's Weekly* than he'd learned in the whole time he'd been in the army.

A soldier could know small things. He might know about the man who got shot standing next to him or about the one he messed with who wasn't in the mess any longer after a battle. What he didn't know was anything about the broader outlines of the war or how long it might last—if the South was getting worn down or if the North was having second thoughts about Mr. Lincoln and his war, which was how John and a lot of the men were starting to think of it. Somebody had told him that Abraham Lincoln had lived not far from Harmony for part of his boyhood. Except for people like the older Owens, who'd known powerful men all over the world and weren't actually Indiana raised, John wasn't sure an Indiana connection was that much of a recommendation for a man—or at least not for one with the job that Mr. Lincoln held. For that matter, he doubted that time spent in Illinois was a useful thing either.

And on second thought, regarding the specifics of things that were right in front of a man, John didn't know how much he knew about even them. Nobody, for instance, had any idea where Felix Edmonds was. Nobody could say if he'd gotten killed or wounded or if he'd taken off when the fighting turned so brutal at Shiloh, and hightailed it for the bluff like all the other scared soldiers who hoped to find a boat to get off the landing. Personally, John thought it was likely that Felix had fled. Ever since Fort Donelson, Felix had seemed spooked. In the tent at night, he would bring the conversation back to the boy who'd died when they lifted him up. "That was a hell of a thing. Just a hell of a thing," he'd say. Then he'd lie quiet, staring at the tent wall as if it were some prehistoric cave he'd come on with pictures of dead people all over it.

There was a disturbance to the rear, and Fred Perkey peered back through the men. "Levi's wagon's stuck again," he said, and John could hear Levi cursing and the sound of a horse whip, and mules crying.

Though Levi could swear with anybody, there was never a man more patient with horses or mules or smarter at handling them than Levi, and his anger at them was unlike him.

John made his way back to see if he could help. The wagon was more than stuck. One back wheel was deep in the mud, and the other, too, except that the axle had sheared off so that the wheel was standing up cockeyed by itself. If the mules pulled the other one free, the whole wagon bed would topple over and send what supplies Levi had managed to get this far straight into the mud.

John considered whether to put his back into the wagon along with the other men who were trying to keep it upright until the men who'd started rigging a temporary axle could get it finished. Or he could help with the mules, who seemed to have gotten more mulelike in all the commotion. The near one was pulling so hard it had rubbed an open, bleeding sore on its neck.

Levi decided for him. "Up here, Jack," he said, getting down from the wagon seat, and John took the reins from him, winding them tight around his hands while Levi tried calming the mule with the bloody neck, which was backing up in the traces. The other mules were straining so hard it felt to John as if his arms were going to pull right out of their sockets. The rain had started again and it was worse than the heaviest Donegal rain. It coursed in streaks down Levi's face. It poured off John's cap and ticked off his buttons and, as Levi worked with the mules and John tensed his muscles to tug back on the reins, the more the mules kept pulling. It was a battle until John felt the wagon shift and felt himself flying straight into the air and then landing hard at a tilt on the seat.

Barrels rolled off the wagon into the mud, and a man screamed. The wagon bed had crashed down on his leg, and while the other men rushed and worked to free him, he made a bleating, animal sound. The mules screamed, too, and John thought he maybe had a mule story to top his Dublin one, though who was keeping track. It was an awful mess here, and there wasn't a barman named Mick O'Gallagher to help him. And there was no Father O'Gallagher to look down from his pub stool and say, "You think too much, lad. It's the pint here that can save you from thinking."

Levi squatted down all at once. Then his legs crumpled and he sat down square in the mud. It wasn't that he'd lost his footing. It seemed that his strength was gone. Or not even that. In favoring his wounded arm, Levi had done something excruciating to the other one. He was holding his good arm, and his lips were white. John thought the two of them made a pair. He didn't see how he was getting out of here with either arm intact except that for no reason he could tell, the mules had stopped pulling. They were standing as stubbornly still as they'd been stubbornly straining.

John yelled through the rain for another soldier to take the reins. Then he climbed down from the wagon and crouched in the mud next to Levi.

"Wrench my arm back," Levi said, gritting his teeth. "Go ahead," he said louder, and John, fearing he would hear something break, went ahead and did it. Levi gasped a little but then pushed himself upright. His pants, which were already hanging on him, sagged further from the mud on the seat.

The men had the wagon righted now and the man freed, and somebody was calling for the surgeon while the injured soldier yelled he wouldn't have one, that they could get him a tourniquet and some whiskey, but no sawbones. John looked at the axle, which was a green branch that left the wagon lopsided. He thought they needed some-body like Frank Bolton from home who'd made carriages for a living and could get the fit right, but Levi looked at it and said it was good enough for now. Then he scooped up some mud and worked it under the harness onto the injured mule's neck.

Lieutenant Boren, who still seemed to John like Lazarus back from the dead, rode over to them, pools of water splashing as he came. He ordered a litter for the injured man and a detail to take him to the rear. Then he looked at the wagon and said the only chance they had of getting anywhere with it was for the men to lift the back up and push on it while the mules pulled, and that even that might not work.

They were a mud-drowned army, John thought. They were sinking into Tennessee, and it wasn't getting any better. He wondered where Harry was, where the 15th Indiana had gone and if it was any easier where they were. He wondered if it was rainy in Harmony and if the river was high and if people were standing on their roofs on the Cut-off Island to keep from drowning and if the cattle were caught in the mud and inhaling water as it rose to their nostrils.

He wished he could transport himself somewhere else entirely, maybe switch mule stories and land in Dublin once more. He thought he'd give anything to swap the war for it. Even with his chin split open, it had been fine that first time in the city with the bustle and racket in the streets and the tall buildings facing each other across the Liffey. It had had the charm of all eager first moments. It was like going to fair day when he was first old enough, his father greeting his friends amidst the herds of animals while John tried to hear all the talk and see whether the men would drink until they argued or argued until they were drunk, or if it was all the same. It was like his first day in Navan, when he thought he'd make a priest and be the one at the altar murmuring Latin that he and God would understand but others wouldn't. And later—when he'd left Ireland—there'd been that very first daybreak at sea when the ribbons of clouds were the same pink as the one piece of childhood candy that had ever been just his own.

Of course, he knew what had been the unequaled first. It had been meeting Ann Bradley, Ann with her aura that all but undid him, that still did whether he wanted it to or not, that would if he could ever get free of this slogging mud and be near her again.

Levi was leading the team from the front and, when John pitched in to help, he looked back at him, and John thought he'd had his mind read. "Ann Bradley came to see me before I left," Levi said. "We walked out a bit with Caroline and some of the other girls. Ann told me she writes to Harry Beal. I don't know if she's your girl, Jack. She said not, but I thought I should tell you. She writes to Rippeto, too. I'm sure there're others."

"I know she does," John said, though he felt the words like a stab. "And everybody writes to Harry," he said quickly—too quickly, he thought—and what he didn't say was that he was already full of suspicions that Harry thought about Ann just as he did. Harry, though, was more apt to cover his feelings with a joke and, besides, Ann wasn't a subject the two of them ever talked about. They skirted carefully around the whole idea of her as if they both knew a real flare-up was possible. Neither one was willing to risk it.

"Is she writing to you, too, Levi?" John asked, trying to sound causal and not accusing, and he wondered if there'd been some sort of message for him in Ann's telling Levi who it was she wrote to. She might be teasing him. She might be trying to make him jealous. What he wanted to think was that she was remembering the afternoon in David Dale's laboratory, just as he did, and keeping his name to herself.

"There's nobody writing to me," Levi answered. "You see any mail for me since I got back? I sure as hell haven't."

The magpies were yammering in the trees, and John wondered if there was an enemy patrol nearby that had come out from Corinth. He stopped to listen for a moment. Then he went on walking, prodding the mules and keeping an eye on the axle. Patrols they could handle, but it weighed on him that Ann had told Levi she wasn't his girl. He didn't begrudge any man a letter, not really, but he didn't know why Ann would tell Levi the men she wrote to. There was no need for it. It was bold in a way that John found unseemly.

Although, could he really have it both ways? Wasn't it Ann's particular daring that had always attracted him? Wasn't it her manner of being ready to do something audacious, even forbidden, that had drawn him to her in the first place, though it unsettled him as well, putting her in those legions of women talked about by all the priests he'd ever listened to. He had a sudden, vivid image of Ann marching with the army, looking back at him over her shoulder with her insinuating laugh and tossing her skirts up devilishly high to keep them from the mud, though his further image of her put her in the actual mud, lying there waiting for him while the rest of the army sloshed on away from them. They were alone under the whole tree-laced sky.

By afternoon, when the captain sent out forage parties, John had decided the army's progress since morning could be measured better in yards than in miles. He helped Levi pack mud onto a bit of sacking and warm it on the fire that was waiting for the foragers' return and, as Levi poulticed his mule with the raw neck, John suddenly grasped his arm.

"Don't talk to me anymore about Ann Bradley," he said, and if his voice sounded harsh, that was just the way it was. "It's nothing personal, but don't do it," he said, and for the instant that he and Levi locked stares, he thought he wanted to fight, not Levi, but Harry Beal, to fight him the way any Irishman knew to fight, though Harry was no slacker. He wanted to fight Harry and hurt him and beat him in the face so that Ann Bradley couldn't stand the sight of him.

But Harry wasn't here—he was maybe in Nashville, or maybe back in West Virginia, where the 15th had racked up fighting hours before they came to Tennessee—and Levi was, and it was Levi who'd said he'd stepped out with Ann. Even if Caroline and a flock of Harmony girls had been with them, he'd still actually done it.

He should fight Levi, John thought. What, after all, was the point of fighting a total stranger, some Johnny Reb who hadn't done a thing to him? Wasn't it time he fought someone who made a real difference in his life instead of the boys he'd actually shot point-blank or run through with his bayonet so the bugle call to fix bayonets stayed a torment in his head that kept him awake long into the night.

But Levi had anticipated him again. "If you said a word about Margret Smith, I'd deck you," he said. "I'd knock your teeth right down your throat, so if you're aiming to hit me, Jack, go ahead, though I'd rather we ate."

John was quiet. "What are you, Levi?" he said finally. "French? I mean on the Flora side. Palatine German?"

Levi just looked at him, and John didn't ask if it was the English in Levi that made him sure an Irishman was always eager to brawl.

Nor did he say how strongly Levi reminded him of Caroline at just that moment—that same even look, that careful aplomb—and he didn't say he didn't believe that he actually fought in just this way anymore, that he would have thrown a punch by now if he did. And he didn't trot out his father and Francis Cannon's well-warmed theory—that men who fought for an idea instead of for passion or sport had their pocketbooks somewhere in the equation. It was beside the point anyway. It was a theory that fit the war, not Ann, though when it came to war, there was the odd circumstance that men would go against their belief not to kill for what seemed not very much. The plain fact was that what John had done in the army was to get right down to the business of killing people because they were standing on the foot of ground that some officer told him was the foot of ground his own feet should be on. "Did you hear anything, Levi, when you were at home?" he said. "Did you hear we might have shot at our men at Donelson? Union men?"

"Did we?" Levi said, and John thought that even if he wanted to, which he didn't, there wasn't a point in hitting Levi just to fight somebody he knew. Maybe he'd already done that very thing. Maybe he'd shot at one of those boys in blue that he'd thought he'd seen in a ravine at Fort Donelson before they were ordered to stop firing.

"Before I left, there were rumors," Levi said. "Mr. Sampson knows a man who heard that part of the 25th opened up on an Iowa regiment. I don't know that he gave the story credence. Especially not with Colonel Morgan in charge."

"What if we did?" John said. "What if we bloody well did?"

"If we did, it's the bloody war," Levi answered. "It means it was nothing but confusion. Jack, are you taking a swing at me or not?"

"I'm not," John said. "Remind me when I see Harry to punch him in the nose—he'd look better with his nose pointed south—but, Levi, I'm not cuffing you," he said, and Levi nodded and started in on another poultice.

John made his way through the mud to the detail that had cleaned the quail the foragers had shot. He watched for a moment as the quails turned on the spit, the fat popping as their skin browned, and he thought just how hungry he was. When the mess call finally came, he sat down on a log next to Fred Perkey, who'd taken shelter under a small jut of rock. Watching water drizzle over the ledge and onto his boots, John bit into a piece of warm and greasy meat. Fred was trying to eat, too, but he was shaking—sick again, sick still—and John got him some coffee and found the thin blanket in his own pack that he'd kept almost dry. He put it around Fred's shoulders.

They would be marching again, marching past sunset to the next muddy bivouac, and John was miserable just thinking of it. He ached all over, not just in his leg, and he was itching again though he tried to ignore it. All the men were in sour moods, he thought, listening. They were sick and tired, and a good number of them had even stopped trusting General Grant. The general had been surprised again, they said. Or they said that he'd sacrifice the whole army if it came down to it, and the cause would be drink. John spit a quail bone onto the ground and then spit out another. He didn't know what he thought right now—not about General Grant and not about anything else to do with the war. There was the one very present fact of a gun-metal sky and mud underfoot that was like the gray, fuzzed world between the battles they'd fought and the ones that were coming. He thought maybe they should all do what Felix Edmonds had done, if he actually had—every last man of them strike out for home.

But they weren't Felix. He wasn't. And even if he should be like him—even if he should give up the fight and be the man in Harmony who was actually there in flesh and blood and not just assumed in a letter to Kate or Ann Bradley—he simply wasn't that man. He couldn't be and, in the end, that was the one clear thing that he thought.

Camp near Memphis, Tennessee
Late August and Early September 1862

12

I took the ladies [who were my companions from the boat] up to the hotel in Memphis and determined to go to the camp of the 25th. It was a long dusty walk. Nobody knew where they were, but I finally found them. Everybody was out on a scout except for Ab Boren, Henry Schafer, Bill Reid, and John Given.

August 29, 1862, entry in the diary of Achilles H. Fretageot

It was warm out, but John, who felt feverish, was huddled in a blanket in the doorway of the command tent. He was working on reports with Lieutenant Boren and half listening to Bill Reid. The band was being mustered out, and Bill, who was the bandleader, was heading home.

"There's the little house downriver, and the ladies with the welcome mat out any hour," Bill said, his London accent turning ladies into lydies. John glanced at him and at Henry Schafer, who'd been sicker than he was, and wondered just what he had missed. Henry, in spite of his deafness, had clearly heard more than he had. He and Bill were both laughing.

John looked across at Lieutenant Boren, who was sitting at a makeshift table with the papers John had given him. He looked more preoccupied than occupied, and John guessed he was thinking about the patrols that had gone out with Colonel Morgan and Captain Randolph, who was still traveling by ambulance. More than that, he had to be worried about his wife. He'd gone home on a brief furlough and, as soon as he'd come back, he'd gotten word she was ill again. John had wanted to reassure him, to say that there was hardly an illness

Margaret Mulhern couldn't nurse a patient through, but he thought such familiarity would be crossing a line. As fair-minded as Lieutenant Boren was, John knew there was a boundary that came not only from service rank but from his place at home. He was careful to observe it.

He dipped his pen and started another page. More and more in the last weeks he'd found himself busy with the paper trail that the regiment and army churned out. He wasn't sure how he felt about it. He wasn't even quite certain how he'd taken on this new role that meant that today he was in camp and the company wasn't. It wasn't that he wasn't a soldier anymore. And it wasn't that he was too crippled to be one. But he'd limped his way through every march since Shiloh, and he'd run, when he had to, with the kind of hoppy awkwardness of a three-legged cat. He thought it had made him more obvious to Captain Randolph and Lieutenant Boren so that it occurred to them both he could write and figure and that they might as well take advantage of it.

Lieutenant Boren stood up and went inside the tent. John shivered and pulled the blanket tighter around him and thought, as he had often had in the last weeks, just how drowning in paper the army was. He wondered if it was that way with the Rebels, if they, too, were leaving their tracks as much in ink as on the ground, though if fortifications counted as a footprint, they'd certainly left enough of those.

He'd gotten a very good look. Two months ago, when the 25th had moved outside of Corinth with General Grant, they'd been close enough that the men could hear the Rebel drums beat. But except for a small skirmish that the men hardly counted as anything, there hadn't been any fighting. One day, the Rebels were simply gone. They'd disappeared, and the 25th had soon discovered they'd been camped scarcely a quarter of a mile from their breastworks, which were vast. For the life of him, John couldn't figure out why they'd been abandoned. He and some of the other boys had gotten passes to go into town, and they had found the remnants of what clearly had been a very pretty little place. It was spread out like Mount Vernon, but with fewer houses than New Harmony.

The imprint of the Confederate army was everywhere. Not a tree was left standing. Every building of any size, whether it was a school or a church or a remarkably beautiful women's college that had caught John's eye, had been converted into a commissary or hospital. And the Rebels had left nothing behind to be captured. The depot, which apparently had been full of everything from wheat to beef to ammunition, had been burned so that it smelled like a combination of gunpowder and charred beef. There were only skeletal remains of wagons and hearses. The Secesh had even burned their cotton so that it wouldn't fall into Union hands. John both heard and saw for himself that the homes that had been used for commissary goods or ordnance had been burned to the ground as well. It was the fortifications, though, that continued to astonish him. He had never imagined an army could be so well dug in. He had wondered if the Rebels meant to fight anywhere ever again since they'd left such a stronghold behind.

When he and the boys who had gone to Corinth got back to camp, they'd found the whole division under marching orders and the regiment already gone to join General Sherman. They'd had to chase after them. They'd expected a fight, but it hadn't come. Instead, the regiment had wound up in camp along the Memphis and Charleston Railroad. It was like Missouri all over again. They'd spent their time patrolling the rails and moving on orders until, finally, at the end of July, they'd marched west from LaGrange and come to this camp below Memphis. Now they were settled in with the other regiments of the division ranged along the river and taking their turns on scouting patrols. Except John wasn't on patrol. This was the first time he hadn't gone out with the company.

"Who's that?" Bill Reid asked, leaning back on his camp stool and pointing at a solitary figure in civilian clothes who was walking toward them in the small cloud of dust that any man's feet kicked up in this encampment. "He looks familiar? Who is it, Henry? Jack, can you tell?"

The person who was approaching them was fingering the watch chain on his waistcoat and there was something about the gesture, the particular roteness of it, that John recognized. Henry and Bill realized who it was at the same moment he did.

"What the devil is Achilles Fretageot doing out here?" Henry said. "Lieutenant Boren? Lieutenant, Achilles Fretageot is here."

John pushed his blanket away and stood up with the other men. Lieutenant Boren had come to the tent flap, and John could see the color leaving that big, florid face. Henry and Bill were still watching Achilles approach. When he reached them, he shook hands with them both, and with John. Then he turned to Lieutenant Boren, and in an emotional gesture that John couldn't read, clasped his elbows with both hands.

"Is it Charlotte?" Lieutenant Boren asked, and for the second before Achilles answered, silence seemed to hang in the air with the dust.

"Charlotte's fine," Achilles said. "Fine, Ab. I saw her with Aunt Sampson before I left, and I've a whole book of letters she sent you. But my brother's sick at Helena. I'm on my way there. And there's something else. A dreadful thing . . ." Achilles looked behind him, and John, taking the hint, picked up his papers and moved away from the tent. He motioned with his head for Henry and Bill to go, too. Lieutenant Boren put his arm on Achilles's shoulder and they went into the tent, the flap closing behind them.

It was late afternoon before the murmur of voices stopped and both men came back outside. They shook hands, and Achilles nodded a good-bye to John, who had put the company papers aside and was writing letters to send home with Bill Reid.

Lieutenant Boren was silent, watching Achilles retreat through the dusty camp. Then he pulled up a camp stool and sat down heavily. "He's catching the steamer to Helena to see Alex. But it's like you heard, John. There's a dreadful thing that's happened."

John waited, wondering if the dreadful thing was something that would be dreadful for him, too.

"It'll go very hard with Charlotte. And hard with her parents." Lieutenant Boren took out his handkerchief and wiped his face. "He told me the *Acacia* blew up on the river near Helena. It's the boat Charlotte's sister was on. Mollie. She was going to see Jule. She was going to surprise him for their anniversary, but the paper Achilles saw in Cairo said that she died."

"I'm very sorry, sir," John said, thinking of the handsome couple Mollie Sampson and Julian Dale Owen had made before they were married.

Lieutenant Boren leaned forward and planted his elbows on his knees. He put his head in his hands and, after a moment, he looked back at John. "The worst of it—or what Achilles heard—is that Jule had his men out diving for survivors and bodies and hadn't an idea Mollie was on board. Then his men brought her trunk to his quarters."

John didn't know what to say. Once he'd seen a drowned woman in Inver Bay, her face swollen and her hair floating behind her like muddy seaweed. It wasn't a thing he wanted to see ever again, and he didn't like the thought of the scene on the river: the burning boat, the cinders shooting into the air, trunks floating on the water, men diving into the freezing, murky river and bursting through the surface to get air.

"John, it's the men who're supposed to die in war. Poor Mollie."

"I'm very sorry, sir," John said again, and he couldn't think of more to say. It was easy to feel shocked, but life was full of shocks now, and he didn't really know Mollie Owen. Kate would likely be sad. And Mollie Owen had been Margaret Mulhern's particular pet in the Sampson family. It would be very difficult for Margaret, and that was unfortunate. Yet John realized, with a certain surprise at his callousness, that his first thought had been that Ann Bradley, who'd written him only once in weeks, might find her own sorrow tempered by the knowledge that Julian Dale Owen was a free man once more.

When Lieutenant Boren got up and went back into the tent, Bill Reid came back from whatever regiment he'd gone off to visit. He took his place on the stool next to John. "So Julian Owen's lost his wife in less than a year," he said, and John looked at him, thinking Bill must have been within earshot until he went on. "It's the headline on the newspaper."

John nodded. He wondered if he should mention the trunk. Then he decided it would end up gossip if he did, and gossip of a particularly sensational kind. For that matter, he didn't know for certain if the trunk part of the story was actually true.

"You're writing another letter for me to take home? If I stay here much longer, I'll have a wagonload of letters to haul," Bill said. "And I guess with your fancy writing, your letters weigh more than anybody else's."

"I suppose they do," John said, thinking he never much minded the teasing about being the man with all the schooling, and he particularly didn't mind it now since he knew Bill Reid offered safer passage for his mail home than he was accustomed to. He was also glad for the change of subject.

"Funny fellow, Achilles Fretageot," Bill said. "I know his father was Madame's son and watched a king get crowned in France when he was a boy. But for all that fanciness and Achilles picking out books on the library board, he and his father are both just men who work in a store." Bill was rubbing at the dust on his shoes. "Did you hear Romeo Keister died?"

"He did? No." John could hear the surprise in his voice. "Romeo? The last I heard they were sending him to Memphis to get discharged."

"They should have sent him home when he got sick like they did with Fred Perkey in St. Louis. Fred got better instead of dying."

"It was Mr. Hugo who went to get Fred. Bill, if you hear about somebody else that's died, I'd appreciate you not telling me," John said, and he really did mean it. He could die himself and it wouldn't be so much—no particular loss to the world that he could see, and certainly no loss to Ann Bradley, if he was any judge—but he'd really begun to hate the way wartime had started out like an empty game board and now was getting crowded with all these pieces that stood for people who were dead.

"I guess Alex Fretageot will be the next Harmony boy to go," Bill said. "Unless one of our patrols gets into it. Where did Henry take off to anyway?"

"I don't know." John quickly finished the letter he was writing to Kate, consciously leaving out word of Mollie Owen so there wasn't a chance he'd be the bearer of that news. He handed the letter to Bill and wished him good luck. Then he turned back to Lieutenant Boren's papers and told Bill he couldn't talk anymore, which was true and a relief, though Bill was a good enough fellow.

In a day or so the troops would be coming back from their scouting trip and, when they did, the camp would be full of bustle. John knew he'd be glad of it. For now, though, the regiment's tents and grounds were empty, and he wanted it that way. He liked the quiet. He liked having the papers before him. Numbers. Something simple. No faces. The familiar cipher.

———

It was two evenings later, sipping from a dipper of foul-tasting water he was thirsty enough to drink, that John realized just how antsy he'd become for the men to return. He did feel a certain importance now that he was helping with the headquarters work of the regiment. He also felt like a shirker. Ultimately, he knew it was the paperwork that meant men got their supplies and ammunition and pay, when it actually came, and that the army rode on the back of these things. But it still had felt strange watching the men, flanked by the cavalry, shoulder their muskets and go off looking for Rebels without him.

He'd finished all the work Lieutenant Boren had given him for the day, and since the men weren't back, he went into his tent and got the letters he'd saved in his pack and lay down to read them again. There was a pebble under his shoulder and he dug it out from under his bedroll and tried to settle himself more comfortably. He ran his index finger over a page, tracing the loops of the handwriting, and his mind drifted over what he'd already read. Since May, life for the regiment had had only a few real changes in routine. They'd gone from toiling through the muddy slog that stood for roads and eating half rations and hacking with colds, to marching on dry roads and getting enough to eat and being almost healthy, if you considered just the head and chest and not the stomach or various limbs. In Harmony, though, the world had been teeming. It had been a real social stir. There were marriages. There were rumors of marriages. He'd heard from his father that Charles Ward wrote letters to Margaret Mulhern sweet enough to make her blush, so of course John had had to plague Margaret through Kate, writing her that the 60th Indiana might be joining them in camp. He said if they did and had to be real soldiers, poor Charles might get killed or, even worse, get his white skin and delicate hands burned to a crisp under the Southern sun. John had meant to tease her more, but a letter came from Michael McShane saying Margaret had gone pale at what he'd written and, after that, he hadn't the heart to torment her any further.

There had been a quilting party at the Smiths'—the one Levi had kept asking and asking about every time the mail came. In her one brief letter, Ann Bradley had written there'd been plays at the Smiths' and they'd had kissing matches, a report that bothered John no end (and also made him consider sending stern warnings to his sisters). Ann had added that I. M. Baker had asked her out to a concert as they were leaving, and John had been doubly vexed, for until that party, I. M. Baker (with his foolish pronouncement of a name) had been his sister Margaret's new beau. There was blackberrying as well, and it seemed to John from the letters he got that the girls in New Harmony were vying too much over the men who were left at home. He'd written Kate to tell Margaret to forget about Mr. Baker, that there were still as good fish in the sea as ever were caught. And he'd told Kate that he feared all the jealousy in Harmony would cause a split among the girls, which would mean that he would have to go home and enforce the laws, compelling the seceders back into the Union. He remembered that particularly, as he'd felt quite witty when he wrote it, though the wit seemed thinner to him now.

Kate's letters were full of other news of New Harmony. Sherd Anderson's children had been put on the county. Caroline Thrailkill had gone to visit her uncle, John Flora, who seemed determined to marry her to a widower. This information had sent Levi into absolute fits. He'd written his uncle, giving him holy hell, and he'd threatened to desert for as long as it took to put a stop to any such marriage. Aside from news of Ann, which John had in only the scanty bits from her, and more news of family and friends in New Harmony, what he'd hoped most to read in Kate's letters and his father's and everybody else's, he didn't find. He'd wanted more specifics of what was happening in the war, particularly facts about what had gone on with the 60th when they'd fled in Kentucky, and just how badly Morgan and his Rebel raiders had given it to them. And with every letter that came, he'd hoped for news that there was another New Harmony messenger on the way like E. I. Rogers, who had brought them a barrel of whiskey and enough eggs to last for two meals (they'd have liked them for at least a dozen). He was also eager for news of the 15th. Some of the 25th had seen them when they were in Corinth and learned that they'd fared about the same as they had since Shiloh. But there'd been nothing since, and that news dated all the way back to early June.

John shifted the letters on his chest and found the one from Michael McShane. He heard a drill call for the regiment camped up the road. He listened for a moment, feeling drowsy and thinking himself drowsy, too. Drowsy. Drowsed. The words of a Keats poem wandered into his mind, and he roused himself enough to remember a verse: *Who hath not seen thee oft amid thy store? / Sometimes whoever seeks abroad may find / Thee sitting careless on a granary floor, / Thy hair soft-lifted by the winnowing wind; / Or on a half-reaped furrow sound asleep, / Drowsed with the fume of poppies, while thy hook / Spares the next swath and all its twined flowers . . .*

John inhaled slowly. *Drowsed with the fume of poppies.* Was that anything like what he was feeling? Or was it like the first feeling from the laudanum he'd had at home when he'd been in so much pain? He loved the words of the poem, the way they insinuated themselves into his brain and even down his spine so that he felt them like music or air. Even if Keats had been writing of autumn, thinking these words was somehow like looking at Ann.

John let the letter from Michael McShane slip down his chest. He closed his eyes, feeling the sound of the poem running through him like waves lapping easily against tidal flats, like waves teasing the bare legs of a girl walking an Irish strand. The image stirred him, yet he was almost asleep when he heard a shuffling at the tent flap. He tried not to listen, but finally he opened his eyes. Thinking that he'd heard a rat, he started to reach for his rifle butt. Then he heard his name.

"John. Shhh, John. I have to talk to you, but quiet, Jack, so the lieutenant doesn't hear."

John sat up. There was a soldier, or somebody with a soldier's cap, looking at him from across the tent. He knew the voice more than the lanky figure. "Felix, is that you?" he asked.

"Shhh, Jack. Yes, it's me." Felix moved quietly across the tent to John and his bedroll. "I've got a letter for you. I've got more than one. You've got one here from Mick McShane and there's others. We can get to that. But can you tell me how it is, Jack? If I'm back, will it go hard with me? Do they put men in the brig still? Do they hang them?"

"What do you mean if you're back? Am I sleeping?" John who'd lain back down, pushed himself up on his elbows. "You're here, aren't you?" he asked, and he thought for a second that he'd dreamed Felix and that the letter Felix said he had from Michael McShane was actually the one Michael had sent with him in June, though John hadn't seen Felix then but only the letter. He'd had the reports of other men that they'd talked to Felix before he'd disappeared once more.

"I'm real," Felix said. "Where is everybody? I had a hell of a time finding the regiment, and it's mostly just you."

"Out on a scout. For four days. They should be back."

"How come you're here? Are you sick?"

John felt awkward answering, but he did anyway. "I'm helping Lieutenant Boren with his paper. And the requisitions. But I'm fit enough to fight. It's not that."

"I'm fit to fight, too. I tell you, Jack, I've been in Kentucky and I'm tired of thinking somebody's going to know I deserted and turn me in. I'd get shot or strung up for sure. Just what're my chances here?"

"I couldn't tell you," John said, and he couldn't. "You know Colonel Morgan's fair, but he's by the book. And if you deserted . . . What happened anyway? Somebody said you got shot. Didn't you get furloughed?"

"I did get shot. But it wasn't bad, and it wasn't when we were fighting. It was at the landing. For all I know, it was one of our boys shooting off his gun to keep anybody else from getting on the boat. Or that officer with Buell's army who rode through and screamed we were all bloody cowards. I know he shot some of us."

John didn't say anything. Part of him (the part that remembered his father saying cowardice didn't rub off on a man) felt he ought to forgive Felix for deserting. Feckless Felix, as Harry Beal called him. But he wasn't in a forgiving mood and, anyway, he realized Felix was more apt to say what had happened if he didn't say anything more. He waited.

Felix gave him a sideways glance and stuck his boots out in front of him. They were as dusty as the camp. Dustier. "I never meant to run," he said. "It's just that everybody was running where I was, and all I could see was the boy you and I picked up that night at Fort Donelson and the blood gushing out of him. It felt like my back was gone. I swear to God I thought I was running with a crater in my back and it was a light-headed thing. I was shaking all over. My bones were chattering like teeth. Jack, you couldn't have proved it by me I didn't just get fished out of the Wabash from almost drowning. I was that out of air and shivery. I didn't know where I was. Well, part of the time I did. But it was mostly like I wasn't there."

John was unmoved. He was tempted to say that he'd held the same boy in his arms and he hadn't run. Instead he stood and pulled his braces up. "Did Caroline Thrailkill marry the widower John Flora wanted her to?" he asked.

"What about John Flora? Where the hell is John Flora anyway? He wasn't in Harmony the last time I was there. Is he out in Missouri?

I told you I've been in Kentucky, Jack. You say Levi's sister is getting married?"

"Not if Levi can help it."

"I liked the one that died. Levi's sister. Amaline. Now that I'm here, Jack, what do I do?" Felix's eye was twitching, a regular tic, and it was something new since John had seen him last. Felix started pacing the tent.

"I could talk to Lieutenant Boren," John said, and he watched as Felix darted him a quick look. The tic seemed worse. "You give me my mail, and I'll talk to him," John said.

"Right. You get your mail, and I wind up in the stocks with somebody shooting buckshot at my backside. What I am is ready to soldier again. I thought you could help me, Jack."

"I could ask him a for instance. I could see what he says."

"Like for instance you got Felix Edmonds in your tent and does he want me in leg irons?"

"I'm not turning you in," John said, still trying to keep his voice low. "But he's going to need me any time now. The men will be getting back."

"I know, Jack, I know." Felix was pacing the tent twice as fast, and John thought he was about to knock over Levi's bookshelf, which was the one bit of civilization they had out here.

"So how good a friend would I have to be for you to help me?" Felix said. "I suppose if I was Harry Beal you'd help."

"If there was some kind of help I could help with. I can talk to Lieutenant Boren," John said again, and he was starting to get annoyed, but it was partly because he knew there was truth in Felix's accusation. If Felix Edmonds was the sort of man he'd consider letting talk to one of his sisters, the way Harry Beal was—the way Harry maybe was—he'd probably think harder about something he could do that might help.

"Here's your mail," Felix said. He'd crouched down and pulled some letters out of his pack, and he fanned them out and pushed them in John's face. "Don't say I never did anything for you, John Given."

"If you could convince somebody you're sick—" John started, but Felix interrupted him before he could go any further.

"Sick how? Sick crazy? I tell you, Jack, I'm ready to soldier again. I need to shoot a Rebel. There was men I might have shot that I didn't. Men that maybe killed somebody like Captain Saltzman."

"You saw Captain Saltzman die? You were on the flank with the Wisconsin troops? You saw him die?"

"I said somebody like him. Who said I saw him die?"

"That's the men coming now." John put his hand up. He couldn't hear anything, but the light leaking in beneath the tent was whiter with dust he could smell.

"Son of a bitch. I can't stay here. If you got some chew, Jack. You know a man has to keep his teeth yellow."

"No chew. I don't have any. But here." John reached into his pocket and took out the bit of money he had that he hadn't sent home. He pulled off half of it and stuck it into Felix's hand. "Your luck could change. Maybe there'll be an amnesty. I hope there is," he said, and he nodded toward the tent flap, and he was ready to stand sentry while Felix slipped out and made his way through the tents, but he could hear Lieutenant Boren coughing right in front of the flap. John motioned for Felix to wait. He listened a moment and then went outside.

"Is Henry Schafer in there?" Lieutenant Boren asked, and John shook his head. "I thought I heard you talking to somebody."

"Henry's not here," John answered. "I think he's off in one of the other regiments. I can go look."

"No," Lieutenant Boren told him. He turned his head. John could hear the distant approach of the cavalry that had gone with the regiment, and Lieutenant Boren was looking in the same direction he was. The lieutenant raised his voice. "We've got a regiment to meet. If it's not Henry in there, then there's nobody who was talking if he disappears when we go to meet the men coming in."

"Yes sir," John said, although he wasn't sure exactly what had happened. He didn't know if Lieutenant Boren had recognized Felix's voice, though he thought he had. But more than that, he didn't know if he and Lieutenant Boren were in league about something now, and he realized he didn't want to know. And he was glad he wasn't an officer. It was one thing to know he wouldn't turn a man in. It was something else to decide to look the other way or to order a man killed, to stand the army at attention while a man was shot like a dog for deserting.

But he was done worrying about Felix. He and Lieutenant Boren started up the road, and he knew Felix would be long gone when they returned. It was exciting having the men riding and marching back into camp. He could see the cavalry advance and the horses high-trotting, eager to be fed. Levi, who was healthier than he'd been since he was shot, would be at the back of the troops with his wagon and team, and John was eager to see him and all the rest of the boys.

It didn't take long to tell that the cavalry was in high spirits. John wondered if they'd gotten into a skirmish or a fight, if they'd done some damage.

"They've been up to something, Jack," Lieutenant Boren said, clearly sensing the same thing, and he left John and went over to talk to an officer in the process of dismounting. The air smelled of men whose clothes were embedded with sweat, and of horseflesh and leather and dust. It was a cavalry smell, which was the closest word John could find for it. He pushed his hands into his pockets. He could hear only a few words of what Lieutenant Boren and the cavalry officer were saying. The one that caught his attention was prisoners. He waited a moment longer, and then made his way down the line of men and horses, listening to the men spitting and talking to each other, and hearing the heavy animal sounds, the horses snorting and shaking their heads and backs as their saddles were lifted off.

The first units of the 25th were in sight now, and John hurried on so he could fall in with Company A. He thought the men would ride him for the gentlemen soldier that he was, but it seemed more on his mind than theirs. They were good-natured in their greetings.

"What do I hear about prisoners?" he asked George Tretheway who, since his wound at Shiloh, rode in an ambulance more often than he walked, though he was walking now. George pointed behind him to the far back of the company ranks and John saw a group of sorry-looking men, some of them mere boys and some of them older than his father and none in any particular uniform. They were dirt-streaked and miserable looking and being herded along like a bunch of sheep on a Donegal road. John looked at George, and George laughed.

"You're a pale and quite ladylike-looking fellow, Jack. Are you over your chills? Did you leave any quinine for the company?"

John, who felt well enough as long as he didn't think about it, ignored the question. "Where did you get those fellows?" he asked.

"We didn't. The cavalry did. And poor sons of bitches they are. They were in a meetinghouse, a bunch of Secesh organizing a company, and our cavalry rode up and surrounded them. They're marching in an army, all right, but it's this one."

John took another look back at the sullen prisoners who were dragging their way along the dusty road. "There's news, George. Romeo Keister's dead. Mollie Owen was killed in a steamship explosion on the way to see her husband. And Achilles Fretageot was heading to Helena. His brother's sick," he said. He wished he could tell George that Felix Edmonds was hightailing it off through the camps, wanting to be a soldier instead of absent without leave. He kept it to himself, though, and since George was a generous fellow by nature and John liked giving as good as he got, he answered what questions he could that George asked.

Soon, the men were back in their camps. The officers' horses and the mule teams were curried and staked in the long grass. Men shaved and asked for the mail. They whistled or shot dice. The sun, which had grown rosy and round, slid down the sky. As dark drew in, some of the men hung lanterns and played ball in the shadowy light. They started their cooking fires. The camp sorted itself into its evening routines. Somebody began a tune on a mouth harp.

John listened. It was the right, plaintive sound and, with all the noise and chatter of camp, it was this sad and simple tune that captured the spooling-out moment he felt he was living in—that he'd been living in since Achilles Fretageot had come walking through the dust, twisting at his watch chain. As the wistful song went on, John thought how good it was to have the men back. They were the counterpoint, the presence to place against the never-ending loss.

New Harmony, Indiana
October 1862

13

I would have consoled with you over the loss of a lover but I heard from some source or other that you had dissolved partnership some time ago. I also heard that Rippeto and you keep up a continual correspondence.

John Given to Catharine Given, September the 1st, 1862

Kate sat frowning at the letter in her lap. It was a mystery to her in more ways than one. Who, exactly, was the lost beau John was referring to and why had it taken Bill Reid a full month to find this letter in his knapsack? And just what exactly had John been thinking anyway? Kate knew that he'd seen Achilles Fretageot in camp near Memphis and that Achilles had told Lieutenant Boren about Mollie Owen's death. She knew it because Achilles had talked to their father. Yet there wasn't a word about Mollie Owen in John's letter. There were questions about who was lieutenant or second lieutenant in whatever regiment and who'd been cheated out of a rank, but there wasn't even a sentence about poor Mollie Owen.

The fact was she'd been terribly shaken by Mollie's death. It wasn't particularly logical, but she hadn't thought people would die like this in America. She'd known they would die in Donegal the way Biddy had or that they would die on the ocean crossing where even the smell felt shameful and dangerous. But she'd had an idea that people would live until they were old in America. That it meant safety. That

that was part of the promise. Instead, people were killed or dying all the time. There was this whole war now just for killing them.

Of course, she had scarcely known Mollie Owen. She had only observed her from the distance that New Harmony placed between someone like her and Robert Dale's daughter-in-law. She'd kept a careful ear out for any comment that Margaret Mulhern might drop, but Margaret had dropped precious few. It could make Kate angry. When Mollie and Julian Dale were married in Evansville before he left with his regiment, Kate and Mary had been enlisted to help with the cake and their mother was asked for her white sweet peas to add to the roses in Mollie's bridal bouquet. But Margaret Mulhern had not even shown Kate the wedding dress when she and Mrs. Maidlow had finished it. For that matter, Kate had had to learn the details of the wedding from Martha Wilsey, who'd told her there'd been officers with crossed swords for the bridal couple to walk under, and that only two days later, the 1st Cav had left on the cars for St. Louis.

And now, just two weeks ago when Achilles Fretageot had brought Mollie's trunk home, Kate had offered as delicately as possible to help with it, and Margaret had turned her down in spite of how good she was at saving things from the damp. Margaret, in fact, had acted as if she'd offered to violate something sacred, while Kate had meant only to be useful, though she had wondered, too, what had been in the trunk. Probably Mollie had packed the rose dressing gown with the filigree that Margaret had worked at the throat. Perhaps, Kate thought, folding the letter in her lap, Mollie had written a sheaf of poems that she'd bound in a book and taken with her to give to her husband.

"Catharine, the dead need to rest in peace," her mother had told her the last evening they'd spoken. "Your concern seems more nosy and morbid than laudable. It's Margaret's business and the Sampsons'. And it's the Owens'. It's not yours."

"I know, Mother," Kate had answered, and she did know. And yet there was still something romantic and haunting about Mollie Owen and her death, which meant it was hard not to be upset with

Margaret Mulhern for her secretiveness and with John for writing this letter without even mentioning her name. It was possible, of course, that John had feared she would get his letter before news of the death had arrived, and then it would have all been on her to tell people or not. Still, John might have trusted her and told her what he knew. And anyway, the news had arrived before John's letter.

Bill Reid she understood better. Londoner or not and bandleader or not, if he was like the other returning band boys, he had his mind in the grog shops and wherever else they had their pressing business. Annoying as it was, it was hardly a surprise that Bill had arrived with a sheepish look and this weeks-old letter. He'd been embarrassed and full of apologies and Kate, who'd been sitting on the bench in the Lichtenbergers' yard cooling off from the day's baking, hadn't moved since he appeared at the fence and gave her the letter.

Now she stuck it in her pocket. She got up and, reaching through the trellis, she began picking up petals from beneath the rose bushes. One by one, she dropped them into a basket so that Mrs. Lichtenberger could make another batch of rosewater for the fair, and so that she and Eliza could make more sachets.

As far as the suitor John had mentioned, she could speculate. There'd been more than one would-be beau who'd come and gone without her telling John, but she didn't know what he'd heard from other people or if he was teasing her about the aging merchants from Evansville that Mr. Cannon kept introducing her to. Probably he had been talking about one of the boys that she'd walked out with with her friends. Somebody, maybe, like the boys who'd joined the 91st in August. Or maybe she'd actually written him that John Flanigan had been very attentive to her for a man Susan Arnoldy considered a beau or that, more than once, John Clarey had carried her basket berrying, though now he was engaged to Ann Armstrong. She really didn't remember. She wasn't sure why, but she'd kept it to herself that she sometimes wrote to Harry Beal. And as much as she'd liked Jim Rippeto and, to be honest, it had been a great deal, she didn't even write Jim any longer. It was an odd thing writing a man who could talk about nothing but another girl, and there was only so much Kate herself had to say about Ann Bradley.

Kate had started cutting roses from the bushes, looking for half-withered ones and stripping their good petals into her basket, when she heard Eliza calling from the porch. "Kate, where are you? I've a puzzle for you. Kate?"

"Coming," she answered. She disentangled herself from the bushes and the thorns that had stuck in her skirt.

"You're a puzzle yourself, Missy Lizzy," she said, herding her inside when she got to the house. She set the basket of petals on the kitchen table and rubbed at a damp curl on Eliza's forehead. "Did you run home?" she asked, and Eliza nodded.

"So what's your puzzle?" Kate asked, cutting a piece of the bread she'd baked and putting out jam. "You licked it. Don't stick it back in the jar," she said, watching Eliza with the spoon.

"It's about Gerard . . ." Eliza started, and then she got a funny look on her face. "I mean it's about somebody," she said. "It's about one of the people who came to Harmony when Mr. Owen founded his community. Are you ready?"

"Go ahead," Kate said, pulling off rose petals from a dying bud in a vase on the windowsill and adding them to her basket.

Eliza was on her knees on her chair. "Who was the *truest* scientist to come to Harmony?" she asked, and Kate turned the bread on its cut end.

"Hmmm. Mr. Audubon?"

"Wrong! Mr. Audubon didn't live here. And, anyway, he was an artist. Guess again, Kate." Eliza pushed herself up so she was hanging over the middle of the table. She leaned down and took a bite of her bread.

"Let's see. Maybe E. T. Cox?"

"No, silly. Mr. Cox was only a boy then. He was younger even than I am. Give up? It's Gerard TROO-ST, of course!"

"Very clever," Kate said, looking for a book to use to press the rose petals. She was thinking of Mr. Cox's wife, who was another

Sampson daughter. She somehow believed that it made a difference the Sampsons had more than one daughter left to count. And the counting was something that, young as she'd been, she noticed when Biddy died. Her mother had always counted her daughters—even if it was only with her eyes and even though she came up short. After Biddy died, her mother had never failed to keep track.

"I know something sad," Eliza said.

"What?"

"You know when Alex Fretageot died of fever at Helena?"

"Yes."

"And his brother, coming home, left the luggage in Mount Vernon and rode here on Dove?"

"Yes."

"I heard Ida tell Alice that Mrs. Truscott was visiting the regiment and nursed Alex before he died. Since Ida was his favorite sister, Mrs. Truscott clipped a lock of his hair for her and sent it back with Achilles in his carpetbag. Ida has the lock in her room. Wouldn't that be the saddest thing?"

"It's a memento."

"I think it's sad. Kate, are you going to the fair with us?"

"You're going with your mother." Kate reached over and locked Eliza's feet together with her hands to keep her from scuffing her shoe heels on the chair. She peered at her, nose to nose. "And with your sisters and your father."

"But are you going?" Eliza asked again, and Kate shook her head. "I'll have things at home to do," she said. She didn't add that her own mother had told her it didn't matter if her father had worked on the grandstand, that that was his job, but she herself wouldn't go to the fair until John was safely home from the war and, while she wouldn't forbid her daughters going, she certainly preferred that they didn't.

But missing it would be a real sacrifice. Kate picked up the bread crumbs Eliza had left on the table. If you didn't count the 25th or the 1st Cavalry, which was still in Helena, almost the whole town was at home. The 15th's band had gotten discharged after the 25th's. The

60th, which had been mostly captured in Kentucky, had been paroled to a camp in Indianapolis, and a lot of the men had wangled a way home. And besides Posey County's best displays of everything from poultry to preserves, the fair would mean horse races with all the Harmony young people at the track to root for the sweepstakes riders and drivers—or to race themselves. Michael McShane would be riding and Kate hoped that that, at least, might carry some weight with her mother. And she did want to go to the ball.

She made a little braid in the front of Eliza's hair. "Lizy Lichty," she said, "you'll have a good time without me."

It was her night off and, after Mrs. Lichtenberger came in with the older girls and Kate had set out a cold supper for the family's evening meal, she walked out into the warm evening to go home. The town was lively. There were clusters of girls and of men on the corners of Church Street, and Kate had a hunch that all the romantic arrangements that were currently in place would soon be shuffled around again. She saw Achilles Fretageot with Rose Owen, Florence Dale's sister. It was hardly unusual since they were friends, but it surprised her that he was out at all since Annie Perkey had told her he was ill with bilious fever and that the family had feared at first that he had the same illness as his brother.

Charles Crew was talking to Susan Arnoldy in front of the Sampsons', and the two of them greeted her as she went by. She almost asked Charles if he was home on French leave since only the band from the 15th had been discharged. She stopped herself in time and thought that John, if he'd been with her, would have complimented her on her discretion. She went on a few steps before she turned around. "And the 15th," she said. "Are the boys all right?"

"She wants to know about Jim Rippeto," Susan said to Charles.

"No I don't," Kate said. "I was thinking of Godfrey Gundrum and Harry Husband. And, of course, George Wilsey and Harry Beal. How's Harry Beal?"

"He was fine the last time I saw him. You can write that to Jack," Charles answered, and Kate said she would, thinking again that she really did need to talk to her mother about watching Michael McShane ride. And about the ball.

She was walking through the crunchy leaves that covered the ground, but most of the leaves hadn't fallen yet and, in the late sun, the sky seemed papered with gold. The evening was glorious. Kate listened to the laughter in the street and wished she could keep this light somewhere inside her. She wished she could capture it to fend off everything dreadful or sad.

The Marshal girls were talking with men from the 60th, which was Colonel Richard Owen's regiment, and Kate went up to them, thinking she'd ask Charles Ward if he'd seen Margaret Mulhern, though it occurred to her then that there was no point, that Margaret would consider her household too much in mourning for her to receive a possible suitor. Even Charles. Kate stood listening to the men bragging about how fiercely they'd resisted when Bragg surrounded them at Munfordville, and she managed to keep herself from asking about the part where they surrendered, which had surprised her since Richard Owen was an experienced officer who'd fought in the Mexican War.

She wasn't really listening to them anyway. Not carefully. She was trying to think what tack to take with her mother. Lizzy Marshal had already told her she could warn her that, at this rate, she'd end up an old maid with so many men off fighting, and that she needed to strike while the iron was hot and men were in town. Kate had some interest in that argument. She wasn't telling, but she'd turned twenty-four in August, and she'd started to think that her years of being a housemaid in New Harmony and, before that, in Donegal Town with Margaret Mulhern—ten years in all—had started to show in her hands and maybe in the tiny crow's feet that her mother said she'd gotten from not wearing her sunbonnet in the garden. But Kate knew that argument wouldn't carry real weight with her mother, for the fact was (and Kate thought she and her father and her aunts in Chicago might be the only other people in America who knew this) her mother had not married until she was thirty-two. As a bride, she'd been a dozen years older than the groom.

Not that her mother had told her that. She'd acknowledged being "somewhat older" than their father, but Kate, before she left for America, had had the whole story from her Aunt Rose. "I like your mother but Ma never did," Rose had said. Then she'd told Kate her mother had loved a boy who'd drowned fishing and had sworn never to marry, but that she'd had her pretty skin and wonderful hair and O'Donnell name, and the lovely voice, and John—Kate's father—had said he would have her for certain, and so he did.

"Ma told me about it when Biddy died," Rose had said. "She told me they named Biddy Bridget for her, but your mother didn't mean it and Ma said it was why Biddy died."

"That's a terrible story," Kate had answered, and the part about her grandmother and Biddy really was, but she thought the rest of it was romantic, and she would stare at her parents sometimes, trying to see the lovestruck boy who'd wooed an other-minded woman so well that she'd married him.

When she got home, her mother was sitting in her chair with her head back and a compress over her eyes. "Kate?" she said, and Kate gave her a quick kiss.

"The headache again?" she asked, and her mother gave a small nod and Kate tiptoed across the creaky floorboards to help the girls in the kitchen. She wouldn't ask about the fair tonight—obviously she wouldn't—but she had to do it very soon.

When they'd finished supper and the washing up, Kate sat near her mother and watched Charley tussling with his setter pup and listened as Margaret read from *Ivanhoe*. She was glad to be home for the evening. She picked up the basket of sock wool, and she'd gotten her knitting needles out when she heard a knock at the door

Mr. Cannon was there when she answered it, and he was red-faced and breathless and clearly full of news. "Ah, Katie," he said, and Kate stepped quickly outside, drawing the door closed behind her. "Your father's not here?" Mr. Cannon asked, and Kate told him he wasn't.

"He's working. He's gone back late to the fairgrounds with Denis."

Mr. Cannon, circled the rim of his hat with his fingers, and told her what he'd heard. There'd been more fighting. "The Rebels attacked Corinth but they had to skedaddle," he said. "They ran into the 25th coming down from Bolivar to cut them off at the Hatchie River. It was a fierce fight. It was short, they say, but it was fierce."

Kate could feel her heart pulse at her temples. "And what about John?" she asked, and she was wondering why it had to be, with so many boys at home, that none of them was John.

"There was nobody dead in Company A. There was wounded again. I didn't hear them say John and I think they would've, for I heard Al Norcross in Company F."

Kate touched her pocket. "I thought they were camped near Memphis. I've got a letter," she started. Then she stopped. "Never mind," she said, remembering the letter's date. Nobody, it seemed, had heard from the 25th in weeks.

"I'll find your father," Mr. Cannon said, and Kate nodded and thanked him and watched him climb into his cart. She went inside and closed the door, leaning against it, and looked at her mother, whose eyes were still covered. If she were more superstitious, she might believe her mother got a sick headache anytime that John had been shot at. But she didn't believe in such things. She was a rationalist, she'd decided, a rationalist like Frances Wright had been, and so she knew that a shot at John on the Hatchie River, wherever that was, couldn't land in a house in New Harmony.

—⁓—

Kate was in the top row of the grandstand watching the horses pounding around the track. She was with Susan Arnoldy and the Marshals, and there were Givens all through the grandstands, though not her mother. Her mother would keep her vow to forgo the fair until John was home—that was written in stone, Kate knew—but on the evening when Kate had told her what Mr. Cannon had said about the fighting at Hatchie River, her mother had sat up in her chair, her compress falling to the floor, and said that life was too short, that since John wasn't hurt (Kate had fudged in her assurances, she knew, though the later dispatches had borne her out), all of her girls should go to the fair. And the ball, too. Or at least Margaret and Kate should.

To Kate's surprise, Margaret had seemed more delighted than she was. "Mother!" she'd exclaimed, bolting from her chair to hug her. Studying Margaret's face as she retrieved the book she'd dropped on the floor, Kate thought they'd both been planning and both been spared an assault on their mother's objections, and that Margaret's eagerness meant she was finally over her wounded feelings about young Mr. Baker. "Your hair is shiny in the lamplight," Kate had told her. "I'll help you put flowers in it for the ball."

Michael McShane was coming down the last leg of the track now and Kate was standing up with everybody else, stretching as tall as she could and peering over people's shoulders. Usually there were Owen men in the races and they had the best horses, the real race-horses, but only Willie Owen was in town now and Willie was fifteen, sixteen at most, which meant Michael had a very good chance. He was within a nose of the lead and his horse was closing fast. It was flying hard across the track, and it took the lead. While Kate held her breath, Michael put the crop to its haunch and the horse surged ahead, open-ing a length and another length behind it. Kate heard herself yelling. She pounded on Lizzie Marshal's shoulder and she watched Michael and his horse hold the lead clear to the finish line. The crowd was roar-ing around her, and Michael rode into a wreath of roses that Martha Wilsey and some of the other Minerva Club girls held up. He was grin-ning in triumph, his hands clasped above his head. Kate clapped and cheered as loud as she could. She wanted to whistle—with her fingers hooked in the corners of her mouth, she could whistle as loud as any man—but she kept on clapping instead. He was a beautiful horseman, Michael was, and Kate felt very proud.

"Do all the Donegal men ride that way?" Lizzie Marshal asked.

"Michael's the best of them," Kate said, thinking once more of that thrilling day on the strand at Meenacahan. She didn't tell Lizzie that in Ireland people like Michael McShane, being Catholic, couldn't even buy a horse that cost more than five pounds, though Michael knew horses and had always found ones that didn't look sound but rode like the wind. "Michael was always the best," she said.

It was a great day all around, she thought. A great three days. Mrs. Lichtenberger had won a second place with her rosewater and had given Kate the whole day and evening off. Her father had entered her mother's peach cordial, and it had won a five-dollar first. Kate had gone through all the handicrafts, looking at the fine laces and intricate cross-stitching, though what she liked best was the crowds and the visiting tumblers who rode bareback, flipping in the air. She liked walking with her father through the farm implements and exhibits and hearing him name the seeds for all the grasses: blue grass, orchard and Hungarian, millet seed and hemp, flax seed and Red Top. It was like the days when there'd been just the two of them and Margaret Mulhern and they hadn't known—not really—if they'd ever see the family again, which was why, when you came down to it, she had a bit of a problem with Michael McShane. True, Michael sent money home, and true, his wife was frightened to come to America, but Kate and her father and Margaret Mulhern had worked as hard as they could as fast as they could to bring the others over. She didn't understand how Michael could be happy without plans for his family to be here—or at least none that she knew of. And beyond that, just how he could wait on the widows or tease her mother that he'd marry one when he had his own wife. Yet this was his day. It was Michael's day. He'd won the riding sweepstakes and it was his day entirely.

Kate kept clapping as hard as she could, and it occurred to her that she felt happy and as young as she'd felt since her birthday had made her feel old. Of course, with the grandstand crowded with so many uniforms, it wasn't really possible to forget there was a war going on. She'd heard rumors about troop movements, and she'd overheard bits and pieces of talk about soldiers people knew who'd been wounded at Hatchie River. In the whole 25th, there were three men dead, though none from New Harmony, and more than seventy wounded, nine of them from Company A. Al Norcross, who was in Company F in spite of the fact he was a Harmony boy, had been shot in the hip. Kate saw friends of Eleanor Wheatcroft, who walked out with him, consoling her at the same time they congratulated her on his being cited for bravery. It was certainly true, Kate thought, that there was no way you could really forget the war. Yet today there were times when she almost had.

She found Margaret and Mary by the track congratulating Michael McShane. Kate laughed and complimented him on his ride, and when they'd watched him tend to his horse, she and the girls started the walk into town to get ready for the ball.

"You're sure Mother said you could go?" Kate asked Mary, and Mary tossed her head, a little like Michael's horse had tossed his, and said that of course she could go, that she'd be fifteen in just days and she was much too old for the children's ball.

"And Mother said you could?" Kate asked again.

"She said I could wear her shawl from the trunk. You're an old nosy bossy, Kate."

"And you're an impertinent miss." Kate pinched Mary's arm and then she gave her a hug. She could see the bright excitement in her eyes.

At home, their mother had set out cold meat and tea things for them. Kate wondered where she had gone.

Mary had put her good dress on, and it had new trimming on the bodice and on the hem. She was trying on the shawl, leaning back to see herself in the glass.

"Kate, where did it come from?" she asked her. "I know from the trunk, but where did it come from first?"

"Grandma O'Donnell," Kate said. The shawl was dark with age, and she thought it looked too old for Mary, but she didn't have the heart to tell her so.

Margaret clearly had no such compunctions. "You look like an Irish crone, Mary. Are you going to a wake?" she said, and she set about rearranging the shawl—tucking up the fringe and turning the fabric over until she found the blue left in it that was the color of Mary's eyes. "That's better. You're more of a lass," she said, and she put the bit of gutta percha in Mary's hair that she often wore herself, and Kate realized she'd forgotten the flowers for Margaret's hair. Dropping her comb, she quickly ran to the garden.

When they were ready to go, Kate thought all three of them smelled of the late gardenias that had nodded against the bellflowers she'd braided into Margaret's hair.

"We should have our pictures made to surprise Mother," Mary said. "And to send to the folks in Chicago and to John."

Kate did the quick figuring, thinking of the bit of money she kept for herself and that she still had more saving to do. "We'll do it. Before long we'll really do it," she said, and she felt that the three of them, with their dark hair, might look as nice, though not as elegant, as Mollie Owen looked in the picture in the Sampsons' hallway. Then their mother came home from visiting Margaret Mulhern, and they were all pronounced fine, and Mary's shawl rearranged once more before the three of them went out into the soft night.

The street was noisy with people walking toward Union Hall, the sound of their laughter punctuated by cricket chirps and the chorus of frogs in the river bottoms. Kate still felt happy. She wondered who she would dance with and if the officers who were home would wear their swords. She'd heard that a quartet from the 15th Indiana band would play the minuets and mazurkas (and whatever other dances people asked for). Since George Warren, their leader, was the finest musician anywhere, she felt especially eager. Mary was the one who was really excited and a little nervous, Kate could tell. She kept rubbing her fingers over the shawl, and then she asked, "Do you think anyone will ask me to dance? Do you think that I'll step on people's toes?"

"You'll be fine," Kate said.

At the hall, they crowded together outside with bunches of people and Kate heard the musicians tuning up. There were candles at the windows and, when the throng moved inside, Kate saw shadows flickering on the walls in the corners of the ballroom. She danced the first set with Michael McShane, which normally would have felt like a waste to her, but everyone was hailing Michael as the hero of the racetrack, and Kate found she liked being a party to the good-natured bantering and to Michael's high spirits.

"It's not the same as dancing at home, Kate, with the fiddlers on the kitchen table, and where it goes all night long. But it will do," Michael said, twirling her round and round.

"Yes, it will," she said, and when Tom Slingen's wife danced next with Michael McShane, Kate danced with Tom, who was Harry Beal's friend. She danced with Charles Ward (and tried making an excuse for Margaret Mulhern, though he still looked hurt); she danced with two boys from the 60th that she'd never even met before and, though she wished John were home, she was glad that he couldn't keep his eye on her. Then she got some fruit punch with all the Anns between sets and drank it outside with the moon shining. The Lichtenbergers had arrived late, and Mr. Lichtenberger looked at her with her cup in the moonlight and asked her if it was moonshine or if she'd paid the tax.

Kate laughed and put the cup down. "If I drank any more, it would be taxing," she answered.

There were more sets when she went back inside. Kate thought Ann Bradley had danced with every single man who was wearing a uniform and even some of the men who weren't. She was everywhere on the dance floor. She was practically twins, triplets even, and Kate knew she was dressed beautifully in the dress from Mrs. Owen that had certainly come from Europe and that, between the dress and her high color from dancing, she had every man's eye. Kate wondered if there would always be an Ann Bradley. It was an idle question, she decided, and it didn't keep her from feeling that she looked fine herself and that there were men looking at Ann she was just as glad were not looking at her.

She turned around to hunt for Mary in the crowd. When she spotted her, she saw she'd gone from the careful execution of her schoolroom steps to a carefree sideline jig. All of her friends were clapping to it. The shawl drifted back. It fell to the floor, and Kate was alarmed and ready to get it but Margaret was already there. She danced by and, bending smoothly from the waist, she picked it up and draped it across her arm. Kate thought what good sisters she had. She curtsied for a new soldier. She took his arm for the promenade, and she went on dancing and dancing until the candles had burned down and the musicians began to put their instruments away.

When she found Mary and Margaret, there were men besides Michael McShane to escort them all home. Two soldiers offered her their arms, and she accepted one and tilted her head ever so slightly for the other man to walk with Mary. Then they went out into the night, which had a first hint of autumn chill.

It had been a reprieve, Kate thought. For the days of the fair and this happy ball, the war had fallen away. It was still out there, she knew, its drums in the far distance of places like Memphis and Richmond. It was out there with men—some that she knew—lying in hospitals until they would die or come home with a leg shortened or an arm gone, like a man that she'd danced a reel with. But the war wasn't in Harmony tonight. They had set it aside as the familiar thing it had become, and if they had danced as though it didn't exist, Kate felt it was all right. Even with John gone and people like Mollie Owen never returning, for one night, Kate thought, everything had been achingly fine.

Camp Davis Mills, Mississippi
Late November and December 1862

14

The Davis Mills Battle was such an amazing feat that it was talked about for years. The Indian mound where the battle was fought is almost gone now. When road construction crews dug into the mound in the 1930's, they uncovered the cotton bales that the 25th used to fortify the position. At first they were puzzled as to how the cotton came to be in the mound.

William Emmick, 25th Indiana Historian

J ohn leaned on his shovel for a moment and, as he wiped at the sweat on his neck with a grimy sleeve, he was thinking of what his Grandpa Given had said the first time they'd gone together to cut peat. *It warms you twice, lad. Once when you cut it and once when it burns.*

Earlier, eyes out for guerrillas every step of the way, the regiment had marched seven miles along the railroad from their station east of Memphis at LaGrange. They were making a new camp now, a thing so familiar to John that he was sure he could do it in his sleep, and probably had. They cut the logs first. Then they dug out a hillside and fit the logs in snugly, and cleanly notched, to make a hut. He was working with George Tretheway and Levi Thrailkill, and he knew they would have it as comfortable as it got for a soldier, for they had a tent for a roof, and George had managed—John didn't ask how—to find a stove.

Strictly speaking, he was not with the company anymore. He was detached to Lieutenant Boren, who'd become acting quartermaster for the regiment. But it was hardly a thorough separation. As often as not, John was with the boys. He marched and messed with them and shared quarters. He did his share of digging and chopping, and he still shouldered a gun. It was really two jobs for one salary (a somewhat theoretical salary), but he was glad enough to trade the boredom of the picket line for the business at headquarters. He also had no desire to get so soft he couldn't soldier when he had to or, for that matter, farm if he ever saw the day when he actually could muster out and go home.

It was supper call by the time they'd finished the hut. John eyed the darkening trees and the hillsides. It seemed to him they had company out there, that it was very likely that the patrols would encounter guerrillas who would attack in some force and pick men off the ranks the way wolves take stragglers from a herd.

John took his plate and sat down on a log next to small Jake Schaen. They talked while they ate their beans and drank coffee. As he listened to Jake hunting for words to say what he meant—and tonight was one of the times when Jake was feeling philosophical—John considered himself lucky: in changing countries, he'd come to one where he knew the language. At home there were people who spoke nothing but Gaelic and, once, it had been all that his mother spoke to him. But English was the more practical language. Beautiful as he thought Gaelic was, he needed English so he could read.

"It's not a thing of surprise," Jake was saying, "that the Dems won so much at the election. Mr. Lincoln's Union is in two entirely—severated, John?—and so what exactly is the cause? It's the horses gone before the barn is closed. I believe a theory. If one part leaves, any part is leaving, too. But they shoot at us, we shoot them. If we shoot them enough and they say what?—uncle?—yes, Uncle Sam—they are sour like cherries that are new. How do they go back on the tree? There was anger, sure—too much for not fighting—but what then? How do we all be back together? I think it is not happening."

"There's a very long history," John started, and he thought of how carefully he'd read the debates between Mr. Douglas and Mr. Lincoln when they'd been printed in the papers, and of how little he remembered of them now. He'd found himself on one side of the argument and then on the other, but he'd finally decided along with his father, who had two years on him in the country and twenty-one in actual years, that the Union was what mattered most. It was the one issue he was clear on, slavery being such a bafflement and the issue that caused fury in both North and South. And, too, there was the nerve of it all: Jeff Davis calling himself president. But John had no real argument with what Jake was saying, and he was ready to admit it. "I can't say you're wrong," he told him. He poked at the bits of hardtack in his beans. "If there was anger before, what is it now?"

"The genie is swell out of the bottle. The box of Pandora is open wide."

Max Munte had been staring at them across the fire and, when it flared up, John saw his eyes glint. "Jake, how come you're fighting then?" he asked in English that was more basic but older and more certain than Jake's, which grew more creative the more he said. "It's because you're short, right? You're Herr Napoleon come to America."

"I'm fighting," Jake said stiffly, "because of you. All of you I have is friends."

"That's a reason," John said. He wiped his plate clean with a mossy rock and then stood up and started for his hut. A few men had begun a game of cards and Levi had gone to see to his mules, but all John wanted to do was sleep. He was weary in his back and shoulders, a weariness that he blamed on his gimpy leg, which always seemed to throw him off kilter when he worked hard and which made him feel that age had flown straight into him with the minié ball. He lay down without starting a fire in the stove. He was wondering idly about Stephen Douglas and what it would have meant if he had actually been elected president and still died so soon after the election. Then he didn't wonder any longer. His eyes drifted closed, and he knew he was falling asleep.

The next afternoon, he was less tired, and the camp felt as familiar to him as if it were any camp. He'd spent the morning helping Lieutenant Boren with paperwork and with detailing men to forage for the animals. A lot of the boys were at loose ends since they'd had marching orders at LaGrange and instead were left to camp here and to patrol the twenty-five rail miles between Coldwater and LaGrange. Many of them took advantage of having the mill to grind corn. Lieutenant Boren told John to inventory what they'd done, and so he got a horse and rode down to the mill. He counted forty bushels. He noticed, too, that the work had put the men in good spirits. They were farm boys, most of them, and they all seemed cheerful with what they were doing.

Riding back in the chilly air as the sun went lower, John caught up with the chaplain, who was coming from the hospital tent. "Reverend Heuring," he said, gesturing for him to take the horse, and Reverend Heuring smiled and shook his head at the offer. John drew the horse down to a slow walk beside him. He asked after the sick men, and he was thinking, as he always did, what a brave man the chaplain was. He'd seen him helping the wounded off the field at Fort Donelson and Shiloh, and even at Hatchie River. The fire had been galling.

Until recently, John hadn't really known him. He'd seen him often, though, since he was working at headquarters and, one day, on the strength of a Latin phrase John thought he'd muttered to himself, Reverend Heuring had asked him, as if he already knew the answer, if he'd studied to be a priest. Surprised, John found himself speaking of things he'd thought he would never talk about again. Gradually—over the days and weeks—the conversations between them had become a regular thing, complete with a complement of familiar skirmishes. They talked of everything from Rome to Martin Luther, who was obviously Reverend Heuring's hero (John's teasing jibe, in spite of the fact that Reverend Heuring was a Methodist) and John's whipping boy-apostate (Reverend Heuring's quick counter, though John had acknowledged readily that he found Luther's rebellion compelling). Lately, though their conversations never slighted more mundane topics, their talks had grown more probing. They'd moved from relatively superficial liturgical differences to the very nature of faith. It was a question for both of them: how faith could be equally live for men who held very different tenets and, beyond that, what it meant to be a man of faith who found himself killing men because of faith in a secular ideal—and with any number of clergy ready to exhort him to it.

"I was reading an old paper the other day—something a man picked up when the Rebels left Corinth—and it had Jefferson Davis's inaugural speech in it and, John, it left me thinking," Reverend Heuring said to him now. He scraped a burr from his pants leg with his shoe. "I'd read it before—probably when he was sworn in—but after all this fighting, the words went deeper. I studied the closing well, it struck me so."

"Maybe I saw it. I probably did," John said, thinking it likely it had made him angry enough that he'd quit reading.

Reverend Heuring stopped walking. He held on to John's horse's bridle so that the horse stopped, too. "It's an odd thing to spend memory on, but here it is," he said, taking a preacher's breath before he started. " 'Let us therefore invoke the God of our fathers to guide and protect us in our efforts to perpetuate the principles which, by His blessing, they were able to vindicate, establish and transmit to their posterity.' " He paused, letting the words sink in. Then he went on to the end. " 'With the continuance of His favor, ever gratefully acknowledged, we may hopefully look forward to success, to peace and prosperity.' "

John was quiet, considering the words. What he thought, after a moment's reflection, was that Jefferson Davis felt God should help the men of the South hand down slavery to their children as their fathers had given it to them. "Does it mean that if the Rebels start losing, Jeff Davis will believe they had God's favor but don't any longer?" he asked when his horse and Reverend Heuring had started moving again. "And why is it nobody ever says he's fighting just because he's fighting but thinks he's got a blessing for it? It's a hard faith, isn't it, that has men fight to keep other men as chattel?" John kept the reins tight and, as he did, he realized it was the first time he knew he believed what he'd just said. Or thought that he did. It was a foreign enough area to him that it still felt a little gray.

"Are you an abolitionist then, John?" Reverend Heuring asked. "Somehow, I didn't think that you were."

John felt a glimmer of something. He was thinking that in twenty-six years of living and of trying to sort out what it was of age and birthright, and of class and distinction that so fixed men's relationships to each other, he'd barely scratched the surface. What he'd done was to stay in a well-trodden vein of thought; it was the pun of his life, but it was no less true for that: so far, all he'd considered was the givens. "I don't know," he said. "I'm fighting for the Union. I don't know that I'm sure about the rest. I don't know if Mr. Lincoln's sure about all the rest or, for that matter, if I'm sure about Mr. Lincoln. My father—and he's three stone smaller than Mr. Lincoln—I believe my father could split rails with him rail for rail. It's an odd way to win an election, isn't it?—saying you can maul a rail in two, and then what's actually split turns out to be the Union. I go hot and cold on it, sir."

They'd gotten back to the huts. John wanted to shrug off his muddle of political thoughts. He'd gotten a letter from Ann Bradley that, for a reason he hadn't figured out, talked of little else but John Clarey buying bedsteads to start up housekeeping with Ann Armstrong. He'd also had a letter from Harry Beal, and it was lot about Charles Crew and how he'd been put in the guardhouse when he got back from the French leave Kate had already written about. As disconcerting as John regularly found it to think about Ann and as little actual interest as he had in Charles Crew's predicament, it was easier to think about either one of them than about the reasons for this war. For that matter, it was easier to think about theology. Yet he'd somehow gotten it all in his mind at once—the thoughts about principles and politics and what was truly just, and Ann's interest in John Clarey and his bedsteads, and what a man, who had the tongue on him Charles Crew had, might do that would stick him in confinement. It was as if he had all these voices, from the most ordinary to the oddly elevated, yammering away in his head.

"Consider, John, that confusion is the beginning of wisdom," Reverend Heuring said, and he laughed as he removed another burr from his leg. Then he turned and headed toward his tent and, as he went, John could hear the murmur of Jefferson Davis's words he was practicing once more as if they were as irresistible to him as a rhyme to a child. The only part that John thought he would remember was the "we may hopefully look forward." It was, after all, his own fervent wish.

⌒

The days that followed in their wintry camp passed by with the usual routines of life in the field. John read whenever he could, taking his turn at the ragged newspapers and old *Harper's Weekly*s and the books that passed from one soldier to another. There was a scarcity of news from home and current war news, and if it was a perennial complaint for all the men, it was still a matter that never failed to irk John. Though they hadn't been in combat since early October, when they'd intercepted Price and Van Dorn retreating from Corinth and fought the brief, furious battle on the Hatchie River, they were still very much actors in the war. They had the battle scars to prove it, and their ranks were thinner than thin. John thought they should know what was going on.

The Hatchie River battle was still very vivid to them. They'd struggled through the grasses toward a high ridge only to be halted suddenly by Colonel Morgan on word the enemy was advancing toward the same point of land that they were. Even now, John felt a chill on the back of his neck thinking of it. Colonel Morgan had ordered the artillery to engage the Rebels' big guns immediately, and they had. They'd disabled them with a fire of shells as loud as any John had ever heard. Then the 25th chased the Rebel infantry full out until they'd actually forced Van Dorn to change his route of retreat.

If the men gradually forgot the small facts of such a battle, things like the broomsedge chafing against their clothes and the weeds snagging at their boots, and the larger ones like men being felled yet again by bullets, there was still never a time when they lost the sense of themselves as men at war. Men in continuing peril. Men who needed to be wary. It was as inescapable a thing as the rank smell of the sinks and the sharpness of the early December mornings that, to John, felt like dawns in the Blue Stacks when the valley lay beneath a skin of hoarfrost.

Yet for all the sense of war—of war as the place where they were—they never knew what was happening unless they'd done it themselves. When the supplies Lieutenant Boren was waiting for failed to arrive, they hadn't an idea why until they got the news—unsubstantiated at first, but finally confirmed by messenger in spite of their communications being severed—that General Cheatham had torn up the tracks. The cars couldn't get through, and the regiment was living on half rations and forage with the rest of Grant's men, Cheatham having "cheated 'em," as the men said, out of their biscuit.

Men became edgier on patrols. There were more rumors, this time that Van Dorn was nipping at the army's rear and that he'd actually taken Holly Springs and—shades of Corinth—burned the depot and, with it, the army's commissary and quartermaster stores. Then there was the certain news a few days before Christmas that he was headed straight for them in force—ten thousand strong and fully prepared to capture their six shrunken companies: the two hundred and fifty men who stood alone to guard the Mississippi Central's railroad lines.

There was general alarm among the men, yet things happened so astonishingly and so quickly, that it was not something they had to consider long, though there was no end of considering it in the days that followed. It was a story for all time, John was certain, a story for every single man and officer who was there—who had been there—and to his great and amazed pleasure, four days after Christmas, he told it first to his cousin Menomen.

He was by himself in his hut, trying to repair his boot heel, when Menomen came in. For a moment, John didn't know him, for his hair had turned gray. Then Menomen laughed and he did know him. They leapt at each other, pawing one another in a great bear hug of the kind that their O'Donnell uncles and cousins gave each other at a wake or a wedding dance. They pummeled each other and exclaimed over finding each other in this isolated place. When Menomen had seen John's new corporal's chevrons and John had noted Menomen's lieutenant's bars and learned that he and the 11th Missouri (Menomen had joined it when the Illinois regiments were full) had arrived with General Hurlbut as part of Grant's army, John made him sit on Levi's bunk since it had the best straw tick.

"Are you a phantom then?" he said, and it was grand to see him—Menomen O'Donnell, who'd always had magnetism the way their cousin James Mulhern had brains. Not that Menomen wasn't smart. "Lord, you look fine. You do, Menomen. And your unit's come here to the middle of nowhere?"

"Center of the earth," Menomen said. "What I heard, you're a dusty little band of heroes."

"Not so much heroes," John said. "Well, maybe heroes," he conceded.

"Tell me about it," Menomen said. He leaned forward with his bright eyes, palms on his knees, and so John told the story for the very first time, and it didn't need embroidering to be a real story, though he did linger over the parts he liked best. He drew them out with the right detail so the story was worth Menomen's attention and the drams Menomen poured them from his flask.

"It wasn't at all like Shiloh," John said. "Or like Donelson. It wasn't a surprise, for we'd scouts coming in to say Van Dorn was on his way and that he had a thousand men he'd already captured from Holly Springs. We knew he wanted us, too. But, Menomen, we've a brilliant colonel. He's Colonel Morgan and regular army, and Van Dorn could have brought a hundred thousand—a whole Shiloh's worth of fellows—and it wouldn't have made any difference." John stopped a moment, wondering all at once if exaggeration really suited him as a storyteller and, though Menomen was still listening, his expression unchanged, John determined to bring it down a notch.

"Though you might not recognize it as such," he said, "for it's a blockhouse since we got done with it and all armored with the railroad ties we pulled up and cotton bales we commandeered—if you spotted the sawmill when you came in, and surely you did, you saw the key part of our defense. It was a straightforward thing that Colonel Morgan wanted to do. For him a thing's as good as done when he's made up his mind, and he'd decided we wouldn't get hurt and we wouldn't get captured and that he'd save the railroad trestle and that we'd just plain play havoc with Van Dorn's men. We turned the mill into the block-house, and there wasn't a man of us who didn't rub calluses through to raw skin for all the hauling and lifting we did and it was officers, too, it was a fierce pace. We made a secure post that sits so you see all of the trestle and the wagon road that comes from the south and crosses the river bridge.

"It's the Wolf River here. You'd have come in over the bridge, Menomen, and it's not seventy yards from the blockhouse. When we were done, Colonel Morgan put Captain Wright and Company H on the inside and we saw to it—Lieutenant Boren and I, for he's acting quartermaster and I'm clerk to him—we saw that the men got ammunition and bread enough to last for a two-day siege. Since Van Dorn still wasn't here, half the men worked until nightfall on Saturday—it's a week ago yesterday though it feels less—and they turned an Indian mound into an earthwork that was stuffed full with more rail ties and cotton. It was brilliant, Menomen. Absolutely. It was a fort, and just 300 yards from the bridge—a little more—and with the blockhouse, we had a perfect cross fire on the bridge. And since Colonel Morgan had rested half the men, there were fresh troops in place by eleven at night, though there was still no Van Dorn. We rested on our arms and at four a.m. we were in full battle positions ready for an attack."

John waited while Menomen poured another dram, and then he went on. "Still he didn't come. We waited, and then we waited more. When the sun was up, we went back to fortifying the mound, which was a bloody mess from the men's blistered hands, and it was at noon when we heard shots from the pickets being driven back in and all of us took our positions again—Company A with four other companies in the new fort. We had an Illinois battery, but only light artillery. There were two companies from the 5th Ohio Cavalry that Colonel Morgan ordered dismounted. He divided them between the blockhouse and fort and to make a guard on the river approach to the west.

"Sitting ducks, you'd think—all of us—and maybe we should have been. When they finally got there and came on the attack—and with all their hellish yowling—we had to stay steady. Nothing else. No moving sideways or back, but concentrating on the firearms and ramming the charge home and making the shot true when the line rushed forward. If they'd had their big guns, we would have been done for, but they didn't."

John had picked up his musket while he was talking. He paused, watching Menomen pull his boots off and stretch out on the bunk. Menomen lit his pipe and, for all the world, it seemed to John he was looking at one of his uncles instead of Menomen. It made him homesick. Really it did. It made him homesick for everybody in Drimarone and the mountain houses where no one could dance away from the other dancing feet and, when night had turned into morning and the dancers kept stepping, his aunts served food cold: oatcakes and boiled leeks. Sheep cheese.

Menomen drew on his pipe, and it was clear his thoughts had turned to Drimarone, too. "They're out on picket now, but there're Donegal boys here with me—Denis Ward from Eglish and Charley Diver, brother to John. But go on. Van Dorn's men must have thought that they had you."

"They did," John said. "They surely did think that. But there were plenty of things that weren't in their favor. The ground was rough. The river was right in their way, and every time their line tried advancing, we'd open fire from the fort and the blockhouse and there was no way they could move forward without getting shot. In a while they had to pull back, and we waited to see what it was they'd do next and it was massing their troops to try to force their way across the bridge. We could see them with all their banners waving and their lines stretched back so far that the road had disappeared.

"The colonel put our best sharpshooters at the prime vantage points, and it was desperate the way those men came forward then—some of them were even forced onto the trestle from the crush behind—but our fire was so heavy from both directions that there was nothing for them to do but to fall back once more. They lost men. Men who were shot. Men who were trampled. And it was a lot of men. Menomen, the year isn't out, but it's a year when I've done a thing I didn't know I would and that's kill men because I can. And more than that, I've gotten used to it and see it like a job."

John looked over at Menomen to see his reaction, for he'd felt the intensity in his voice. Menomen was quiet, his eyes and his pipe still glowing. John paused a moment longer, wondering if Menomen might say it was that way for him too, that, like it or not, it was part of them. He didn't, and John went on. "We had the sky overhead, but it didn't seem so, it was so tight in that earthwork and, as much as a soldier stinks on a regular basis, it was worse being confined in that way. All the men breathing, and some of them wrenching, and the dried blood smeared on the cotton bales we were leaning against. And the Rebels weren't done yet. They'd fallen back, but there were more and more of them out there and they had a huge front that went even beyond the railroad. They never stopped firing. We thought we'd soon have a roof of lead.

"We kept up firing, too, and the wonder of it was we never ran out of shot. There were parties of Rebs trying to cross the river in any number of places, but they couldn't do it. Our fire was too heavy, and so they massed up again with all their battle flags and tried another time to cross the bridge. Their muskets were pouring fire from their whole line onto the blockhouse and onto our fort—and we were so sure of our works by then that we sent up volley after volley. It was no surprise to us when they all fell back again, but they made another assault in short order and, this time, some of the men made it across the bridge, though there was no place for them to go. They had to hide beneath it away from the fire.

"I couldn't have said how much time it all took, but later Colonel Morgan said it was three and a half hours of constant firing at us before the enemy withdrew. They left their dead on the bridge and by the railroad tracks, and it was up to us and our surgeon to care for their wounded that they couldn't take with them, which is what we did. But before that, the men under the bridge surrendered and we let them shelter in our works and they were quivering with fear, some of them, boys that thought we'd likely shoot them, that Yankees are savages.

"The Rebels had one more plan. They wanted the trestle gone and so of no use to us. We saw them pouring turpentine on cotton balls and lighting them to hurl at it, but the boys in the blockhouse aimed so well they couldn't do it, and so they finally gave it up. When the retreat was called, those troops and the ones that had shielded themselves next to the trestle surrendered, too, and it was a smart thing as there was no way they could have made it safely over open ground.

"They left twenty-two dead and, counting men taken off on horseback and in ambulances or left on the bridge or in a house behind their lines, they had more than three hundred wounded. And as soon as they retreated, their general sent a man out with a truce flag to ask for our surrender, which you can imagine Colonel Morgan quite heartily declined. We hadn't a man killed, Menomen, and just three wounded and those only slightly. And that's the whole tale."

John finished the last of his dram, and Menomen stretched out his arms and cracked his knuckles. Then he swung his legs from the bunk and, standing up, reached as tall as the tent roof would let him. "So the 25th are monarchs of all they survey. You've got a story for your grandkids, Johnny Given," he said. "Make sure, now, that you stick around to tell it."

Of the whole war, it was the days with Menomen that John remembered always with real fondness. When they weren't on duty, the two of them spent their hours quite happily together. At times, they stayed by themselves talking of everything from the rough ship crossings to the wildness of New York and Mick disappearing, and the Irish gangs who seemed harder than any men they'd known at home. They spoke of what it was like to farm in America where the fields were bigger and there were swamps but no peat. "It's a lot of trees," Menomen said, "and the wrong rocks for building fences."

Mostly, they talked about old times, of how often they'd walked over the Blue Stacks helping their fathers drive cattle to fairs, and how they'd stopped at houses on the way for a night's sleep and then were off again at daybreak. Menomen knew things that John didn't. He knew why Mary Mulhern, Margaret and James's sister who'd been a favorite of John's when she was a grown and pretty girl and he a small lad, had gone north from the Glen and never come back.

"Her apron was high and the man wouldn't marry her. It was likely a Molloy, and him leery that Daniel Mulhern would flay him and weave him into a sack. Or so me old aunt thought."

Menomen had a memory, too, for things that John didn't, like going with Michael McShane to his uncle's to break horses in the sea, and the horses floundering when the water came up to their shoulders and how the men could handle them then and, finally, ride them onto the strand. Menomen said that sometimes they would break a horse with a wooden bit they screwed down on its lip so its nerves went haywire and the horse all quivery.

"I've watched Michael ride his horses out on the strand," John said. "Kate and I both have. But I don't remember a time he was breaking them."

Menomen had gone to Scotland, working with men and lads who dug potatoes and with girls and women who, following behind them, sorted the potatoes into the baskets of good ones and the baskets of pig feed. They saved what pay they could to take home.

"Blistering, bloody work," Menomen said. "We'd take the boat for the crossing and they'd lower horses to the boat deck with a fall-and-tackle, and those horses were wild from the sea rocking and they lurched about. But the girls were jolly on those trips. You were off with the books, John. Were there jolly girls where you studied to be a priest?"

"If I'd seen a real girl then, I'd have thought her a figment," John said. "But we've fine girls in New Harmony."

Often, when they were all off duty, he and Menomen joined Charley Diver and Denis Ward. "Now I understand why the Given house is loud and full of talk," George Tretheway told him. "Together, you Irishmen talk the fastest and the most and the hardest-to-understand English I've ever heard. What does *slan* mean?"

"It's not English, " John said, "so why would you understand it? But all it means is good-bye."

John had had an even harder time recognizing Denis Ward than he had Menomen. In spite of the army, Denis was a great deal fleshier than when he'd known him at home. But there wasn't a better fellow than Denis, and he talked always about Michael McShane's kindness to him in Liverpool when they were both there working to earn their passage.

"It's East Dublin, or it was with Michael to show me the ropes," Denis said, and John wrote that in his letters back to New Harmony when he sent Menomen's greetings to the family and to Margaret Mulhern and Michael McShane. He told them, too, what he knew they would all want to hear, that Menomen had had a letter from Jackey, everybody's favorite O'Donnell. The folks about Drumboarty were all well.

Aside from his long talks with Menomen and just being with him (he still remembered how he'd tagged after him when he was a lad and how Menomen had never minded), what John liked best, what took him back the most was listening to Denis Ward when he got out his whistle and played his airs, for all of the Wards could fall out of bed and make music. It was just that easy to them, and Denis could float John far out of Mississippi and clear over the ocean and back to Donegal with his jaunty tunes. Maybe even more with his sad ones.

"You need my mother to sing with you," John said. "One day for sure, you'll come to Harmony and bring your whistle."

"And your father will get his fiddle out?"

"He will," John said. "And Mr. Cannon will get his out, too."

They had less time than they wanted. Menomen had the responsibility of his men and, with both rations and communications still cut, John was busy at headquarters keeping track of the details that were ordered out to kill hogs and cattle and to grind meal. On New Year's Day, they spent from morning until night in line of battle, but they heard through the grapevine, which was how they got all their news now, that there was no fighting nearer than Jackson, Tennessee.

Maybe it was true, and maybe it wasn't. Given the day, they could hear that both Vicksburg and Richmond were taken (or they weren't), that Burnside's army had been slaughtered to a man (or they weren't), or that Bragg had taken both Columbus and Paducah (this would mean they were still cut off from their support, which they couldn't disprove), and Rosecrans had completely defeated Bragg at Murfreesboro with the 15th in the fight (or that Rosey hadn't and the 15th hadn't been and Burnside wasn't even whipped).

"Did you ever wonder, John," Menomen asked him one night when they'd been sitting around the fire and wishing they had old potatoes and knew how to make boxty pancakes the way their grandmother did it, "just how it is that we ever got here?"

John motioned with his cup at the trees and tents around them. "*Here* here?" he asked. The cup was still warm with his coffee dregs. "Here in the war, or here in America?"

"In the war," Menomen said. "Do you think we joined up, Johnny, to show we'd earned the right to be here—to feel like Americans? It was a bandwagon thing, sure, signing up with all the high feeling. It's a sociable thing in the regiment with the lads. And what Irishman would walk away from a fight? But do you ever wonder, John, if we really have a horse in this race?"

John was quiet, not certain just what Menomen was asking.

"Look at this." Menomen reached into his breast pocket and pulled out a creased piece of newspaper and spread it open. He pushed it closer to the fire. John saw it was a cartoon, but before he could really get a look at it, Henry Schafer walked up, cup in hand, and saluted Menomen.

"What's the cartoon, Lieutenant?" he asked. "Is it one of the nigger on the fence? Or is it the ape in the tree? That's it, Jack. It's one of you Irishmen. He's got your ears, even if your arms aren't as long." Henry laughed, pleased at his joke. Then he poured his coffee and went off in the direction of the sinks.

"He's a good man, a good soldier," John said quickly. "You'd want Henry any day in a fight. But what do you mean, Menomen? You mean we're at the bottom of the barrel here the same as the black man?"

"Maybe. I'd be lying, John, if I didn't say I like the army, and I'd be lying if I didn't say I thought it would do me good down the road if I fought beside my neighbors. But here's a question. Where does an Irishman come out if the slaves are set free?"

"They've no education," John said, not adding what he knew, that Denis, his own brother, hadn't either. And not Denis Ward for that matter. Not many Irishmen. "And you made your fortune and can keep it here. What kind of threat could any man, black or white, be to you, Menomen?"

"But the core of the thing is something else. We could win every battle. We could beat the South to its knees, and the only way the war would ever end is if the real cause of it—and it's slavery, John, it's always been slavery—is entirely uprooted. And that likely leaves other Irishmen with less luck than you and I've had."

"You think it's set—that Mr. Lincoln means to free the slaves? Free them when they're written into the Constitution as not free?"

"I don't see he's got another choice. Not when the South has a million able-bodied blacks to feed armies that are killing Union men. Slavery isn't just the cause of this thing. It's part of what made it possible. It's Mr. Lincoln's duty to seize property—and, John, that's what the black men are—when it's used to undermine the safety of the nation. And for him, seizing the slaves means to free them."

"So you say we're fighting for abolition, Menomen? And even if it means Irishmen's jobs?"

"I said why I'm fighting." Menomen pulled the cartoon out once again. He looked at it. Then he tossed it into the coals. "I've been here longer than you, John, but it's still not long enough to understand the bitterness that made this war what it is. And, yes, what it means for an Irishman. But I've cast my die. When I went home to Ireland, as much as I still loved the land, I hated the poverty more. It's why I kept Mary and the children here and brought the others over. Yet it's true the one bitterness I really feel—the one that belongs to me—is for the injustice I still saw. A part of me thinks I should have made my fight in Drimarone. A part of me wishes I'd stayed."

John turned his cup over. "As you say, there was all the excitement and being part of it when the war started," he said, pressing the cup rim into the dirt. "Yet I've wondered a hundred times if we shouldn't have let the South go. I can understand it's a wrong—a sin, slavery—but I can't sort it all the way through. It still has an unfamiliar feel." John picked his cup back up, and it occurred to him that Menomen thought more than he remembered him doing, and it occurred to him, too, that he should tell him that his best friend was a Yorkshireman. He let it go. "If we weren't cut off, we'd know now if Mr. Lincoln went ahead with his proclamation," he said.

"We would," Menomen answered, kicking at the coals.

For days afterward, the conversation stayed with John, though it was something he and Menomen backed away from when they spoke again. Denis Ward brought word that another regiment—either a Minnesota or Wisconsin one, he wasn't sure—had a quartermaster who was a brother to Dan McGroarty of Letterfad. John wondered what the full roll call of Irishmen was in General Grant's army—just how many lads from Drimarone, how many from Donegal, how many Irishmen who'd cast their lot with America and, having made a safe passage here, found themselves fighting.

"I don't ever want Denis in this war," he said to Menomen later. "I made Father promise to keep him at home. It's his back I put my foot on, for I went off to school while he helped Father. But Charley's done well. I've a letter from Charley I've kept, and I'd admire it if I could read what captain he said had been home on leave."

It was a damp January day when the 11th Missouri and the rest of its brigade headed back to Corinth. John was up early to say his farewells. He had written letters to New Harmony and Chicago and to Drumboarty, and he handed them over without a word, for he'd already talked with Menomen and Charley Diver about the chances for mail getting through. The dawn was chilly. There were sprinkles of rain in the breeze, and it reminded John of Donegal and the mud-colored fog and scent of sheep manure.

He stood with Menomen. For a second, it was hard for either of them to say a word. Then Menomen grinned a sly grin and slapped him on the shoulder.

"I heard you'll be headed for Memphis," he said. "Be careful, John. There's a world of women there. They'd every single one of them like your name."

Memphis, Tennessee
June 1863

15

*Kate, from the remark which you made relative to our being sent to Utah
I infer that you have heard some pretty hard tales about us boys here in
Memphis. I will acknowledge that there is no scarcity of women here and not
a few of them are very pretty but I have not made the acquaintance of many
of them yet. I know that some of the boys have married "during the war" but
Posey County is clear of that yet, as far as our regiment is concerned.*

John Given Jr. to Catharine Given, Sept. 2nd, 1863

I believe Harry Beal was right," John said to Bill New. They were on their way down the levee, and John had been trying to pry information out of him.

"Right how?" Bill asked, putting a plug of tobacco in his cheek.

"He wrote me that you and William Taylor spent your furlough at the grog shops. It makes sense you've nothing to say about Harmony if the whole of your leave was a drunk."

Bill snorted and then laughed. "And what does he know, him home on sick leave, though I'd say he was a well enough fellow. Jack, you're not married. If you had a wife and a leave, you'd look for a grog shop, too. Unless, of course, you'd a chance with Ann Bradley."

John looked quickly at Bill. Then he focused anew on the girls who were walking ahead of them. They seemed happy. They looked spirited. They were hoopskirted and bonneted, and carrying parasols, one of them pink, and they were clearly ready for the day's ceremony to mark the year since the Union capture of Memphis. John slowed down behind them, and so did Bill. The parasols nodded ahead, the girls chattering, and John believed he'd not seen a group of young women as much like the girls in New Harmony in all the time they'd been here in Memphis. And odd as it was that Tennessee women would participate in a ceremony like today's, John had an explanation. In fact, he had three. The young women of Memphis seemed eager for any sort of social gathering; some women were less Rebel than Southern and would sign General Hurlbut's Union oath without flinching; some were probably real Unionists.

Not that it was ever entirely evident where any given person stood here. In the months since General Hurlbut had replaced General Sherman as commander of the District of Memphis, and the 25th had arrived on the cars to serve as provost guard, John had found himself alternately puzzled and intrigued. Though he still believed that life in the wide-open spaces suited him better than anything, he'd come to like the city's noisy busyness. He also liked the contrasting things it embraced. It had its quiet areas like parks and the tree-lined walks that could wind into mazes. It had gardens and fishponds. But what John felt most—and he thought the other men did as well—was the pulsing energy of the city. It was mostly about buildings and tight quarters, and so very, very many people. Soldiers and officers filled houses of all descriptions (some of them turned into hospitals), and the camps near Fort Pickering, and the barracks on McLemore Street that had been the state's women's college. Men were on every street corner and street and on each bit of space on the levee.

Every day a vast number of soldiers arrived and a vast number left. Near the water, companies stood in formation. They were flanked by mounds of baggage tied with heavy rope, all of it ready to be hoisted onto steamers for soldiers who were leaving, or onto wagons that waited for troops who were ready to disembark. There were men with Northern accents and civilian clothes—merchants who, against all regulations, were pirating Northern goods to Southern buyers in Atlanta and New Orleans and Baton Rouge in exchange for cotton that was illegally sold. Some of them were sharpers or dandies who wore fine suits and gleaming rings; more were men who looked very much like the men who sold goods in the stores in Evansville and Harmony and Mount Vernon.

John had watched the city's matrons, many of them keeping their children close as they went about their daily errands or lined up at Union commissaries to ask for food. Some waited at headquarters to request their homes or servants back or to demand that their furniture and queensware, now in use in the grand homes commandeered by Union officers, be returned to them immediately. Many of them had a determined grimness about them, and it was not just the ones who were dressed in mourning, though John had started to realize that as much as a third of them were.

More often, the women he saw made John remember Menomen's light warning. For the whole war, it had been a rare camp they'd made without its camp followers. There were plenty of men who had had the usual bouts of soldiers' illnesses complicated by syphilis or gonorrhea. Yet in even his most vivid thoughts, John had never imagined such an array of easy women as Memphis had. It was not like the alleys of Dublin where, as a lad going out to relieve himself, he'd sometimes seen women with bodices down and skirts hoisted, backed against a wall with a man. Even when painted, women on the streets of Memphis looked clean, and they were far better dressed than such women in Dublin. And they were everywhere. It was as if they'd multiplied like mice, as if every other building must house a warren of them. Because Lieutenant Bennett had become assistant to the provost marshal, the 25th had had early word of the April order to close all the brothels. But if the order had meant some bawdy women had headed north, it was impossible to notice a difference.

And it wasn't just these women and the soldiers and Yankees who'd come South who'd crowded into Memphis. In the first weeks after the 25th's arrival, John had found himself plainly gawking. Though he'd begun to grow used to the black men in the Tennessee camps who'd become servants to regimental officers and even to some of the men, and though he'd seen the many black women who had greeted soldiers in the countryside and sometimes, half curious and half friendly, offered them home-cooked food, there was a far wider description of Negroes in town. John couldn't stop himself from studying them. It was impossible to settle on a single color for the darkest skin. It was neither black nor brown but more a steely charcoal that carried a blue sheen. It was like train metal in the bright sun, a color so dense and rich that he found it amazing. And yet it was no more striking than the lightly bronzed tones of the octoroons in silk dresses, the women most likely of all the prostitutes in Memphis to be seen on the arms of Union officers. John knew from reports at headquarters that the city was flooded with slaves who'd escaped from plantations farther south, or had been freed in the unoccupied areas thanks to Mr. Lincoln's proclamation. The Union authorities had put them to work at various construction jobs around the city. Other workers were Memphis slaves who'd hired themselves out despite the fact they weren't free. And some of the Negroes in town had been free all along. Yet whether their English was a dialect or a patois that he couldn't make out or was close to book-perfect, as it sometimes was, John knew that nearly half of the background voices he heard—lazy talking in that Southern way or wheedling or raised in anger in the fights outside the grog shops and brothels—were bound to be Negro voices. It was part of the vitality of the city and, though it alarmed him at times and made him unsure, he grew daily more used to it.

"Who do you think those girls are?" Bill said. "That one carrying the pink parasol looks like Lydia Hinckley to me. Or when she turned around. They seem a lot like Harmony girls out for a walk. What do you think, Jack? Could it be they're not hookers?"

John laughed. "If it's Lydia Hinckley with them, they're not," he said, but he knew what Bill meant. The girls had an air about them as if they might flirt, but nothing more. "I can't complain," he said, "at having the sight of them. Kate would imagine them spies," he added, remembering how she'd demanded every detail about Ginnie Moon, the Confederate spy who'd been caught in Memphis with morphine quilted into her skirt. When they'd first arrived on the cars, the story had raced through the 25th, and John had had more than one vivid dream in which Ann Bradley was Miss Moon and he the one asked to search her.

"What if they were hookers?" Bill asked. "What if they are? Does it really make any difference?"

"It would if they were Harmony girls."

Bill was spitting through a space in the crowd. A flock of crows swarmed up from a church spire and they both watched as the crows circled around and then settled on the steeple and on the treetops. "I mean, in your book, Jack, how long is it that a man needs to keep himself on hold?"

John didn't answer but kept on walking.

"So you're a priest or a half a priest or whatever you are for a man who likes the girls so much, but this is the land of milk and honey. Look around you, Jack. What are you waiting for? What's the good of a bayonet and balls if you don't try a little skirmish?"

John laughed again. Still, though, he didn't say anything. He had no answer to make to Bill New for, irritable debating society of one that he'd become to himself on this very subject, he hadn't found his own answer yet. And, anyway, if he had, he didn't know that he'd volunteer it to somebody like Bill New.

"So tell me again, Jack," Bill started, and John thought he'd raised his voice to get the attention of the women who, for a time, had disappeared into the crowd and then had re-emerged just yards away from them, easy enough to spot from the height of the one pink parasol that rose above the rest. "Jack, how was it again that you got yourself busted back to private?"

The girl with the pink parasol turned to look at him, and John felt his face color from the fury he felt. He wanted to deck Bill New. He wanted Bill's words erased and to not feel humiliated, though he knew there was nothing he could do.

The fact was he hadn't really lost his corporal's chevrons for cause. Before they came to Memphis, he'd been sent on patrol with Dave Vint. They'd split the men into details, and Dave's men had broken down the front door of a plantation house and helped themselves to featherbeds and food and whatever else they could carry. A Secesh woman had ridden up to Colonel Morgan the next morning and demanded restitution, and Colonel Morgan had been absolutely livid. He'd read Dave out and reduced him to the ranks, and he'd fined him besides. John, who was silent under questioning (which he would have been in any case but actually had to be since he knew nothing of what had happened), was demoted as well. Though Dave was back to his sergeant's rank by January, John seemed to be stuck. Not that there was anything on his records. They were clean, and he suspected Captain Boren had had something to do with that. But he wished if he wasn't to be a corporal, that Menomen—and these Memphis girls— had never known that he had been.

"Your wood ticks, Bill? I've a fine, dull knife. I'll be glad to cut them out for you," he said, and Bill grinned.

There were more steamers on the river than usual, their stacks sending up black clouds of smoke above the bluffs, and John could see that some were at anchor waiting for the ceremonies to begin. He and Bill had gone past the companies of soldiers who were massed on the levee below the city's icehouse. Then they'd turned up Court Street, which was thoroughly festooned with flags and bunting, and headed to Court Square. It was where the parade was to start before making its way through the streets to the Esplanade for review by General Hurlbut, who would make the day's final speech at the commandant's house. John knew all this because he'd seen the day's program. It was different from what he'd expected, which was a reprise of the ceremony of a year ago when the city was taken in a gunboat battle: a military parade, bands playing patriotic songs from the horsecars as they moved through the city, men raising the Stars and Stripes atop the post office roof, which was six stories up if a roof was a story, and the ladies of the city presenting a wreath. He'd read about that, too.

Though it was his day off from duty detail, John was on a specific assignment. He had orders from Captain Boren, who'd become captain finally and officially in February three months after Captain Randolph (sick of being carried around sick in an ambulance) had resigned his commission and gone home. John was to check the platform staging, where the Union Committee would start things off by offering patriotic resolutions for approval, and he'd gone to the government shops and found Bill New. As often as not, Bill did smithing for the army, but Bill was a first-rate carpenter, and John needed him to be sure that everything was done right.

When they got to Court Square, which lacked any real courthouse though there were certainly fine buildings in Memphis, they put their packs down and began working. Bill added braces to part of the staging, while John examined the rest.

A crowd had started to gather for the kickoff ceremony, and soldiers were installing a topiary arch, an eagle trimmed into it. A statue of Andrew Jackson stood at the center of the square, and another soldier was draping a ribbon across the place where someone had chiseled away all of the "Federal" and part of the "Union" in Jackson's words: *The Federal Union, it must and shall be preserved.* There were flowers on the statue, the nameless wildflowers—or nameless to John— that grew among the rocks in the woods out past Fort Pickering. John assumed they'd be wilted or dead before the first person even stepped up to read.

"Have we got time, Jack?" Bill asked. "We could get a beer and meal at the Eclipse Stable. They've a fine lot of horses, and the men tell a good story. Do you know, Jack, if George Warren and the Evansville Band are playing today?"

John shook his head to both questions and put a wedge under the last riser to level it. "They're gone," he said. He gave the wedge a few taps with his hammer. "They're off on their tour."

"There's not a band here to hold a candle to them."

John pulled some jerky from his pack and shared it with Bill. "That's true," he said, for he knew there wasn't a better bandleader anywhere than George Warren, and that today's celebration could be as fine a display as there was, and still not provide half as good a time as they'd had the previous day with the Evansville boys. Colonel Morgan had rolled out a barrel of beer. The band fellows were entertaining to a man and, before they'd left, George Warren gave John a song he'd asked him to copy for Margaret Mulhern. John had already sent it off in the letter to Kate in which he'd written that the woods on the far hills had caught fire just before sunset and the band had played with the fire bells ringing in town. It was a fine melee—noise and excitement with nobody shot.

It was only later that he thought how much the fire looked like the bog fires in Donegal—blazes that lit the horizon and set the turf flaming and smoldering so the gorse burned a dry black. He wished he'd written that to Kate. He didn't know what happened in Tennessee, but in Donegal, such fires flushed out the moor fowl and snipe. They panicked the curlew and grouse.

John splashed water from his canteen onto his face and looked around to see if he could spot the girls they'd seen earlier. He couldn't.

Bill New eyed him. "I can't find them either," he said, "and there's nothing going to make you any prettier, Jack. You're as lost a cause as the South."

For all of the day's activities, it might as well have been the Fourth of July. Mingling with the crowd, John listened to the Union Committee resolutions, and the letters read from General Sherman and General Ben Butler and Edward Everett, the great orator. Governor Tod of Ohio gave his own speech. John didn't recognize the dignitaries assembled for the parade, but he knew without counting that there were thirty-four young women dressed in white, one for each state. They carried banners of red or white or blue and were mounted on horseback. For a second, he envisioned them each riding with a parasol turned golden in the sunlight, but they looked splendid as they were, even better, he thought, than the float carrying the Temple of Liberty, which was surrounded by attendants and escorted by the National Union Memphis Guard. And they looked better than the floats with patriotic scenes and the painting of the Battle of Memphis. There was a band, of course, and various officers and a straggle of citizens, some of them clearly inebriated. John half expected a gun salute from the river to point out once more that the Union controlled this city—or at least that it made the rules. From what he had seen of Memphis—and as part of the provost guard, it had been a great deal—he didn't think it was a city that was subject to actual control.

At the ball in the evening there were little flags everywhere, some of them tucked into the gowns of the ladies. John tried to think how it would be if the situation were reversed and the Rebels had taken New Harmony. He couldn't imagine the townspeople fêting them all day, and then his sisters and their friends, or even Ann Bradley, waving the Stars and Bars and flirting with Rebel soldiers at a ball. Just considering the possibility made him angry. It didn't, however, keep him from dancing. The fact was, he felt he had a kind of permission. He'd thought so all spring and now in the summer, for when Mrs. Boren had visited Captain Boren in March, John had called on her in her room and she'd pressed his hand, and then looked fondly at her husband and said, "Absalom, dear, do see that it's not all work and no play for Private Given. War or not, no one should waste a youth by not dancing."

John had liked what Mrs. Boren had said. He liked her. He thought she was brave to visit her husband when her sister had died on the way to visit hers, and he thought she was pretty and welcoming, too. She'd been very natural with him, telling him how Kate argued politics daily with Clarence Bruner's mother when Mrs. Bruner called at the Lichtenbergers'. Then they'd all talked politics themselves. Mrs. Boren and John were in agreement that Mr. Lincoln's Emancipation Proclamation had the potential for causing great chaos, and John thought that Captain Boren, solid Lincoln man that he was, had actually gotten badly used up in the argument.

"It's hardly thought out," his wife said. "Where will they live? They've no education. None. Even Frances Wright took Nashoba's slaves to the Caribbean."

"Is that what Kate says to Mrs. Bruner?" John asked, and Mrs. Boren shook her head.

"It's what Mrs. Bruner says to her," she answered, pouring the tea. "Is it news, John, that your sister's become an abolitionist?"

It *had* been news, John thought, presenting himself to a laughing Memphis girl for a waltz. It was news even now. While he'd known

Kate had launched herself on a serious course of self-education, including asking him to see where Nashoba was built when he first got to Memphis, she'd not ever written that she'd adopted the side of Mr. Garrison. It was possible, though. She had a restless imagination and a soft heart and, together, they made a romantic of her, and that was Kate. She might have her rough hands and the hard-learned dutifulness of a serving girl, but the idealistic Kate was also the real one. He would not have her another way or, for that matter, have her see the sights of a city like this one that might make her anything else. And not for the whole world would he have her hear speeches like the one shouted this very night by a drunken officer he'd seen shackled and being hauled through the streets to the Irving Block: "What a bloody town that's filled up with whores and niggers and all you filthy Irish."

"Private, would I be giving aid and comfort to the enemy and be locked up by you provost guards if I said a Southern soldier would never mind his thoughts more than a lady's feet?"

"Excuse me," John said to the girl he was dancing with.

"Excuse me, *ma'am*," the girl answered, and she turned on her heel, lifting her skirts away, and left John standing alone. For a moment he remained there awkwardly. Then he made his way to the wall, hot-faced and no longer in the mood for dancing. He'd known all evening that the girls here didn't really attract him. Walking back from the day's procession, he'd discovered himself face-to-face with the girl with the pink parasol. She had black eyelashes and a graceful neck and, though she didn't know him, she seemed as willing as Harmony girls to chat and to flirt. Yet he'd quickly realized they had nothing of interest to say to each other, that if they spent not a second more together, it wouldn't bother him at all. He'd tipped his cap and moved on.

He looked out across the dance floor. He watched the swaying gowns and the flash of the officers' swords. There'd been a time when he'd felt that Harmony girls put on airs, and he still thought some of them did, but it was their curiosity that he missed—the sense he'd always had that they liked fun and were ready to learn something new.

There was an eagerness about them, but an innocence, too—even, in her way, an innocence about Ann Bradley.

John eased back farther against the wall. There was innocence here as well. He was sure that there was and that it was unfair not to recognize it. Yet he had no idea how to read it. He could not distinguish between insinuation and some plainer charm. He thought it wasn't his fault exactly but something to be ascribed more to the city. It was the tenor of the place. It was the fact that so many people were here for a temporary, wartime reason. And too, there were the indelible scenes in his mind of the women, clearly not innocent, who lolled on the street corners and hung from the windows as they called out to soldiers. There were the women he was forced to look at on the gruesome nights he was detailed on guard duty at the Irving Block and sat next to the dingy, airless room that housed the female prisoners. They were shrill and quarrelsome. They were crowded together on dirty beds in disheveled clothes, and it had tainted all of Memphis for him so that he thought he had come to the inferno described by the Savonarolas of his seminary years and found it—just as they said he would—occupied by women who'd been created by men. And worse, there was something sordid at the heart of it all—something embedded in the very breath of the city—that he found disturbingly alluring.

John nodded at Levi, who danced by with a fresh-faced girl in his arms, and that made sense anyway—a man whose father had been born in Tennessee dancing with a Tennessee lass. His thoughts wandered to the map that hung above the desk at headquarters where he worked on the daily troop returns. It was a map of Memphis before the occupation, but with colored boxes added for all the Union encampments and the headquarters and posts. John knew it by heart: Beal Street (which he'd written about to Harry). Chickasaw and Hernando. Gayoso and the parallel streets, which were named for presidents, with Jackson the farthest north. When he'd gotten sick at the end of May—a relapse caused by his plagued stomach—he'd found himself unable to concentrate on his work, but he'd stared at that map. It was the fever, he thought, but all he saw were the tiny squares marked in color the whole way across it. They looked like so many little Trojan horses set throughout the town and it seemed to him that the women of Memphis were the real Trojan horses, something ready to attack from the inside out, though he thought, too, that a counterattack was warranted, a skirmish, as Bill New had said, even if John knew that he'd pulled back whenever the opportunity offered itself.

If there had not been the dance music, he might have pondered more what he meant about Trojan horses, just as he'd fixed on the map when he was so sick and wondered why he'd written his parents he was finally well and done with the attacks that were made on him for the express purpose of keeping him at his fighting weight. His eyes blurring on the map, he'd collapsed. Flat on the floor and gazing up at the tin ceiling, he'd reached back through the fevered, mucky swamp in his head to whisper for quinine and to tell the boys who carried him out that he wanted his cot and not the hospital again.

Yet he was well now. He was here. There was dance music in the Memphis night, and the beguiling, recurrent tune that he'd copied for Margaret Mulhern, and both were less a diversion from the hidden, dark throbbing of his body than a prod to it: a tattoo of sound so strong that, finally, John had to turn and slip away.

16

We all loved her; fell down before her; her very appearance seemed to enthrall us . . . she was more than beautiful; she was grand! It was not feature simply but soul–soul. There was a majesty about her.

Walt Whitman on his childhood memory of seeing Frances Wright at the Hall of Science in New York

L ooking at his latest letter from Harry Beal again, John thought that Harry had done exactly what he'd wanted to do himself: gone home on furlough, though now Harry was back in Louisville, half-invalid with his game leg, and half-orderly at a hospital there. John wished he could see him. He wished, too, that he had more than Harry's word for it that things were fine at home, that his sisters were still good company and that the girls a fellow might think of marrying were still to be found. He'd been sure he would have a furlough himself by now, but General Hurlbut had countermanded the order that allowed them. It meant, John and the other men assumed, that they should expect a fight in Memphis or nearby, though what else was new? They'd antici-pated a fight since March and, if Vicksburg fell, they would expect it even more. The Rebels would be in desperate need of a base on the Mississippi to provision themselves.

The men here would do all right in a fight. Hurlbut went in on his muscle. He fought in front with the troops, and it meant they were always ready to fight for him. But it was clear they weren't going to Vicksburg. Other regiments had had their orders, and Memphis was crowded with men arriving from various commands for transport downstream as reinforcements. Part of Burnside's command had been ordered to Vicksburg and the rumor was that the 91st Indiana (with so many Harmony boys who'd signed up last August) was among them. The 25th expected them at any hour—people like John Corbin and Enoch Snelling, who were officers, and John Smith, who was part of their company. Levi let it show how concerned he was about proving his faithfulness to John Smith's sister Margret. The result was mischief among the boys. They put a lacy handkerchief in his pocket that he pulled out when he was eating. They had a messenger bring him a box of lingerie that had come from New Orleans. They sent a horsecar to camp with two giggling, perfumed women wearing bows that said, "Have a thrill with Thrailkill." They even smuggled a girl into his cot.

At first, Levi being Levi, he was as hot as hot could be. He was ready to fight half the regiment. But as one prank followed another, each more ingenious than the last, he finally joined in the joke, or at least acted as if he had. "I'll tell John to tell Margret she'll just have to wait in line," he said.

A day went by with no 91st. Then another. Then more. After a week, John concluded they weren't coming. He asked around at headquarters and found that Burnside had sent his 9th Corps to Vicksburg and kept the 23rd Corps in Kentucky, which made it official: no 91st. John was disappointed. Everyone was, except maybe Levi, who was very busy in his free time writing letters to Margret. Instead of the 91st, they had to settle for a brief visit from John O'Neal, who'd resigned his second lieutenant's commission in the 60th, but was headed back to the army in Vicksburg. There wasn't time for Mass before he boarded his steamer, but he wanted to go to church, so Captain Boren had John take him, and John gave him a quick tour of the center of Memphis on the way. At St. Peter's, they went in the side door and a priest heard their confessions.

Afterward, they stood outside and John O'Neal lit a cigarette. "It seems like there's a lot more in Memphis to confess than at home," he said. "Jack, in case my letter goes astray, when you write your folks, will you ask them to let my wife know that I got here?"

"I will," John said.

Later, Levi took him aside. "You don't think, do you, that John Smith would have believed all that talk if he'd come? You don't think he'd have told Margret? I maybe danced with some girls is all."

"Of course he would have. He'd have believed every bit. And sure he'd tell Margret. I would have helped him with the letter," John said, and he ducked away when Levi swung at him, and then he laughed and laughed until their yellow camp dog stood on its hind legs and licked his face and rolled him over in the dust.

With no more anticipation of seeing the 91st, camp felt utterly dull. Once more it was the same routine day in and day out. Or day on and day off, which was how the duty roster worked. On a Monday, John might stand guard with a patrol at the landing or a supply depot; on Wednesday, they could be at a street post or the paymaster's office or at some general's headquarters. More often than not he clerked on the days he was supposed to be off. And sometimes on his duty days there was so much paperwork that somebody else was assigned to his detail so he could stay at headquarters. He'd come to hope for paperwork on the days of the worst assignments so he wouldn't have to go to the Irving Block or break up the irritating, nasty fights that, in spite of the fact it was General Hurlbut's headquarters, erupted regularly at the Gayoso House.

It wasn't their usual duty, but occasionally details from the 25th manned checkpoints on the Hernando Plank Road or the Raleigh Road and, even though they were stuck at crossings those days, John liked being out in the countryside, far enough from the city that it almost seemed as if they were in the field again. Yet even that made him of two minds. He liked the idea of change, of something about to happen, which was the way he felt in the field. On the other hand, he'd seen enough combat that he had no desire for more, although he would have told the boys in the 91st if they'd actually headed to Vicksburg—and he would absolutely have meant it—that every Indiana man should know what real soldiering was before he went home. You could try, but you just couldn't tell someone so he'd understand what it was like in the thick of things with the noise and confusion and people killing each other. How you learned if you could stand fire. How, in all the horror and fear, you could feel both fatalistic and incredibly alive.

He thought he knew what John Smith would have answered: "If it's like drinking Eagle Whiskey with Harry Beal, then I'm ready." And it was like that, John thought, yet it was something much more.

On the days that he spent in camp, more than anything John looked for the mail or wrote letters. He wrote to Kate and his parents. He wrote Harry Beal. He wrote back and forth with the folks in Chicago and, from the letters he received, he thought a good deal of Mr. McAuliffe who'd married his Aunt Ellen. He scarcely wrote, though, to anyone else for he mostly followed his own rule of not writing a letter he didn't owe, and it was weeks and counting since he'd heard from Ann Bradley. On the day the guerrillas stopped the mail boat, he wondered if his letter writing was becoming pointless anyway. Earlier, the *Platte Valley*, which was full of prisoners, had kept right on running through the fire from the Rebel batteries, but the mail boat had retreated, stopping once again at Memphis.

John read the newspapers, which they got in camp every morning and every night, but he considered them entirely misnamed, for they were papers without any news that he could find. And he always read *Harper's Weekly* when he could get it and the well-thumbed books that other soldiers had finished. He'd bought his own new copy of Byron—now very tattered—because he liked the poems and because the reference to New Harmony and the Rappites in *Don Juan* amused him and made him feel less homesick (if he actually was homesick— he wanted to go home but he thought that was something else). In the city, there were plays every night, and he and Levi and George Tretheway went regularly, and sometimes Fred Perkey. As often as not, they'd make up the endings between them on their way back to camp—and the more ridiculous the better—for curfew was at ten o'clock, and if a play was long, they had to leave the theater before the final curtain.

There were circuses in town, and John went occasionally because he liked the clowns and because he could write home about the trick riders and the menageries of animals that his father always loved to hear about. Sometimes he walked around just trying to place himself—to see the camp in relation to both the city, spreading to the north along the river, and Fort Pickering with its sight lines for battery fire, which were clear since the neighborhoods between the fort and the city had been demolished to make them so, hard luck for their black families notwithstanding.

When he thought about it—how much work he had to do and the variety of activities that Memphis actually offered—it seemed to John as if he shouldn't be bored, but the fact was that he was. Everything seemed repetitious. The days passed like one long and muggy monotony. When the idea came to him one Saturday to ask for a day pass for Sunday and to try looking for Frances Wright's Nashoba as Kate wanted him to, he didn't have to think twice to decide to do it.

He'd kept the letter she'd sent and he found it in his tent and read it over again, amused at her eagerness, at how smitten she was with all things Fanny Wright, though it didn't dissuade him from forming his plan.

"You're a Harmony boy. You know where Nashoba is," he said to Fred Perkey at supper. Fred looked blank, so John added it was the place where Frances Wright had tried to train slaves to be free and that it was around here somewhere, that Kate had said it was on the Wolf River.

"I might have heard of it," Fred answered, "but you'd better ask Levi."

John found him in a tobacco-spitting contest and looking as bored as John felt. The upshot was that early in the morning they had a regular scouting party together. John thought the worst that could happen was that they'd have a hike and a picnic and get shot at by guerrillas. But it was getting out of camp. It was getting out of Memphis and hugging close to the river on a hot day. He and Levi and Fred and George Tretheway and Al Norcross, who was still a Harmony man, though he was in Company F, took their guns apart and cleaned them and put them back together and had their haversacks ready. Levi said they were headed near Germantown, that he remembered it from one of his father's maps, though they weren't to hold him to it if he was wrong.

"We'll see if the chiggers are still sweet on us," Fred said.

They left camp, walking past the pickets and past rows of cedar saplings that an earlier regiment had planted on its outskirts. The morning songbirds raised a loud chorus and, ahead of them, the world was all green hills and small valleys. John, for a fleeting moment, imagined that they weren't soldiers, but their citizen selves off with some Harmony girls and hunting for wild strawberries.

They tramped for a while. After a time, they drew near the river and found an old wagon road. When it narrowed into a horse track, it was still wide enough to walk two or three abreast. "So what are we looking for?" George asked. "Old bones? What? Did she bury some gold?"

"We're looking for where it is," John said, and the truth was he wasn't quite sure what it was they were after. Evidence, he guessed. Some proof, as if it were math or *Don Juan*, that could show them once more that New Harmony's stories were fact and not myth. It meant more than that to Kate, he thought. For Kate, some physical remnant of Nashoba would be the link she needed between what she wanted to believe in: Frances Wright—beautiful, generous, and brilliant friend to Lafayette attempting to create a utopia for black people—and what she knew: Frances Wright, launcher of a communal experiment as bumpy and chaotic as Robert Owen's had been in New Harmony. There were, however, more generous ways to judge things. Without Mr. Owen, there would not have been what came afterward: the geological surveys and kindergartens and Robert Dale Owen, if it was more than a rumor, having the ear of Mr. Lincoln. And, of course, the five of them here, walking through the woods once more.

The horse track was more like a footpath now, and so close to the water that the footing was uncertain. They headed for the higher ground, and John thought how it had never frightened him as a boy, he was so used to it, that the ground in the Blue Stacks simply disappeared beneath your feet, but that it might frighten him now. He listened to the river below them slapping and churning its way across the rocks.

At noon they stopped to eat, and John pulled out two pies he'd bought from a peddler before they left. Al Norcross got out the boiled eggs he'd brought, and they pooled the leftover berries they'd found along the way. Fred dangled over the river to fill their canteens while Levi held his feet. Then they all sat leaning against the trees and swatted at bugs while they ate. Without two years of soldiering behind them, John thought they would have slept or swum and made whistles from the grass, but they were used to the discipline now. They were accustomed to the miserly breaks and the focus on where they were going. When they'd finished eating, they shouldered their guns and sacks again.

"It shouldn't be far," Levi said awhile after they'd started off again. "We need to ask somebody. Do we try that cabin or follow the sound of the ax?"

"The ax," John said, for he could see the scrawny old man who was swinging it as they started down an incline.

The man, noticing them, straightened up, shading his eyes, and waited as they approached. Al Norcross took the lead, heading off the track to speak to him. A moment later, he was back saying that the man knew nothing of Germantown, let alone Nashoba, and John considered talking to him himself but decided there was no point. He was one of the countless country people they'd encountered since the 25th had been in Tennessee, and John didn't know if they were taciturn by nature or from wariness or if, maybe, they all had sons with the Rebels. They were the way his grandfather had been when the land agent came. Afterward he would get the milk pail and set his cap straight, and then he'd lean over and speak right into John's face: "He can tell me his master owns me own land. He can ask for his rent. But there's nothing, lad—John, are you listening to me?—there's nothing that says I should talk to the eejit!"

In a while, they saw a black woman coming up the path, her hair springing out from beneath her kerchief in wiry gray strands. She had a young boy beside her. This time Levi asked the questions. He was down on his knees and drawing in the dirt.

"Fanny Wright's great social experiment. Wasn't it mainly about how the beds got mixed up and who wound up sleeping together?" George Tretheway said. "From what I've heard, it was a bit of an outpost, but maybe Memphis's first brothel and Fanny's own very fine bundling colony. Or bungled colony. Didn't Mr. Owen draw them like flies, Jack? The fuzzy thinkers. The fuzzy planners. If Fanny wanted to end slavery, she'd have had more luck if she'd bred a bug to kill cotton."

"And you'd be half naked. We all would," John said, not bothering to concede the rest of the argument: no cotton to pick, no need for slaves. Finally, no war.

"She knows where it is, Jack," Levi said, coming back to them. "Or she says that she does. She's sending the boy to get someone."

John fiddled in his pocket for a coin as he watched the boy going off. He was worried it was all a wild-goose chase. "It's about Kate," he told Levi. "Kate and her curiosity."

When the boy returned, he brought a black man in a tattered shirt who called the woman mother. John didn't know just what relationship that signified, though the woman looked older than the man. For that matter, she looked older than anybody.

The man stood in front of them. "Mistress dead. Young massa gone to war. We beats the locusts that come."

John nodded. "About Nashoba," he said, not sure if he'd just heard a biblical reference or a physical and entomological fact. "It was a settlement near Germantown. Years ago. Can you take us there?" he asked, and he was dubious when the man nodded and took the coin from his hand.

As they started after him, the woman and child resuming their slow trek in the other direction, it occurred to John that he'd brought himself and his friends on a fool's errand. It wasn't that he doubted Nashoba had existed. As well known a traveler as Fanny Trollope had described it, saying most memorably that the chimney caught fire every hour. Kate had told him in her letter what he already knew, that the plan had been to teach the colony's children on the Lancastrian model and to have the slaves work for their freedom while being educated for it, and then to colonize them in Africa.

But Fanny Wright had gotten sick. She'd gone off to Europe to recover, leaving matters in the hands of her sister and two men, and her colony had quickly proclaimed itself against religion, against marriage, and happy to announce the cohabitation of one of the slaves with a white leader. It was a huge scandal, and the start of the doom of Nashoba, which had ended with Fanny's return and some kind of expatriation of blacks to Haiti. Yet Fanny Wright, with her otherwise generally illustrious career, was still one of Harmony's own.

"Apple trees," the Negro said, pointing when he'd taken them up higher above the river. John looked uncertainly at the orchard they'd come to, thinking—not for the first time—that they'd have to make the trip back on the double quick or get written up for missing curfew.

"We were looking for this Nashoba place," Al Norcross said.

"She planted an orchard. My mother told me she did," Levi said. "There were the rain trees in New Harmony that Thomas Say planted, and the apple trees at Nashoba."

And cedar saplings around their Memphis camp since people always plant things to mark a settlement, John thought but didn't say. "Is there anything more?" he asked. "Anything specific? Anything like an artifact?" He was searching for a simpler word, but their guide turned and led them to the edge of the orchard.

"When old massa young, we helps a sick lady," he said, and he nudged his foot into the tall grass. John could see a bit of rotten foundation.

"This was one of the buildings?" he asked with a little stab of excitement. He followed the foundation line with his eye to the collapsed boards that had made a corner.

Fred Perkey was looking at the sun, which was moving lower in the sky. "All right. Say Fanny Wright did set her fanny down here. We've seen it—not her fanny but the place. I say we get a move on."

John was still poking around at the boards. He thought he could see the layout of two buildings—not very large ones—and he had a sense of where a garden might have been.

"In a minute," Al Norcross told Fred. He took out his sketchpad and quickly drew some lines. He smudged in the trees and river below. He made the rough lines for the houses and garden in just the places where John had pictured them. "Eleanor will like it when it's finished," he said, closing the pad, and John, for the first time, understood why Al Norcross had come along. He was on a love errand. Eleanor Wheatcroft, with her family roots deep in the Owen community, would have a drawing of Nashoba as Al Norcross had imagined it from these ruins. She would show it to her friends, and then hang it in their home when she and Al were married.

John pulled out another coin for the guide, and a penny for him to give to the boy. "Ready?" he said, and the five of them started back along the river. They moved quickly and steadily as though they were on a forced march to a battleground, but with the unspoken satisfaction that they weren't. The sun began to set, a skimpy peach glow in the sky and, when they paused, it was only for long enough to fill their canteens from the river.

By the time they reached their picket lines and were done thinking of guerrillas, the night was starry with fireflies, and Memphis a huddle of faintly gas-lit shapes beneath the moon. Tired with the fine weariness that comes from a long day's tramp, John stopped for a second to take in the scene. He listened to the silence. Then Al Norcross gave the signal for the picket, and John followed him and the other men into camp.

He wished he could thank Kate right then for this day when life, briefly, had felt unexpected. Maybe they had seen Nashoba; maybe they hadn't. But they had walked into a version of the past, and it had been like taking a deep breath on the first day of spring. A day when everything feels new again. A day when every single thing seems simple and interesting and full of possibility.

New Harmony, Indiana
July 1863

17

*I spent last Sunday afternoon at my aunts and after supper I and Flanigan
went out to your house and took a walk with the girls and had a first rate time
of it you may be sure.*

Harry Beal to John Given, May 11th, 1863

H er parents had gone to the Wilseys' with Mr. Cannon,
Denis and Charley were out with Margaret and Mary,
berrying with friends, but on her Sunday off, Kate was
in the attic room at home making two lists. Her papers,
which she'd stored in the rough crate where she kept John's things,
were scattered on the floor by the window, the afternoon light falling
on them, and one of her legs was asleep. She stretched it out, letting
it tingle half awake. Warm as she was on this hot July day, she kept
on working—sorting papers and jotting notes, her shoulder against
her bed.

In a while, she stopped a moment to read. The two lists were
actually related in her mind. One was the record of the year's events
so far. There were the big things like the Emancipation Proclamation
and the start of the draft and, just this month, the fall of Vicksburg
and the bloody Union victory at Gettysburg on the Fourth of July. The
list also included smaller things, or at least things that were closer to
home like the death of Florence Cooper, who had nursed the troops
in Evansville and come back to New Harmony to die of a fever. Some
people said it was diphtheria and others erysipelas (Kate had practiced

the word until she could say it easily), though no one really seemed to know if it was either one. Robert Dale Owen was rarely in town, but the mansion was still draped in mourning for his daughter, and everyone knew they had séances there for, when he'd been ambassador to Naples, he and Mrs. Owen had both become ardent spiritualists.

Kate, going back over her first list, put a star next to Vicksburg. John had written their parents that he'd heard from Charles O'Donnell, Menomen's brother, that Menomen had been a real hero. The Confederates' wall had been built so well that the Union soldiers had reached the fortifications in only a few places, and Menomen was with those who did. Or rather Menomen had been in front of them. He'd led forty-four men, only half of whom had made it to see him scale the earthworks and plant the flag of the 11th Missouri. Minutes later, after the Rebel bullets had knocked it down, he'd planted it again.

Kate could imagine it. She could easily see Menomen, wild and determined—an O'Donnell chieftain in full fury and completely impervious to Rebel fire—but she couldn't see him with gray hair as John had described him. In her mind, when her cousin pushed the flagpole into the earth, his hair was still the same shiny black of cut peat.

Kate traced her finger over the other star she'd made on the list. It was for Harry Beal's furlough home in May, and she wasn't sure that it merited a star except it had stayed in her mind and, given how circumscribed her life was these days, what had happened seemed like an event, certainly for the embarrassment, but also because, small as it was, it still seemed so present.

Kate stretched a kink out of her neck. She let her finger stay on the star. It had been such a lovely day when she'd set out on her errand to see Harry. He'd only recently come home, his leg still mending, though he'd been wounded at Stone River after Christmas. The one time she'd seen him, she'd been in town with her father and she'd promised Harry leftover pens from the fine ones Margaret had made the last time the geese molted. With Kate trying unsuccessfully to shush him, her father had told Harry he should get the war over soon, that he should take matters into his own hands if he had to so the boys could come home and marry all the girls. Harry had laughed and Kate had flushed but, of course, she herself would not really consider someone like Harry Beal. It was true that she'd always found him funny and handsome, but did she need another man in her life who was in love with Ann Bradley? Did anyone? She meant to see him just as a friend.

As it was, she'd almost made a wild-goose chase of her trip. A block from home, she'd realized she'd picked up right-handed pens, and Harry was left-handed. She'd run back quickly and switched the light packet of quills. Starting off again, she was thinking with pleasure of how perfectly the quills were stripped and how carefully the nibs wrapped, when Michael McShane stopped on his horse and offered her a ride. They chatted amiably as they went but, halfway to the John Beal house, Kate decided she wanted to walk. She thanked Michael, remembering to tell him her mother expected him for dinner on Sunday, and she got down from the horse. Then she set off on foot. She thought she would surprise Harry with her visit, and she was confident she would find him, for Mary had heard he was making a cedar hope chest for Robert Clarke to give Emma West. Kate was certain Harry would visit his aunt, who was in mourning now for Mr. Beal, and sure he would be busy in his uncle's workshop making the chest.

She was pleased at what she was doing. It was partly, of course, that she liked going to the Beals' in the hills south of town. She'd taken Eliza and her sisters there often to see their grandparents, though of course Mr. Beal had died in April, and Kate hadn't been at the house since he fell ill. She hoped Mrs. Beal had kept up her garden. She planted it in ovals like a Rappite garden and, when it was in full bloom, Kate thought it had the texture and color of an elaborate rug.

The air had grown fragrant with the peach and apple blossoms from Mr. Beal's orchard but, as she came in view of the house, Kate could tell from the tall patches of weeds that the garden had been neglected. She saw the black wreath on the door and she stopped a moment, smoothing her hair and patting her neck with her handkerchief. She said a few silent words for Mr. Beal. Then, quill pens in hand, she turned in at the gate and started toward the workshop, her skirts brushing the paving stone.

She was hurrying as she went. At the workshop, she leaned her elbows on the window and shielded her head to see in. The arc of the sun curved back at her, blue and purple in the glass. She could make out a hat left on a peg by the backroom door and sawdust under the workbench. She thought the hat was Harry's, but she didn't see him. She tapped on the glass. She waited and then tapped again, but nobody came, so she walked around to the door and knocked. She heard something, maybe sandpaper scraping, but there was still no answer. She knocked once more. Finally, when nobody appeared, she lifted the latch and pushed.

Standing in front of the open doorway, Kate saw she was in a beam of sawdust the sun had striped in the air. She smelled dust and new wood. She was ready to sneeze, but she still wanted to surprise Harry and she stopped herself, tightening the muscles in her face and squeezing her eyes shut. She pinched her nose until the quick snatches of air that wanted to be a sneeze had eased away. Gingerly, she lowered her hand, making sure she was quiet. Then she stepped forward and edged softly across the room.

Cedar. The scent was unmistakable. Kate wondered what Emma West would put in the chest that Robert was giving to her. She wondered how fine it would be. She had the strong desire to look at it—to see if it was anything like Mrs. Lichtenberger's amazing carved chest that her father had made. She was almost ready to call out Harry's name and to walk quickly to the backroom door. She wasn't shy, and Harry was *never* shy, and she didn't really have to surprise him. Yet something made her reluctant. She hesitated longer. Perhaps she was wrong. Perhaps Harry wasn't here. Maybe it was someone else making the scuffling noise behind the wall. Maybe it was squirrels or a bat.

There was the sudden noise of something falling on the floor, and that did it for Kate. Her dress swept the sawdust in front of her as she hurried forward. "Harry? Did something happen, Harry? Harry, it's Kate," she said. She pushed open the backroom door, and what she saw wasn't the chest, though the top of it was leaning against the wall. What she saw was a lace blouse lying in the wood shavings and a knocked over sawhorse and, for a frozen second, she thought she'd found Harry and Ann Bradley. There was a fair-haired man, head down and hips pumping in a sprawl of skirts on the floor.

Kate heard herself inhale. Her feet seemed stuck to the floor, and she wanted to make an apology for barging in, and she wanted more to yell hussy—hussy, hussy! What was Ann Bradley doing here? And with Harry! With Harry! And then, through a bleary-eyed haze, Kate realized it wasn't Harry at all. It wasn't Ann Bradley. It was Harry's cousin George. It was one of John Beal's other nephews that he'd taught to carpenter because his brother Walter had died, and he'd no sons of his own. It was George Beal on the floor with his wife, Hectorina, and they were both staring up at her, their breath short, and with looks of total astonishment.

Kate edged backward. She thought she muttered an "excuse me," feeling for the doorframe and then trying to pull the first door after her. She wanted to be outside and down the path. She wanted to be clear through the garden arch and making her escape and, the whole time, she was thinking of how she could never look at George Beal without remembering that his brother had died of typhoid in Missouri with the 25th, and how she'd never be able to look at him again—or his wife!— without seeing him thrashing away in the sawdust. She was ready to stick the quills in her hair so she didn't have to carry them and, no matter how hot and breathless it left her, run all the way home. Yet she was no sooner outside than she heard someone coming down the walk from the house. She listened to the gimpy tread.

"Kate?" It was Harry himself, and Kate knew that her face was the shade of the crimson flowers that were tangled in the garden weeds.

She hadn't stammered since she was a child but, even though she swallowed first, she knew she would stammer now. "I—I brought you your quills," she said, and she handed them to him.

"You brought me pens here?" he said. "I mean I'm glad to get them. Thank you very much. But how did you know I was here, Kate? I didn't know I was coming myself."

Kate pinned her stare on the nearest tree in the orchard. "Mary said you were working on a chest for Robert Clarke."

"Me working on something Robert Clarke would buy? George is. George is the carpenter and I'm the miller, in case you forgot, Kate. But George is probably here if you want a look at a hope chest."

"No, I don't," Kate said quickly, thinking that she would kill Mary as soon as she had the chance, or do the same thing—tell their mother she'd caught her smoking a corncob pipe, which she had.

"He'd show you. Or we can look if he's not here. Come on," Harry said, starting toward the workshop, and Kate grabbed at his sleeve.

"No. Please," she said, covering her mouth and the awkward laugh that escaped it.

Harry paused. "Oh," he said then. "He's here, isn't he?" He looked at Kate with a cocked eyebrow. "George and the lovely Hectorina?"

Kate nodded, waiting the long second for Harry's reaction. She thought he was going to tease her or at least get that devilish Harry twinkle in his eye, which maybe he did a little before he pushed his hands in his pockets offhandedly as though he were considering rain or maybe the market price of hogs. Then he told her he had a boy with a wagon who could give her a ride home. Kate, aware she was still blushing, thanked him and brushed at her dress. Then she watched quietly while he went to get the boy.

———

In the stifling attic, Kate stretched her legs out again and looked at the scatter of papers. She sighed. Such a woolgatherer she was. She traced Harry's star one more time, then willed her thoughts to the latest news about Ann Bradley. Since Mrs. Owen had cut back on her household, Ann was working for the Beattys, though Kate had heard that the Beattys had had their own reverses and were going back to Kentucky. Kate thought she might feel sorry for Ann and her reduced circumstances, but she didn't really. She touched the star one last time. Then she leaned over and looked at both of the lists in front of her.

She needed to decide how it was the lists fit together. She was certain they did—there was a sense that she had—but she hadn't quite managed to make the juncture. It was partly that the second list, which she picked up now, was more complicated than the first. This second one was about thoughts more than events. She'd written down her ideas on what she'd heard or read about why there was a war and if it was more about slavery or about union, or if the two were entirely intertwined. She'd been thinking particularly about whether having freed the slaves in the rebelling states without the kind of first steps that people like Frances Wright had believed in would mean mayhem, or if freeing them had been a simple moral necessity. There was the question, too, of whether the South had had a cruel advantage—the ability to make a crop from slave labor while white Southerners were free to fight. John had written her that Menomen believed that was so.

These were all the things that started this harder list but Kate was actually getting a glimmer of how the two went together—a feeling that her lists were really illustrations of each other. They were both about where the war had come from or about what it meant and how it was playing out. Though perhaps that was too simple a connection. Facile, as John might say. It was a word she could use as well. *Facile.*

She put the second list on top of the first. She had a growing pile of papers that didn't belong to either one, and she set them behind her on the bed and, for the moment, out of the way. It wasn't that they fell into the category of miscellany. They were the notes she'd been assembling about New Harmony (all so laboriously made; how she wished she had John's easy writing and handwriting skills). Though there were still all the Harmonist buildings and people in town who were descendants of Father Rapp's German followers, she knew most of what interested her, and what she'd read, had to do with the Owenites.

John always told her she was just impressed at how well connected they'd been, and with the way Robert Owen had educated New York society and Washington leaders about his New Harmony plans, model phalanstery in tow.

It *was* impressive, of course. Not just anyone could visit Thomas Jefferson at Monticello. Not just any man could have a thirty-six-square-foot design for a cooperative village on actual display at the White House. And how many people could miss giving an announced lecture and have the president-elect (it had been John Quincy Adams) return to the hall the next day in hopes that the lecture had been rescheduled? The Owens had certainly been acquainted in high places. In fact, they still were. But what Kate had insisted to John, and what she really felt, was that it was the brilliance of the people Robert Owen had brought to New Harmony that was so appealing. That and the fact that they'd simply been added to the random collection of fortune seekers and farmers and laborers who'd descended here. Kate had always been amazed that William Owen, at barely twenty-one, had been left alone to handle the chaos, though, of course, he'd written panicked letters to his touring father. John said the whole enterprise had been exceptionally naive, and probably it had been. Yet Mr. Owen's desire to make a society based on an idea that the right environment could shape people to be good people had been so very, very hopeful.

There was the whole bunch of them who'd come—the scientists and artists and teachers whose names every New Harmony schoolchild knew by heart and that Kate had learned so very well, though she'd never quite gotten straight just who had arrived from Philadelphia on the "Boatload of Knowledge," the keelboat *Philanthropist* that Mr. Beal had built. Her favorite name was still the longest and most exotic, and the one she loved to practice to herself: *Guillaume Sylvan Casimir Phiquepal d'Arusmont*. He was the Pestalozzian teacher who'd married Frances Wright and who'd actually taught Mr. Fretageot when he was a boy in Paris and, the rumor was, done so harshly. There was Fanny Wright herself—reformer, writer, lecturer, and experimenter at Nashoba. Kate had studied the drawing of her in the library. She saw beauty in the slightly flattened lips, the slightly padded chin, but mostly in her confident air. She had always imagined Fanny Wright as a majestic woman dazzling crowds in New York with her presence and mind, giving her lectures on women's emancipation and writing away at the newspaper she and Robert Dale had run though, for herself, all Kate could remember of New York was the stench and noise and the men she didn't know and didn't want to know who pressed against her in the streets.

Joseph Neef was another of the Pestalozzian teachers, although Kate had sworn she wouldn't mention that to John again for finally he'd simply laughed and started reciting Pestalozzi's math tables, which he'd learned in school. "I know," he'd said. "Pestalozzi's schooling is meant to be learning with objects and nothing rote. It's supposed to be all kindness to children. For a boy in Dublin, it wasn't. Did you ever think about this, Kate? As different as the Rappite and Owenite communities were, they were also alike. I mean they both even had pietism behind them. Rapp did, but it was also part of Pestalozzi's background. And both had leaders who met Thomas Jefferson, though with different purposes. Rapp had his hand out for land, and Owen wanted to make a convert. And then there was the millennium. They all expected it, though Owen thought men shouldn't wait but actually create it."

Kate considered the other famous Owenites. There was Madame, of course, which was how everyone referred to Madame Marie Duclos Fretageot. She'd been another teacher, and she was also Mr. Fretageot's mother. There was William Maclure, Madame's great friend, who'd invested in New Harmony and, unlike Robert Owen, believed in education and scholarship for their own sake and not just as a means of reforming society. Maclure had thought people should be taught manual trades, and he'd left his mark so thoroughly on New Harmony, right down to the Workingmen's Institute, that many people thought he was even more important than Robert Owen himself.

The names went on, and Kate had them very much by heart, and she didn't care that John liked to tease her that she did. They included Thomas Say, who was usually called the Father of American Entomology, and Charles-Alexandre Lesueur, artist and ichthyologist, and Gerard Troost, who was the pioneer among New Harmony's group of geologists, though it was David Dale Owen who, at one time or another, had drawn virtually all of the country's distinguished geologists to New Harmony. It interested Kate that George Warren's father, Josiah, had been a prolific inventor, and had also devised the "time store," a very complicated scheme for trading labor for labor. Mr. Audubon had had a protégé in New Harmony, for Lucy Way Sistaire, an artist and scientist who had married Thomas Say, had studied with him before he'd painted his famous birds. Of course John, poking gentle fun at Kate's enthusiasm, had told her that Lucy might have dropped the Sistaire and then been Lucy Way Say.

Kate pushed back a damp strand of hair that had worked its way loose. She touched the sweat on her neck and folded a paper to fan herself with. All of these people were important to what New Harmony had been—to what it had become—and it mattered very much to her to know about them. Yet her lists were still a separate thing. The items she'd included on them didn't involve New Harmony's luminaries (with the exception of Robert Dale). They concerned the more immediate sphere of living during wartime and what for her, personally (and as an eager, but undeclared suffragette), was basically the politics of the thing.

That was it. Yes, that. Quickly, Kate scratched onto her pad, trying to hold her thought, to catch the nub of it—of what she meant by politics—and to think of what it implied before it slipped away. Yet neither the pencil in her hand nor what she had written was enough. After a moment in which her mind stayed blank, she tossed the pencil away and flopped back against the bed. She so much wanted to get this right. It was Mrs. Boren, really, who had given her the idea, saying that she'd become such a student and so good at arguing her points with

Mrs. Bruner and all comers, that she really should write something for the Minerva Club. She couldn't promise a membership or even an invitation to a meeting. That was all under Constance's thumb and Constance, married to Reverend Runcie or not, was still very much Constance Fauntleroy. But Mrs. Boren had said she would do what she could.

Kate hadn't told a soul. She hadn't even told her mother, although when she'd first thought she would write a poem, she'd tried out various rhymes until her mother had looked at her quizzically and asked if she was getting a head start on next Valentine's Day and was it really wise to consider the Valentine heart in such a bloody fashion? (Kate closed her eyes and remembered one of her less satisfactory couplets: *the shot so piercing his gallant heart / he froze in time like a startled hart.*) Her mother had been suspicious, she thought. More than suspicious. She'd talked to her about not neglecting her work and about still seeing her friends and about how she would certainly hurt her eyes from reading too much and, even worse, run the danger of spoiling herself with profane knowledge, her worry, as usual, that Kate was losing her faith. And Kate had not been able to tell her not to worry, for it would be worse if she told her (and heaven help her if anyone told John) that it wasn't about faith or any lack of it, which was a whole different matter. It was about walking into a Minerva Society meeting at the Fauntleroy house with the debutantes and St. Mary's students and girls who'd traveled abroad and been educated in Munich.

A poem had seemed impossible in any case. She had lines and scraps of lines that she'd tucked away, but she could no longer imagine constructing an entire, reliably metrical poetic edifice on such a large subject, for whatever precisely her subject was, it did seem quite large. She had thought of writing a story, for she knew that that, too, was customary for the Minervas, but a story presented its own problems. It was particularly vexing trying to decide what characters to use. An essay of sorts seemed the only real option, and she'd had one idea that both intrigued her and intersected with what she'd learned of New Harmony.

She'd thought she could start by talking about both utopias—both of New Harmony's—and how the two of them had, to one degree or another, been about marrying or not. Mostly not. The Harmonists, of course, had had Father Rapp's revelation to guide them. They were to be celibate while awaiting the kingdom of God. But for the Owenites, there had been a different twist. Robert Owen had made his "Declaration of Mental Independence" in which he'd condemned private property and most religions, and then added a condemnation of marriage since it was linked to both. Robert Dale, on the other hand, had advocated early marriage as a curb against illegitimate births, but with the important antidote of easy divorce if a long marriage grew wearing. He had also had such a concern for the rights of wives that he and Mrs. Owen at their own wedding had signed an actual contract to honor them. For their part, Fanny Wright and her sister had believed that marriage wasn't necessary, although both of them had eventually married. William Maclure, who'd owned land in Spain, was said to have been opposed to marriage entirely. There had been all these antimarriage statements and attitudes among the Owenites, and hot on the heels of the Harmonists, who weren't to marry at all.

The connection Kate had wanted to make was to the slaves—that they couldn't marry legally—and to the strange knowledge she had from John that there was every possible color of slave in Memphis so that it was necessary to imagine that white men had children with black women and lighter but not white women. If the war, as some said, was as utopian an idea as New Harmony had been, in some hidden way it was also, as New Harmony had been, about how men and women were and weren't together. There were men, Kate realized, who were actually fighting for an institution that made their own children slaves.

She had thought she would shock someone like Constance if she said such things, and so she'd decided that she wouldn't. And anyway, she hadn't gotten the whole thing straight in her mind, which made her question how clearly she could think and regret her lack of word skills and the schooling she'd missed. Yet the whole matter—scattered or not—was on her mind, and it was partly because she believed that the war was killing off marriage altogether for girls like her, girls who had no bias against it. It was threatening her and her sisters with becoming old maids.

She was sure her mother thought so, too. She didn't say it directly, but she'd stood staring glumly at her yarn basket. "How odd," she'd said. "A house with no babies or, with Charley so old now, not even a real child anymore."

And her father, Kate suspected, wanted a grandchild. He was sweet with the little ones. And, too, it was still in her mind what he'd said once more to Harry Beal when Harry, near the end of his furlough, had come to the house with John Flanigan. Harry was chatting and flirting with her sisters and her father had practically bellowed at him. "Get this war over, Harry. We need you lads to come home and marry these girls."

Kate had been listening from the kitchen. She wasn't avoiding Harry exactly, but she felt as though things were up in the air between them since she'd gone to the Beals', and it made her feel awkward. It even made her feel cross. Part of her had really wanted to say yes when Harry called into the kitchen to invite her to join them for a walk. Part of her wanted to act as if nothing had ever happened, but the part of her that still felt uncomfortable meant she'd said no.

She'd seen Harry at the ball right before he left, however. He had signed Ann Bradley's card and then, because he was angry with Ann for stopping writing to him, he'd skipped the set altogether. Some gallant officer had had to rescue Ann, though Kate didn't see who it was, for a left-footed fellow had stepped on her skirt, pulling it clear off the waist. She'd been off with the girls getting it pinned back on.

"Is it your leg? Does it hurt?" Kate had asked when she blundered into Harry as he was leaving, and he'd told her that it hurt like hell but that it wasn't the reason he wasn't dancing. Kate didn't mind that he swore in front of her. He didn't say anything rough, but only what he thought, and she liked that spirit in him and that he didn't treat her like some wilting violet and that . . .

Well, really, she was wilting now. She pushed her papers aside and went down the steps. Outside at the pump, she couldn't find the dipper and so she took a long drink directly from the pail. She splashed water on her neck and forehead. She filled the pail again and dipped her fingers into it, making slow figure eights in the water and thinking she was hardly any closer to knowing what she would say to the Minervas. In a while, she heard the sound of her parents' voices in the street. It startled her, for she'd meant to have supper begun when they got back. The afternoon had already slipped away.

Kate set the pail down by the pump and walked across the grass. As she rounded the house, she saw her parents standing in the yard, hand in hand, her mother's head just tilted against her father's shoulder. It was a rare sight, and yet not unexpected. There were still times when her mother seemed almost young, still almost beautiful, and her father looked at her—charming man that he was—as though he'd won every single bet that he'd ever placed on a race day.

Kate moved back into the deep shadows at the corner of the house. She could call out to her parents. She could simply make a sound, and she wouldn't be alone anymore. Except that she would be, and that was the real thing about war, she thought. About all of it. It made a girl feel so very, very alone.

18

Sapientia gloria corona est

Motto of the Minerva Society, New Harmony, Indiana

Kate was in a great flurry. She'd gotten home from the Lichtenbergers' early and she'd started getting ready in plenty of time, but while she was reading John's latest letter again, she had first put a stocking on inside out and then, pulling it off, snagged it on her crate. She'd had to darn a hole big enough to put her thumb through. Now in the downstairs mirror, she saw how flushed she was. There was a red spot on the lower side of each cheek and her bonnet strings slashed both spots with a gray stripe. She pulled her gloves on, trying to remember if she'd forgotten anything and then, her paper gripped firmly in a gloved hand, she called her good-byes to her parents and the girls and went out the door.

In the street, she spied Charley and his friends, who were out for a walk after supper. They were hopping on the cobblestones, dodging the horse droppings, one-footed, and waiting for somebody to fall. She thought of scolding them, of warning them about their boots and trousers, but she'd promised John yet again to see to Charley especially, to be big sister and brother both. In her view, that strictly included indulging him.

"Kate, watch!" Charley was jigging his way around the largest pile of manure and he swung his arms and landed out of the street and onto the grass, still on one foot.

"Watch you when I've time for nothing at all? I'm late, Charley Given." Kate swung her skirts away from a bush in her path and lengthened her stride.

"The Minervas are meeting."

"Miss Given's a goddess. An honorary goddess."

"Charley, she'd notice if you'd take a spill."

"You'd be mustard-plastered all right."

Kate listened to the voices that followed her, boyish voices and one ready to crack, but she didn't turn around. The sun sat on the turret of David Dale's laboratory like one of Charley's red lollipops.

When Kate reached the Fauntleroys' house, Lizzy Marshal, who worked there, opened the door and Kate found herself momentarily nonplussed. From what she'd heard of the Minerva meetings, and admittedly it came only from gossip and overheard conversations, she knew they followed definite rules. They had an actual constitution and officers, and the girls were expected to read their friends' compositions before the meetings and be ready to critique them. The programs often had book reviews and music, and there was usually a subject for debate. Standing at the door, Kate felt she should explain herself. She should at least tell Lizzy that Mrs. Boren had invited her to come, and she was here for the actual meeting. But just like Charley's friends, Lizzy already seemed to know. She told Kate to come in, and she took her bonnet when Kate undid it—the dove-colored summer bonnet that had been her most extravagant purchase ever—and motioned her toward the parlor.

As Kate feared, the meeting had already started. She could hear Mrs. Preaus speaking in earnest tones and wondered if perhaps she was offering a prayer, though from what Kate understood, prayers weren't part of the meetings. Mrs. Preaus was making an exhortation of some sort— some encouragement to the Minervas to remain steadfast in the face of the sobering losses that had accompanied the victory at Gettysburg.

Kate wondered if she should wait for her to finish. Lizzie, though, nodded toward the parlor again, a little impatiently Kate thought, and so she tiptoed along the hallway. Taking a breath, she slipped through the doorway, hoping to move silently to a seat at the back.

She wasn't in luck. Martha Wilsey was seated next to the aisle the chairs made, and that was the end of a silent entrance. "Kate, I'll move down for you. Kate," Martha whispered, and Kate winced. To her—to everyone, she was sure—Martha's whisper was as loud as a shout and her chair groaned ominously as she extracted herself, all hips and skirts, to change places. Not for the first time, Kate wondered how Martha had made it into the Minervas, Harmony lineage notwithstanding.

Mrs. Preaus paused. She was one of the older Minervas who'd been included in the club to give it a greater degree of respectability and seriousness, and she'd been a Fauntleroy and was some kind of cousin to Constance. Kate could feel her waiting as she sat down. She wished for her bonnet strings, for curls like Eliza Twigg's rounded against her own cheeks to cover the red. Not that Eliza Twigg was at the meeting. From what Kate had heard, she was still in Evansville nursing troops at the hospital.

Kate sat frowning ahead to keep Martha silent. Then, slowly and carefully, as Mrs. Preaus resumed her reading, she eased her back into the chair. When she felt people had stopped noticing her, she began to look around. She had been in this house. She had been on the back porch and in the kitchen. She had been at the start of the hall and looked at the staircase, which curved around balusters at the bottom, making a sort of newel post. It was lightly decorated at the ends of each riser. Even for New Harmony, the house was not unusually large or finely crafted. It was a house, though, that seemed to carry itself (if you could say that about a house) as if it had brushed against grandeur. Or at least the illusions of it. It was the house where Constance's mother had held her school for young ladies.

Once, looking in an old Harmony paper, Kate had seen an advertisement for the school. What had struck her was that at the very same time she'd realized Biddy wasn't as strong as she and John were and had the premonition she might one day slip away, girls had come to Mrs. Fauntleroy's school to benefit, indirectly, from all the education her father, Robert Owen, had lavished on his children. A girl in this house would have learned history. She would have studied geometry and composition, as well as natural philosophy (Kate didn't know what that was) and astronomy and botany. She would have heard lectures from Mrs. Fauntleroy's brother, Dr. David Dale Owen, who would have illustrated what he said about chemistry or geology or mineralogy with experiments and apparatuses. And the piano in this very room—Kate could see the shadow of one heavily carved leg against the wall—and the harp, with its fine wood and its bronzed column and copper strings, would have been the heart of the musical education. And because it was a school run by an Owen—Mrs. R. H. Fauntleroy as the ad said, but Mrs. Jane Dale or Mrs. Jane Dale Owen Fauntleroy to everyone who spoke of her (or simply Mrs. Fauntleroy now that she was dead)—there would have been instruction not only in French and in drawing, but in dancing, which the Owens loved almost as much as they loved racing horses. And, too, because it was a school run by an Owen, its goals were idealistic. In her ad, Mrs. Fauntleroy had promised nothing less than physical health, kindness and moral feelings, and well-informed minds in her students.

Looking at the newspaper, Kate had added up the charges. For all this education—and the added cost of boarding, bedding, and washing—it would have been sixty dollars a quarter per girl, a third of that for the use of the piano and harp. She'd shown John the ad, and perhaps she'd sounded a little envious, for John had told her that, as fine as Mrs. Jane Dale seemed to be, her school would not have been worth a penny of Given money if it had turned a single one of his sisters into a person like Constance Fauntleroy.

Kate stared at the daguerreotype of Mrs. Fauntleroy hanging above the table next to Mrs. Preaus. In it, she was pretty and delicate in her widow's weeds. Kate thought of the stories of her mourning her husband's death inconsolably, and yet still managing to take her children abroad for them to finish their education and to see their grandfather, Mr. Owen, who'd returned there much earlier and, like his son Robert Dale, taken up spiritualism. There was real history in this house. The fact was, as her father would say, it was just plain lousy with history. Kate felt a prick of eagerness simply in thinking of it.

Martha Wilsey's breathing had grown heavy, and Kate, nudging her, thought Mrs. Preaus's admonition on the duties of wartime had grown long for Martha, too. But she was finishing now. "And that, ladies," she said, "is our part: to continue on the home front those efforts toward gentility, toward wisdom and art which our brave men seek to defend. As a finer voice of our town has said before me, 'May the light of Truth continue to emanate, and at length shine out so refulgent, that Error shall fly trembling before it.' "

With that, Mrs. Preaus was done. She took her seat to applause, water glass in hand. Kate was dismayed at herself. Not only had she not listened to most of what Mrs. Preaus had said, but she was still distracted and as fidgety as a child. Though the windows were open and a light breeze blowing up a thin veil of dust in the street, it was warm in the room, and her leg itched from the darn in her stocking. Just what had she missed? For that matter, why was she here if she wasn't to have the benefit of it? Her paper, of course, but she did want to concentrate.

It was Rachel Fauntleroy's turn to speak—William Fauntleroy's wife who had been Rachel Homer when Kate had first known who she was. Kate commanded herself to pay attention. She meant, after all, to write to Harry Beal about this meeting, for even if Harry wasn't easily impressed, and didn't care to *be* impressed (he was a latecomer here, after all, with only a year on her in New Harmony), he still had ties to this part of the community since his uncle had built the *Philanthropist*. Kate wanted him to know that she'd been here. She wanted him to know that she could hold her own with the Minerva girls and women. Not that Harry was one for philosophy, and probably not even the Emerson essay that Rachel Fauntleroy was discussing, which was all about self-reliance.

Kate, however, was interested in her method. First Mrs. Fauntleroy read a sentence of Emerson (the one that struck Kate was the one she began with: *to believe your own thought, to believe that what is true for you in your private heart is true for all men—that is genius*) and then she explained it in more homely terms, as if all of Emerson's ideas were essentially about the talents the Owenites or Harmonists had brought to New Harmony. Teacher that she was, she had props. She tapped bells when she said that "sculpture in the memory is not without pre-established harmony." She worked a sliding triangle to emphasize that Emerson had taken aim at three categories of men when he said, "A foolish consistency is the hobgoblin of little minds, adored by little statesmen and philosophers and divines." She manipulated an abacus and said he believed that children make no calculations before their actions, while adults have an arithmetic that computes the "strength and means opposed to our purpose."

Kate wanted a closer look at the beaded bracelet with the scarlet flowers Rachel Fauntleroy held up when she proclaimed, with Emerson, that for nonconformity, "the world whips you with its displeasure." Kate was not sure she understood the argument entirely, but small as the bracelet looked from where she was sitting, it had caught her eye. It was beautiful, she thought, beautiful and vivid in the manner of Mrs. Beal's garden in its prime.

Kate measured her wrist with her fingers, then unrolled her paper and placed it on her lap. She was suddenly nervous. Mrs. Boren had given her a smile of encouragement when she came into the room, but she didn't know if that was enough. If she was to read the first essay she'd ever written in her whole life aloud to New Harmony's most cultured young women, there was no way she couldn't be apprehensive, though she was excited, too. After all, if she did well, Constance Fauntleroy might be impressed and ask her back. Maybe she would even ask her to join the society, which Kate would certainly do. What better way could there be to improve her mind? Of course, she would expect a tart letter from John about it if she did for, proud as he was, he was always wary of his sisters trying to make friends where they might not be wanted. And he'd mocked the Minervas.

"What's this slogan again?" he'd asked when he first saw it in a book Martha Wilsey was carrying. When Martha gave him the translation—*Wisdom is glory's crown*—he shook his head and laughed. "It doesn't say that," he told her. "Where's the possessive in the Latin, and what would it mean anyway, that wisdom is glory's crown?"

But Kate was not going to worry about John. She was here as a guest. She'd been invited and if Rachel Fauntleroy's presentation was the one that would be discussed—the one that was being discussed now—and Kate's paper was meant as something extra to round out the evening, it was simply a matter for Kate of reminding herself that, though she wasn't educated, she was smart enough. She was from a family of bright people, from John with his superior education—as good or better than anyone's in New Harmony—to Dennis O'Donnell, who'd bumbled at becoming schoolmaster in Drumboarty but still done it, all the way to James Mulhern, known as a mathematician throughout all of Ireland. In spite of her endless battle with spelling, Kate thought she had nothing to be ashamed of and if she was to fail here, which she wouldn't—she wasn't going to—it would not be because she hadn't prepared well and not because she'd not held her head up, wobbly as her knees might become.

The discussion had moved from the specifics of the Emerson paper to Emerson himself and to the brilliance of the Transcendentalists, and then on to Brook Farm. "Grandfather Owen's community was earlier and more ambitious, and the phalanxes at Brook Farm were quite derivative of his phalanstery, even if you consider Fourier's," Constance Fauntleroy said (it had been two years, but Kate thought she would never get used to Constance being a Mrs. and a Runcie). There were murmurs of assent but no further comments. Kate was holding so tightly to her paper that she could feel the thumbprints she'd left in it. She still had to wait, for there was a fine harp and piano duet to listen to, though the truth was that she scarcely heard a note until Constance Fauntleroy stroked her hand across all the harp strings and then let it fall at her side and sat motionless before raising her head for the applause. Finally, Constance stood up.

"Charlotte has asked that we suspend the rules and have Miss Given say a few words to us before we adjourn," she said. "We have no copies, but I believe she'll address our ongoing debate on whether war or slavery is the greater evil." She turned to Kate. "Your brother went to Nashoba?"

"With Al Norcross," Kate said, glancing at Isabelle Wheatcroft, Eleanor's sister. She'd turned in her chair and, now that she could see them all, she took in the whole group of young women. They had basically stuffed the parlor with their broad expanse of skirts, and Kate thought that, in Donegal, if there'd been dresses like this at a country house hooley, there would have been room for only one woman. She took a breath and stood up in her place. "There was just a bit of the foundation left and the corners," she said, "and he wasn't sure of it. A slave took them there, John and Al Norcross and three other boys. There was an apple orchard in the woods, and it was the best proof of it for Frances Wright planted an orchard."

"And they've no other orchards in Tennessee?" she heard someone whisper and Kate, swallowing, felt herself flush again.

"I've written on war as a utopian tradition," she said, moving to the front of the room and making the effort to look out into all the faces that were looking at her, "and how it is that so many people who feel a change is needed in a given situation—whether it's Catholics in Ireland as my family were, with very few freedoms and opportunities, or Frances Wright wanting to end slavery—how they assume that the right plan, if it's acted upon, will bring a utopia, that the removal of a burden or an injustice will create the opposite circumstance: a condition of pure justice or of . . . unfetteredness." Kate hesitated, wondering if she'd made up a word. Then she quickly looked down, hunting in her paper to find her place.

"So Miss Given is bringing coals to Newcastle," Anna Owen, David Dale's daughter, said in a clear voice from across the room.

Hearing her, Kate was flustered, not sure if she was supposed to respond. Then she realized she was in luck, for her answer was ready in her very next line. "It's not about New Harmony," she said. "It's not about the Rappites or Mr. Owen's community. It's the utopian idea, the idea that something will be changed so that it's fixed forever like a greased wheel that never stops rolling. If there could be such a thing," she added.

Kate sensed a rustling in the room, the shifting of all those fine dresses, and she saw Miriam Elliott and Anna Owen stand up and go into the hall, where it had to be cooler, and where Lizzie Marshal had set out cookies and pitchers of iced tea. Kate picked up the pace of her reading and moved so she faced the group more from the corner and could address the hallway as well. "We could say," she continued, "that the war itself is a utopian venture, for of course it is about reaching for an ideal—the sort of platonic ideal that Sir Thomas More sketched in his *Utopia* and what Mr. Lincoln has called 'a more perfect union.' For the South there is likely such an ideal as well: a way of life unhindered by Northern meddling or restriction. And perhaps, as many have said, the conflict has been irresistible.

"But what can it achieve when lives are interrupted and lives are lost in a seemingly endless series of battles that keep our soldiers, who are our own loved ones, far from home—or even kill them? What can be gained that is ideal or utopian?"

"Miss Given, you are saying you oppose the war?" Miriam Elliott stepped back into the doorway as she asked her question.

"No," Kate said, trying to make her voice as firm as she could. "That's another matter. What I am saying—and I've written it here farther along—is that reality, by its very nature, will fall short of any ideal." Kate looked down at her paper and then back at the room. "Certainly that happens in the process of war when men head off intending to plant the colors for a cause, but die of something as ungallant as typhoid."

"You think, then, that Alexander Fretageot's death was ungallant?"

Kate felt her eyes twitch. "No, of course not. I didn't mean that at all," she said. "It's my larger point that we need utopias to strive for. I didn't mean anything about people dying from typhoid. Perfection can't exist, but our own everyday dissatisfactions can still push us toward hope that it does. We can make changes that move us away from feeling trapped. Which means we can feel we've made progress." Kate turned a page and then went back two and quickly scanned her handwriting. "But I had an example about the draft, if I could offer it. If I could read it."

There was more rustling in the room, and Kate found the section she wanted. "If a soldier volunteers to fight for what he believes in, we can say that he has cast his vote for this utopian idea: that blood spent for a cause will purify it and somehow bring a reign of honest peace. But if a man is drafted for a cause that he has not made his own, he lives with resentment rather than hope and so we see—"

"The draft riots?" Constance Fauntleroy, who had joined the others in the hall, had come back to stand in the doorway. She looked sharply at Kate, her long face and just rabbity chin not even close to seeming pretty with the frown on her face. "You've come to justify the draft riots your countrymen have visited on New York, Miss Given? Is that it?" She stood just leaning forward in the doorway as she spoke. "Have you seen the pictures in *Harper's Weekly*? Did you see the Negro hung from a tree? Did you read about the Irish looters and Irish throng that burned the Aged Colored Woman's Home and an orphanage for black children? Is this the utopian impulse that brought the Irish to our shores? A people lacking in freedoms you say, but isn't it because of a religion that allows such things?"

In all her life, Kate had not heard words of such venom, and yet there was a tone to Constance Fauntleroy's voice that suggested she felt she was not being rude but simply forthright, merely stating the obvious (and it was true, of course, about the orphanage and the Irish rioting). Kate tried to gather herself. She thought of attempting to finish her point, but she had no idea of how to retake the reins of her argument. She thought that perhaps Constance had spoken merely to stimulate debate and that someone else would jump in with a comment. She heard only silence. Martha Wilsey, who was the one person here that Kate had thought was her friend, had turned toward the wall, clearly embarrassed. Mrs. Boren didn't turn away; she was, however, gravely still. The others in the room seemed to be waiting for Kate's reaction and Kate was waiting for it herself, her face burning. She looked down at the pages in her hands. It seemed now such folly to her that she had written them, and she was suddenly very angry. At Constance Fauntleroy. At everyone in the room. Mostly, she was angry at herself.

"Yes, of course," she said. "A religion that urges us to such acts. Give me a Negro orphan, and I'll set fire to her myself so she doesn't threaten my job. We're like that, we Catholics, we Irish. But Miss Fauntleroy—Mrs. Runcie—if I might remind you, it's not my brother who's paid three hundred dollars for a Negro to take his place in the war."

In her mind's eye, as if they'd come to stand at the window like a Greek chorus ready to cry, "Oh, Kate!" she saw her mother and sisters and all the Smith girls and Margaret Mulhern. Kate brushed her hand across her mouth. She touched her lips. Slowly, she folded her paper in two and ran her fingers the length of the crease. Too late now, she wished she'd taken John's advice that she not go where she wasn't wanted, and that she keep her too-ready sword in its sheath. Her words had been cruel words, she knew, for even if Arthur Fauntleroy had chosen not to fight, the year before the war, Constance's brother Edward had died in California.

She could not backtrack, though, or take back her words. She lowered her eyes and, without raising them, put her paper under her arm and, passing by Constance Fauntleroy, walked out of the room. In the hallway, she took her bonnet from the table, glad that Lizzie Marshal was no longer there to hand it to her. The silence had turned to whispers, but she did not look back. She went out to the porch and, as she pulled the door behind her, she knew, with a growing darkness, that she was closing this particular door forever.

Not that it had actually been open. In truth, Kate thought as she turned up the street, it had always been quite firmly shut.

New Harmony, Indiana
November 1863

19

Memphis, Tenn., 29 Oct., 1863

*Private John Given Co. "A" 25th Indiana Infty is hereby detailed to accom-
pany Major John T. Walker of said Regiment going north on sick leave.
Having performed this duty Private Given will return to his Regiment with all
possible despatch.*

**By order
Brig. Genl. Veatch**

I f he ruled out the larger sorts of animals such as camels or
elephants, John was sure that he and Major Walker had been
on practically every form of conveyance known to man. Since
they'd left Memphis a week ago—John ordered to accompany the major home on sick leave—he'd used all his wits trying to
arrange transport that would keep the major at a minimum level of
discomfort. His best had hardly been good enough. The major was
weak and in great pain, and when at last they'd boarded a steamer
with fresh air to breathe and the clean scent of the river as it lapped
against the boat, he'd told John that he no longer had a sense of smell.
John hadn't said anything, but he'd realized what a terrible irony it
meant for a man who was tormented by the raw stench of the cars
they'd ridden that were taking captive Rebels north to Chicago. If
only things could have been reversed.

The major was asleep now, though it was a fitful sleep at best.
They were very close to Evansville, and John hoped the telegram he'd
sent from Paducah had reached the major's family and that someone
would be waiting at the landing with broth and blankets and a carriage
to take him home, that there would be a doctor as skilled at caring for

him as Major Walker, the surgeon of the regiment, had always been with the troops. And as long as he was hoping, John hoped, too, that he wouldn't be needed for long and could quickly catch the stagecoach or the mail packet or another boat to New Harmony.

In all the Memphis months that the 25th had spent as provost guard and as many captured Rebels as he'd watched in Memphis, for John there'd been something particularly bothersome about the hollow-eyed men he'd seen on the cars he and Major Walker had ridden. It was because of Levi, he thought. In fact, he was sure it was because of Levi. A month ago, Levi and his team had been taken when they were on a scout with the regiment east of Memphis. At headquarters, before the regiment had gone out, there had been general concern about increased activity among the guerrillas. When John warned Levi as he harnessed his team, sweat already soaking his shirt, Levi had made light of it. "If they capture me, they'll have to leave these mules behind. They're lazy bastards. There's no Rebel could drive them."

John wished it had been true. He wished the Rebels had left the mules. He wished they'd left Levi. But the story he'd heard from Max Munte when the men returned had made his heart rise into his throat. Max, who'd recently come back from his furlough a bridegroom, had been pale even for him. "Jack, I thought I'd made Mary Taylor a widow," he said, and then he'd told John how Captain Darling had sent a detail foraging for pumpkins and the guerrillas had appeared out of nowhere, their guns blazing. Max had gotten away but, Levi, who was well in the rear with no cavalry around, had been an easy target. The guerrillas had hurled the pumpkins off his wagon and forced him to turn it into the woods. "It was a huge mess of smashed pumpkins," Max said. "That's what they left."

John wasn't over feeling guilty that he'd been at headquarters working on papers when it happened. He still felt the same intense dismay. He could picture the scene. He could hear the pumpkins thunking and popping. And as much as he was looking forward to the short time he could spend at home after he had Major Walker situated, he wasn't at all eager to see Levi's mother. He knew he could offer the usual platitudes. He could tell her what he'd written to his parents—that she was much luckier than mothers whose sons had died, for she would see Levi again. And as much as John wanted to believe that was true—and as much as he believed that it was—he still thought captivity would go harder on Levi than most men, for confinement of any kind had never suited him. Caroline had confided to Kate, who had confided to him, that Levi was a dreadful patient when he was home wounded. He was too unsettled and tossing about to mend quickly. John thought he was restless by nature.

But if he was not looking forward to seeing Mrs. Thrailkill, he could still scarcely wait to be home. It had been nearly twenty months since his leave after Fort Donelson. As the boat angled across the current and edged toward land, he could see Evansville. The sight of it seemed so sweetly Indiana that his first impulse was to cross himself. Instead, he put his hands on the rail and watched the buildings grow nearer and larger. The boat shuddered in toward the landing, and John realized that, for all his anticipation, he still felt ambivalent, and not just because of Mrs. Thrailkill. He was of two minds about parting with Major Walker, for he'd worried as much over him since they'd left Memphis as if he were an infant to care for. And, more than that, he was feeling a little gun-shy about returning to New Harmony and trading the name on the packages that had found their way to him in Memphis, for his actual self right there for any person to make inquiries of and wish well or ill. And he was eager and nervous about Ann. That was the main thing.

John felt his heart lurch with the boat. It was all starting to feel real. He was going home. He was practically there, and that was the wonderful fact of it. Really, he couldn't help but laugh to himself at the pleasure he felt and at how Kate had prodded him in a letter to do everything he could to get a furlough since the men she'd encountered at balls from other regiments had done just that. It was "griping," as she'd put it, for those who had friends in the army to see others come home when they couldn't see the men they loved themselves.

Done, Kate, he thought. He'd finally gotten himself considered dispensable at headquarters and the best man, with his knowledge of procuring transportation, for getting Major Walker home. Soon he would be back in New Harmony. He would actually be there.

Major Walker stirred beside him, and John reached under the blankets into the major's pocket for a rolled cigarette. He lit it, holding it for him to smoke as the boat moved in close.

"We're here," he told him. "We'll be tied up at any moment. You've come home, sir."

John scanned the throng of people and stacks of parcels on the shore until the crowd had thinned out and he was certain that no one was waiting for Major Walker. There wasn't a carriage. There wasn't even a rude wagon hired to meet him. John cursed the man he'd paid to send his telegram in Paducah. He thought of the story the troops all knew about General Grant, of how he'd angered General Halleck and nearly lost his command after Fort Donelson when a Secesh-leaning postmaster in Cairo stole his dispatches, and General Halleck thought he'd left his post to go to Nashville without notifying him. There was nothing in the communications line that a man could rely on in wartime. Nothing at all.

John considered what to do. He could take the major to his home and hope there was someone there to care for him. Or he could take him to the hospital and know that the major would get whatever help the doctors and nurses could offer him while John set about finding his family and letting them know where he was.

Major Walker tried to raise himself but fell back against his cot. "Look in my bag, John. Is there morphine?" he said between shivers, and John pulled his blankets up to his neck.

"There's not, sir." John shook his head to make sure the major understood him. "But we're going to the hospital."

Which was why, after getting the aid of two deckhands who helped him lift the cot up like a stretcher, John found himself once again in a ward of sick and wounded soldiers, a ward that stretched on and on, its sheets—cleaner than anything a soldier would ever see in a field hospital—moving like white caps on a very slow sea. He had heard in a letter from Harry Beal that Lydia Hinckley worked here with the Red Cross, and he wondered if he might find himself thinking once more that he was seeing her in the distance, yet uncertain it was really her. Instead, to his surprise, he encountered Eliza Twigg, who at first acted as if she hadn't recognized him—and perhaps hadn't—but then quickly answered his request that she find a doctor to attend to Major Walker. After the doctor had seen to him, she bathed his face and hands herself. Then with John helping, she got him into a clean shirt.

When the major was asleep once more, his hair so smoothly combed against his pale skin that John kept staring at the part, Eliza spoke to John in quiet tones, and it was really the first time they'd ever had an actual conversation. She was William Twigg's daughter, and her mother was Virginia Poulard Dupalais, who had come to New Harmony on the famous boat and, along with Lucy Sistaire, been under Madame Fretageot's care. John thought the first story he'd ever heard about New Harmony had been about Miss Dupalais, who was now the elderly and ill Mrs. Twigg. It was from the Count of Saxe-Weimar. He'd visited New Harmony in 1826 and written that he'd seen her playing the piano and singing quite beautifully and then—because she had been brought to a community of equality—being interrupted at her music to take her turn milking cows. Enraged, and with rebellious tears, she had stormed her patrician self outside to do it.

"It's only me here now from New Harmony," Eliza said. "Florence Dale died, of course. And Ellen and Lydia Hinckley have gone to their brother in Sacramento. Adino. Did you know him? They're working in the mining camps. They teach English to Chinese men. Ann Bradley's in town, staying with her sister, but I haven't seen her here at the hospital."

John let the name register without an overt response. He thought Eliza had glanced at him from the corner of her eye when she said it, but he wasn't sure. He was startled, however, unnerved he was already in the same town as Ann and suddenly looking foursquare at the unpleasant but undeniable fact he'd preferred to avoid: if he had a life for every letter Ann Bradley had sent him since he'd been in Memphis, he'd still have just the one life he'd started with.

Eliza laughed all of a sudden. "You should have seen Susan Arnoldy and Ann in the play this spring. Such melodramatics—from Ann in particular."

"I heard about it," John answered, but he didn't tell Eliza Twigg that, in an attempt at wit that would provoke a response, he'd written Ann he would give more to see Susan's grandmother come onstage in pursuit of her old cow than to watch her and Susan perform after a twelvemonth's study. He stood up. "I need to find the major's family. You've been extremely kind," he said, and he realized just how tired he was. For all the foul smells and moaning around him, he would have gladly taken a cot so he could lie down.

When he asked her where the commander's office was, Eliza told him. Then, looking at the major, who had fallen into a deep, morphine-induced sleep, she added, "Leave his trunk if you need to, but take his medical bag and his watch. There's nothing's safe here. We've good men and we've men that, I'm quite sure, would get up from their deathbeds to steal from their mothers."

John did as she said. He slipped the major's watch out of his pocket (how very long ago it seemed since General Veatch and his adjutant's watches had been stolen in St. Louis), and he put it in the bag. Then he shook hands with Eliza Twigg and saluted the major as he slept and made his way through the crowded ward, wishing with all his might that he could head straight to New Harmony, and take Ann along with him.

Instead, he made inquiries until he'd found the major's house and gotten Mrs. Walker to the hospital. By the time he'd arranged for the major to go home by ambulance and had waited in the interminable line at the post commander's to see to his and the major's paperwork, another day and two precious dollars for a hotel room had slipped away. He had learned where Mary Armstrong, Ann's sister, lived and had made his way there, but no one answered his knock. Not on the first visit. Not on the second. If he'd been a white-gloved fellow with cards, he would certainly have left one. Since he wasn't, he wrote a short note that took him longer to compose than he wanted it to, standing exposed as he was on the Armstrongs' porch. He left it weighted down by a rock, wondering what Ann would make of his offer to call on his return to Evansville. Then he went back to the hospital and looked for Eliza Twigg. When he didn't find her, he finished his business and, checking his purse, decided on the stagecoach home.

Finally, then, he was riding shotgun on the road west and listening to the coachman, who stunk worse of tobacco juice and rotting teeth than any soldier John had ever smelled. He went on and on about the fair. He talked about the big Shoe there'd been in New Harmony that had more than a hundred horses. It was a story John would rather have heard from his father.

"Barely a fraction of Shiloh," John said, "the number of horses, I mean," and an image of slaughtered horses suddenly assaulted him.

"What?" The coachman turned with his rank breath, and John shook his head.

"Nothing," he answered, though he could all but hear horses screaming once more, an ungodly mixture of angry whinny and the fierce explosion of air when the bullets struck. His mind stayed for the longest time on a horse's eye that had changed, as though a shadow had passed over it, from glassy to a clouded gray.

To his delight, when the stage came into New Harmony, John spotted Mary walking down Main Street. If it had not been for her slightly broader nose and slightly lighter hair, he might have thought she was Margaret, she had grown so much. He'd just missed her birthday, but he had brought her a small gilt picture frame from Memphis for turning sweet sixteen. He had presents for all of the family, though not what he might have liked. His clerk's pay was thirteen dollars a month—steady pay, to be sure, if it was actually paid, but griping, to use Kate's word, when you knew that your brother who was eighteen made twenty dollars harvesting tobacco and Charley, young as he was, earned twelve.

The stage stopped in front of Fretageots', and John called Mary's name at the same moment that she saw him. "John, oh—John!" She gave a little shriek and he caught her off the ground in a hug when she ran to him and twirled her around before he put her back down. "You're really home? Aunt Mary was coming from Chicago. She'll feel so bad she put off her visit. Father thinks she'll never come. They never do visit, John."

"I'm here, though."

"And I've got you first! Kate will be so jealous. You look thin, John."

"And you've grown up," he said. "What have you done with my little sister?"

"You really think I'm grown?" Mary looked at him with excited eyes and John laughed, for she seemed the same child that she'd always been.

"Of course I do," he said, draping his haversack over her shoulder and thinking how different it was coming home this time when nobody was really expecting him and he had two sound feet on the ground. Or as sound as they would ever be.

"We should go to Mother first," Mary said and, as they turned off Main to start up Church Street, she kept up her chatter. She talked about the fair and about the men in the 15th who people thought were in Chattanooga with Rosecrans and would fight a big battle soon, and how lucky Harry Beal was he was still in Louisville, though he'd hoped to get home for the fair. She said Mr. Miller, the postmaster, was harassed and poked fun at for trying to get Max Munte hung as a Copperhead on the strength of a letter he'd written (Mr. Miller had denied actually opening it), and she told him what he already knew about Max marrying Mary Taylor and having to report to Captain Darling at Evansville before he could even say good-bye to her. Kate had been very angry, for she'd fixed a wedding supper at the Lichtenbergers', and there was a bride but no groom.

Their father, Mary said, had called John Hunt Morgan, the Rebel general, a sneaking coward as well as a horse thief for deserting his men in Ohio, though it hadn't done Morgan a bit of good since he'd been caught and was in prison now, and John knew, didn't he, that Jim Randolph and Martha Wilsey were engaged? Waltzing had become so much the rage at balls that she and Margaret were practicing it with each other. Kate Marshal had gone for the body of Jacob Schaen when he died so suddenly in July (one more painful reminder for John of losing his fine little friend), and she'd done it in spite of the fact she didn't know him, that Mr. Wilsey had sent her since Jake had worked for him. There was word that Fred Perkey was sick in St. Louis. He was in the hospital once more, and Annie and her mother hoped he'd be back in New Harmony soon so they could nurse him well. Most surprising of all—and Mary didn't even know if John would believe it—Margaret Mulhern had gotten so nervous and excited about Charles Ward coming home on furlough that she'd actually scorched the gown she was ironing for Mrs. Maidlow to be laid out in.

And there was something the matter with Kate. She got snappish and on her high horse, and she'd spent all her time reading at the library and then she'd quit reading altogether.

"Mary Given's Catalogue of Comings and Goings, and Death and Destruction," John said. He laughed and took back his haversack, which she'd been shifting from side to side.

"I just told you there were some people that got married, or at least they intend to." Mary looked at him with a slightly hurt expression, and he laughed again and gave her a hug.

"You've no idea what a sound you are for sore ears. Go on ahead. Have Mother sit down."

In the evening, the house was full of celebration. His mother had held on to him so long when he walked in the door that John thought she would cut off his circulation. His father had just kept pounding him on the shoulder, and Kate had burst into tears, but by suppertime the house was full of neighbors bringing food and offering so many toasts that John thought he was tighter from drink than he'd ever been since he joined the army. The Thrailkills didn't come, and of course Ann Bradley wasn't there, but he remembered that, sometime before the guests had left and he'd fallen asleep in front of the fire, he'd danced a wild jig with Francis Cannon while his father played the fiddle. In the night, more than once he woke up panicked that his gun wasn't next to him, and in the morning his head was fierce, and he doubted he was even a Given, he minded a hangover so. He thought how much his mother must have missed him, for she gave him coffee without a reproving word, though she had a lot of them for Denis.

Everyone was the same, John thought, but everyone was different. He could tell that before he'd gotten through even a handful of his Memphis stories, which were possible to tell if he left big gaps and only talked about the swarms of people and soldiers and the river clogged with boats and the music that was stirring in a way he'd rarely felt before. Twangy. Loose. "There's banjo music everywhere," he said. "You'd like it, Father. Five strings, and it's dandy for a jig."

"And I'm too old to learn a new trick," his father answered.

His mother seemed not even to hear him when he mentioned Memphis. "We wished you home so much at fair time," she said. She stroked his hair, and he saw that her own hair had gone a shade closer to white from its sheeny gray.

"But he wouldn't be here *now*, Mother," Mary said, keeping her proprietary air as the one who'd brought him home, and John thought again that she was prettily grown in spite of the little girl who remained. Margaret was pensive, more apt than ever to drift into her own dreamy world, and Denis had the muscles of a dockworker, and Charley had shot up into a string bean. But Mary was right. Of all his brothers and sisters, Kate was the one who seemed to have changed the most.

For one thing, she seemed to be avoiding being alone with him, and he didn't know why, though he expected it had something to do with whatever it was that had altered her disposition enough that it felt unfamiliar. It was so much her nature to be impulsive that, though she was the oldest of his sisters, he'd assumed she would always seem youthful and, in some way, happily exuberant. In other words, she would stay Kate. But there was something oddly dispirited about her now. She reminded him a little of the young women he'd seen who'd gone from being the liveliest girls at the dance to the worn and faded mothers of many small children.

John thought she would talk to him when she was ready, that she'd shake her mood. But when he handed out the gifts he'd brought to the family, and gave her a story on Nashoba, which he'd copied from an old Memphis paper, and a piece of apple wood from Fanny Wright's purported orchard that he'd carved with Fanny's profile—the distinctive lips and chin—she thanked him, but very somberly. Then she folded everything away in the paper he'd brought it home in. "Did you want French lingerie instead?" he asked her, teasing, and even that didn't bring a smile.

"You were very thoughtful, John," she said, but that was all she said, and it occurred to him, watching her, that his furlough might be over and done with before he even knew what was wrong. He thought he had to press her.

In the morning he got up early and found her in the kitchen getting ready to go to the Lichtenbergers'. She had a slice of bread on her plate and was drinking her tea.

"I'll walk with you," he said, cutting some bread for himself. "We'll walk in the dark like we did to Grandpa Given's when we went with him mornings to tend his still."

"It wasn't a still."

"Of course it was. Did you think it was water we carried home in the jugs?"

Kate picked up the last chunk of her bread and got her cloak from the hook by the door. "I have to leave," she said. "If you're coming, come along. I won't be late."

John followed her and closed the door when they went out into the street. It was a pre-reveille, chilly sort of dark, and the air was damp. "Is it getting old, Kate, minding other people's children and another woman's house?" he asked, not waiting but trying a frontal assault.

"When I might have my own?" Kate said. She gathered her cloak around her and pulled it up so it hooded her face. "No, John. Whatever you're suggesting, that's not the case. And, anyway, the Lichtenberger girls are hardly children any longer. Alice has a regular set of young women she goes about with, and Mary will soon. Eliza's still a pet, but even she's already nine."

The milk wagon rattled in the street beyond them and, listening to it, John had to catch himself to realize where he was, to remember that all the quiet houses along the street sheltered families and lives that were about something very different from the war. "Listen, Kate," he said. "We can skirt around this—whatever this is—wiggle it like a loose tooth. Or you can tell me what's happened. You know you'll tell me sooner or later, and you might as well start now. And I'd thank you to do it so I don't have to spend my furlough watching you look glum."

"A person can't be reserved without being accused of being glum?"

"When were you ever reserved in your whole life, Kate Given? Yes, you're glum. You're glum as can be."

They were walking quickly up the street, and Kate stayed silent. John thought that he'd made a tactical error—played his big card of her threat to his furlough and gotten her back up instead of gaining her sympathy.

"I saw Eliza Twigg at the hospital in Evansville," he said, changing his tack. He wanted to draw her into the town gossip and see where that went, but she looked at him sharply.

"What did she tell you?"

"That the Hinckley girls are in California with their brother and that she found Susan Arnoldy and Ann Bradley amusing in the play. What do you think she would she tell me?"

Kate said nothing. They were almost at the Lichtenbergers', and John reached out for her arm and drew her to a stop. "Kate," he said.

She wouldn't look at him when she spoke. "You don't have better things to do, John, than to badger me and make me late for work? I don't want to spoil your furlough. Not at all. But I've nothing to say. Have I asked you about your time in Utah?"

"My what?"

"Utah. Memphis. Whichever you please."

"Is that what's bothering you? I'd think you'd believe me, Kate, when I said the girls in Memphis were pretty, but there weren't hard tales on us Posey lads. I wrote as much to Harry Beal and you can ask Harry if you've decided that you won't believe me.

"And what did Harry write you?" Kate said quickly, and John gave her a frowning look, and then he laughed, an odd sound even to him in the dark street.

"I gather there's a regular army of people privy to knowledge I'm not?"

Silence again.

"If I'm badgering you, I'll stop," he said. "It's just that I count on your being happy. But, of course, I can't make you happy if you aren't."

"And you'll make me less happy if you tell me that I'm not. Mrs. Lichtenberger has her lamp on. I really have to go." Kate started across the street, and then she came back. "It's not important. Not really," she said. "But did Harry say anything about seeing me when he was home?"

Harry Beal twice? The sky was just beginning to lighten, and John looked past Kate at the trees as they started to take form. "Just that he had a good time visiting at the house. Nothing else."

"He didn't say I was at his aunt's house? Not in the house. But there?"

John shook his head.

"You're sure?"

"I'm sure," John answered, and Kate's face softened a little, and she pulled her skirt away from the droppings the milk cart horse had left and hurried across the street.

$\sim$

For all that he had longed to be home and as short as his furlough was, John found himself feeling dull, and it wasn't just because of Kate's mood and the lack of Ann Bradley. Michael McShane was working on a job in Mount Vernon and, except for those of his friends who'd seemed to grow old in his absence and never even wanted to leave their houses, almost every man John really knew was off at the war. There were young men in town, of course, but they were people like Achilles Fretageot and Horace Owen, who weren't in the army and wouldn't be, whether it was from not having their names appear in the draft or from buying their way out as Horace had the year after his father, Colonel Owen, sent him home from the 60th. John didn't really hold it against them. Mr. Fretageot had already lost his oldest son and the Owen family, from Colonel Owen on down, was well represented in the Union ranks. And, too, John wouldn't be a hypocrite about it. He didn't want Denis enlisting or being drafted, and so he wouldn't judge another person's motives. Yet he couldn't help feeling he'd lived in some way that a man like Achilles Fretageot had not and, even if he'd moved in the same circles with him and Horace Owen, which he certainly didn't, he doubted he would ever find much to talk about with them. From what he could tell, their lives were filled with ventures and frolics. And Horace, although he'd been an officer, seemed to have all but forgotten the war and so had Achilles. They both seemed a part of another world.

His main errand, aside from escorting Major Walker home, was delivering the packages and letters Captain Boren had sent to his wife. When he called at the Sampsons', it felt odd having Margaret Mulhern open the door to him and lead him to the parlor to wait while she called Mrs. Boren and then disappeared into the kitchen herself. He wanted to call Margaret back, but of course he couldn't. He promised himself that he would take her for a long walk to cemetery hill and ask her to tell him everything Charles Ward had said to her when he'd had his furlough, although it had been August when Charles was home. It might seem like old news even to Margaret. He wanted to ask her about Kate, too, though for some reason he thought she wouldn't have an answer and he thought, as well, that just asking would seem disloyal to Kate. Then, while he was considering all this, Mrs. Boren came in, her hand extended in a gracious greeting, and John spoke with her almost as easily as he had in Memphis. She had him sit down to open his pack, but he didn't stay long. He left her with packages on her lap and opening a letter.

The evenings, he found, were better than the days, for there were always gatherings at people's homes and lots of girls to talk with. He had the distinct impression that Mrs. Thrailkill, who seemed to take trouble harder than just about anyone, could not bear to see him at all. If they ended up at the same gathering, Caroline apologized to him with her eyes, which were really quite expressive. Then she left with her mother, though once she did manage to slip over to John and tell him it was just that Levi had been home, too, on his last furlough, and her mother felt bad seeing John without him.

On these evening visits, John tried to put Ann Bradley out of his mind, though he kept wondering if he would get a response to his note—or if Ann might even turn up in New Harmony. At times, the whole Ann situation felt distasteful to him. He didn't like pursuing a woman who had so much less interest in him than he had in her. He didn't like it either that his best friend was as interested in her as he was, though with basically the same result. He particularly hated it that, with Ann, a person didn't really know what fellow she might decide to toy with next, and he certainly found it annoying that, in spite of all those things, he was constantly bedeviled by thoughts of her, which were even more frequent now that he was back in New Harmony and in frequent sight of David Dale's laboratory.

But the worst on the Ann front caught him totally unprepared and it came to him in a roundabout fashion through his sister Margaret. She'd enlisted him to help her put feathers in the new tickings on an afternoon when their mother had gone to bed for the two hours she allotted herself to get over a cold. John had taken bags of feathers down from the loft in the chicken coop and Margaret, in spite of their mother's warning not to waste any, had managed to get stray bits of fluff and feathers all over her dress. John flapped his arms and crowed at her. She clucked back at him and they were both laughing, and she was talkative for Margaret, and surprisingly ready with her observations.

"I certainly wish Kate would get back to being herself again. It's so tiresome when she's not," she said, and John listened as she told him what Kate hadn't. "But it *was* her fault," she went on. "Mother doesn't know about it, and she shouldn't, but it really was Kate's fault. I don't mean because of all her reading or because of her being so enamored of Fanny Wright and that ilk, though she won't always even admit that she is. And I don't blame her for saying yes when Mrs. Boren asked her to talk at the Minerva meeting, which Martha Wilsey says they've stopped having now because of the war, though personally I think Kate took the wind out of their sails, and their snobby little boat finally just went dead in the water."

Margaret turned her head and opened another bag of feathers, holding it away from her while the dust puffed into the air. She pulled the ticking over it, bunching it around the neck so the feathers wouldn't fly out when they upended the bag. John helped her squeeze the feathers into the ticking and, when they'd started the more tedious work of pushing them into the corners, she went on talking. "Martha thinks it wouldn't have been as bad if Kate had just agreed with Constance Fauntleroy and quick finished up and sat down. She thinks there were girls who were curious about what Kate had to say and would actually have taken her side against Constance even if they didn't do it to her face. But you know Kate. She had to speak her mind. She always does."

"And what did her mind say? What did it have to do with Harry Beal?"

"Harry? Not anything." Margaret looked at him, uncertainty creeping into her voice. "Kate didn't tell you about what she said at the Minervas?" She paused, sucking her upper lip under her lower one. "Then I shouldn't," she said, and John waited, though not for long.

"Well, certainly she can say what she said a lot better than I can repeat it when I didn't even hear what it was, but it was just about you not hiring a black to do your stint when Constance's family has.

Or when Arthur did. But I'll tell you, John, it's not the easiest thing being a Given in this town when your sister insults the Owens and the Fauntleroys, and then Ann Bradley, for sport, reads letters to all your friends from your brother who's making love to her."

John breathed in so suddenly and so hard that he thought he had chicken feathers all the way down in his lungs. He was coughing and sneezing at the same time and trying to keep the feathers from spurting out of the ticking. Margaret leaned over him, ready to thump his back, but he frowned in the midst of a sneeze and motioned her away. "I mean you must have heard about Ann Bradley," she said. "Oh dear, John. Oh no. Like sister, like sister."

John coughed a soggy bit of feather into his sleeve. "If there's a fault, it's not yours," he said when he could talk again, and he tried to sound as if he meant it, but he wasn't able to cover his anger. "Feel free, though, to finish these tickings yourself," he said, and he thought that, slow and unwilling as he'd been to pick up on their hint, he understood now what Kate Marshal and Annie Perkey had meant when they'd told him that if a person—Ann Bradley, for instance—was to make fun of someone's confidences, they would think less of her, but certainly not of her victim.

In a black mood, John went out to find Francis Cannon and have a drink with him since Francis could carry both ends of the conversation without even noticing. John sat turning his glass in the tavern. In a while, his father came in, too. He was carrying the *Mount Vernon Union* and, after he'd gotten a drink, he stayed standing and cleared his throat to read the words aloud that Mr. Lincoln had said at the cemetery at Gettysburg. When he'd finished, he got another drink and, in silence, studied the words a while longer.

"It's a short speech," he said then, "yet there's something here. He's not Daniel O'Connell, but he's his own way with words. Still, it's a terrible carnage that's going on. You'd think it was a whole country of fighting cocks. Or us Irishmen set on each other."

Yes, certainly not Daniel O'Connell, John thought, remembering the words every Irish boy was taught: *Not for all the universe contains would I, in the struggle for what I conceive my country's cause, consent to the effusion of a single drop of human blood, except my own.* Yet Daniel O'Connell was a fierce constitutionalist and Mr. Lincoln was one as well.

Francis Cannon and his father were already well into their cups, and since John wasn't eager for another hangover, he got up and went out. He walked the streets idly for a time, saying hello to acquaintances, though not stopping to talk to them. He didn't feel at all like calling on anyone, and so finally he walked down to the river and watched the ferry easing across the black current of the Wabash and making its crossing from New Harmony to the Cut-off Island. He was chilled standing there, and it reminded him of the blowing drizzle of Donegal and the North Atlantic coast, a memory tied in a way he felt more than understood to an image of himself looking at a tangle of leaves between the Cumberland and Tennessee Rivers. He was clawing uphill in the snow. He was smelling the wet earth his fingers touched as a Rebel scream shrilled down on him, and he wanted to escape that scream. He wanted to be at home in his own bed, and this night, he thought turning around, he actually could be.

He was less than happy when Kate caught up with him as he was walking back. "I'm glad I found you," she said. "Can I ask a favor? May I?" she said, and she went on speaking without waiting for him to answer her. "You needn't have harassed me, but it made me think, and I've a letter written. I'd like it if you could see about the spelling."

"Is it to Harry Beal?" John asked. "What should I know about Harry?"

"It's to Mrs. Runcie. To Constance Fauntleroy. I made a mistake, John. I thought I could go to the Minervas and, if I'd worked hard and written something they might admire, they would admire it. But Constance was dreadful and said the Irish were burning black orphanages and old women's homes because we've a religion that encourages such things and is the very reason we lacked freedoms at home. I was horrible back and said her family were the ones who took advantage, buying her brother out of the draft. You're right, John. I'm too quick to speak and I don't stop to think of how it might hurt someone. Not that I mind really about Constance Fauntleroy, but Lizzie Marshal has to work there. So I've written that I'm sorry. It's all here in the letter. That I abused their hospitality and that I know that Colonel Owen, and Alfred Dale and Julian Dale, and William Fauntleroy and the others are serving nobly in the war, and that I didn't mean to suggest otherwise."

John looked at the envelope Kate was holding. "Do you have your paper?" he said.

Kate shook her head. "I tore it up."

"You'll have to tell me what you wrote," John said. "In your paper. I'd like to know. But don't send that." He motioned at the letter. "Don't give her the satisfaction. And anyway, she won't care. You may have thought of little else since, but she'll have gossiped over it for a day and then forgotten it. Kate, if I'm harsh, I'm harsh, but it's what I'd hoped you'd have learned by now. To Mrs. Runcie—to someone like her—we're none of us so much as a single flea on a dog. Get angry with me all you like, but cool in the same skin that you heated in, for what I've said is plain fact. And it's true, as well, that if you knew I thought I had written to a friend in writing to Ann Bradley, and that I didn't think I was writing public documents to be read all over town—if you knew what she did with my letters and didn't tell me, how can I trust you, though I always believed that I could. It is getting very hard, Kate, to be a judge of you girls."

Kate looked surprised. She was very quiet, but John felt her like a small volcano beside him as they walked. He picked up a pinecone and pitched it over the roof of the nearest house, wondering as he watched it fly, if soldiering had ruined him for everything else. "Tell me," he said, "was Caroline Thrailkill there when Ann read my letters?"

"I wouldn't know," Kate said tartly, and John counted the silent beats before the volcano's eruption. "If you're judging girls, John, I'd ask you to leave me out. How would I know what Ann read or what person she read it to? I don't sit waiting on her as there are some of us that have a life without Ann Bradley at the center. If you're going to mistrust me, John, you'll need to find a better cause. And as far as Harry is concerned, if Harry Beal was gentleman enough to be silent about a silly embarrassment that had nothing at all to do with you, I would think that you—my own brother—might be as kind. Have you decided not to be kind, John?"

John picked up another pinecone and skimmed it across the street and thought that whatever there was about Harry, he wasn't going to learn it tonight, unless he counted the fact that Harry was on Kate's mind. "Actually," he said, "I wouldn't have minded being a fly on the wall at the Fauntleroy house. I'm quite sure you got the best of Mrs. Runcie."

"I did," she said. She reached down for her own pinecone, but she picked at it instead of throwing it. "Mother's right. It only lasts an instant. The satisfied part. Revenge goes sour in your mouth—"

"And it's your mouth that you have to live with. I have my own letter to write, and if I ever consider Mother's advice, it won't be until it's written and mailed."

"A letter to Evansville?" Kate flicked bits of pinecone at his cheek. "Do we have to be angry with each other, John, when we can both be angry at Ann Bradley?"

"Why should you be angry with Ann?" John put his hand up against the pinecone assault, glad it was silent and without the whizzing noise of a minié ball.

"If she's been unkind to you—"

"You're sly, Kate."

"Sly and untrustworthy. I suppose you'll tell me next that my eyes are shifty like a liar's."

"Let me look," he said, peering in at her and then crossing his eyes, and Kate laughed, a silvery sound in the growing dark.

She sighed then. "We'll find Father drunk and Mother still sniffling and Margaret still fuzzy with bits of chicken feathers—"

"And Denis and Charley falling asleep from bagging corn at the mill."

"And Mary wondering how she got into this family."

"Does she?"

"Only part of the time."

Banter again. The string tuned almost true once more. John tossed a last pinecone. He knew what the next days would be. He would hear his parents out on the issue of what he would do if there was still a war when his term was up. He would spend time with Michael McShane when Michael got back from Mount Vernon. He would teach Charley what he'd learned of the finer points of baseball from playing in the regiment, and he would work another day harvesting late corn with his father and Denis and Charley. He would also spend more time with the girls in the evenings, though he would hang back a little, determined that when he came home again no person should be afraid to talk to him because he used to go to see his wife. And he would write the letter that was already half written in his head, and have the fun with it that would leave a certain person feeling rather shabby and—if she had any principle of a lady about her—certain to return his letters, which he would then have the pleasure of burning. And he would tell his mother, who had caught her cold from him (his had nagged since Memphis), that yes, he did go to church in Memphis, and he would be telling the truth when he said it, though not as large a truth as it might have been if he'd gone to church more often.

And then, with a small concern that he'd overstayed this furlough, indeterminate though it was, he would leave again. He would check once more on Major Walker and, if he passed near the Armstrongs', restrain himself from calling, which he desperately wanted to do, wounded as he still felt. He would retrace his journey, perhaps in the company of soldiers he knew, perhaps even someone who'd been missing like Felix Edmonds, while New Harmony—this New Harmony with its evening sounds of laughter and clicking pool balls and horses nickering softly and music moving in a fading, discordant relay from house to house—New Harmony would slip from the present to the picture he held in his memory: a now bright and now dim stage with dramas as small and as pressing as this odd one he'd played out with Kate.

Southern Tennessee and Mississippi
December 1863 and Early 1864

20

Q. M. Office, 2nd Brig. 4th Div.,16th A. C.
Hopefield Arkansas Opposite Memphis, Tenn.

Some say that we are to go along the Tennessee River and march to Athens.
Others say that we are going to Washington and join the Army of the Potomac.
I do not care where they send me so that I have not to traverse some old path for
I would like to see as much as possible of the country for the next four months.

John Given to Catharine Given, March 17, 1864

I t seemed to John that he'd spent so much of his usable life in Tennessee that he was practically a resident, godforsaken country that it was apart from Memphis, which was godforsaken in its own way. But on the Tuesday four days after a Christmas that the regiment had spent in readiness for yet another march to yet another camp along the Memphis and Charlestown Railroad—fresh meat and a single dram their only celebration—he wanted nothing more than to stay in Tennessee.

His reason was quite sound, he thought. They had been tramping around from Lafayette to LaGrange and Grand Junction in no particular order that he could determine. On Sunday he'd been sent to LaGrange to draw forage, and by the time he returned to Grand Junction, the regiment was loaded into the railway cars to head back again to Lafayette, its purpose to intercept Forrest, who was expected to cross the tracks there or at Moscow. Since the regiment was traveling on the cars, John was left with the charge of the horses and wagons, and Lieutenant Smith with the charge of the camp and of the guards who remained with camp property. They had no men for picket duty, and John didn't mind admitting to himself or anybody else that he'd been more than ready when the order came to move back to LaGrange where there was a larger force. He was quite happy when they'd actually arrived, for he had no desire, as he wrote home, to see Richmond before the Army of the Potomac did.

Capture was on his mind. It wasn't just the uneasy stillness that he'd felt in the camp at Grand Junction with its skeleton guard and lack of pickets to warn of guerrillas or approaching troops. First and foremost, there was Levi's absence, but now there was also news from home that Eugene Thrall of the 60th was a prisoner and Tom Richardson had barely escaped being caught. And the hard word in camp at LaGrange when John arrived from Grand Junction was that Captain Boren himself had been captured.

John knew the whole story and, at its heart, it seemed the usual wartime mix-up. With Lieutenant Bennett still in the provost marshal's office, Captain Boren had been sent back to Memphis to see about procuring horses and equipage. Colonel Morgan wanted the regiment to be mounted, a fact that made John believe they would be scouting around this dismal land for the rest of his enlistment. (He hadn't decided yet whether to join the Veterans' company and get the thirty days furlough and the bonus; some days he was going to, some days he wasn't.) When Captain Boren returned from Memphis, John handed over the letters from Mrs. Boren that had arrived in his absence. Looking at the captain, John thought he looked as tired as he'd ever seen him, though he'd gone to work right away.

John was sure that fatigue was a factor in the captain's getting caught. He'd left with the regiment on the cars when they moved to Lafayette. On Sunday, he and Captain Darling of Company B had gone to a house close to camp intending to sleep for the night. Instead, there were marching orders at four in the morning. Two men went to rouse them and, aware that the Rebels had been driven off the night before, the four headed straight in the dark, thinking that the transportation they were approaching was the 25th's. To their sleepy surprise, it was part of the Rebels' rear guard and wagon train lagging behind. All four of them had walked right into their own capture.

John thought what a stir the news would make in Harmony. It had made a stir here. Yet despite the concern, there was the possibility of good news about Captain Boren that was also the result of more wartime bungling. A messenger had come for Lieutenant Smith and, while the lieutenant got ready to leave on horseback for Lafayette to take command of Company A, the man had told John the story about it that amused and pleased him enough that he made sure he was the first to tell it to everyone he could, and not just to the rump guard from the 25th.

"Are you pulling my leg, Jack?" Henry Schafer asked him and, when John assured him that he wasn't, Henry made his own way through the account again.

"So a Rebel quartermaster comes up to our picket lines and asks for General Forrest's headquarters thinking our boys are his?"

"Yes."

"And a smart boy on picket asks him what he wants the general for?"

"Yes."

"And this quartermaster says he has a wagonload of bacon to deliver, and so the guard takes him and his bacon to Colonel Morgan's headquarters where it's received?"

"Warmly."

Henry was laughing. "And disposed of as soon as they get it. We should've been there, Jack."

"You're right," John agreed, eager to tell the story again and, though there was a good deal of talk about Forrest having feinted toward Moscow and managing to move a very long wagon train across the tracks at Lafayette despite trains running constantly between Memphis and Corinth—such an improbable escape from the part of the 25th that was chasing him that men thought somebody was at fault and that body not less than a general officer—most of the men left at LaGrange were soon talking more about the likelihood of the quartermaster and a Rebel officer being exchanged for Captain Boren and Captain Darling. John was nervous about it. He was keeping his fingers crossed. He had written to Kate about the capture, but he'd cautioned her not to talk of it unless she heard it from another source as he didn't want either of them to be the cause of worrying Mrs. Boren.

In the meantime, camp had an air of confusion with men still waiting for orders to join the regiment or waiting for the regiment to return, which seemed the likelier option to John as he thought it was pointless to expect infantry to overtake cavalry that had an open road for retreat. There was also the dismal sameness that had dominated life since John had gotten back from New Harmony and the 25th had finished its provost duty in Memphis. At home, he had felt ashamed of himself that he'd not had more money to give to his parents. He knew that the fondness he'd developed for card games was part of the reason he'd found himself short. It wasn't that he was a committed gambler or a particularly bad one. It was more that he was a bored one or, more accurately, a bored soldier who did what bored soldiers do.

There were definite moments when he chastised himself that he wasn't making more of his time. He could read more. He could memorize long passages of *Paradise Lost*. He could acquaint himself with the affairs of the rest of the world by reading the foreign news in the papers that made their way through camp. He could spend time with Max Munte working on German. His correspondence had fallen off, and he thought he could try to increase it again by sending off letters to all his aunts in Chicago (his Aunt Ellen was having another baby soon, but Mr. McAuliffe was still good about writing). He could write to friends and family in Ireland and even try to stir up some mischief for Michael McShane—Michael who'd grown quite happy with his bachelor ways. He was tempted to write to his wife and say how much Michael missed her and that she should really try once more to come out to New Harmony. John guessed if she said she would it would push Michael over the edge, if he wasn't already pushed, so that he signed up with the new hundred-day cavalry regiment. And there were always letters he could send to people like Menomen and the girls at home he counted his friends and to Harry Beal in Louisville.

Yet he found himself with a certain lassitude. As he occupied himself with the busy work of drills and headquarters paperwork and the likelihood that he would soon be saddle sore, he found he'd been diverting himself more and more with the easy pursuits of cards and baseball, though in baseball to get on base he had to swat the ball with all his might just to give himself the chance at getting to first with his stiff run. Since returning from Harmony, he'd felt very little desire to talk with Reverend Heuring. He had actually experienced what he decided later was a sort of spiritual malaise, although it had started as something more like an awakening, a thing that made him feel very American even if he'd not been ready to shake and speak in tongues unless it was the Irish tongue and the bit of German he'd learned from Max. And Latin. He could always speak Latin. Perhaps, though, he had avoided Reverend Heuring with his clear voice and steady, blue-eyed gaze because he was a man who inhabited his vocation so thoroughly and comfortably that it had started to make John troubled over his own. Or the lack of it. The loss of it. The loss of it in Ireland and the more permanent loss of it that had come with his feelings about Ann Bradley. He'd wanted an open field where Ann was concerned; he'd rejected the impediment a vocation would mean when it came to pursuing her.

He was not sure, though, that awakening was really the right word. It had been more of a revelation, more a moment of spiritual surprise. When he'd gotten back to Memphis, his cold still nagging him so that he'd been chilled and basically wretched the whole journey, he'd felt gloomy that he'd not made more of his furlough and found more in New Harmony to engage him. He wished he'd been a better son and cousin (he still owed Margaret Mulhern a walk to Maple Hill), a better brother and friend. In Memphis, the regiment had had only one Sunday before they were done as provost guard, and he'd absolutely promised himself he would trade assignments or just about anything to get to Mass, for he felt he owed it to his mother to make his word as good as she trusted it to be.

And he had gotten to Mass. He'd taken Communion and prayed afterward for a long time, for he felt the need to pray for every man that he'd shot. He tried to remember each face—or the semblance of it—for it was the only way since he didn't know any names. Afterward, in spite of the arrests their patrols often made in the rough backstreets of Memphis, he had started back to camp through the area where many of the city's blacks had crowded into ramshackle places when their own homes were leveled to make the clear-fire range from Fort Pickering. As he walked, he realized that he had come upon another Sunday service. It was not in a church. It was in one of the dilapidated houses, its windows opened partway—obviously for air for the crowd of people inside. As he got closer, he felt himself drawn to it by the most amazing music. He would have been drawn anyway, for he knew that Reverend Heuring sometimes preached to black congregations, a tough task John thought, even with the Bible to offer texts such as the one he used from 1 Corinthians: "Art thou called being a servant? Care not, for it, but if thou mayest be made free, choose it rather."

John knew the thrust of what Reverend Heuring had to say— that slaves should obey their masters so that it did not go harder on them, that the Almighty, for whom a year—even a thousand years— was as a day, would break the slaves' chains in His own time, but that liberty carried its own responsibilities and toil. A free man must, by work and example, dispel any slanders against him. John understood what the sermon would be. What he was curious about was the delivery. He did not know how a man of Reverend Heuring's learning and assurance would address such an audience—if he would speak down to them or speak level. He knew that even without the sound of the music, he would have looked in a window of the house on the off chance that Reverend Heuring was there.

He wasn't. The music had swelled louder and John had felt it like a hot rush of wind into the wintry Memphis day. He'd stepped back from the window and leaned against the wall. He could feel the voices through the wood even as he heard them with all their stirring power. There was an aching quality to them and, for John, it heightened the beauty of the music to something that was nearly thrilling. Well, it was thrilling. There were so many voices, men and women singing solo and in a drummy unison. As John followed the words, he was sure it took a full twenty minutes for them to be thoroughly sung, and in every possible musical variation: *Jesus gonna carry, carry me home.* He felt the desire in the voices, a thing that did not break down barriers, didn't even cast them aside, but simply existed in a full and open space. He knew what it was: the music was ecstatic. It was transfixed in a glorious moment in the way that saints who mortified their flesh and were held in rapture were said to be: made other, freed—through agony—from the pain-inflicting shackles that had held them to the earth.

After a long time, he moved on, jostled in the morning crowds as he made his way back to camp. The music, though, wouldn't leave him. For days, for longer, even though he couldn't quite hear it, he felt it is as a kind of lingering immersion—a new surface on his skin. He lay on his cot, remembering a voice that had sung the word Jesus, stretching it out as though pulling on an infinite thread. The pitch of another voice, a soldier's perhaps as he passed in an alley, would bring back a trace of melody and he would search his mind for the elusive next note. Always, he kept an ear out. And he was haunted, too, with what the music had finally seemed to illustrate—with the memory it had freshly etched.

In Dublin, in the rooms near Trinity College, rooms that were so acrid from pipe smoke and coal dust from the open window that his sleeve had grown sooty as he leaned on the table, John had listened to William Reeves, who had allowed him to read with him for the pounds the family had cobbled together when Bishop McGettigan suggested it. ("As long as you don't take the soup, John," Bishop McGettigan had said, using the old famine expression for going Anglican in exchange for food. "Learn what Reeves has to say about theology and any other subject, but tend to your faith.")

John had. He had learned every bit that he could, and he had stayed scrupulously Catholic. Noting that, William Reeves had never said a word that clearly proselytized, but he had challenged John with an idea that had come back to him on that Memphis Sunday morning:

If a passion exists for religion, it is directly proportional to one of two things—the degree to which that religion seems threatened, or the degree to which that religion is bound to a personal, and often political, desire for power. It was a proposition that left out the question of faith and spiritual comfort, John had always thought, though perhaps the word passion excluded such a consideration from the start. Yet the statement had had new resonance for him in the sound of those voices. There was such longing in the music and in the words—*Jesus gonna carry me home*—a longing for freedom, which John knew for himself—and from what his grandfather and father had taught him—was a political thing at its core, yet in such a setting so completely spiritual.

The music had been his awakening. He'd been moved in a way that he'd not been for a very long time. On his cot, he turned on his bedroll and thought of what it was he had lost, why it was that he had let his own passion for what was sacred (if it was that and not just a chance for influence and being revered, and for pleasing his mother)— why it was he had let that disappear, the way the sound of the voices had stopped in the air, cut off by distance and time. He knew the ostensible reasons—first son with a chance at education but not the necessity for taking Orders; young man who, ordained, would not be able to marry and have children when it seemed so much in his blood to do so; son and brother who, in watching his father and Kate leave, had realized that he loved his family more than anything. Was there any way he could have stayed in Ireland in a black cassock parceling out blessings and sermons with his whole family gone?

He knew the answer was no, but why couldn't he? Why hadn't he? Why hadn't he stepped entirely over the line of the secular sphere and into that great, transporting mystery? Why had he always *thought*? And why was he still so troubled by the image of Ann Bradley who, even if she would love him, might always seem as tainted to him as the back-alley women of Dublin and the brazen women of Memphis who were the vivid reminders of the women harangued about by priests all his life, Eve's fallen daughters, who brought forth their children in sin?

Why could he lose his vocation—and possibly even his faith—and still hold on to this conviction that something so physically compelling was wrong for him to have? How could he so easily divide things so that his mother and the women and girls he knew who did not carry Ann Bradley's aura could all share the assumed purity of the Mother of God?

He didn't know, although he thought the answer was about being Catholic and about having walked so close to the threshold of the priesthood. He also thought that, in some way, it was about being Irish.

It was this uncertainty that spawned his malaise, which was as enveloping as the music had been, although it was certainly not thrilling in that way, not thrilling at all, but rather something quite dark. He felt particularly grim while the regiment was off on its chase after Forrest. He went about his tasks. He did all that there was that could occupy a soldier stranded as he was in the countryside of Tennessee, including debating with himself about whether he would sign up to join the Veterans' regiment, which was an argument that, inevitably, returned him to a wilderness of unsettling questions. He would start by wondering if he had a duty to his friends to re-enlist, though the Harmony boys in Company A, from what he could tell, were mostly going home. Then he would wonder if the Union needed him to put itself back together, and if he could stand New Harmony with the war going on without him and if he would feel as if he had quit something again because of cowardice, for perhaps it was cowardice if he didn't see the thing through to the end and cowardice that had kept him from being a priest and cowardice that prevented him from rejecting what the priests had taught him and simply acting impulsively for once, acting as though he had a body, which he did, acting without checking the tracks he would leave before he made them.

And yet there was something at least in theory (he understood the principle of the thing) to be said for restraint and for offering himself to a wife as someone who had waited for her. And, too, he had not been a physical coward in any battle or skirmish or at any time in his life that he could remember—even if he had been afraid at times—and so perhaps it wasn't that he was a coward but that he was too proud and too wary of some very different kind of risk, one in the category of irrevocable mistake. At the least, he thought, he needed to get drunk or pick a fight with one of the boys in another regiment and give that man a beating or be beaten himself and wind up in the guardhouse. There was no startling music here. Guardhouse, or whatever it might be, all he could do in this camp was to settle for a new variant of boredom.

It took most of January for John to shake the sense that he was bound for hell, which he realized finally was what he'd been feeling. The change began with the regiment's return to LaGrange just after New Year's. They were filthy and stinking and full of blisters, for they'd marched twice as far on foot as they'd ridden in cars. They'd seen nothing of Forrest, and they were grousing and irritable and ready for food that was at least cooked if not fresh. With every complaint, John recognized how glad they were to be back, and how much better camp was with his friends returned.

"It's winter. Can't we just stop here until spring?" George Tretheway was combing what looked like part of a bird's nest out of his hair and warming his backside at the tent stove. John could see the hole in Max Munte's boot where water had seeped in and frozen. He watched as Max took his boot off and cut away what was left of his sock so he wouldn't pull off more skin.

It was Henry Schafer who spoke up to answer George. "Find General Veatch and ask him. Find General Sherman and give him your opinion. Tell him we're behind you," he said, and John could hear from his voice that Henry was glad, too, to have the boys back, though it was strange having them here without Captain Boren.

"That puts you in the fire, Henry," George said, freeing up the last of his hair.

"You get paid, Jack?" Max asked. "We got paid in the field and I'm ready for a game."

"You could send your money home to your new wife," Henry said, and Max looked at him without saying anything, for Henry's own wife had died in November.

In a moment, though, Max took out his purse, and John, glancing at Henry and deciding he was all right, considered only briefly whether he was a reformed card player or not. He got out the deck.

It wasn't until the middle of the month that he felt a bigger and even more welcome nudge toward being himself again. Though he'd been starting to think that the mail had been discontinued for the rest of the war, a steamer arrived that had letters for every man from New Harmony. Max Munte got the main haul, and the men told him that Mary, in lieu of herself, had sent him her weight in paper and ink, and that he should be imaginative. John scanned the mail quickly for a letter from Ann Bradley, and then went through it again. Instead of a letter from Ann, there was a letter from Caroline Thrailkill, and it was the second one since his return from home. She'd dated it the seventh of January, and the first part was all about New Harmony's concern over Captain Boren's capture. She wrote that word had come through Mr. Hornbrook who'd heard in Evansville he'd been taken, and that Mrs. Boren was certain the news wasn't true, just as she'd been certain he hadn't been killed at Shiloh. John wished he could talk back to the letter and tell Caroline to tell Charlotte Boren that, in spite of the fact that the capture had been real, the exchange was complete. Captain Boren was headed back to the regiment.

He was more interested in the other things Caroline had to say. She talked about Christmas and said that she'd skipped the balls because she wasn't in the habit of going to them and that, anyway, her mother wasn't well. She'd spent her Christmas reading. She'd reported, too, on the usual Christmas mayhem—boys breaking down fences and gates and blockading the street. From what she'd written, they'd been particularly creative this year, taking an old buggy and putting it on top of William Fauntleroy's shop and breaking up one of Dick Ford's wagons to make a pig pen that they filled with an old hack and dray. She talked about New Year's, too—and of how cold it was—and said that snow had started on New Year's Eve and was still falling as she wrote. John could easily picture the scene. Some people would have stayed inside at their fires, but others would have bundled up against the snow and cold to go out into the drifting streets and make the usual New Year's visits, while the boys, still full of mischief from Christmas, shot their pistols into the air. John imagined Denis among them, though Caroline hadn't said that he was.

He frowned when he read there was still no word from Levi. He had heard about the prisoners exchanged from Richmond—five thousand of them—but, like Caroline, he'd seen no reports of exchanges from other places. Levi was still a prisoner if he was held in Atlanta, which Mr. Thrailkill thought he was, and which John hoped he was since one of their surgeons had visited the prisoners there and said they were well treated and well fed, partly with rations from the North. Caroline wrote that her mother grew more worried by the day, frightened that they would never see Levi again, and that his own mother was uneasy about him, worried that he would become a prisoner, too. Reading that, John made a mental note to censor himself in writing home. At the least, he could save his stories when they were about things like camps with no pickets.

It was the final section Caroline had written that John read over every time he took the letter out of his Byron. The part about the Blackburn child, of course, for it was so riveting with its tale of John O'Neal finding the child dead in bed with another child sick beside it—a horrible sight for him, Caroline wrote—and all of the family nearly starved, and Mrs. Blackburn unwilling to cook the food people gave them and the county having to bury the child. Then people taking the other children away from her. It was the next part, though, that John read particularly, the bit right before Caroline mentioned her good health and wished him the same. She told him she'd recently addressed two letters wrong and thought it quite likely her mind was woolgathering. Perhaps, she said, she was distracted by thoughts of some young man, that it was unlikely the distraction was an old man as she didn't often bother herself with thinking of old men. John smiled at both her phrasing and meaning. He smiled, in fact, every time he read it.

What brought him fully back to himself, however, was just being a real soldier again. The regiment moved a little way to Moscow. Then, on the twentieth-eighth of January, they set off marching for Memphis. He was traveling light, for he'd given his Byron to a soldier who was stationed in Mount Pleasant, though he'd made sure to take the letter from Caroline Thrailkill out of it first, folding it into his pocket and telling himself it was as close as he could get to having a letter from Levi. He liked the tramp. It was an easy distance, and he had hardly a blister raised. All the men were ready to be back in Memphis, but no sooner had they arrived than they were on the way again. They caught a steamer to Vicksburg. John was eager to see the town and the towering bluffs, and he did see them, but they stopped only briefly. They were off once more, this time heading east with General Sherman's column across Mississippi in the direction of Jackson. And they were on foot. In spite of Captain Boren's efforts, the plan to use horses had been scrapped. There'd been a dispute between the senior officers about mounting the regiment, and the upshot was that the 25th was still just plain infantry. John didn't mind. The roads were good, and he was just as glad he didn't have a horse to be bothered with. His one regret was the loss of his Byron. With saddlebags, he would have kept it.

It was part of his job to keep the march log for Captain Boren, who listened to the men's frequent comments about wagon trains (impertinent remarks like how to tell a wagon train from a railroad train), with a basic good humor, though John thought he seemed even more tired and more subdued after his brief stay with the Rebels. As an officer, he'd been treated like a gentleman, but he'd told John in passing that there was little difference he could tell between the men in blue and men in gray except that the gray uniforms were far more threadbare (and usually more dust-colored than gray) and their wearers much thinner. "They're just boys. Just more boys," he said. "And some very fine officers."

"But not Lincoln men," John responded, and the captain had nodded, his face the red Kate called whiskey-colored (for the skin, not the whiskey) though John knew it was his natural coloring. He had never known him to drink to real excess, or to drink at all on duty.

"It would be over if they were, John," Captain Boren said. "The war would," and John had to agree.

Along with the written company log, John kept his own mental list of new names and new places. The division had sailed from Memphis on the *Kenton* and *Mars*, on the *Emma* and the *Commercial* and, at Helena, they'd seen a Wisconsin regiment boarding the steamer *Choteau*. They'd camped near Clear Creek and halted on the Big Black River. They crossed the Pearl River, where their brigade destroyed the pontoon bridge behind them. They marched through or to or near Brandon and Morris Mills, Line Creek, Shockalo Creek, Hillsborough, Talla Bogue Creek, Anticola Creek, Tuscalameta, Bollabush, the Coonahatta, the Little Chunky River, Tallisha Creek, Bogue Filliah, and Oktibbeha Creek. Each name meant encampments with dates and times and marching distances written in the log for Captain Boren. Some entries even had notations of skirmishes and, in the case of Decatur, Mississippi, the fact that it had been on fire when they reached it. But the names themselves were what stayed with John. He collected them all the way to Meridian, which was most of the way across Mississippi and, with good roads, eleven days' marching time from Vicksburg. Then, on the fifteenth of February, their section of the column turned north along the Mobile and Ohio toward Marion, and their real work began.

As they moved forward, they demolished stretch after stretch of railroad, tearing up track and piling ties into raging bonfires. At Marion, a part of the regiment was shot at and, with the help of men from the 32nd Wisconsin and its battery, they drove the Rebels' cavalry clear out of town. Then they occupied it. John knew they looked like wild men from their march. He himself had hair that had gone oily brown under his cap but was very blond where it stuck out beneath it. When they stopped to mill grain for bread, his hands were the color of the Wabash in a muddy spring.

For three days they stayed at the mill. Then the 25th headed out again, this time with Colonel Howe of the 32nd Wisconsin and all of his men. They went past Lockhart's Station, sticking close to the Mobile and Ohio as if they might follow it all the way north to Corinth. They destroyed a station building, and every single bridge and culvert in their path. They set fire to the lumber they found that Rebels might have used to replace what had been ruined, and they sent even the Rebels' large hospital buildings up in a blaze. They burned all of it. Everything. Their clothes reeked of charred wood and smoke. In the night, when they turned south again and marched back to Marion, bits of papery soot darted in the air like tiny bats.

That was the heart of their raid. When he thought about it later, John believed they'd proceeded like regular barbarians. Yet even at the time, he'd understood it hadn't been about killing. They'd hardly shot at a Rebel. There wasn't a dead man in the regiment. But every last one of them was astonished at how much physical damage they'd inflicted and in such a short time. Captain Boren was grim-faced, his hair and cap and shoulders covered with the ash and debris that had floated down on all of them. "What if it was New Harmony, John?" he said. "What if it wasn't just a block that burned in a normal fire, but somebody burning the granary and the mansion, and then Fretageots' store and Corbin's mill and the ferry all in a day? It would feel wanton, John. I see no end of this now that it's started."

John had considered what he said, and yet in the exhilaration of the moment, he was struck more by the sheer physical feat—they had felt like giants—and the amazing pyrotechnics display put on by their engineers. He didn't understand it entirely. He didn't really want to. But the pure recklessness of it had somehow made him breathe freely again.

When the men discussed it, they said it was a different kind of war now, and the change was due to General Grant having gone to the Army of the Potomac and General Sherman being in command. They'd all believed that General Grant would sacrifice any men he had to to beat the enemy, but General Sherman somehow went deeper.

Whatever stood between him and victory was fair game. He seemed bent on annihilation—on whatever it took to win. John, who was feeling an odd combination of fearlessness and fear of that fearlessness, thought they'd created their own version of something like the *Iliad*. They'd entered a world where the warriors were unstoppable, and war—pursued like some uncontrollable *aristeia*—no longer had bounds.

George Tretheway put it more plainly. "I never knew I'd like being an arsonist."

Max Munte nodded. "Yes. I am a Hun."

The new orders from General Sherman were to move back to Vicksburg. The line of march, as they returned westward, curved north and south with the roads and terrain. John added new place-names and rolled off the old ones—that staccato rhythm—backward to himself. They encountered enemy cavalry engaged with the guard for the train from Decatur. The 32nd Wisconsin burned the Mississippi Central's lines. The brigade stopped to grind more cornmeal, and John, glad for the chance, calculated they did it at forty pounds an hour. But little else happened except marching. It gave him an angry knee and a lot of time in which to think. It gave every soldier time to think. By the evening they stopped at Canton, it was clear to John that not a single Harmony man from Company A would join the Veterans' unit, but only the two first lieutenants, Gilbert Smith and James Bennett. Maybe George Ham. For that matter, he doubted Gilbert Smith would serve more than his original term even if he did sign up again.

The men talked about it among themselves, both in large groups and small ones. They were tired. They were full of lice and every other kind of vermin. They'd been sick and knew they were going to be sick again. They were disgruntled about how infrequent their paydays were. Some of them felt that Mr. Lincoln couldn't manage his generals and still thought he'd seriously hurt the Army of the Potomac when he'd removed General McClellan from command. Many of them were Democrats and were hoping Mr. Lincoln would lose in the fall so the war would come to an end, if it hadn't already by election time.

Some expressed outright bitterness that, ever since the Emancipation Proclamation, the war seemed more about destroying slavery than saving the Union. Some thought that if they were going to level the South, the idea of having a normal Union again would disappear for good. Others wondered—the usual complaint—just what freed black men would mean for their own jobs, although a young soldier in Company E—a boy who had family in Dubois and Spencer Counties, where Abraham Lincoln had spent the Indiana part of his boyhood and read his first law book—said he'd been to a Negro ball in Memphis and he'd found it quite splendid. He claimed that he, for one—regardless of cost—would not begrudge any race a single instant of freedom.

What the men in Company A didn't talk about was how many people they'd lost, though John thought about it, and more often than he wanted to. He was sure everyone did. He kept his own roster that ricocheted about with the other lists inside his head. Edward Beal had died in Missouri before he could ever fire a shot. Romeo Keister was dead of typhoid and so was Jacob Schaen. Nobody would be surprised if Fred Perkey, still sick in the hospital in St. Louis, didn't make it this time. John Hugo and Michael Chancy had been killed at Fort Donelson. Levi was captured, and Felix Edmonds had deserted, though he was back now and court-martialed and sentenced to two years hard labor. (John hadn't seen him, but when the regiment started its rampage toward Marion Station two years to the day since John had been shot at Fort Donelson, Felix—with all his ghosts—had caught up to the main column and turned himself in.) The band, with people like Bill Reid and Eugene and Walter Thrall, had been discharged long ago—even if Eugene Thrall had gone into the 60th. It was almost two years since Robert Clarke had been discharged at Corinth, though he, too, was back in the army as an officer in the 85th while Emma West, now his new wife, waited in New Harmony. Captain Randolph had resigned his commission because of his health. Jacob Jordan and Henry Myer had been killed at Shiloh, and John didn't think the company had ever recovered from Captain Saltzman's death there. The loss roll went on and on. The company was a remnant of itself, and it was fair to say that those who were left had long ago given up their enthusiasm for war.

John thought it might have been different in Company A if Captain Boren had decided to join the Veterans. There were men in other companies who hadn't agonized at all about signing up again. Al Norcross in Company F was one. He'd told John that, when he'd been home on furlough, he could hardly wait for it to be over for he'd had the sense that nothing would happen in New Harmony that hadn't already happened before. Even if Eleanor Wheatcroft was waiting for him to marry her, and even if he did, which he said he meant to, he was a soldier first and foremost. He'd learned that about himself and, besides, he was Captain Larkin's right-hand man. He really was needed.

John knew that Captain Boren wanted to be at home, that he was one of those men who was miserable away from his wife, and that he worried about her health. From talking to him, John had believed all along that he would resign his commission when the bunch of them mustered out. He'd grown even more sure of it after the captain's capture at Lafayette and, now, since their raid past Meridian, there was no question left. It was an odd thing about Captain Boren, John thought. He could take battle casualties—not easily—but more or less in stride. War meant war to him, and he was fatalistic about men and boys being wounded or killed. Yet what had happened at Marion Station and on the railroad on the way north had been profoundly unsettling to him. It was as if the war had finally exceeded what he considered allowable, for it was no longer just men who wore uniforms that were fair game. It was all the things that men made, and the things that helped them provide for their families. Considering it, John felt odd himself. He wondered if their short foray into Mississippi had been too much for him, too. He wondered if it had been too much for all of the Harmony boys—both the attraction and repulsion of it—and if it was what had meant, finally, that none of them was staying in Company A.

They rested at Canton. There was a full review that made it official: the part of the regiment that was re-enlisting signed up again and the rest didn't. The 25th Indiana Volunteer Infantry was now the

25th Indiana Volunteer Veteran Infantry, and it left those of them who were counting on mustering out in July feeling very much at loose ends. They didn't have a furlough coming, as the other men did, and when the 25th marched into Vicksburg once again, it meant there was general chaos, with the regiment broken entirely into fragments.

John found himself bouncing from post to post. When it all settled out, he had been briefly a part of the 89th Indiana, along with most of Company A, and then he'd been transferred to the division office until Captain Boren's brigade quartermaster made a switch to get him back. In the meantime, all the regimental remnants, and that included him, had been taken by river transport back to Memphis and then across the river to Hopefield, Arkansas, which was where they made camp. It was his job both to wait for Captain Boren, who was forwarding the rest of the regiment's transportation from Vicksburg, and to do all the business that he and Captain Boren usually handled together. He was also in possession of a dozen letters from Mrs. Boren for her husband and one from Kate and one from his father that included a letter from his Uncle Charles in Donegal.

The good news was that Levi had written home, though the letter was delayed and he'd written from Richmond to everyone's surprise and to John's wary dismay. Michael McShane, without a bit of rascality from John but for a harder reason (and a blackly ironic one to John)—the word from Donegal that his wife was dead—had signed up for a hundred days in the 10th Cav. There was also a short further litany of death: Charles Randolph had gotten himself murdered in Louisiana while he was still with the 60th; Susan Stephens had died of winter fever; Fred Ribeyre had drowned. There was nothing more about the starved Blackburn children, although Kate's letter contained a very handsome, unsigned Valentine that John suspected came from a person who was quite well versed on the subject.

In exchange for this information, which scarcely seemed like enough to satisfy even a whit of his curiosity, he began a letter to Kate (with instructions to share it with their father) and told her the most recent news from the regiment—that the Veterans, as they were called now, were about to leave for home, and that since Captain Boren hadn't re-enlisted, there'd been an election to replace him, with Lieutenant Bennett voted captain over Gilbert Smith, though it was hard to say when Lieutenant Bennett would receive his actual commission. He told her where he might finish out his enlistment and where the regiment had been, but he didn't give her any particulars of their raid into Mississippi.

Then he put his pen down and, for a long time, looked out past the tents of the camp and toward the broad Mississippi that separated him from Memphis. If all went well, in four more months he would be done with the army and headed home himself, and headed home for good. He was eager for it—more eager than he could possibly say— and yet he was so used to all of this: to the army life; to the city life in Memphis that he might swim his way to if he tried; to the whole state of Tennessee—godforsaken, yes, to a Union man, but as familiar to him now as the back of his hand. There was this whole large enterprise he was so much a part of and—with the Veterans elsewhere—increasingly apart from. It felt very strange. It was confounding, actually, and since he couldn't explain it to himself, he didn't try to explain it to Kate but picked up his pen again and wrote one more variation of his usual closing:

> Hoping that in four months from now I may be enabled to see you all again, I will now conclude with love to yourself, Father, Mother, and the rest of the family and Margaret Mulhern. My respects to all inquiring friends, ladies in particular.
>
> I Am Dear Sister
> Your Affectionate brother
>
> *John*

Decatur, Alabama
Spring and Summer 1864

21

Tomorrow will be the Fourth of July. Our first in the army was spent in Mississippi. Our second in Tennessee and our third and last will be in Alabama. God only knows where we may pass the next. You will have, of course, a gay and festive time in Harmony on the Fourth and as I cannot leave here before the 19th of August you must give me a true history of the proceedings in detail.

John Given to Catharine Given, July 3rd, 1864

I t was not a skill that he needed often. In fact, John hadn't used it since the days in St. Louis when some of the boys in another regiment had brought him a sack of cracked and damaged fiddles that they'd received as one of the war's odder donations to its fighting men. They'd gotten his name through the grapevine as a Donegal fiddler, which he wasn't, and as somebody who could fix pegs and sound posts and generally repair a fiddle, which he could. He'd learned how from his grandfather, who'd repaired fiddles for the Ward men, who were always musicians. *Always.* John hadn't made it through a third of the sack before the regiment left for the field, but it was one of the things that he'd always associated with St. Louis: the top of a fiddle pried carefully off and laid on a small shelf in the barracks, the smell of glue and varnish, and finally, the satisfaction of tuning an instrument when it was whole again and ready to play.

Now he had another fiddle to mend. Captain Larkin and Lieutenant Shannon in Company F had had an argument, and all John really knew of it was that a fiddle had been the loser. Lieutenant Shannon had brought it to him, and the truth was that John liked the fiddle more than Lieutenant Shannon with his swaggering ways and bulbous nose and his cauliflower ear. But it was the fiddle that John was spending the time with, when he had the time, and it gave him a surprising amount of pleasure. He liked the puzzle of the thing. He liked analyzing what the damage was and how he could best fix it. He liked putting his mind on a problem that required all of his concentration and patience, as well as the skill in his hands and, often, the right piece of wood. It was what he looked forward to when he was done with his long day's work at headquarters and the ordered drill after drill he could do in his sleep.

He had had very different expectations when they came to this place. While the Veterans had set off for their furloughs home, he and the remnant of Company A had followed in their wake through Cairo. They'd steamed up the Ohio and for one noisy hour, all the boys had hoped they'd go clear on to Mount Vernon, though of course they hadn't. When they came to the Tennessee, they'd turned toward Savannah instead.

It was All Fools' Day that John remembered the best. They'd boarded the boat after a pointless three-day march from Williams Landing to Purdy and back. When the wagons and mules and horses were finally loaded, they were ready to head off at daylight. The pickets, though, had had their fun with them. At first light, they'd given the alarm so every man rushed to arms and the gunboat commenced to shell the woods. They waited longer while a reconnoitering party went out, but there wasn't any enemy to find, so the steamer started off. In less than an hour the men had pushed toward the railings, and the boat grew quieter than quiet. For the first time in two years, they were steaming up on Pittsburg Landing, with its bluff and the two small buildings still standing below it. John was next to George Tretheway.

"Bloody April," George said quietly, and John thought he could see the tents again, stretching on and on in a billowing white until the cannonballs of Shiloh blasted them down. The boat kept on. He felt the breeze and remembered bullets whipping past his ears. He stared at the bluff and the open space beyond it. There was not a trace of the battle's carnage, but he was sure the grass grew thicker at Shiloh than at anywhere else along the river.

They stayed on the steamer until they got to Waterloo. Then they marched to Florence, Alabama, and back into Tennessee at Prospect. When they crossed the Elk River, they saw the first Union troops they'd seen in days. Then they tramped some more, going on to Athens, which was Alabama again. John was looking forward to Decatur simply to get there and be there, but he'd also assumed it would have some of the attractions and liveliness of Memphis, though on a smaller scale. Instead, when they crossed the Tennessee on a pontoon bridge, they found a small Alabama town that he thought must match Captain Boren's nightmares. It was being dismantled bit by piece by Union soldiers intent on being the first to find materials to build their cabins. There was still a fine Doric-columned bank, which was Union occupied for running the post. There were a few handsome houses that were safe from destruction since they'd been taken over by Union officers, and a smaller, clapboard place that reminded John of the Fauntleroy house.

But otherwise, the town was desolate. It had been built on the high ground commanding first the river and now the Nashville and Decatur Railroad, which was absolutely crucial for General Sherman's supply lines. The trees had been downed to build a fort to protect the railroad and, when they first arrived, John thought the brigade was extremely vulnerable with their transportation and most of their stores still on the other side of the Tennessee. But they hadn't been attacked or hadn't attacked the Rebels themselves and, soon they had a large fort, a mile in circumference, which was not an accidental figure, for the people of Decatur and the country people for a mile around had been ordered to leave. The town had no people at all if you excluded soldiers and cotton speculators from the count, which John did.

And the men wanted discipline here. John thought it was partly because Colonel Morgan had resigned his commission to go to Washington and Hancock's new corps. Whatever the reason, the orders from headquarters grew more strident each day. John had yet to see one as severe in tone as the command the guerrilla leader Richardson had given the Rebels the year before to enforce Jeff Davis's conscription act in West Tennessee. Richardson had proclaimed that every man capable of bearing arms would be taken, that any person leaving his home to evade the draft would have his property destroyed, that any man who tried to flee would be shot and left where he fell, and that anyone making forcible resistance would be kept in his own house, with the doors and windows guarded well until he was finally entombed there.

It was the cruelest order John had ever heard and, to him, it made the case against the North for military despotism look paltry by comparison. Yet he wondered, after a time, if they needed a kind of Richardson here. It had been a Union town, Decatur. It had been entirely pro-Union like the rest of this part of the country all the way to western Tennessee, and now there were Union soldiers whose looting of the town had gone so far that John knew of men who had dug up actual gravestones to use as doorsteps for their cabins. He would have killed a man with his bare hands who dared to steal the stone his father had carved for Biddy and that he'd scratched her name on, but the war had made brutes of men, and there wasn't a woman in sight to tame them. It didn't help in a single way John could think of that there weren't any. And as far as the local Union sympathies went, he assumed they were history.

On a dusty May morning at headquarters, John rehearsed all these general miseries, and then added specific ones. He was half-choking on the air. He wished the Veterans were back from their leave. He wanted new mail, for he'd had just one letter from Kate since he'd left Cairo, her only real news that Al Norcross and Eleanor Wheatcroft were getting married before the end of Al's furlough. She didn't say if anyone had heard from Michael McShane off in the 10th Cav or if there'd been word from the 91st; she didn't tell him how many New Harmony men had re-enlisted in the 60th. She also didn't say if Ann Bradley had returned his letters.

John's finger kept going to the mustache he'd grown, following the lay of it. He was doing the paperwork by himself this morning, though earlier Hamilton, the Negro clerk Colonel Howe had assigned to the main office, had been here, too. He was the first black John had ever worked with. He was the first one he'd really known at all, though he'd gotten accustomed to black men in camp working as servants to men who were eager to have somebody brush their uniforms and polish their buttons, a thing John didn't understand either for the expense or for the idea of it.

He'd found that he liked Hamilton's company. He was civilian, not army, a composed sort of fellow who worked hard and kept to himself, though when he said something it was usually acute or humorous. John was curious about him, about where he'd been educated and how he'd come to this godforsaken town. He didn't know, however, if it was either his place or Hamilton's to be exchanging personal histories. He didn't know what their places were in relationship to each other.

For most of the morning, men and officers had been in and out of the office, which was how it usually was, but today the traffic had dwindled even before George Tretheway, who was orderly to Colonel Howe now, had come for Hamilton to go with a detail to the storage depots. Now there was nobody here. John closed the door against the swirls of blowing dust. It was quiet enough he could hear his pen scratch, and he wondered how many more words and numbers he would write before he'd have writer's cramp as a regular thing. He expected another cheeky letter from Harry Beal warning him of a spreading rump, and the piles from dysentery that every soldier had, growing worse from sitting all day.

John stretched a little, thinking that he liked headquarters better with Hamilton working next to him and how much that fact might have surprised him even a month ago. He wondered if Hamilton had gotten his brains from a slave-owning father, or if he was simply a black man who was intelligent and felt no need to hide it. The fact he was black was the most obvious thing about him, and it made John wary any time men gathered in the office to talk. He didn't want a repeat of the recent morning when a group of tobacco-spitting soldiers had stood not ten feet from Hamilton's desk and exchanged loud and pointed comments about white soldiers routing Rebels from their positions and then building fortifications in which "Abe's Darlings" took their place out of reach of the bullets.

Hamilton had shown no reaction at all, but John had been uneasy, for it was a subject he'd joked about himself, saying the reserve was clearly the post of honor if the better class of soldiers was entrusted with it. He didn't want Hamilton to hear that joke—particularly if it was attributed to him—and he didn't want him to hear the loutish comments from the men who resented anything that put the Negro soldier in a better light. One rumor had had a Negro regiment under an Indiana colonel losing six hundred of nine hundred men in capturing a battery and, when it was proved untrue, the fact it had even been a story had outraged a number of men. John didn't want it to come up in front of Hamilton. He just didn't want it to.

He was still alone when he heard what sounded like a dog scratching itself backward into the door. He heard it again, and this time it was followed by a sort of scraping sound at the latch. When he looked up, he saw Captain Boren, his reddish face turned a chalky gray, hunching himself through the doorway. He caught at the stand by the door to keep himself from falling.

John was up in an instant. He knocked his chair over in his hurry to get to the captain's side. His first thought was that the captain had been shot, but there was no blood when he ran his hand over his uniform and touched the back of his head. John was trying to brace him up and to think of what he'd ever known about apoplexy. It did seem the captain was having some kind of fit. His breathing was rough, and he smelled like metal. He was leaning heavily against John, who managed to tip the chair upright with his foot and help him into it.

"Sir?" John said when the captain seemed more or less stable in the chair, though he was slumping to the side. "You want water?" he asked and, without waiting for an answer, he ran to get it, for it was always water that a man who was wounded asked for. And even if the captain didn't have a wound, John thought it might bring him to himself.

When he hurried back in the door, Captain Boren seemed to have recovered a little. John carried the dipper to him and lifted it up. The captain leaned forward, still short of breath, and he seemed almost to bite at the dipper's rim, but with John holding his head, he managed to choke down a swallow or two.

"I'll get the doctor," John said, easing the captain's head back, and he was about to leave, but Captain Boren, still working to recover his breath, caught at his sleeve.

"No," he managed, his eyes staring as he kept hold of John's shirt, and John thought he was dying, that he was having a heart attack—even his grip was weakening—that he would crumple dead and slide off the chair.

"Please," John said, "I can get him. Please, sir," but Captain Boren seemed once more to have caught his breath, and it was enough so he could tell John no, no absolutely, that the attack would pass off if he got to his bed.

John was thoroughly frightened. Even if the captain could speak, his eyes looked as if they couldn't focus. They looked as if they belonged in two entirely different heads. John thought that if this was an order he was ready to disobey it, but the captain had managed to push himself up. He leaned on John and started toward the door, and John was pulled along with him, moving like a crutch with the captain's heavy arm draped over him.

"The doctor, sir," John said again, but Captain Boren was clearly headed for his quarters and, since he wasn't dead yet, John thought he might live. He was walking, after all, and John kept on with him until he'd gotten to his room. He helped him into the bed. When he was settled, lying back against his pillow with his hand on his chest, John got the flask that was on the top of his bureau. He held the captain's head as he gave him a drink. He felt the dribbles of whiskey fall into his sleeve. Then he waited and watched as the color slowly returned to the captain's face.

"I really should go for the doctor, sir," he said, still holding the flask. Seeing that the captain wanted to speak again, he leaned down to listen.

"Since Shiloh," Captain Boren said, his eyes closed and his voice barely more than a rough whisper, though little by little he got the words out, telling John that he'd had these episodes since the ball had bruised him over his heart, and that he wasn't to tell anyone, that he wouldn't have his wife know for anything. He wouldn't have her know for a thousand dollars.

John nodded his agreement and then agreed out loud. He stood waiting by the bed.

After a while, Captain Boren opened his eyes again and looked at him. "I'll sleep. You can go," he said. John hesitated awhile longer but, seeing that the captain's color was better and his breathing easier, he went on out of the room.

There were several soldiers and officers milling around the area near his desk and a spitting contest in progress—Alex Hugo in the lead—when John got back to his ledger book. The brass spittoon in the corner was the target, and so he moved his chair to get out of the way. He had decided after leaving Captain Boren that he would tell anyone who inquired that the captain was working on private correspondence in his room. He was silently rehearsing something brief and unremarkable to say, when he heard another commotion outside. His first thought was that it was the captain again, and he was up, his heart pumping faster as he headed for the door, but then he made sense of the sounds—it was wagon wheels creaking and men shouting—and he was sure it had nothing to do with Captain Boren.

All of the men in the room were heading outside. John had pushed halfway through the door when the wagon slowed to a stop in front of it. George Tretheway was riding next to the wagon driver and he leapt down, yelling for somebody to get the doctor. For the shortest instant John was confused, thinking that this really was about Captain Boren, and that there was the matter of violating his express wishes and ignoring his anxiety for his wife, but he realized as quickly as he thought it that George was concerned with something else entirely. There was blood dripping out the side of the wagon. As soon as John saw it, he took off running after Alex Hugo to look for Dr. Thomas.

They found him in the sinks. The doctor was still pulling his braces up as they ran back. When they got to the wagon, George Tretheway and the other men had the wagon gate down and were huddled around it. All John could see was a man's boots sticking out, but when Dr. Thomas got up onto the wagon bed and ordered everyone else aside, John realized that he recognized the boots. They were the ones that tapped silently on the floor next to him when he was working, and the boots that extended out across the floorboards when Hamilton leaned back to stretch. And there was blood on them now. Blood was still dripping from the wagon side.

"Get my bag," Dr. Thomas said. Then he turned around and waved off the man who'd started to obey him. He shook his head. "Save your legs. His skull's kicked in. He's got no blood left to speak of. Your man's dead. Did a horse or a mule kick him? It looks like a horse."

George Tretheway and Lieutenant Shannon, who'd been in the wagon, too, were telling the story, but John couldn't listen. He was staring at the blood, which was oozing now more than dripping, and it looked exactly—exactly—like all the blood that he'd ever seen. He took a step closer to the wagon. He could see the nappy hair over the ebony forehead, and the eyes fixed skyward the way that dead men's eyes stare.

"Have you got his glasses?" John asked, for it seemed important to him all at once that Hamilton have the glasses he'd always adjusted so carefully before he started to work.

"What's his name?" Lieutenant Shannon asked, ignoring John's question. "Was Hamilton his first name or his last? Or was it Hamilton Hamilton? Or Hamilton Washington? Or Jefferson Hamilton?"

John didn't answer. He wouldn't have if he could have, although it was true as well that he didn't know the answer. It seemed the tip of the iceberg of all the things that he didn't know. "I'll see to him," he said. "I'll see to the body. I'll talk to Reverend Heuring. And if there's family—"

"He's only a nigger," Lieutenant Shannon said. He was checking Hamilton's boots for wear and, apparently satisfied with his inspection, he stripped them off. "An all right boy. We'd have saved him if we could've, but it still doesn't change things. Boy's nothing more than a nigger."

John, standing in the dust, leaned over and closed Hamilton's eyes. He waited a long moment and then got up on the wagon seat and told the driver to move on.

———

It was the week after Captain Boren's attack, the week after John had led the detail that buried Hamilton—Reverend Heuring saying a few words over the grave and John finding a stone to mark the site—that the Veterans came marching across the pontoon bridge and into camp. They were full of stories from their furlough. There was a great deal of talk about girls and picnics and general visiting and carousing. It was actually true that Al Norcross was a married man. John offered his congratulations but later couldn't help writing to Kate (who, in the one recent letter he'd gotten of the two she claimed to write each week, had returned to being her usual enthusiastic self), that it seemed the folks in Harmony must have served Al pretty badly while he was home. He'd looked a perfect ghost when he returned. Or else, John wrote, marriage was the cause.

With the regiment back together and all of them quartered in what John considered the last place in the world to live, it struck him even more how blasted Decatur was. It was very easy to get tired of looking at nothing except a soldier's face and, without women, there was a singular lack of beauty. And color was missing. Clothes were the sea of uniforms, faded to a vague blue, which the men, in the heat, shed as often as they could. In a place where a normal year would have meant a host of summer flowers everywhere, the ground was unplanted—chewed up and battered by the boots of so many men. There were no blossoms of any color. There was no foliage. There was only the wasted, treeless town and the mud and wood of the fort.

The one thing that did seem to grow was the grapevine. There were rumors, as there had been ever since John had gotten here, that they would be heading soon to Atlanta or Chattanooga to rejoin General Sherman. The men who'd returned as Veterans were eager to know if they were going and when; the men who weren't Vets were hoping they would be well out of the army before any of it could happen.

John was as eager as the next man to get home alive and intact, but he had his own additional concern. He was unhappy at headquarters. It was an airless and cheerless place. There was far too much work since Hamilton's death, and every time he heard a noise at the door he had a sudden image of Captain Boren staggering in in his fit or of Hamilton lying frozen-eyed in the wagon.

He did his best to divert himself. He played cards when he had the chance. He asked around for another fiddle to mend when he'd finished Lieutenant Shannon's. He also spent more effort on his correspondence. In a letter to Kate, he wrote an elaborate dissection of Mr. Lincoln designed expressly to fluster her and to leave her dumbstruck when it came to making Mr. Lincoln's defense. He thought he'd made a good job of it and, before he mailed it, he read it over several times, once to George Tretheway. George was less impressed with his cleverness than John thought he should be, but he mailed his letter anyway, certain at least that Kate would study it.

Nothing that he did seemed to rid him of his restlessness with his job. He decided, finally, that he wanted out of being a clerk and that he'd take his chance in the company as a full-time soldier for the time he had left in the army. He didn't know if Harry Beal even got his letters, or if he was still in the guardhouse, where he'd landed after some hell-raising, but the case he made in writing to Harry, and to people like Henry Schafer in person, was that a soldier made thirteen dollars a month clerking and a civilian a hundred and twenty-five. As he put it, the wages and work no longer tallied well enough for him to continue. But the real case he made to himself was that he wanted out of headquarters entirely, even if it meant standing a picket line in the hot sun.

It took him a while to engineer the change, and he tried not to think whether he was letting Captain Boren down, but on a hot evening in late June, he reported back to the company for duty. Saluting Lieutenant Bennett, he felt like a new recruit. For twenty months (and he'd counted those months the way he'd counted every day in his soldier's life)—for all those months, he'd had a dual life, which meant that, dull or not, he was often at the hub of things. He was never on a picket line, and now he would be and with newer men who'd joined the company after Shiloh, even after Hatchie River, and so had not even seen a real battle. That could change, he knew, for a strong detachment had gone out once again hoping to find Forrest.

The sky had pinked up over Lieutenant Bennett's shoulder and, not for the first time, John thought how odd it was that a man of this lieutenant's calm and bookishness was spending his time as a soldier instead of following the kind of intellectual pursuits New Harmony offered. It was about the cause, John decided. In nearly three years, John had never talked politics with James Bennett, but he was sure he was a Lincoln man and a man who, if asked, would say without hesitating that he favored abolition. John thought it was something they might talk about one day. For now, he saluted again and, glancing at the garish, candy-striped sky, shouldered his gun. Then he went off, as the lieutenant ordered him to, and joined the pickets.

On his first night back out, it wasn't the enemy that he encountered. It was their own men coming back. They were in markedly good spirits. John caught a bit here and a piece there of the night's story from the groups of men who went by him after they gave the password. They had surprised the Rebels all right. They had caught them in their camp and fallen on them before they could get to their arms, though the Rebels had run fast enough that they'd avoided capture and had only five killed.

"They were in a real hurry, Jack," Henry Schafer said. "To ske-daddle, they jumped on their horses bare-backed, and bare-assed as well. If you want a Rebel's underdrawers, you can help yourself off the seven wagons we took."

John laughed. "That many pairs?"

"Food and ammo wagons. The drawers we just tossed on board. You see a man running in the buff, Jack, you can be sure he's a Rebel."

"By the light of the moon," John said, looking up at the sky, and remembering nights when there wasn't a cloud and men brought poteen down from the mountains, their faces and jugs reflecting an otherworldly glow. Somewhere in the Alabama woods, he assumed there'd been that same streaky gleam.

By morning, the weather had changed drastically, and Max Munte was busy sorting foodstuffs he'd moved into tents out of the torrents of rain. "We should've beat them by now," Max said. "If this is their food, they should be starved or poisoned. The biscuit alone's more weevil than flour."

"We'll eat it anyway," John said, and Max nodded, and the two of them looked out at the men who were splashing through the puddles, Rebel underwear on their heads.

What John was waiting for took a long time to arrive. He was expecting Kate's report of the Harmony Fourth of July, for he'd read in the *Evansville Journal* that there'd been a demonstration by Copperheads, though the Union Leaguers and Crescent City Band had carried the day. When Kate's letter finally came it said only that there'd been "a little party jealousy," but nothing worth mentioning. She wrote, too, that John Pulleyblank and the other boys of the 15th, who'd mustered out and gotten home (though not Harry Beal, who was free of the guardhouse at last, but was working on fortifications instead of being released), had decided to form their own league, which John assumed would be a Lincoln and Johnson league. Kate, to his mild aggravation, reported nothing about John Smith, who'd been very ill, and nothing about Robert Clarke, though Lieutenant Smith had said he was wounded again, which made the boys in the company very anxious to hear from him. There was nothing about Levi. Kate, being Kate, saved the hurtful news for last, putting it off as long as possible. She'd phrased it carefully—or as carefully as she could. Jim Rippeto, she said, had proposed to Ann Bradley and, to everyone's surprise, Ann had said yes, though of course nobody could know for sure about Ann.

Reading the words, John felt stung. He read them again with a sudden fury at himself that he'd not haunted Ann's sister's house until he'd actually seen her, and with an even stronger wrath at his loss, for it did feel to him he could lose something even if he'd never really had it. He tore into his tent and got his paper and pen. He wrote back immediately to Kate that he would think Miss Bradley would be in as great a hurry to get married as Mr. Rippeto was, that certainly there could be no person in the 25th on whose account she would postpone her marriage. He changed subjects then, attempting to make it seem that he didn't really care—and as if Kate wouldn't care about Jim Rippeto. He said that he did not expect fighting as there hadn't been any since he'd rejoined the company and that the family shouldn't be uneasy on his account, that he thought they wouldn't be sent to any battle before they left for home, and that Forrest was too busy in Mississippi to come to them.

But then he couldn't restrain himself more or stop the swell of bitterness he felt about Ann. He added a final word. "At all events, if I do get killed, it won't have killed any big things," he scribbled. Then he closed the letter as usual and, with an irate flick, tossed his pen aside.

⌒

Since January, the 25th had been brigaded with the 17th New York, but now that Colonel Grower of that regiment had taken command of the entire brigade, it was definitely something new under the sun. John liked the change. Maybe he was partial—he was sure that he was—but he had always firmly believed that two thousand western troops would make a tougher army than three thousand eastern ones; in fact, he thought the Rebels would rather fight even a thousand eastern Yankees than a hundred from the West. But he did make one caveat. He had watched the eastern troops who'd gone through Memphis on their way to Vicksburg, and they were better drilled and better disciplined than any western soldiers he'd ever seen. Now, with Colonel Grower in command, the 25th had the benefit of the eastern army's kind of discipline. There was another positive factor in the mix. Colonel Grower was a strategist, and John suspected the battle-hardened 25th, which was used to going in on its muscle in a fight, might be in for a surprise.

And a fight was what they were headed for. He'd been wrong in his letter home. On the 25th of July, with three days of rations, their brigade set out from Decatur. Including the two hundred fifty men of the 25th, they were a thousand strong. To John, it was liberating to be marching as just a soldier once more. He didn't have to care about records or transportation or the logistics of the thing. He just had to keep his powder dry and put one foot in front of the other. He also didn't care that it was an all-night march. He liked the greenish black sky and the sounds of the bullfrogs and owls and the various insomniac insects. It was a racket that kept him awake, or in a condition close to wakefulness, and it had a certain cheerful silliness about it.

The word in the ranks was that they had twenty-two miles to cover, that they were moving close to Courtland, Alabama, where a number of Rebel regiments had made a rendezvous. As dawn finally neared, John took a drink of tepid canteen coffee in an effort to stop a fit of yawns and to wake up his feet. Light broke to the sound of trees being felled, and it occurred to him they were decoying the Rebels into thinking they were setting up a permanent camp. Then Dave Vint passed the word that their scouts said the Rebels were getting ready to leave their encampment at Pond Springs. The men groused at the thought of more marching, but a moment later Colonel Grower rode down the column and sent them all on the quickstep to take cover, to actually hide in the woods in the underbrush.

It wasn't a normal kind of hiding. They were setting a trap, John realized. The colonel had sent a small detachment of their cavalry, who were Tennessee Union boys, forward to draw the enemy toward them, while the rest of the men lay waiting and quiet. By the time most of the men were trying to fend off sleep or to shift a leg or arm in the brush without making the noise of twigs breaking, the cavalry reappeared on the road. The horses were flying. John saw the muscles in their legs as they thundered up the road.

Nobody was sleepy now. A long minute went by. Then another. John heard more horses approaching and, almost before he was sure that his gun was ready, there were two horsemen, a Rebel lieutenant and sergeant, in front of them on the road. They were near the center of the line of hidden men, which was where John was. When they stopped, they weren't ten feet from the muzzle of his rifle. It was clear they hadn't an idea there were men in the underbrush. The lieutenant spat his tobacco in John's direction, and it landed on an elephant ear. Then both men began shooting at the cavalry, and they were screaming their awful yell.

They were full of taunts. "You damned cowards. You damnable bastards. You afraid of two men? There, you—Abey's babies! Are you fuckin' afraid?"

John didn't move, but he looked sideways out of the corner of his eye. Alex Hugo had a bead on both men that he thought could kill them with one shot, but there was no order to fire. The gibes and gunfire kept up, yet the cavalry didn't advance. When the two men finally seemed to think they were getting nowhere in setting their own trap, they clapped spurs to their horses and headed back in the direction they'd come from. John heard a low, soft whistle up the line, but nobody moved. Nobody spoke. He could feel the men waiting to see what would happen next, and it occurred to him that he had a front row seat (if lying on the ground beside a line of ants marching up an elephant ear could count as a seat) at the strangest and most fraught play that he'd ever seen.

He was watching the ants when he heard horses again. They were louder this time. It was the same two men, but with four more men accompanying them. They resumed their firing and shouting, their horses doing a jittery dance in the road as their riders held them. A speckled gray stallion pawed the road right in front of John. He might have shot a hole through its haunches without even moving his gun. The horses stomped and backed on the road, as mindless and defenseless as their riders, who didn't know they were so close to death that a fully live man couldn't get any closer.

John blinked the sweat out of his eyes. He blinked again. It was a wonder to him that all the men lying in the underbrush were so still not a single Rebel had noticed them. Of course, these Rebels were making a furious commotion and, too, it was overcast so there was no sun to glint off the rifles in the underbrush, nothing to give the light-flash warning that they were here.

John didn't know how much longer the men lay without firing. Maybe it was as long as a half an hour. It was certainly long enough that he knew each of the Rebel's voices. It was long enough that he could tell which was the best horseman and which was best at insults and swearing and which one would have the most swagger out of his saddle. John looked at the horses' legs and the boots and stirrups and dust churning together. He watched as the Rebels took turns firing at the Union cavalry. When, finally, it was clear they wouldn't advance any farther, Colonel Grower gave the order to shoot.

Later, when they had abandoned the brush and fallen back into the woods and out of line and the men were guzzling from their canteens and digging into their haversacks for food, it seemed to John that every man had his own version of what had happened—his own jabbery need to tell the story. What those stories came down to in nearly every case was that the men had breathed easier when they hadn't opened fire on the first two men at the end of their muskets for it would have seemed like murder instead of killing. As it was, John had still had a split second of indecision when the colonel's order finally came, but there was more distance then in terms of time and the position of the Rebels and more of a sense that they were a military unit of some threat. Yet John was still relieved when it was all done and only one Rebel lay dead—not the swaggerer, he thought—while the others, trying to flee, had been captured by the cavalry who, by then, had circled around and come up in their rear.

"We could have killed them all, every cussed and cussing one of them," Dave Vint said, and John thought Dave would have liked to do just that, but that he was distinctly in the minority.

By nightfall, they were back in the line of march, proceeding westward toward Pond Springs once more. As they drew close, John eyed a fine, large house that was partly visible through the distant trees. He wondered if anyone was left living in it until Gil Smith said he'd heard it was General Wheeler's house, the Confederate cavalry's Fighting Joe. The camp itself, when they came to it, was deserted, but with a good deal of evidence it had been left in a hurry, though hours ago. Abandoned laundry was strewn and dried across the bushes. The cooking fires were cold.

"We're after a naked army again," Max Munte said to John. "These Secesh boys have to spin more cotton. Or else get Sambo to do it."

It was only a short while—hardly enough time for the men to think of resting or poking around in the litter—before the cavalry scouts rode up and reported the enemy in force at Courtland. On orders, every soldier formed up again in the line of march. They headed quickly onto the road, the lines of troops moving forward with their wagons rolling behind them.

They might have been headed into a major battle. John thought that they were; they all thought that. As it turned out, they weren't, and by the next evening John had a very good idea of what the official history of this brief westward march might say. Since Colonel Morgan was gone, the command of the 25th had fallen to Lieutenant Colonel

Rheinlander, and John thought he would make a short report, probably noting that there'd been a spirited engagement in the morning at Courtland, that it had lasted half an hour, and that the regiment had taken no casualties and returned to Decatur on the twenty-eighth. Colonel Grower, in a longer report on the action of the whole brigade, would likely say that the Rebel pickets, falling back, had opened fire on their forces as they entered the town, shooting with small arms from the streets and the houses, but that they had been quickly dispersed. He would also certainly include that the main Rebel force and its battery in the old breastworks outside of Courtland had fired on their brigade before retreating. And perhaps he would mention that the Union cavalry that pursued the Rebels had had to chase them with tired horses over a road strewn with pistols and blankets, and haversacks and canteens, and that they'd eventually turned back.

John was confident that what he remembered most of this short expedition would not find its way into any report. The men would still talk about it, of how tense and exciting it had been to lie hidden while those few smart-mouthed Rebels had strutted their horses before them. Even though the people of Courtland had reported the ambulances full of wounded when the Rebels retreated, Colonel Grower's ambush created a far more indelible memory than the fight in that town. Not a building had been burned. Only two men of the brigade and a handful of Confederates were killed.

For John, what also proved indelible was the scene in Courtland after the fight. Every man and woman and child was Secesh, and even the Negroes were Rebels, though Rebels or not, pressed into Union service by a detachment of Negro soldiers who'd gone with the expedition for precisely that purpose. John heard one soldier ask an old black man why he wanted to stay with his master instead of becoming a freeman and the answer made absolute sense—that the man wished to go along in the worst way but that he had his family to consider. The interview grew comic then. The soldier asked how much of a family the man had and the answer was lengthy. There was his wife, he said. And then the four gals. There was Aunt Sarah and her two gals. And there were four more boys and the baby. Listening, John had smiled, thinking he'd found a family to rival those in the mountain homes of Drimarone, but in the morning there was the old fellow trudging along in the ranks of pressed Negroes and his whole family following him the best that they could.

There was a last vivid image that, for John, was linked to the expedition, though it was more in the way of a postscript. When they got back to Decatur, a single, broken violin was waiting in his tent. It was lying next to his books, and he looked at it silently for a moment. Then he ran his hand down the just crooked neck and over the flinty pegs. He touched the varnished top; he felt for the glued joint with his fingers. Then he took off his cap and sat down to start work. He wasn't sure about himself, he didn't know at all about Ann Bradley, but this was a thing he could make whole again.

The Siege of Atlanta
Late Summer 1864

22

Company A, Monday, August 10, 1864
Absent—Enlisted Men 23; Present for Duty or Detached Duty—Officers 3,
Enlisted Men 46, Aggregate 72

Consolidated Morning Report of Twenty-fifth Indiana
Commanded by Lieutenant Colonel John Rheinlander

Company A, Monday, August 17, 1864
Absent—Enlisted Men 10; Present for Duty—Officers 2, Enlisted Men 19,
Commissioned Officers Died in Action or of Wounds Received Thereof 1,
Enlisted Men Discharged by Expiration of Service 40, Aggregate 72

Consolidated Morning Report of Twenty-fifth Indiana
Commanded by Major Victor C. Larkin

In a way, John believed he had started an exodus. The men on detached duty at headquarters in Decatur were coming back to the companies one by one, day after day, though it was not that they had asked to be returned as he had. General Sherman had laid siege to Atlanta, and what had been rumored for weeks, now verged on certainty: all of the men in camp would be going there, and very soon. It was obvious General Sherman meant to use every possible soldier, which included men like John who had only days before their enlistments were up. John didn't know if the men were more bitter or downhearted. They were both, but generally they seemed resigned.

For the whole summer, the need to sustain the discipline of a fighting force had meant a variety of efforts at policing the camp. Some had been successful, some not. But the business of camp was now more immediate than maintaining fitness for duty or ensuring that men didn't desert or wind up in the brig. Men who were very ill, Henry Schafer among them, were sent to the hospital in Nashville. Every man wrote the letters he needed to write; every private was mending his boots and cleaning and oiling his gun until he knew it would make him a marksman.

On the third day of August, two weeks before the time John had thought he would be headed home, the order came down from Colonel Rheinlander. They were to move to Atlanta. They were to join the 4th Division, 16th Army Corps as soon as transportation could be provided. Commands were to be kept at readiness to move on twenty-four hours' notice.

They had forty-eight. John hurried to fix the violin he'd found in his tent. It had come from Al Norcross, who had purchased it from a sick man who'd been sent to Nashville. John repaired what he could, though it was clear the varnish would have to wait until later. On the evening of the fourth, Al came to his tent and sat on a crate while John finished thinning and sanding the bridge.

"I'll ship it to Ellie," Al said, watching him. "I promised I'd learn to play for her and I will—after the war. This is part payment on the promise. Have you ever read *Ivanhoe*, Jack?"

John shook his head. He held the violin in the light from the open tent flap.

"Alex Fretageot told me it's one of the best books in the English language. He played the violin. Of course, his pa still does." Al ran his fingers across the grain of the crate. "Alex and I talked books. Sometimes astronomy."

John wound the E string around a peg. He was trying to remember Alex Fretageot's face, though he couldn't really. "I didn't know him," he said, pushing in another string. He tightened the peg. "Will you play Bach for her? Bach? Or dancing music?"

"I'd be lucky to play 'Yankee Doodle.' Harmony seems a long way away, Jack."

"It does," John said, and he took the two dollars that Al handed him. Then, considering the orders for Atlanta, he gave it back and asked Al if he could send it and more of his money to his father with the violin when it was crated.

Al nodded. He picked up the violin while John got the money for him. "Sometimes I wonder . . . you know, if I was quick to sign up again," he said, putting the violin under his arm. Its neck touched the chevron of red and blue braid on his sleeve, which was the official emblem the Veterans wore. He shook hands with John. "But it's a done thing."

It was still dark when the 25th left with the brigade, their long lines moving across the Tennessee on the pontoon bridge. They were headed for the cars on the other side and then to Chattanooga, though the train wouldn't start there until full daylight. Waiting on a siding, John found himself crouched on the floor of a car playing chess with Lieutenant Bennett, a horde of men pushed in closely around them. They had as good a match going as any he'd had in the army, but the men started to get obstreperous in the tight quarters, and Lieutenant Bennett, looking around, got up to restore order.

"We'll play at home sometime," he said, leaving the game, and John nodded, though he wondered if that was true—if the difference in their rank in the army and the pecking order in New Harmony would make that unlikely. Or if something about this war actually meant it could happen.

When the train lurched into Chattanooga, the men were sprawled in all sorts of positions, asleep and awake. The air in the car had the particular smell of a cramped army space: a mixed stench of farts and spat tobacco. The men got off the cars in squads, but at sunup they were moving again, on to Allatoona. There was one more early-morning ride to Marietta, and over the Chattahoochee, and then they were finally there. They had moved into the reserve at Atlanta within shouting distance of Peach Tree Creek. Once more they were back with General Sherman, their orders to be ready to move to the front, which was less than a mile from the Rebel works, and their job to help finish the capture of Atlanta, which would be a symbolic capture— of the heart of Georgia, of the heart of the South—and a substantive capture of the place that was the South's main granary and manufacturing center.

They were, however, late to the ball. The siege and approach had been going on for weeks. Everywhere that ridges of trees hadn't yet been sheared off by cannons or turned into abatis, well-entrenched encampments lay in the shadows of branches. John saw an astonishing number of trenches, and seemingly endless chains of supply trains snaked among them with mules and mule drivers adding their particular din to intermittent fire that kept the men on edge as they made camp. It was the most dug-in army John had ever encountered. It was extraordinary, and it seemed to him that fighting had changed in some fundamental way since the war's early days at Fort Donelson and Shiloh. Now the face of the army was far less apt to be the actual faces of men than the sudden artillery shells and sniper bullets that arrived from out of the blue.

The men knew that there'd been an intense fight at the end of July, with battle lines arrayed beside the shattered forests. The reports were that fighting had continued for days in fits and starts, but had never been conclusive. John wondered if that was because the army didn't go in as much on dash and muscle as it once had. Instead, after the hardest fighting, men moved back to their barricades and trenches, which was all right with him. In theory, it seemed a less hazardous thing, though unnerving in its own way. There were reports of soldiers falling dead in the process of crossing a bit of open ground or in the middle of eating a meal, not ever realizing there'd been someone to fire on them and make his shot. John thought it caused the men to be careless. This sort of imminent death was too random to guard against.

There was still a very large army in place—as many men or more as there'd been men at Shiloh. But there was a city here, and not just a meetinghouse and a few lowly buildings, which made it quite different. General Sherman was intent on bombardment. Many, even most of Atlanta's residents (though certainly not the "all" that the general claimed) were reported to have fled. Some had been packed into railroad cars. Others had left in a vast exodus of mule-drawn wagons loaded with furniture and personal possessions. John wanted to find Captain Boren and ask him what he thought of the shelling, of laying waste again to the things men made. Hobbling them in that way. Pushing them back to a life of cavemen, as Max Munte had said. To John, it seemed a loss that would take incalculably long to undo— not just the building and rebuilding of structures, but the chipping away at a deep resentment that rebuilding had to be done at all. And considering all this, it seemed odd to John that men might get over the fact of killing each other when they stayed alive themselves, and yet feel a seething rage that everything they'd worked to build was gone. Death, he had started to think, was too personal for real mourning to attend it in any way but in the most immediate situation: the loss of a brother or father; the loss of a best friend and comrade in arms. Those things a man could feel. But a whole army? To lose that was a stunning idea but not something one would take inside and feel. Instead, John thought, it would work on the mind and in a way much like the loss of these tangible things.

Every fifteen minutes, another big shell—the Atlanta Express, the men called them—roared toward the city. The troops who'd been entrenched here made a sport of it, cheering the shells as they went overhead. Even as newcomers, the 25th got into the spirit of the thing. There was excitement that they'd finally left desolate Decatur and come to a place where General Sherman, with his red hair, could be seen walking among his troops. They knew he was intent on taking the city. Or at least what was left of it.

Whether the city would fall before the non-Vets made their departure for home was an open question. John believed that if they weren't forced to stay in the ranks beyond their muster-out date, the sporadic nature of the attack meant they were unlikely to see Atlanta much closer than they already had which, in his opinion, was close enough. As it was, they were on the front line or out on the skirmish line, where they lay the whole night of the ninth, listening to shells and the bullets that hit the ground or, twice, soldiers. John heard the men yipping in pain and being carried to the back of the lines for the surgeons to go to work on them, and both times he thought it was an odd thing, being shot while you were lying on your belly. Already, there had been horrendous casualties in the fighting here—eight thousand on their side alone, he'd heard, though he was no longer privy to the official reports at headquarters that would let him know for certain.

On the long night on the skirmish line, in spite of the fact Levi's one letter home had been sent from Richmond, John couldn't push it out of his head that Levi might have been in Atlanta, that he might even be here now. As he lay on his gun, its familiar stock pressing into his chest, he thought of General Sherman's mission he'd heard rumors about—the scheme to send men behind the Rebels' lines to free Union prisoners. Sweating in the hot night and waiting for the big shells, John made his own fanciful plan. He would find himself a mule he could tether at the back of a cellblock (in his mind it looked very much like the Irving Block in Memphis), and leave it there while he and the men he took with him overcame the guards. They would free the prisoners, every one of them, and he would hoist Levi onto the mule—weak as he'd be—and bring him back to their trenches. He'd see to it that he got a good meal and all the coffee a man could drink and whiskey if he could buy it.

Then John would give him the news that would make him grin and puff up a bit, that the kinsman of his brother-in-law, Captain Bill Barton, was a major general now: General John A. Logan who, on General Sherman's orders, had rushed off across the field on horseback from his old post with the 15th Army Corps to take command of the Army of the Tennessee during the fighting here. He had rallied the troops, brilliantly counterattacking against Cheatham's corps and hurling them back after they'd punctured the Union line. In telling it, he would skip how General Logan had been removed from his new command only days later, not for any deficiency but, as seemed to be the frequent case with general officers, for something political.

John thought of other things Levi would want to know. When he'd exhausted his ideas and realized he'd been clenching his jaw for the long minutes he waited for another Atlanta Express, he found himself thinking once more of Ann Bradley and wondering if she'd thought better of Jim Rippeto's offer now that he and the other men of the 15th Indiana were home. They were a sizable number of the Harmony friends he had left—Harry Beal and John Pulleyblank, Godfrey Gundrum (who generally lived up to his given name), and Harry Husband and George Wilsey. Handsome as the girls thought Jim Rippeto was, John doubted he had the name or prospects to make Ann happy, though she'd clearly not made any progress with Lieutenant Colonel Julian Dale Owen. John had even considered the possibility Mrs. Owen had let Ann go, not for financial reasons, but because she'd sensed her interest in her nephew. Perhaps, with her station reduced, Ann was panicking and ready to settle for Jim. Yet John could easily see her changing her mind. And if she did, mightn't she as well change her mind in favor of him? Not that he thought seriously of marrying her. But he would like to be her beau long enough to drop her and, really, long enough before that to have the pleasure of walking out with her on his arm and feeling the light pressure as she leaned slightly against him, and smelling the lilac scent that came from her collar, perhaps her neck—a little spot just behind her ear where a man might find a way to loosen her well-wound hair.

John reached for his canteen and drank some coffee, glad it was cold. He listened to hear if the other men were breathing heavily into sleep. Lying here with Atlanta smoldering before him, it occurred to him that Ann might have meant no harm in reading his earlier letters aloud—that they pleased her—that she was proud of them—and he knew Jim Rippeto could not write the letter he could. Perhaps Ann had been wounded by what he'd last written and yet had still kept his letters in a box in a drawer, not imagining she would return them. Maybe she'd even accepted Jim Rippeto from hurt or spite, though if Ann would turn fickle on Jim—whose fine appearance Kate certainly had noticed—what could John expect? When he was of sound mind, which he couldn't entirely claim at the moment, and when he was being honest with himself, he knew that the most he would ever get from Ann Bradley was that single hour in David Dale's laboratory when he'd kissed her fingers and felt the overwhelming desire to hold her against the wall—to kiss her and kiss her until, slowly, she slid to the floor, laughing and skirmishing and then no longer pushing him away but prying at his buttons, the fossils and bottles on the shelves shaking and clinking together and then falling.

John stared at the fires rimming the lower sky with their bloody glow. He remembered the evening horizon the day George Warren played in Memphis with the Evansville Band and he'd thought of the gorse fires in Donegal when the children gathered round calling *the bog's aflame!* and the wind swirled the flames into a blazing peat fire that might have warmed the county's worth of hearths. John thought he could feel the heat from the Atlanta fires, though it was partly the unlifting heat of the southern summer and the particular heat that came to him in thinking of Ann. He should feel lucky, he thought. He was seeing the country as he'd hoped to, even if he lay with the ruins of Atlanta before him and the mosquitoes bothering him more than the odd bullet that landed close to him while the big guns launched their shells.

His mind was on Levi again. He would have to tell him he'd heard from Caroline, that his sister had a particular way of sending a man the kind of information he was eager to learn and a way of making him feel her interest in him, yet without being forward. Though perhaps the distinction would be lost on Levi, and he would take it as an insult to his Catty, dear sister. Being Levi, he might call John out for a fight so that they would have to interrupt their escape and settle things right there on their way out of town, though John would pull his punches and duck Levi's until he could push his skinny ass back onto the mule and pin his arms to his sides and just hold on to him, it would be that good to have him back.

Day finally broke with smoke twisting its way into the lightening sky. Their relief came, and the men crawled back over the ground and then made their way, as they could, back to the reserve. At their bivouac, John could hear how much his ears were ringing and realized that the night, as it had worn on, had seemed almost silent to him, he'd grown so deaf from the general din. They were on half rations for breakfast. For as many supply trains as there were, the lines of support were still stretched thin, and it was the business of people like Captain Boren to see that they didn't break. It was the business of people like Max Munte to see that they went hungry but not so hungry that they starved. It was the generals' business to see that General Hood didn't cut their railroad lines and leave them stranded here in the South with no breakthrough to Atlanta and no way to make it, if it came to that, back to the rear.

John missed it a little, being in the flow of things at headquarters, though he thought it felt honest to leave the army, as he'd come into it—and as Levi would have—with just plain soldiering. But even as soldiers, it was not fighting they were doing so much as scuttling back and forth with Atlanta in the foreground. The reserve moved up a hundred yards and onto the front lines again. Company A and Companies F and D were on the skirmish line for twenty-four straight hours, and at least one man was wounded. Yet for all the immediacy of the siege, John had the feeling that the actual fall of Atlanta, which seemed all but certain, would be something he learned about only from reading a newspaper in New Harmony. Unless, of course, one of the sniper bullets from the enemy found him first.

They were holding the line. They were filling in for men who had died, all with the intent, John knew, of starting the Confederacy falling in on itself the way a wind-felled tent corner starts a general collapse. It meant that the whole enterprise felt momentous, though John didn't see how the role of the non-Vets in the 25th was anything but peripheral. In a way, it reminded him of how he'd been a student at Trinity. He'd been at it but not of it, and the same thing was true here. He had no real bragging rights to Atlanta. None of the non-Vets did. If it hadn't been for the burning skyline, which they could turn their backs on and ignore at will, they might have been on a skirmish line anywhere.

As it was, there was mostly confusion. In moving back and forth from the reserve to the front line, John wasn't always even sure of the day. One after another, the officers who hadn't re-enlisted submitted their resignations, and it was never certain who would be next to give the regiment and company their orders. Colonel Rheinlander left first. Then two captains and at least five lieutenants were gone. John was afraid that no one would be left to see that the men whose terms were up were given the papers they needed and their transportation home. He wasn't the only one who was concerned. There was skulking in the reserve. There were men reporting sick and at least one deserter. In talking to Lieutenant Bennett, who was waiting for the command to send the non-Vets to the rear, John could tell he was worried that the regiment would be left as nothing more than a skeleton force. Already, not only were officers missing but details were undermanned and the troops edgy, wanting to leave for home or, if they were staying, to finish the job instead of waiting uneasily on the skirmish line or in the trenches.

The weather turned wet, which might have been a relief, except that it stayed hot. When the raindrops stopped for even an instant, mosquitoes took their place. John and the other men were busy swatting at them at first light, which was when they seemed the hungriest and when the flurries of bullets started from the Rebel trenches. He didn't know which he hated more, bugs or bullets, until he saw a man up the line from Company F raise his head and get thrown instantly backward. It was a deadly shot and, when John learned it was Seth Johnson who was killed, a boy he hardly knew, he hoped he was the final person he'd see shot and that he'd always remember his name for just that reason.

But the fact was that he didn't know who the last man was that he saw die while he was still on the rolls of the 25th. Try as he could, he couldn't remember. He didn't know if he and the other non-Vets had been lying wretchedly on the skirmish line and had seen the next lethal shot, or if they'd been huddling in the rear and waiting for the cars when they learned the horrible news. But learn it they had. Lieutenant Bennett had been killed. John could scarcely believe it. He felt it like another crater ripped in his life. But as much as he hated that death—such a terrible waste, James Bennett, a brilliant man and all of his knowledge lost—he couldn't feel it as keenly as the news about Al Norcross. Al Norcross had been leading his men, and Al was dead, too.

John didn't know how it had happened. He couldn't remember that either, and he wouldn't ask anyone to tell him, though he wished that he knew. All he really had left of the time when the regiment had dwindled to a shadow of itself was a gray space in his mind that he couldn't fill. He wanted to remember when things had occurred and where he fit on the coordinate of events between the moment when Seth Johnson had sprawled backward in death and the later moments when he knew that Lieutenant Bennett and Al Norcross were dead.

Nothing was there. Instead, what he remembered, and what was burned in his mind next to the word Atlanta, was the constant downpour when the crated bodies of Lieutenant Bennett—breveted a captain in the field—and Al Norcross, who had died a sergeant, and Seth Johnson, an ordinary private, were put on the train. John had watched. He'd rubbed his hand nervously up and down his rain-soaked sleeve and wished very hard that he had Al's violin back. It needed varnish, it really did, and as he climbed into a boxcar with the other men and their guns and packs, the smoke from the engine puffing and streaming through the rain, he regretted it keenly—that the last tangible object Eleanor Norcross would have from her husband was a thing he had left so unfinished.

⁓

For an instant, John thought he was flying. At the crossing point between sleep and consciousness, the Rebel cannon he'd touched in his dream turned into a circus cannon and he was its missile. He was shot into a crowd of gasping and shrieking spectators. Then, with a hard and jolting thud, he was fully awake. The car's wheels no longer clattered beneath them. Trying to right himself and to find something to stand on, he realized that his lingering sense of being airborne and the startled yells and bodies crushing against him meant the train had left the track. It had tilted and then plunged and then slid. Then it had stopped.

The men were swarmed together in a messy sprawl of legs and packs. Muddy water oozed in through a gap in the car. A pistol discharged, its bullet ripping a man's cap off, but not his head, though he checked with a careful hand. A din of shouting and cursing, already loud, grew earsplitting.

Dave Vint had a foot on John's hip and his other leg caught behind him. John tried pushing him off. "Get the goddam door open," Dave yelled and, for a moment, John thought that he meant the door he was lying against, which was impossible since it was obviously jammed into earth. Then he saw Dave was waving at the other door while he shouted out orders. In spite of the fact they were all citizens since being mustered out at Chattanooga, the men did what he said. They hoisted each other up to undo the bar which, along with the door, was jacked skyward. John thought they looked like leggy bugs climbing and sometimes losing their hold on a trellis. Finally, they'd managed to do it, to grab the bar and slide it over and to shove hard so that, with one long metallic groan, the door opened on trees and on the sky itself.

John watched, amazed. One man pulled himself up and out into that sky. More men scrambled up behind him. It was as if they were going over a parapet once more. It was as though they were clambering up that long ago hill at Fort Donelson with General Smith, his mustache flying as he urged them on. It was so steep, so slippery as they clawed up the snow, Rebel screams shrilling down on them through a tangle of leaves.

Sudden tears stung at John's cheeks. He brushed them aside. They were getting out. The men were. They weren't crushed or killed in this car but climbing free of it so that it wouldn't end this way, and they would still go home. They wouldn't be like Lieutenant Bennett and Al Norcross, but they'd be back in Harmony alive and he would hug his mother again and stop in the street to scratch the ears of a stray dog or sit in a parlor and dandle Emma Clarke's baby, which was surely a girl for he had always considered Robert Clarke a manly fellow, and his grandmother had said it takes a real man to father a daughter. He would see all the girls who'd waited for all the men, girls who didn't know that the war was a heavy, unyielding thing that still lay inside them.

"Get off me, Dave. Off," he said, and he hunched his side up and torqued his hip until he was out from under Dave's foot. Then he righted himself, though he thought a man needed sea legs just to stand here. He moved with the knot of other men, inching his way across the car side, which was the floor now—a canted floor—and then crawling as he could. With a boost from Max Munte, he managed to pull himself up toward the opening. He used every single bit of muscle he had, and finally he was through the door and, steeling himself, he dropped down after George Tretheway and landed with a splash in water that came up to his thighs. He winced, absorbing the shock to his knee. When he could, he waded to higher ground. The men were still muttering and cursing as they milled about. It didn't seem anyone was really hurt, but Alex Hugo had a giant shiner, and there was a general assortment of bruises and bumps. John looked behind him. The train was entirely off the track, and the car he'd been in, along with a second one, had gone about six feet down the embankment and landed in a gully.

George Tretheway was working at a wet cigarette paper that came apart in his fingers when he tried to roll it. John stood watching him, remembering the first soldier's trick he'd ever learned—to light a pipe with the wind at his back. George threw the paper on the ground. "Are we still in Tennessee?" he asked, and then he answered himself. "We're always in Tennessee. A nod of the head to Alabama. Five minutes in Georgia to get the lieutenant and Al Norcross killed, and here we are again. It's a bloody lifetime in Tennessee."

John actually thought they were in Kentucky by now, though he didn't say so. And who was he to know where they were, having been stuck with everyone else inside a boxcar and, before that, left on cars that were uncoupled and stranded at stations all the way to Chattanooga and again en route to Nashville. "It's the leaning car that the coffins are on, isn't it?" he said, and George nodded. John looked around him. "You think there're guerrillas?"

"Why not? Why wouldn't there be? Probably Forrest himself since he's everywhere. He's like the whole goddamn state of Tennessee."

"I don't see Captain Boren," John said, though he knew that finding Captain Boren wouldn't necessarily help. They'd gotten a ride on the cars from the army, but little else. Their tents were still in Atlanta with the Veterans. They'd had food enough for three days, but they'd taken four days in getting to Chattanooga and they hadn't gotten any more rations. John doubted, too, if anyone had enough ammunition to make more than a single pinging shot at a boxcar.

The last of the men were being pulled out of the other upended car, hauled up with a rope like lassoed horses. John thought there was a good chance that one of the other cars would tip over and into the gulley, but at least there were no men in it. The whole train had emptied out after the derailment. The field, which stretched to a brush of green trees on the far hillside, was full of tired soldiers. Ex-soldiers. *Ex*-soldiers. John was still trying to get used to it.

He spotted Captain Boren and went over to him. "What about the coffins?" he asked. "If that next tilted car falls into the gulley . . ." John stopped. He knew he didn't have to describe the picture he had in his mind. Coffins splitting open. The car filling with water. Bodies floating free, puffed up and ridgy like fingers in a dishpan.

"We'll get them out," Captain Boren said. They started toward the car, and John touched his pocket, checking as he had ever since Chattanooga, to make sure he had his discharge papers. He was scanning the field, too, looking for Reverend Heuring.

The train's forward cars had jumped the track into a patch of vines that had already begun to change to their fall color. They made a meandering stripe of red. It looked like blood from a wound that had flowed as far away as it could get from its source. John stared.

It reminded him of something, though it took a moment before he remembered what. Then he knew. Once at headquarters in Memphis, he'd heard a general say that the mark of the Southern states was miscegenation, that it ran clear through them like a bright red thread so that the South, with its florid tales of chivalry and fine Southern womanhood and the whole rest of its elaborate mythology, was largely just kidding itself. John had been struck by the comment. He remembered the conclusion he'd drawn for himself: that the red thread was the mixed blood that kept coiling back to the heart of the South, but that it was mixed only in terms of idea. He had seen Hamilton's blood—the elegant clerk, and he *was* elegant—and it was like any other man's blood. It was exactly like the whole river of blood he'd seen in this war.

"Are you coming, John?" Captain Boren asked, looking back at him, and John nodded and hurried to match stride with him. "We need a detail," Captain Boren said. "We need four of the lightest and strongest men we've got. And the biggest men to sit on the door side for ballast when the coffins get moved."

It was a minor engineering job, but after the fifteen minutes or so it took to round up a detail and follow Captain Boren's directions, the car was still tilted at the same angle and as close to unmoved and stable as anyone could have hoped. The coffins were clear. Men on the higher ground grew quiet as the detail brought them up. Some spread ponchos out to set them on. One man rigged a flagpole and hung a handkerchief on it, which was a far cry from their faded and bullet-ripped flag with its silver threads dangling in the holes where the stars had been—the flag with the battle names on it that had stayed with the Veterans. George Tretheway printed 25th Ind. V. Inf. on the handkerchief, and the men saluted. John saw one of them make the sign of the cross, which he made, too, with the slightest movement of his fingers on his chest. He spotted Reverend Heuring with another group of men and thought they should ask him to say a prayer. Then the moment passed. The men moved away, and rain started, drizzling on them and the coffins and the makeshift flag.

Later, the men argued over how many wet and hungry hours they'd spent waiting for new cars and for a crew to fix the track. Ten hours? Fifteen? Men tried to sleep, but a harder burst of rain kept them awake. John thought it was all wretchedly fitting—to leave the army in as much discomfort as they'd served it, though he could easily have skipped this latest miserable development.

Alex Hugo, who was sitting on a stump, let out a long yell. It was the same banshee scream he'd made when his brother was killed, and John wondered if he was reliving that moment at Donelson or if he'd simply had enough of it all. If everybody had. For himself, if he'd had a thing to eat in his pack or the money promised to be waiting for them in Louisville, he thought he could make his way home by foot and by boat. It would be faster and more certain than waiting for a repair crew and another train, though there were still raiders and guerrillas to watch for. When it finally came down to it, he got on board the cars with the coffins and everybody else. He sat in a corner and listened to the train as it swayed and jolted along, and he tried to believe it was really happening, that the train he was on was taking him ever farther from the war. That, with luck, he was going home.

New Harmony, Indiana
Fall 1864

23

In the name of the Benevolent Father of All I Francis Kannon of the town of New Harmony County of Posey in the State of Indiana do make and publish this my last will and testament.

Item 1st: I give and devise to Mrs. Mary Armstrong wife of William Armstrong for her own use the sum of One Hundred Dollars.
Item 2d: I give and devise to Ann Bradley sister of the above Mrs. Armstrong the sum of fifty dollars.

From the will of Francis Cannon, January 14th, 1864

J ohn was in the hammock Denis had tied to the trees by the house. He was under strict orders from his mother to rest until he stopped hacking, which was something he no longer even noticed he did. He was reading the Evansville paper and doing it in great comfort since Mary, doting little sister that she'd become, was fanning him while he drank lemonade. He thought he might look either lazy or content to passersby, and he hoped that he did. He read slowly through the pages and then stopped at what the paper said about their regiment's return: "A considerable number of the 25th Regiment who did not re-enlist arrived at home on Sunday night. We regret that we had no notification of their coming, else there would have been a grand reception given them."

John read it once more and then, folding the paper back on his chest, looked up at the crown of rain trees that stretched down the street. He thought what it would have meant if there really had been a celebration in Evansville. He was curious just how the citizenry would have toasted their ravaged band of returning warriors. He wondered if Ann Bradley would have come out, or if she would have been too busy entertaining Jim Rippeto or, by now, some other fellow.

When they'd finally gotten to Louisville, and when the word went around that there wasn't a chance at all they'd get paid, John had helped Captain Boren arrange for a steamer that took them to the Ohio and west toward Evansville. There was air to breathe again. They were going home. They didn't, however, expect any particular welcome, rump part of the 25th as they were: men who had left a battle and war and were taking the last of their dead home with them.

At Evansville, John had wondered if Ann Bradley was there, and he'd thought seriously of trying to find out. But coming up on the steamboat landing where he'd brought Major Walker ten months earlier, he knew that he had to stay with the men. He felt honor bound to go back home to New Harmony with the same boys he'd left with. Or at least with the ones who remained. And, anyway, it was hot as the devil in Evansville. The whole town looked limp. It looked as if it hadn't recovered yet from the dull Fourth, which had been described in the same paper that reported on the Crescent Band and the handful of Copperheads at the parade in New Harmony. In Evansville, the rockets and Roman candles had fizzled out as if there really wasn't much to celebrate.

When they got home to New Harmony there'd been a ball, though it was the oddest kind of party John could have imagined, hard on the heels of the burials on Maple Hill. There was also the whole incongruity of the thing: the idea that a man could turn the page so abruptly and close the book on a war, when it was like some deep cistern of roiling sound that didn't go away. John had been polite at the ball, but he hadn't felt like dancing. In fact, hardly any of his comrades had taken the floor. And anyway, Ann wasn't there.

"What will you do now, John? Will you work with Father or work your own land or maybe clerk in a store? Or will you set up housekeeping with some lucky girl for your wife?" Mary had stopped fanning him and she was looking at him with a teasing eye.

"You'll be setting up housekeeping before me, little girl," he said, and he thought that, for all her American accent, Mary, with her lovely black hair and quick, laughing eyes, had the most Irish look of all his sisters. He swatted her skirt lightly with the paper and thought once again what a lively and pretty grown girl she'd become. He was glad of it, and yet he hoped that she and all her friends would not take all the men who were left so that girls like Kate and Margaret Mulhern, who had worked so diligently all through the war—all through every-thing—were passed over.

"What will you do?" Mary asked again, and John told her he would go to the fair and take their mother so she'd have the pleasure of entering her canned goods herself now he was home and she could lift her self-imposed stricture against fairgoing. His thoughts, however, followed the larger meaning of Mary's question, which was very much his own. If Michael McShane weren't off somewhere in Alabama or Tennessee with the 10th Cav, he believed the two of them would stick their heads together and come up with a plan to put money in their pockets and give them a stake. If Menomen had gotten home, there was always the possibility he could join him and Charles in Illinois and farm or explore some business prospect, and certainly Menomen had proved that an Irishman's prospects were better where he was than in New Harmony. There was also Harry Beal, who was milling in Grayville. He'd been discharged—and honorably—at the beginning of August, mustering out basically straight from the guardhouse and his work on the works. John didn't have much interest in milling, and he was sure Harry would be hard pressed to afford another man but, if it came to it, he knew they could have fun together regardless of the amount of work they did.

The most obvious option was just to stay in New Harmony and work with his father and Denis and put himself in the thick of things with all the returning men and the girls who were welcoming them home. It would go against his mother's thinly veiled hint that there was still the seminary, that a man could become a priest in America, not just in Ireland, which was a thought that had crossed his own mind, though not very happily.

"I feel very sorry for the Thrailkills," Mary said. She picked up her tatting instead of the fan, and John assumed he'd used up his chits with her for one day at least. And since it was Mary, there would be chatter instead.

"Because of Levi, you mean?"

"Well, yes, Levi. Of course Levi. But Caroline's sister—Mrs. Barton has been so ill, and Caroline's gone to take care of her and the children, and Margaret said she was very worried at leaving her mother who still takes it so hard that Levi is gone. They don't hear from him at all. And Margaret tells me that Caroline is hoping Captain Barton will be home soon so she can come back to Harmony. Or at least for a while. She had to give up her place for the fall. She was teaching the youngest children in the free school. Is it true, John, that Captain Barton is kin to General Logan?"

John looked up from his chair and registered the real import of what Mary had said: that there was a reason why he hadn't seen Caroline Thrailkill and a reason why he might not see her soon. "I've heard he is," he said.

"And is General Logan part Indian? Someone said that he's descended from Pocahontas, and of course Captain Barton has very black eyes."

John laughed. "Then he must be," he said, and he picked up his paper again.

———

The fall, as it unfolded, was much more diverting than John had had any reason to hope. The expected word arrived that Atlanta had fallen to General Sherman. From reading the papers and *Harper's Weekly* and talking to people, John had the definite feeling that any waffling sentiment in the country was once more shifting firmly behind the Union cause. He had his own sense of satisfaction at the outcome of the siege, along with a small bit of hope that Eleanor Norcross and the Bennetts might feel there had been some reason for Al Norcross and Lieutenant Bennett to die. He had called on Eleanor at her parents' house, offering to complete his repair of the violin, but Eleanor had looked at him with the same brimming eyes she'd had when she entered the room and told him no. She wanted the violin just as her husband had sent it to her.

The fair started. Though it was smaller than it had been before the war, it was lively enough, and John and his father managed both their late harvesting and their customary odd jobs of paid bookkeeping for the Ag Society (John's job) and work on the stables (his father's). When John went to the exhibits and events, he attended with Kate and her friends and with Godfrey Gundrum and John Pulleyblank from the 15th and with George Tretheway. He also made a point of accompanying his mother when she entered her preserves and flowers, and of taking Margaret Mulhern to see the evening races. He was quite sure that if Margaret weren't so careful saving her money for the church at St. Wendel's and for the church in Donegal Town and to help her siblings and their children, she might have placed bets on the ponies. She loved the races. She loved them so much that it made John think it was Michael McShane's O'Donnell blood that had made him a horseman. It wasn't a passion in the O'Donnells he'd known—Jackie and Dennis and his Uncle Charles or all the rest. But Margaret had it.

Except for his work at the stables, his father, who'd always gone to the fair with Francis Cannon, wouldn't go this year, and John didn't press him on it, for Mr. Cannon had died shortly after John's furlough (he wondered sometimes if their drunken fiddle dance hadn't driven a nail in the coffin). John saw how testy his father was when anyone even suggested he should go, or said that he'd still enjoy himself. It was getting crowded on cemetery hill, John thought. He knew far too many people in the graveyard.

As November drew closer, there was electioneering everywhere and, from what John could tell, Posey County was evenly split between the Democrats who supported General McClellan's candidacy, and the people who were Lincoln men whether they were Republicans or not. There were political rallies in Union Hall and a speech by Robert Dale Owen. There were rallies in Mount Vernon. There was more politics than smoke in the tavern when he went with his father or his friends for a pint. The arguments continued out into the street when the tavern had closed. There were times when John found himself wondering if democracy was really all it was made out to be. Men had the oddest reasons for their allegiances, and they were not only loud and immovable about them but got a vote to cast like the next man. Some people even thought that returned soldiers who'd fought for the Union should get two votes. John didn't say it, though it crossed his mind that the men he knew who'd come home from the war had already begun to create a sort of mythology about their experiences that certainly had grains of truth but had turned them into wiser and braver people than he'd ever known them to be.

The fact was that the politics that excited him the most was decidedly local. Whether it was Captain Boren's good word or the fact that Achilles Fretageot was leaving town on a tour east and was temporarily unavailable for the post, John heard his own name put forward to be secretary of the Workingmen's Institute. He was certainly flattered at the attention and aware that, unlike some others who might be considered, he actually was a workingman. He didn't believe, however, that his candidacy was serious. Not amidst the luminaries of the town—all those people who were Owens or descendants of Owenites or Rappites or people with artistic and intellectual pretensions who had come to New Harmony well before he had, and none of them Catholics or Irishmen.

Still, he went to the election, and then to the meeting where the tellers announced the results. At the end of it, when he knew that James Chadwick and Bill Baldwin and Colonel Henry Fitton had been made trustees, and John Chappelsmith treasurer and Charles White librarian again, John waited to hear who the new secretary was. He was thinking about the piece he'd admired on Byron that John Chappelsmith had written for the local paper before the war. Then the tellers read out his name loud and clear: JOHN GIVEN JR. He could scarcely believe it. He'd won. He actually had. He was the secretary, and he felt prouder than he thought he ought to feel and then wondered if this small bit of fame would go to his head. He didn't care. He was eager to surprise Kate with the news, eager to think what this new distinction might mean for him.

"So one of us Givens has moved up in the world," Kate said when he told her, and then she laughed, though he thought her eyes held a hint, not of jealousy, but perhaps of old wounds, old slights.

John gave her a hug. "If I could, I'd make you a workingman," he said.

The hard thing was that, in spite of the WMI election, and in spite of New Harmony's social life and his pleasure at being home, he felt unsettled. Unsettled and uncertain. He wasn't alone. Some of the men who'd mustered out of their regiments had been so fidgety at returning to civilian life that they'd already headed east intending to hook up with new units. John thought it was partly that they were bored with the familiar routine of life in New Harmony (although he didn't know what could be more boring than most of a soldier's life), and partly that a few weeks or months at home had made the bonus money look much more appealing. It was also that the ordered camaraderie of the army seemed a different thing from the camaraderie of men at home. Mostly, though, it was that they smelled a coming victory and at least one more big fight to bring the war to a close. Some men couldn't stand the thought they'd miss out on it.

When John went to Grayville to see Harry Beal, they talked about it.

"So why would I go?" Harry asked. "In the end, all I was good for was hospital duty, though not even that for long but stuck in the guardhouse or working on fortifications. I lack your restraint, Jack. I rub the officers the wrong way. Anyway, what about your knee?"

John didn't answer the question. "It's just if an opportunity came up," he said. "If there was something. Not soldiering but something."

Harry gave him a drink. "Have you seen Ann Bradley?" he asked, and John told him that he hadn't, that there was no point in either one of them discussing a woman engaged to be married. Though it was what he said, it wasn't entirely what he thought. And it wasn't even true that he hadn't seen Ann. He hadn't talked with her, but he had seen her. The morning after John Smith was buried—John Smith who'd never recovered from the soldier's illness that had brought him home months earlier—Ann had been in town walking with Jim Rippeto. Though John had wanted to approach her and had considered the pretense of offering congratulations on their engagement, he hadn't. He'd simply stared after her from afar with a complex of emotions that was somehow as much about the war as about Ann.

The nights grew cooler. The fall was slipping away. With remarkable suddenness, Election Day arrived. The speeches were finally done, though banners were still everywhere and the flags were out. With his friends, John went to vote, walking up the street in the just brisk, new November air. He thought of the men from the Army of the Potomac who had paraded so smartly on their way to Vicksburg. General McClellan had been the one to polish them to a sheen, and it was McClellan who had been removed from his command in the same high-handed way General Frémont was in the early days of the war, although their politics were vastly different. As a candidate, McClellan seemed to have a plan to end the war and to put the Union back together without doing anything radical. And, too, he was a Democrat and so not in league with the moneyed Northeasterners who would like nothing more than to use a Republican victory to run roughshod over a workingman's rights.

John thought all that, rehearsing it to himself as he got ready to pick up his ballot. Yet there was another voice in his head, and it was Kate's. The evening before, he'd come home and found her sitting in their parents' kitchen, her cloak still on and her bonnet pushed back and hanging by its strings. She was pulling a splinter from her finger, but she'd clearly come on a mission.

"I'd like it if, when you vote, John, you'd vote for me," she said. "Not for me personally, but for how I'd vote if I could. If General

McClellan wins, it's as though the war stands for nothing when I think that it does. Mr. Lincoln could always be wrong, but if there's anyone I trust to be thoughtful and right, it's him. He's like you, John. He thinks down to the very bottom of things."

And so he had this dialogue—the point, counterpoint—in his head as he stood with the other men waiting to choose their ballots. He let himself drift farther to the back of the line, surprised that he was still uncertain. He thought of the pictures he'd seen of the men he was choosing between. Kate was wrong about him, he decided. It was often not his thinking that settled him on what he would do, but his instinct. At the moment, he imagined the tens of thousands of Union fires dotting campsites in a great arc from the South to the North and the men around them who might mock Mr. Lincoln and yet, as a group, sense his pull at the center with his brooding eyes and lifting words: the language he spoke that honored their dead and, through everything, stayed fiercely hopeful that life as they wished it to be, would not perish even if they did.

Finally, he had to step forward and choose his ballot. When he'd entered beneath the polling place bunting and his name was called, he crossed the room. Still, he hesitated. He looked at the printed name at the top of the strip, considering once more, and it wasn't his own voice or Kate's that he heard now, but his Grandfather Given's just as though he were standing beside him and talking quietly into his ear: *You can vote, John! You can vote for freedom for a man! Then do it, lad. What are you waiting for!*

Yet he still wasn't sure. It was only a guess when he folded the ballot with Mr. Lincoln's name on it and slipped it into the box.

Later he felt he had cast a die, and it was a sense that stayed with him for days and made him feel all but personally solicited when he read about a new call for civilian clerks from Major General Meigs, the army's quartermaster general. General Meigs wanted men with experience, which John had, and men who could soldier when they had to, as John certainly could. He knew it was a real opportunity, one he had to take seriously though he was reluctant to leave New Harmony so soon after the WMI election. He was sure something important for his future lay in that vote.

The future, though, hadn't arrived with the war still on. The war was the present (and all-encompassing thing) and, even if he wouldn't re-enlist—he wouldn't even consider it in spite of the fact that Harry Husband and George Tretheway and Vic Miller already had—he thought he might be ready to try his practiced hand at clerking once more. He could head back to the army until the war was done. It was more where he wanted to be, and it was a way he might cure his restlessness and earn more money than he could in New Harmony. He thought it would be a good decision, though it bothered him that it would disappoint and worry his mother and Kate and the rest of the family. And he was hanging back for another reason, although he didn't confess it to himself until he answered a knock at the door and saw Ann Bradley standing before him, her shawl drawn over her hair and snowflakes from a new snow glistening in the weave.

"May I come in, John?" she said, skipping her usual "Mr. Given."

John was sure he'd been staring when he'd recovered himself enough to hold the door open. "Of course," he said, embarrassed at his slowness, and Ann came inside, pushing her shawl back so it fell on her shoulders.

"The girls are out. Sorry. And my mother," he said. He reached instinctively for his cap and, when he realized he was bareheaded, he tried to cover the gesture by smoothing his hair back. He stuck his hand in his pocket. "This is—it's just me," he said, and he asked Ann to sit down and nodded toward his mother's chair.

"Thank you, but no. I've come to see you. And your father, too, if he's here."

John shook his head.

"If you could give him this." Ann reached into the cloth satchel she was carrying, and John took the moment she spent digging to study her face again. It was thinner, perhaps, and lovelier, if possible, and it seemed to him that she had a new seriousness and maturity about her.

"I've just come from Mr. Duclos's," she said when she looked up. "My sister and I went to see him about the final settlement of Uncle Frank's will. Uncle Frank was generous with us both, but of course he had very little. Mary was his pet. He's given five dollars to each of her girls and ten to young Francis, which was sweet. And he left money for the care of our cousin's child. But what I've brought is his Bible. He wanted Francis to have his fiddle, and Mary's given it to him, but we both thought your father would want this."

"He's not a big Bible reader." John looked at the worn cover. "Of course, I'm sure he'll like having it," he added quickly and then laughed as Ann opened it. "An Irish Bible," he said, seeing the whiskey bottle that lay inside. "Mother will thank you."

Ann smiled but didn't laugh. "They were very good friends," she said.

"Yes."

"And I've something for you, John." She reached into the satchel again and brought out a packet. "I didn't know that I had these still, but they're very fine letters. I thought you should have them. And if I read parts of them to others, John, I didn't mean harm."

John looked at the letters she was holding. He could feel the old surge of anger rising inside him. He could feel his face growing hot. "But you did, of course. Cause harm, I mean."

"By letting others hear your cleverness? Do you really think so?" Ann tilted her head at him and gave him a small smile, which he only found more maddening.

"I do! By God, I do. You were sharing what I wrote you, Ann. What I wrote, clever or not, was for you, and not the whole town. And it wasn't just about cleverness. It was what I felt about you."

"And you think it was mocking you if I read such things aloud?"

"Judge for yourself. But how could it be otherwise?"

"I did judge. Otherwise. Perhaps I was wrong."

"Perhaps? Ann, if you admit—"

"I admit nothing. And there's no need to be patronizing. If I'm to judge, *that's* what I'll judge." Ann had the letters in one hand and, with the other, she'd begun to tug the shawl over her head.

John glanced toward the kitchen and back. "You needn't go," he said. He ran his hands over his hair again. "I was going to fix tea. Or we could try out the bottle. We could drink to your uncle."

"Such a fine offer. Are you trying to be amusing or cruel?"

"Not cruel. Ann, I know you've another offer on the table—or accepted actually—but if you should think better of it—if you should ever change your mind, we could perhaps spend time together." John stopped a moment, but then he plunged on, astonished at what he was doing. "Even a good deal of time. Perhaps you would think about marrying me."

He could tell that he'd surprised her. He'd surprised himself. Very carefully, she was arranging her shawl. When she spoke, it half muffled her voice. "If that's a proposal—"

"It is! Believe me, it is."

Ann took a step back. She eyed him coolly, but he did not think she was hostile. "John, you deserve someone who cares for you a good deal more than I do. And I've someone who pleases me very well. I'm sure of it. I'm sure I'll be fine."

Soldier that he'd been, soldier that he still felt himself to be, John saw an opening to press. "But are you, Ann? Are you?" he asked. "I know you lost your position with Mrs. Owen. I know it's hard to find a good place with the war. You've been helping your sister, of course, but are you all right? Are you sure that you are?"

"You do keep up with me," she said, the dryness clear in her tone. "Mr. Given, if it's any real concern of yours—and I don't know that it is—I am absolutely and entirely fine."

She had pushed the shawl away from her face again and was staring straight at him. John saw the bluish and lilac flecks in her eyes, and her expression, which had started to harden.

"Ann," he said, but the moment of openness—vulnerability even—that she'd carried with her from seeing Francis Cannon's will a last time was entirely gone.

"Don't leave," he said. "Ann, please don't."

"I shall consider myself flattered, if you like. And tell your father I'll think of him raising a glass to my uncle's memory."

John nodded without speaking, angry again, though more at himself than at Ann. He was wondering what more he could say. There were so many things that he felt but, to Ann, he knew they all would seem slight. And he was sure he would make a perfect ass of himself if he mentioned the WMI election or anything else of his prospects.

He wanted so much to touch her face. Her beautiful face.

Since the whole line of her body told him he couldn't, he gripped his hands behind his head. He looked toward the window. There was another thing he could add. It wasn't about him, and he thought it was something she would do well to hear. "Ann, listen," he started. "I don't know that you did, but if you had your cap set for Julian Dale Owen—if you're in some way just settling for Jim Rippeto—Jim's a very good man." John lowered his hands and turned back to her. "And, Ann, if any man would think less of a girl for being Irish, I would say he's a man a girl could think less of herself."

She didn't answer at once. Instead, she gave him a steady and measuring look. Then she spoke, and her words were like darts. "You've forgotten perhaps, Mr. Given," she said, "but I'm not Irish. I'm American. I was born in New York. Here's your sister now. Margaret's come home." Ann was looking out the window, and John heard the brush of her skirts as she moved toward the door. Then Margaret came in, snowflakes dotting her shoulders like clusters of tiny stars.

"If you'd take these letters for your brother," Ann said, pushing the packet into Margaret's hands. "He seems unable to accept them himself." Ann laughed—not her throaty laugh but a laugh John thought carried a hint of scorn. Then she went out, leaving him to glower at Margaret as snowflakes melted on her and the letters.

He took them and put them straight in the fire. They caught and flared up. "That's an end of it," he said, the heat on his face. He watched the flames, the ragged soot marks that etched their way through the paper. He poked at the letters until they were ash, and he thought that even the WMI and what it might promise was not enough to keep him in New Harmony now. It infuriated him that he felt that way, but he knew himself. He couldn't bear the idea of seeing Ann again or of spending each day wanting to see her, which he certainly would. It would be better, he thought, if he just left.

In the end, he didn't so much talk over the clerkship in General Meig's department with his father as tell him he was going and then ask him to please try to square things with his mother.

"When there's chances to be had, a man has to take them," his father told him, and then he grasped John by the shoulders and squeezed them so hard that it hurt.

The day before he caught a steamer for Louisville, Margaret arrived with a request from Caroline Thrailkill, who had just returned from her sister's house. She asked that he please come to see her.

When he went, John found her waiting for him. She didn't ask him inside but stepped into the cold, glancing back over her shoulder as though to make sure her parents wouldn't overhear.

"Margaret told me you're going east to the army. And with the rumors we've heard that General Grant will finish the siege of Petersburg soon and take Richmond—if you could find, Levi, John. We've not heard from him. If you could find him. If you could bring him home. If you could just find him . . ." Caroline stopped speaking, trying to compose herself. Then she reached beneath her apron and drew out a letter. "And if you'd give him this so he'd have a message from home right away."

John saw the tears in her eyes. "Of course I will," he said quickly. He put the letter into his pocket and, light as it was, he felt its weight beside the one he still carried there. "Yes, of course," he said.

Virginia, with the Eastern Army
Late March and April 1865

24

To Major Jesse W. Walker, A.A.G.
November 26, 1864, by Telegraph from Louisville:
Can you obtain for me a clerkship in the Q.M. office
Answer

Jno. Given Jr.
25th Ind

A s distractions went—and it meant a great deal to John to avoid the sharp clutch of air that came with every thought of Ann Bradley—the siege of Petersburg worked really quite well. He had come to the center of a bustling universe. The wharf, which fronted on the James, looked out on as many ship masts as he'd seen in New York harbor. Maybe more. Whether it was the heart of day, with muscled laborers unloading supplies, or a sunset with boats at anchor and their riggings shaping the sky into triangles of pink-tinted light, the port was invariably crowded. It was full of energy. It was full of people. City Point, where the Appomattox met the James, housed everyone from General Grant in his cabin to the hundreds of clerks and craftsmen in the quartermaster repair shops, while the log huts and tents of thousands of Union troops stretched far across the plateau. The Confederates were here, too, dug in for months in front of the Union lines. They were protecting Petersburg and, beyond it, their capital. *Richmond*. It was the object of Grant's army and, since he'd left home, it was John's as well.

In the months that he'd been here, he'd been clerk in the 9th Army Corps to Captain John Batty, assistant quartermaster of the Third

Division's First Brigade. John knew he'd had a stroke of incredible luck. Captain Batty, an Indiana man, had gotten his position through the offices of no less a personage than Governor Morton himself and at just the time John had arrived with his own letter of introduction. John didn't know how Captain Batty felt about joining the eastern troops, which western soldiers generally considered a discouraged lot. They'd been thwarted so often in their attempts to take Richmond; they'd had so many of their generals replaced. For himself, John was amazed at the whole enterprise, and not just the activity on the wharf and in the camps. It was the entire scale of things here in the East.

The supply lines were the most obvious example. Inventory alone took far more time than John would have thought possible. He'd written it all down in a letter to Kate. It was their job to account for everything that covered an army: Sibley and hospital tents, wall and shelter tents. Drawers and trousers. Stockings and hats. Caps and shirts. Coats (great and regular) and blankets (woolen and waterproof). There were the sundry other things a man needed, like hatchets and bed sacks, mess pans and canteens, and the part ceremonial, part crucial things like bugles and guidons. And all of this was before keeping track of the army's forage and the miles of railroad and the number of locomotives and cars and every single horse and wagon. It was the whole kit and kaboodle that had kept the army in the field or, in this case, laying siege to the city of Petersburg.

His main job with Captain Batty was to provide for the Pennsylvania soldiers in the 1st Brigade—three regiments of older men who'd signed up in the fall for the bounty, and young lads who were as green as green could be. When John wasn't doing paperwork, he was usually on errands out to the regiments. He liked the trip. The army was so near the water that, stilled or just rustling, the air had the softness of sea air. It was also the windiest place he'd ever been. On one night, the March winds blew so strong that, even with the tents nailed to log houses, half of them had blown away. The men had held up their shirts against the sand and chased the tents as they set sail.

John thought that he'd never seen snow in a snowstorm being blown about in greater quantities than that sand. It had turned the cheeks of all those recruits a blushing maiden's red. And yet the weather here suited him. His health was good—it was far better than it had been at home—and even if he sneezed sand, which he sometimes did, he wasn't hacking anymore. By his own standards he was practically fat. When he was home again, he thought he might well tip the scales outside Fretageots' store at close to a hundred forty though, as he'd written to Kate, he wasn't fat enough for it to hurt yet.

He had gotten very well settled here, but in recent days it had been all flurry and preparation. Every bit of the brigade's surplus baggage and artillery had been removed and shipped to Washington or Alexandria. Since the siege had gone on busily month after month, John didn't know why the current arrival of messengers and the stream of wagons going northward past empty fields and lopped-off forests made him feel something conclusive was about to happen, but they did. He believed that the deluge of orders meant a real fight was coming, and likely a decisive one.

He was more than ready for it. It was an extraordinary thing that a battle here in Virginia could mean a fight that would end the war. In personal terms, it meant that Levi would be freed, and Michael McShane, who'd been captured three months ago chasing Rebels with the 10th Cavalry after the battle at Nashville. Kate had written he'd been taken near Hollow Tree, shot in the leg and dragged in his horse's stirrup, which was the last position in which John could ever have imagined him. There'd been no further word, and it made John anxious, though now he felt hopeful. In the not too distant future, Michael and Levi would both be released, and soon they would all of them be home again. And though John couldn't say just what it would mean for him, New Harmony would no longer be the place Kate said was forever waiting and waiting to see what would happen—the place where everything was put off for the war. The war itself would be finished.

With the camp's new watchfulness, and his own anticipation, there was one nettlesome problem for John. He had trouble sleeping. He'd begun to have nightmares that woke him before reveille or at midnight if the pickets scattered fire at one another between the lines. Half conscious, half in the dream, he always found himself in the same place. It was a cavernous room with the narrowest of barred windows, their light scarcely reaching beyond the shadows of the few men who were close enough to them to be illuminated. Other men huddled or lay in dim corners, the condition of their clothing a rough measure of just how long they'd been prisoners.

There was a stench to this dream: an acrid mixture of human waste and fetid wounds and a smell of men whose breath made it clear they were starving. John would lurch into full wakefulness just to escape that bitter smell, but the faces would stay with him when the dream was gone, those gaunt and pallid faces distorted by mangy beards and blackened eye sockets and empty gums. He hunted quickly through them, trying to search each one before his memory of the dream slipped away. Once he was sure he saw Michael McShane. On a different night, the face that he recognized was his Uncle Mick, lost more than seven years ago in New York. At one midnight's waking, there was a woman among all the men. She was draped in black and, though older, her face was the face of the boy who'd died in his arms at Fort Donelson. John wanted to speak to her. He wanted to ask if she'd gotten the letter from her son.

But in all of those faces, as hard as he looked, he could never spot Levi. That was the thing that kept him awake. Desperate as the men of his dream appeared to him, he knew that Levi needed to be one of them.

It was because of the dreams, and the accompanying insomnia, that John felt relieved when Captain Batty said they were moving from their lodgings on the wharf out to the brigade. The captain would be at headquarters and John would be there, too, but at night he could mess and stay with the Irish lads he'd met, soldiers whose only combat experience had been in February slashing timber and holding the works at Hatcher's Run. John thought they could use the steadiness of a hardened campaigner, while he would be happy to have their company. It would be like being with Charley or Denis.

And he'd have a rifle for a pillow once more. He knew he would sleep.

———

While many of the names scattered among the German surnames on the brigade rosters were Irish enough that they might have come easily from a census in Ireland, Pennsylvania's real Irish contingents in the 9th Army Corps weren't the units who had a scant six months of soldiering under their belts. They were the ones who'd been the first out the door for the fight. That meant men like the coal miners in Schuylkill County's 48th—the soldiers who'd dug a shaft under a Rebel fort and blown it sky high. They were famous here. There was a crater thirty feet deep and nearly the length of a Harmony block that the men in General Parke's command had been eyeing through their field glasses since July.

When they spoke of it, men said the Union forces should have charged past the corridor the blast opened, and seized the church and hill at its end. They were certain it would have given the artillery command of the whole city and finished the Petersburg siege right on the spot. But the battle plan had been botched when the black troops trained to carry the front were kept in the rear. The crater had turned into a Yankee death trap, and afterward General Burnside had been relieved of his command. John had heard all manner of opinions since he'd come to the East, but the one he heard most was that General Grant had a better plan now—one that was sure of success.

As he came back to the regiment from headquarters one evening a few days after he and Captain Batty had moved, John was considering what such a plan might be and factoring in his own experiences. When it came to big battles—and certainly with General Grant in the field—he knew the Confederates had a habit of springing surprises. At any time, the men of the 208th Pennsylvania, Company C, who were making the raucous sounds that grew louder as he approached their tents, might need to be heroes. Coming into the light of a campfire, John watched them. They'd spent the day repairing defenses and now they were shaking lice from their clothes, watching them pop in the fire or, if the lice fell out of the flames, lining them up for races to bet on. There were boys down on their bellies urging their racers on.

"You got a louse in this fight?" a boy named Delancy asked John.

John laughed and got himself a plate of beans. He poured some coffee. "Is Captain Dalien in the regiment tonight?" he said turning to a man named Feeney, and Feeney looked up from his plate and then shook his head.

John nodded, but he was disappointed. He had hoped for a game of chess with Prosper Dalien, the brilliant officer with the French-sounding English, who'd given him the best game of chess he'd had since he'd played with Lieutenant Bennett on the cars on the way to Atlanta. For the briefest second, he considered what it would be like to be a Frenchman himself, what it would mean to have been trained in a military academy like St. Cyr and to have gotten medals from Napoleon III for gallantry in Italy, and even what it would be like to be detailed to General Hartranft's staff as an engineer. He was sure it would impress a man like Achilles Fretageot. He was certain Ann Bradley would take notice.

Not that he really cared. He was growing more certain each day that he didn't.

As it happened, the Confederate surprise John had expected arrived just before daybreak. He had fallen asleep while the boys in the tent were talking about girls he assumed were younger even than Mary. He'd half-listened for a time, counting every one of his twenty-nine years. Then he dozed off and on and gradually fell into a deeper sleep. He didn't know what woke him. Since the wind carried sounds away from their lines, he doubted he'd actually heard a gunshot signaling a Rebel attack. But he was sure he'd heard a horse gallop away from General Hartranft's headquarters. He'd even felt it in the ground. The *thunk-thunk*.

Quietly, he roused the others. They didn't ask questions but fumbled themselves and their guns together and out into the nippy air. John, who was wearing his clerk's black coat, reached into a pocket for the soldier's cap he'd acquired with his gun and pulled it on. Jimmy Cassady, a sixteen-year-old with a teepee of hair, mumbled something about his canteen and went back into the tent. John studied the sky. There wasn't a moon, but Mars was visible, and the constellation Crater.

"Let's go," he said when the boy returned with his canteen. He led the men and one curious dog over frosty ground up the row toward the officers' tents. To the north, a puff of white smoke had risen against a blue-black sky.

Jimmy Cassady had moved up beside him. "Jesus," he said, fingering his gun.

"You're ready," John said. "You'll soldier fine," he added, and he believed it, although he couldn't promise more. It occurred to him he should find Captain Batty, that there were things Captain Batty would want him to do. It didn't matter, he thought. He'd signed on for a job that asked him to fight if he was needed. As he saw it, the boys here meant that he was.

Reveille sounded. The rest of the camp began to stir. John kept his eyes hard on the horizon and watched for more smoke. He heard the faint and then pounding-louder noise of a horse's hooves, the horse and its rider returning.

"Someone's bringing the alarm," he said. He was listening for the same pop-popping from a picket line that he'd once heard near Shiloh Church, that same thin and distant rhythm of muskets. In the first light, he could make out only the sound of the horse and the wind blowing northward, but he saw more puffs above the horizon. Then he couldn't hear the horse any longer.

Their camp wasn't far from the Avery house, which was brigade headquarters. Listening, John was certain that that was where the horse had stopped. Other people were listening, too, and John thought he might be hearing guns beneath the wind. Lieutenant Keller of Company D ordered his men into line. There was the sound of the horse again. It was loud and growing louder. It was thundering closer. As it came into view in the grayish light, John saw that Captain Dalien himself was the rider. He was shouting for the lines to form and deploy. In his odd, unstressed English, he was telling the officers that the Rebels, in force, had broken the Union line—that they'd taken Fort Stedman and two batteries.

John felt a jolt of recognition. Admiration, too. The Union and Rebel works were not only close to each other at Fort Stedman, but Fort Stedman was near Meade's Station, supply depot for the 9th Army Corps It was a wonderful stroke if a man was Rebel. If the Confederates could defeat the Union troops who were supposed to protect the station and rail lines, General Grant would have to pull in his left to oppose them. And, if he did, General Lee's flank might escape south and join General Johnston's command.

With Captain Dalien rousing the regiment and the lieutenant detailed as aide-de-camp at brigade headquarters, the second lieutenant in Company C mounted his horse to give the company orders. It was Albert Corl, and he'd been sick and was still pale but, watching him, John felt a certain, almost cool detachment. He knew that the boys and men falling into line had their stomachs in their throats. He knew they were scared their guns wouldn't fire or that they'd turn tail and run under fire. To him, the whole scene was far too familiar for such feelings. He was fatalistic, he thought. Whatever happened to him would happen, and it wasn't as if he was here with men like Levi and Henry Schafer that he'd gone to battle with in the 25th. And it wasn't as if Ann had said yes and he had a fine future to protect himself for. And the devilish irony of the thing was that if Ann had said yes—if Ann had held out even a sliver of hope—he would have stayed in New Harmony. He wouldn't be in Virginia at all.

The drum rolled. The company began its advance with Lieutenant Corl checking the line. As they moved forward, John felt an unexpected surge of emotion: he didn't mind marching with these men. He hoped he wouldn't see a boy like Jimmy Cassady get shot, but he was glad he knew how to fight.

It was a hazy dawn that saw them over old bits of corn stubble and a thin shell of frozen mud that cracked and oozed underfoot. John was between two Joes—one young, one as old as Michael McShane. When they came up on the Avery house, both were already lagging behind.

"Joe. Hey, Joe. McAfee. Feagan." John motioned with his gun. He could hear the breathing of McAfee, the older man, as both men caught up, and he felt a quick pang for Michael McShane, dragging from that terrible stirrup.

As daylight came, their batteries opened on the Rebels. It had grown light enough that John could see officers on the lines issuing their orders. He assumed they were following General Hartranft's commands (3rd Division) or General Parke's (9th Army Corps), maybe General Meade's (Army of the Potomac) or possibly even General Grant's. From Shiloh and Fort Donelson—from any battle—John knew that communications could be cut, that a general officer could be detained, that almost anything could happen. But a man followed the orders he got, and the word now where they'd halted beyond the Avery house was that the 208th was to push north to the breach in the line and go in on the left. They were to fight the Rebels where they found them, which was fine with John, though he thought it likely the 200th Pennsylvania, one of their regiments, had already made contact. He'd been hearing a lot of musket fire.

They'd hardly paused before they started again. Joe McAfee was managing to keep up, and John was glad. He had a hole started in his boot and McAfee, being a shoemaker, was the one man in the company likely to carry decent leather in his pack. For the moment, they were moving uphill. They'd passed Fort Meikel and Fort Morton. They passed several batteries along the Union breastworks, and John realized he'd stopped feeling cold. To his surprise, he felt a glimmer of the old excitement coming back. The battle thrill. Once it had felt alarming, but now it seemed merely inevitable and the way he got on with things. The way every soldier did.

The regiment was at the corner of a woods. They had almost crested the hill, and suddenly the Confederate line was right before them. It was advancing, still in good order, the men coming forward with white bands on their chests. They looked startling—bandaged—and John wondered if they'd worn these stripes of white cloth so they'd see one another when they'd made their attack in the early darkness.

A ripple of low sound went through the line. John couldn't tell how far the Rebels had come from Fort Stedman. They'd certainly gotten past the first line of rifle pits in the rear of the breastworks. And they'd seen their regiment now. They were opening fire.

"Blackbirds, is it?" Joe Feagan was staring wild-eyed at the sudden scatter of shot in the sky, and John did for Joe what Henry Schafer had done for him at Fort Donelson. He hooked him with his leg and pulled him down.

"Bullets. Easy. Mind your gun," he said.

On order, they fired back. There was a blaze of fire along the line. The sky blurred with a thin wash of smoke, and John smelled the black stench of it. As he handled his gun, the crucial, familiar motions came back to him: tearing and charging the cartridge, ramming it home. Moving the gun into firing position and priming the cap. Cocking the hammer and taking aim before he fired. He knew there were cavalry units that had repeating rifles, that they'd made war a very different thing. But this was war as he was used to it: men in formation; the blue glint of metal as they raised their guns to fire at each other and then lowered them to load once again.

Another volley now. Then a third. It was methodical. It was numbing, which was what let a soldier see men catapult through the air or plunk head first into a muckish stream, and all the while keep loading. John saw the sudden, red shock of wounds. He smelled a man near him who'd soiled himself.

For twenty minutes, for half an hour, they kept their position. Some of the Rebels had begun to shrink back. They were taking shelter in a ravine, but the gunfire kept up on both sides. From what he'd seen, this enemy seemed a threadbare bunch and, for the briefest second, John thought how much smaller the task of inventory had to be in General Lee's army. Then he heard the order for the regiment to charge.

"Stay low. Fire low. Keep low when we go forward," he called to the men who were near him, and they were off on the double-quick and heading straight for the Rebels. John could feel the fever, the blood rising in the line as the men charged ahead.

Yet to him, the faster things happened, the slower they felt. Their flags moved like drifting kites. Feet disappeared in a smoky haze and appeared again only when the haze lifted. When he drew closer to the advancing line, bullets still flying, John saw the Rebels who remained in the center of the line loom larger—their faces gradually acquiring features—while the men on the right and left fell out of view. He heard Lieutenant Corl order the line left, and as he started the move, he felt a rifle butt crack his head from a boy who'd turned the wrong way. He shook his head once. He shook it again, but he knew it was clear. Really, it was as clear as it had ever been in battle. Clearer, for he was aware of so much. The jumbled racket. Yes. Yes. He recognized the noise of bullfrogs and owls and insects—how amazing to lie next to an elephant ear while the Rebel cavalrymen hurled out their taunts—and rain pummeling the cars as the men hoisted coffins on board, and Felix talking. Did Felix never stop talking? Felix saying *we killed him, Jack. Oh, Jesus holy crap.*

Such a choir. The sooty, opened mouths growing wider and louder by the second. And what was he hearing? *You've forgotten, Mr. Given, I was born in New York. How could I be Irish?*

But you are! he wanted to shout. *You are! And these lads. Feagan and Feeney. Delancy (creaking as he is from the rheumatism he got from sleeping on the ground). And McAfee is. O'Neal is. And Jimmy Cassady, who's too fast to catch up to.*

He could take off his cap, John thought. Stuff it back in his pocket, and the Rebels would never know him for a Yankee in his clerk's coat.

He could slip into their line and use his bayonet like a dagger left and right. It was kill or be killed, and it hardly mattered anymore unless these lads themselves were killed. He would take it very hard if they were. But to hell with Ann Bradley. To bloody hell with Ann. In all his life, he'd never been so angry. He was here because of her, and would it get him killed now, her voice running in his head?

"Are you shot?" a man asked beside him as the line halted. John reached up to touch his head. His hand came away with blood on it, but he wasn't shot. It was the smart blow from the rifle that had left him bloodied. Knowing it settled him down.

"I'm fine," he said, spitting the blood off his hand. He stared at two band boys who were pushing by with Lieutenant Keller of Company D, a terrible wound in his stomach, the boys struggling to carry him.

Beyond them, the Rebels had started fleeing from the ravine. They were scampering for cover inside a battery. Some of them fell as they ran, struck by fire, but a few managed to get shots off, and one flew past John's ear. Others ripped away their white cloths and waved them to surrender. In the distance, John could see still more of them in the Union camps near Fort Stedman. They were trapped with Union troops in their front and shelling in their rear, though it was such a crowd of Rebels, John didn't think the Union officers could actually deploy their commands. The whole thing had a feeling of chaos.

For a while the regiment held its position. The sun was in John's eyes and his head throbbed. He tied his handkerchief over the gash and pulled his cap down to cover it.

"What are we doing now?" Joe Feagan asked him. "Are we done fighting?"

John told him no. A moment later he saw the battle flag of another regiment and the whole regiment—the 211th Pennsylvania—advancing in perfect order in full view of the enemy.

"We'll go now," John said, watching as what was left of the Confederate line began to waver. He could see a colonel on horseback raising his arm.

"*Charge!*"

They were on the move. The men held steady in the line, but it was a brutal thing still. Running, John wondered if it was possible to die not shot, but destroyed simply by the noise of a battle. He'd wondered it before. He could tell the fire was taking a toll, though he didn't look to see who in the line had been hit, what fallen soldiers were being dodged or hurdled like some ancient dog who'd wandered into the army's path and fallen asleep. The men had started toward the occupied batteries. They were rushing forward, guns flashing in the sunlight. John thought the Rebels must see them as one great blue wave.

When the line came to the first battery they'd been headed for, there were Rebels crouching or backing up, hands in the air. John took a sidearm from a captain and waved him into a huddle of Rebels who were already under guard. When he turned around, Jimmy Cassady had come up beside him. He had two pistols stuck in his belt, and he was drinking from his canteen. "I shot a man," he said, wiping his mouth. He grinned. "Maybe two."

After that, the work was almost routine. The regiment had retaken two batteries and much of the line. They were gathering prisoners by the score, by the hundreds, and John saw a colonel and adjutant among them. A color bearer from another regiment ran by carrying a whole collection of Confederate battle flags. John thought he'd helped himself to trophies that were rightfully the 208th's, just as he assumed the men from the 1st Division, 9th Army Corps, who'd appeared just minutes ago claiming to be provost guards, were taking prisoners to the rear they'd try to steal credit for capturing. John had to smile. He knew the boys in the 208th were sure to protest, but it hardly mattered to him. It wasn't even nine in the morning, and whichever men of the 9th Corps had been in this fight, they'd already nipped the Confederate plan in the bud.

The officers were restoring order to the units that had broken up as they came through the bombproofs and earthworks. John counted heads as he could, looking for the boys he knew, and relieved every time he saw one. Besides cocky Jimmy Cassady, he'd accounted for

Patrick Feeney and Joshua Delancy and he'd seen both Joes. Still, he knew their losses had to be high. Already, large numbers of men were being detailed to see to the dead and wounded.

John pulled his hat and handkerchief off to see if he'd bled anymore. He hadn't, and he thought himself lucky to have only been clunked in the head, maybe dazed a little. He'd survived whether he needed to or not. They were done fighting. Soon the Rebels would send out a truce flag and cross the fallow cornfield between their lines and Fort Stedman. They would hunt for their men among the bodies scattered on the field and in the grove of shattered trees.

John shouldered his gun. He started the trek toward the Avery house to find Captain Batty. His eyes had been dry as dry could be since he'd come to this place, but they were misty by the time he reached headquarters. Walking the line, he'd heard that James O'Neal of Company K, the big sergeant from Bloody Run, was wounded and Lieutenant Keller had died. He learned that Colonel Diven, their brigade commander, had been shot and replaced in command by Lieutenant Colonel McCall. He confirmed that the 200th's men had been the first part of the reserve to counter the enemy, and that its men had attacked two times and suffered a fearful toll. Twice, he'd startled at a name: division privates, one named John Levi and one with the first name of Levi, had both distinguished themselves. Another time, he looked back to see a line of carts carrying bodies toward City Point, where men said President Lincoln himself was staying, here on a visit from Washington. And he'd heard as well that Captain Dalien, who'd brought the alarm before dawn and put the 208th into position, had gone immediately to the aid of the 200th, that he'd had his horse shot from under him and, hurrying forward on foot, was shot in the lung. He was certain to die.

Sitting down on the porch of the Avery house, John lifted his boot and looked at the hole that had worn clear through. If he'd been superstitious, he would have blamed himself for playing a game of chess that had doomed one more fine officer. As it was, he vowed that he was done with chess and officers. For the war. For as long as it took. For the duration.

Amazingly, after this morning, he didn't think it was going to be long.

25

*Fondly do we hope, fervently do we pray, that this mighty scourge of war
may speedily pass away. Yet, if God wills that it continue until all the wealth
piled by the bondsman's two hundred and fifty years of unrequited toil shall
be sunk, and until every drop of blood drawn with the lash shall be paid by
another drawn with the sword, as was said three thousand years ago, so still
it must be said "the judgments of the Lord are true and righteous altogether."*

**Abraham Lincoln, Second Inaugural Address, Saturday,
March 4, 1865**

Exhilaration. A week since Fort Stedman and exhilaration was exactly what John felt as the horse he was riding came up on the vast and empty Rebel works that had seemed so impenetrable only hours before—whole forests of logs built into them and a honeycomb of tunnels that stretched to Petersburg, maybe even to the Appomattox and the James, maybe even to Richmond—yes, the whole way along the lines to the Rebel capital. John was in a pack of exuberant men whose horses leapt over the lowest traverses and redoubts and jumped or skirted trenches and the chopped-up abatis. All the men were yelling as they went and shooting guns into the air like a bunch of roguish boys on Christmas Eve. John knew the officers would rein them in soon, but this exhilaration was the nearest thing he'd felt to pure joy since he'd come East.

He hung low on his horse's neck as it jumped a trench. If riding around these works with the men who had stormed them at dawn meant the Army of Northern Virginia was well on its way to being vanquished—the men could smell it, really, like blood—it meant, too, that Richmond would fall with no lines to protect it. Its prison would be taken. It would yield up its men so that John could search

among the ragged figures until he finally heard Levi's voice: *Given.*
John. John Given, over here. Are you a month and more late with my
valentines, Jack?

They were on Confederate mounts they'd caught near abandoned artillery, and John pulled up beside a soldier who'd stopped
to look back at the entrenchments. John heard the awe in the man's
voice: "I wouldn't believe they could be taken. Not ever. And I say it
though this morning I passed over them myself."

John nodded. He agreed that it seemed impossible. In all his
years as a soldier, he'd never seen fortifications that compared even
remotely to the defenses of Petersburg. And yet Petersburg was a
Union town now. Once more, it flew the Stars and Stripes. It had surrendered as Atlanta and Memphis had before it: lock, stock, and barrel.
The 1st Brigade had been the first unit to enter the city. It was cause
for a celebration to beat anything, though it seemed there wasn't time
or place for that. With nowhere to stop, they were headed back to their
old camps by the Avery house. The command was to ready itself to
march in fast pursuit after Lee. John wondered what road they would
take in the chase. He wondered if they would go through Richmond
and if he'd find Libby Prison and give Levi the letter he was carrying in
his pocket from Caroline.

In the days since Fort Stedman, from Jones's Farm to White Oak
Road, from Dinwiddie Courthouse to Five Forks, General Grant had
been testing the Confederate line with battles and skirmishes and
moving his troops into position. Yesterday, which was the day after
All Fools' Day, was the real blow to the Rebels. The fighting had been
unbelievably fierce. Shelling and gunfire had started before dawn with
the 9th Corps beginning the attack. The boys of the 208th had been in
the advance of the assault made in front of Fort Sedgwick. In vicious,
daylong back-and-forth fighting near Fort Mahone, they'd acquitted
themselves like veterans. General Wright's 6th Corps had followed
the 9th's attack with a huge breakthrough in the Confederate line
and later, Gibbon's men of the 24th Corps assaulted Fort Gregg. They
went like madmen, scaling walls into a galling fire. Unable to shoot as

they climbed, they'd flung sand and rocks at the Rebels who, in their own thoroughly savage turn, threw cannon balls and shells with lit fuses onto the Union men who were crawling up from the ditch below. Soldiers who'd survived it said the combat in the fort itself was unbelievably desperate, man-to-man fighting with guns broken and barrels and stocks used as clubs, and sword fights, too, and all of it amidst the wildest exchange of screaming and swearing. Bodies lay everywhere in pools of blood.

Most of John's time had been spent carrying orders to and from Captain Batty and seeing to it that detachments got ammunition to the companies. For him, it was a long day of dodging bullets and making his way around half-emptied cartridge boxes and stumbling over abandoned pouches and belts. He'd seen men killed, watching them fall to the ground in that oddly familiar way, like marionettes whose strings are severed. He'd seen men he knew get wounded. Patrick Feeney, who was married to a woman born Ginnavin (which was what Feeney called him—*Hey, Ginn-a-vin!*), was wounded freakishly in the groin when a shell hit a cord of wood. A flying chunk of wood tunneled inside him. In Company D, John Gaugler was shot in the face on the picket line. And Jimmy Cassady had been shot in his trigger hand. John had seen him holding his fingers out and staring at the trickling blood, and he'd thought *good*. Jimmy wouldn't fight anymore; he wouldn't get killed.

In the evening, still under heavy Rebel fire, their division had orders to move the enemy's abatis and chevaux-de-frise so they fronted their lines instead of protecting the enemy. In theory, it was a job for the engineers, but the rest of the men felt like sitting ducks with the bullets flying. They pitched in. John did, too, cutting the wire that joined the sections of chevaux-de-frise and then pulling them back like opening a gate, though an unwieldy one. The work was extremely hard, but the men went at it with a will and, to John, it felt as good as anything he'd done. He liked the sheer, brute force of it.

It was late when they finished. John was sure the real push to take Petersburg had started, and he feared the next day would bring more horrific fighting. He left the regiments in their waiting columns and went back to Captain Batty and Avery house, which was a hubbub of messengers with orders and stories about the day's attacks. Artillery fire kept up all night long, but in the morning when John returned to the line, he discovered that the 208th had already moved well forward. He could see battle flags far ahead across the parapets. Hurrying over the earthworks, it occurred to him that the Union troops had already taken Petersburg, that the Confederates must have withdrawn under cover of darkness. He kept on going, and he might have gone all the way to Petersburg except that he'd run into these jubilant men who'd already been to Petersburg and back and were helping themselves to horses.

Officers were coming up now, ordering the men back into line and telling them to guard the prisoners they'd found crouching in the works when they came back through them. They told the men to turn over their appropriated horses, which was where John came in, clerk-of-all-trades as he was to Captain Batty. But he was really more interested in Richmond than anything, and the officers were full of news. It was burning, they said. The flour mills had been fired by retreating Confederates, the flames spreading quickly to other buildings, and magazine after magazine of stored munitions exploding so there was a continuous rumble. A returning messenger from General Weitzel's corps, which had entered the town, reported that the streets ran and reeked with liquor, that women and children were pulling furniture from burning houses, that Capitol Square was gray with smoke and cinders and crowded with miserable people—the ones who weren't piling drays high with their worldly goods and trying to get out of town.

John wondered how much of it Levi could hear. He wondered if Levi had made sense of the sounds, or if he thought the town was being shelled instead of blowing up from its own ammunition. He wondered if Levi knew that the war seemed to be rushing finally toward an end, or if he'd heard the Federal bands marching into Richmond or knew that a regiment of U.S. Colored Cavalry had arrived, that they'd drawn their sabers and shouted in triumph when they passed the main hotel. They would talk about it, he and Levi would, when they saw each other. John would tell him, too, of the speech Mr. Hunter had made in the Confederate Congress in Richmond when it voted to grant General Lee's request to enlist slaves.

John thought it was a remarkable speech coming from a senator who supported slavery even as he spoke. Within virtual earshot of Levi, Mr. Hunter had said that the South had fought for a belief that Negroes were happiest as slaves and that two races could not live together without one being master of the other. He'd insisted that for the men of the Confederacy to deny that now would make them outright hypocrites. Yet, with even that strong word, he wasn't done with his argument. He said that if slaves were made soldiers they could no longer be slaves, that scarred by war, they had to be free. The human heart demanded it, he'd said, and John wondered if that feeling was in his own soldier's heart. He thought that it was, and he wondered if it was in Levi's, too.

When they got back to the Avery house, Captain Batty was there, and he ordered up a detail to help John sort out the better horses to use for the captured Rebel artillery. John was doubtful they'd be wanted. With Lee's head start, he thought the army would travel light: a few days' rations in men's haversacks and whatever supplies a handful of wagons could carry through the Virginia mud.

He went to work anyway. He and the other men had half a corral of more or less able-bodied horses—ones without foot rot—when the order came for an immediate movement after General Lee. He'd been right, though. The horses and artillery were staying behind, and it meant he was in the line of march again. In all but name and uniform, he was a regular foot soldier once more. He thought it wouldn't go hard on him, that he would like the march (old and foot-calloused campaigner that he was), although he'd wanted to see the streets of Petersburg. More than that, he wanted to go to Richmond and find Levi, though it was well off their route. He was torn, but he had a job in General Grant's army, Ulysses S., and they were after serious prey and following the lead of the 6th Corps and General Wright on the River Road.

By nightfall, Petersburg was a good ten miles behind them. After that, John knew it was just a race. General Lee still had the lead, having slipped his army across the Appomattox in the dead of night, but John thought Sheridan's cavalry would be nipping at him wherever they could. He was sure as well that General Grant would think of everything possible to block Lee from his provision depots and from gaining a clear road to Johnston and his Rebel army in North Carolina. For John, it seemed simply a matter of marching hard and anticipating victory, though with the knowledge that he or any one of the 9th Corps boys he knew might be the final casualty of the whole campaign, even the last of the entire war.

Then, in an instant, their orders changed. Late on the afternoon of April 4, a messenger arrived with a dispatch for General Parke directing him to separate from the 6th Corps and to move to the Cox Road. They were to guard the trains. They were to perform picket duty along the railroad and mend the tracks as far as the rear of the army. The irony wasn't lost on John. He'd started the war guarding the rails with the 25th, and it seemed he would end it the same way with the Army of the Potomac. It was a joke he thought he could save for Levi. He had little time to consider it, though. He was occupied entirely with Captain Batty's charge of seeing that the men from Sutherland all the way to Farmville had the tools they needed.

Road crew that they were consigned to being, the men hung on any word of the forward troops. They heard that General Lee had planned to meet supply trains at Amelia Courthouse but his trains had mistakenly gone on to Richmond without unloading food. His hungry troops were sent foraging when they might have been marching. John didn't know if it was true. He also didn't know how much credence to give the stories that the Army of Northern Virginia was bleeding men, leaving stragglers in its wake and men who fell exhausted from the ranks, unable even to get up again. As the armies moved west, reports filtered back of skirmishes and battles at virtually every crossroads. The men all wondered how soon it would end and how it would end, and if it really would. Could General Lee be wily enough to slip away again? Nobody thought so, yet nobody was absolutely sure.

Later—much later—when John had read about Lee's retreat in *Harper's Weekly* and pieced it carefully together for himself, though he was still excited that he'd seen all he had when Petersburg fell, there was one story he really wished he could make his own. While he'd gotten as far as Farmville, the westernmost point that any 9th Corps troops had reached, he hadn't arrived by April 7 when General Grant set up his headquarters in the town hotel. John remembered the veranda. He could also imagine what he hadn't seen—General Grant seated while the troops of the 6th Corps marched down the street three abreast and then, having caught sight of the general on the porch, passed in review. Saluting him. Cheering him as night began to fall. Lighting tapers from bonfires and marching up the street in torchlight. How he would have loved to have been there—a fly on the porch wall—watching Grant watch the men while his cigar glowed in the darkness.

John knew, of course, that this was not the most important part of the story. It was not the final confrontation at Appomattox when Sheridan's cavalry moved aside to reveal the host of Union infantry that had come up and stood in Lee's way. It was not the hour in the McLean house when Lee and Grant negotiated terms, and Lee actually surrendered his army. It was not the Rebel stacking of arms or the day that the weeping color guards gave up their flags, hastily tearing off pieces for souvenirs. But it was the moment he liked to think of: the stolid general, the troops almost on a lark, the spring night that was like one last deep breath before everything stopped.

———

Four days after the surrender, writing to Kate from Nottoway Courthouse at the end of a tramp southeast along the railroad from Burkeville, John didn't know about the scene in Farmville, though he did know about the surrender. When he'd come up the muddy rails, the courthouse, which was red brick in the Virginia style, looked serene in its narrow valley, the mountains beyond it brightened with young foliage. He'd stopped, gazing around him, thinking what a beautiful place it was and of the people he'd like to show it to. Kate, certainly, for she was interested in Virginia's presidents. And Levi if he didn't mind seeing more of Virginia when he got out of Richmond. And Ann. Still, whether he liked it or not, Ann.

In spite of the mud, the men were soon sprawling and camping everywhere, and the courthouse was overrun. Lying on his pack as he wrote, John kept both that initial peaceful sense of the scene and the sense of exhilaration, quieted but still there, which had started when he rode around the works at Petersburg. He bragged a little to Kate, telling her how very much he'd enjoyed the march from Burkeville and how he could laugh at the boys he was with who complained at the long march since they weren't at all used to it. The exhilaration had broken through then, and he'd told her that he loved this kind of semicivilized life, that he loved it better than any other. Then he put his pen down and looked out across the mountains and wondered if there was a lake close by of the kind he'd swum in with his grandfather. All these years later, he had the same feeling he'd had swimming with him as a boy—that sense of being really and truly alive.

He finished his letter (which was part elation and part record of events and part concern over his father's bad knee) with a warning to Kate that she mustn't let curiosity overcome her so much as to want to know everything in a man's letters. He told her that, in that regard, he could only say that whatever Harry Beal had written him recently had no reference to her or any other person in particular and that perhaps she would as soon not hear it.

It was Maundy Thursday when he wrote, which he would not have remembered later except that it was two days before the Saturday he couldn't forget. It was as vivid to him as any time in the war. They were still at Nottoway Courthouse, and he'd finished the day's paperwork from Captain Batty. He was waiting to get into a card game with some of the Pennsylvania boys and officers who, after looking for a place where they wouldn't be stuck in the mud, had taken over a barn and made it their personal headquarters. The conversation was about whether they were going to Petersburg and what would happen to Parke's corps if Lee's surrender prompted a general peace. It was also about the terms of that surrender, which had been greeted hotly by both officers and men, a fact that made John believe the eastern army still understood very little about General Grant.

They were arguing over it once more when a commotion started in the camp. The boy sent to investigate came back ashen, the blood totally drained from his face. John could just make out that the president had been at Ford's Theatre the previous night, and his first thought was that it would scandalize his mother, Mr. Lincoln going to a play on Good Friday. That thought, though, was instantly erased by the rest of the news that had come by messenger and been delivered by this shaking boy—that the president had been shot in his box at Ford's, that Secretary Seward had been stabbed in his bed, and that the president had lingered for a few hours, unconscious, and now he was dead.

It was a horrible moment. John could not have imagined one more horrible. Some men were stunned into quiet. Some ran out to look for the messenger themselves. One man stood in the middle of the barn, his arms crossed over his forehead and his mouth fixed in a silent scream. Others swore and threw things and cried. John knew how frightened and suddenly rudderless they felt, for it was how he felt as well. He sat on an empty barrel, striking it methodically with his heels. Then, downing a drink that a man offered him, he went out to the stricken camp. He wandered aimlessly in the muddy dark, and he couldn't push it out of his mind how much the president's words had always been at hand, printed in the papers and ready for debate. It had made him a real presence, someone to talk to, and John realized just how much he'd relied on that private dialogue to help him think. He was reflecting still on the words of the recent inaugural—moved certainly, but mostly perplexed by their troubled darkness. He needed more words from Mr. Lincoln if he was ever truly to understand what he'd meant.

And now he wouldn't have them. They were gone.

Virginia and Washington, D. C.
Spring and Summer 1865

26

Mrs. Maggie Walters, 532 12th Street, Washington, D.C., Number of Inmates: 14; Class 1 (Best)

Military provost office's register of bawdy houses in Washington, D.C., for 1864–65

I f you did not count such things as dead cats and the other decaying matter that floated in the city canal and the thermometer standing at ninety-five in the shade or the sweltering summer nights without a touch of coolness or breeze, there was something, John thought, to be said about a place like Washington. In May, on his first visit to the center of things, he found an oyster house he was particularly fond of. He saw the federal buildings and generally approved of them and, just in case Kate got interested in New Harmony history again, he made a special point of going to the Smithsonian Institution to see what it was that Robert Dale Owen had gotten funds appropriated for when he'd been in Congress, and what David Dale Owen had helped to design. On later trips, he walked through the teeming neighborhood from the president's house to the Capitol and found it dense with milling soldiers and every one of the temptations they were looking for. There were shops, of course, and even factories, and a man could always find a theater to attend or a place where he could drink or brawl or gamble. There were certainly as many brothels as there'd been in Memphis. John liked the bustle of it all. And the truth was that, when it came to considering the temptations he'd so far resisted (and there were still some), he generally found himself rather like the border states early in the war: he was poised on the fence with perfectly good reasons to fall off in either direction.

In most of the time since Lee's surrender, John had been far too busy changing bases and doing his work to think of much else, although he'd certainly noted the various events that had marked the close of the war and start of the peace. The sorting-out of troops meant the disbanding of Mosby's Raiders (they'd helped keep General Lee in the fight) and the negotiated surrender of General Johnston to General Sherman in North Carolina. The end of hostilities in the Trans-Mississippi saw units of soldiers either mustered out and sent home or ordered west to garrison forts or fight Indians. There were significant captures. John Wilkes Boothe, the actor who'd shot President Lincoln, was found and killed by a New York cavalry platoon. Jefferson Davis, on the run, was surprised in a nighttime bivouac.

Word of some of these things came officially, word of others through the grapevine. The 9th Corps had been severed from the Army of the Potomac late in April. When John had learned he would be headed for Alexandria with Captain Batty, he was at Petersburg, which he'd finally gotten a look at, his duties putting him frequently in the heart of town. They were to join a new brigade and new division, though they'd stay in the 9th Corps. To John, it seemed unsorting and winding the army down and finishing all the paperwork and seeing to the transportation of the regiments going home meant even more quartermastering than there'd been while the war was at full pitch.

In the middle of all that busyness, a letter arrived from Caroline Thrailkill saying her family had still had no word of Levi. It made John desperate again to go to Richmond. Or more desperate. It had never left his mind. He'd been half-consumed with guilt that he hadn't gotten there and half with the certainty that it had been impossible. With Caroline's letter, he determined to go however he could and thought he might finish his work in Petersburg in time for a hurried trip before he and Captain Batty caught the boat for Alexandria.

To plan anything, John knew he needed to talk with Captain Batty first, but he found himself reluctant to broach the subject. He was aware how busy the captain was because he was aware how busy he was himself. And, besides, this was personal. He didn't like asking for favors. There was another matter, too. He'd been thinking for so long what it would be like to find Levi and to see he got home to his family and to receive the warm thank-you he knew it would mean from Caroline, but what if he couldn't find him? It had been forever since anyone had gotten a letter from Levi, and John hadn't heard a thing about prisoners being sent home from Richmond. He half assumed that the men were being fattened up and any medical problems attended to and their papers put in order for their release, but he had no idea if that was really true. The fact was he didn't know at all what he might find in Richmond.

When he'd decided he couldn't wait any longer, John took a sheaf of papers he'd finished to Captain Batty's quarters to tell him about Levi and to ask permission for going to Richmond. The captain was in the middle of dressing to go to dinner with some of the brigade officers. He listened to John while the Negro valet, who'd attached himself to him in the last week, polished his boots and then his sword. "So your friend was in Richmond," the captain said, and John nodded. "And you want to find some record of him?"

"Sir, I was hoping to find him. Or at least to find what arrangements have been made to get the prisoners home. Or if they've been sent home. His sister wrote me that they've not heard at all."

"He'd be in Georgia."

"Sir?"

"There're none of them in Richmond." The captain leaned down to pull a boot on. He paused while the valet buffed the toe once more. "They've put their own men—the criminals—in Libby Prison and there's to be some sort of refugee camp on Belle Isle. Our men were sent to Georgia sometime ago."

John froze. When he could, he cleared his throat. "I've thought my cousin must be in Georgia. But when Levi wrote, it was from

Richmond," he said, and for a racing second, he wished that he'd made a real plan and gone through with it in Atlanta, that they'd had the raiding party he'd imagined and that he'd rescued Levi and Michael McShane both. "Are you certain, sir?"

"I'm certain if your friend's in Richmond, you won't want to know it. If he's there, he'd be in the graveyard."

"But why wouldn't I know that?" John asked, the panic he was feeling creeping into his voice. "Not about the graveyard, but why wouldn't I have heard if they sent all the prisoners south? Wouldn't it have been in the papers?"

Captain Batty pulled his other boot on and sat down at his table and started writing something. It was just a few lines, and he added his signature and blotted the paper and held it up to John. "When you get to Richmond—and go ahead, go see what you can learn—take that to the commandant's office. I don't know what papers you've read but I hope your friend is in Georgia. You know when we're leaving."

"I do. Thank you, sir." John saluted in spite of his civilian clothes. He took the paper, folding it into his wallet, and he thought it was at least something, that there was something he might do.

Late as it was, when he left the captain he headed straight for the pasture and the brigade horses. Since the roads were sloggy again from so much rain, he picked himself a decent mudder. Still, it was a slow ride and well after midnight when he finally got into Richmond. He rode through the dark streets and found a livery stable where he could board the horse. He would have slept on a pile of hay in the corner but the stable man he'd awakened told him to find a room at the hotel. He took two dollars from his wallet and got a bed for the night and spent a restless few hours dreaming. He was back in the cavernous room with its gaunt and starving men. Once he thought he saw Levi from the back, but when the man turned around, he had no face at all.

In the morning, he had an early breakfast in the hotel and asked directions to Libby Prison. Then he set off walking on the street near the river. More than once, he stopped to look up at the burned-out district and to show his papers to a patrol. He was in the process of stepping over yet another filthy gutter when he saw the prison sign right in front of him on the corner of a building. He read it twice and, after eyeing the building's forbidding upper stories, he went ahead to the doorway. A guard was there, and John took out his papers and his letter from Captain Batty and, then, operating on his own theory that a soldier would know more about the place he was guarding than anybody else would, he engaged the man in conversation, asking if a friend—a Federal soldier—might still be imprisoned there.

"Officer or enlisted?" the man asked. He looked at John's papers, and when John answered him, the man handed the papers back and told him that the enlisted men had been on the island which, in this weather, was nothing but a marsh. "They crowded the men behind the deadline. And they were shot if they crossed it," he said, pulling to attention as an officer passed.

John tried to disregard the movement in his stomach. "What about records?"

The soldier shook his head. "Ask inside if you want, but the records went to the War Department. You look like an Irishman who'd ask anyway."

John ignored the comment. He started to go in the door when the soldier caught at his sleeve. "They're bringing a batch of colored women to the island to make a troop laundry. You don't find your man, wait around and you can find yourself a woman," he said, and he was laughing as John entered the prison.

Inside, John found four offices on the ground floor. At each one, he showed his letter from Captain Batty. Eventually, he pieced together a sort of verdict. The guard was right that it was only Federal officers who'd ever been imprisoned here. Unless an enlisted man was sent to the building's hospital, the one time he might have come here was for a night's stay in a holding room on his way to Belle Isle. And, too, although there was a cemetery with headstones on Belle Isle, a great many men had been buried on a sandbar, and their bodies carried off in the freshets.

John felt grim when he went back outside. He stood a moment to get his bearings. The guard had disappeared, but there were groups of soldiers in the streets now. Most of the civilians he saw were black men, many with small bundles on their backs, and all of them going about their business as if it was what they had always done. John could see the mills by the river, and the charred remains of railroad bridges and the stone piers they'd been built on, but the only standing bridge was newly built. It was crowded with people on foot, and with omnibuses, and with wagons hauling freight. From his queries at the prison, he knew that the pleasing-looking hill that rose from the river below him was Belle Isle. He knew, as well, that the prisoners' actual camp—and Belle Isle had been tents and a few shacks, never a barracks—was not on the slope but on a flat that went out into the river. It was so low that high water would have touched it.

The clouds had lifted with the morning, and John walked quickly down the hill, the risen sun warming his back. It was hard, really, to reconcile the two things: the river that a soldier would have seen from Belle Isle was quite beautiful with its brisk rapids and a host of small green islands that looked like so many giant lily pads. And yet what a treacherous camp it must have been. It was so open to the elements, and there would have been thousands and thousands of prisoners closed in by an embankment, and a trench that held them on acreage the size of a small orchard.

When he came to the cemetery, John thought he'd found the muddiest place in the whole of Virginia. The gravestones were scattered. Many of them had been knocked over or had slid sideways and, with the poor footing, he was sliding, too. He resolved, though, to look at them all. He started with the row closest to the water. Uneven as the rows were, it took all his concentration to keep track of where he was and which stones he had seen. Some of them were a project in themselves, the names on them covered with moss or mud, and by the time he'd made his way down the first section, his fingernails were bloody from scraping. He took out his knife and, being as careful as he could not to mar the stones, he cleared off the mud and cut at the moss. It was miserable work. His boots were damp through to his socks and skin; his clothes were drenched with sweat, but he was determined to keep going.

It was nearly noon when he'd made his way to the farthest corner of the graveyard and looked back across the ground that he'd covered. He was as sure as could be that he hadn't missed a single stone and he hadn't seen Levi's name. He understood, though, that it didn't really prove anything. Names could have been chipped off or eroded. Stones could have washed away. For that matter, who could be sure that every soldier who had died here had been placed in a marked grave? John thought it was all but certain that many hadn't been (his mind stopped uneasily at the memory of Confederate dead he'd watched piled into shallow graves to keep them from rotting in the air). He did know, however, what he could tell himself and what he could write truthfully to Caroline Thrailkill: he had looked at all the tombstone inscriptions on Belle Isle. Levi's name wasn't among them.

Yet it was hardly a stopping point. Though he was greatly relieved that he hadn't scraped one of these gravestones down to Levi's name, from the standpoint of the task at hand, his work was still cut out for him. He might hope that Levi would make it home on his own—that he was even home now—but in the meantime he had to make more inquiries. He wasn't clear where. He supposed he could start from the idea that Levi might really be in Georgia, as Captain Batty had thought he would be. Michael McShane, after all, was surely in Georgia, and nobody had heard from him either.

John cleaned his knife on some leaves. Then he dried it on his pants leg and put it in his pocket. For the first time since he'd appeared in his dream, he thought about his Uncle Mick and realized he'd always felt grateful they'd never learned what had happened to him. He'd feared that, whatever it was, it would be more than his father could bear.

But this was a very different matter. It had to be different.

Everyone had to know what had happened to Levi, for Levi had to get home and tell them himself.

It was this thought John took with him when he collected his horse and rode out of Richmond and back to camp to make his boat trip with Captain Batty. For Levi's sake—for Caroline's—he somehow needed to hurry Levi's homecoming. He stewed over it the whole steamer trip— down the James and up Chesapeake Bay and to the Potomac. When he and Captain Batty finally got to Alexandria, he stopped just worrying and went into action. He asked around about the 25th and learned they'd arrived in Washington with Sherman's army. They were in time for the Grand Review of all the troops, scheduled for the end of May, and John himself was eager to see it. He was even more eager, though, to see the 25th, and he went straight to their camp and to George Ham, who was the new captain in Company A. When he found him, he asked if he'd make inquiries of the War Department on behalf of Caroline Thrailkill who, as John told him, was acting for her parents. George told him he would, and then John spent a raucous time catching up with the men.

Afterward, he was glad he'd actually done something, although he was increasingly doubtful that anything would happen fast at this stage of putting the country back together. The fact was that, with all the Northern troops eager to go home and the government and army working overtime to get most of them there, and with the Southern states still reeling from Sherman's assault and their railroads and rolling stock said to be in terrible shape, John didn't know how even a company of men could be moved from the South, let alone a whole stockade of prisoners. If Levi was in Georgia—even if George Ham found that he was—John didn't think he'd be going anywhere soon. And if a paper trail led to Belle Isle—well, he didn't know at all what that would mean.

In the meantime, John struggled through a mountain of paperwork for Captain Batty in Alexandria, his eyes growing so tired that he sometimes stood outside and stared at the far horizon just so he could focus clearly again. He expected to wait a very long time to hear back from George Ham, and it occurred to him that he might not have the patience to wait, that George had his own business to attend to. He thought he might have to go to the War Department himself, starting from the bottom with his questions and working his way up the command to find the Belle Isle archive and Levi's records, if indeed they existed.

He was so sure nothing could happen quickly that he was caught off guard when a letter came from George Ham in just days. At first, he thought it had nothing at all to do with Levi but was other business left over from the non-Vets 25th. When he read it, though, he had a hard time swallowing. It was a request that he forward its enclosure to Caroline Thrailkill, which seemed ominous, and, though he'd been trying to smoke less to get rid of his cough, he quickly rolled a cigarette and smoked it clear down to his fingers. He rolled another one and, lighting it, took a slow, nervous turn up and down the muddy path near his tent. Finally, he rubbed his hand across his scalp and, taking a deep breath, unfolded the paper and started to read:

Camp 25th Ind. V.V. Inf.
Washington D C June 2/65

Miss Thrailkill

I have just Received a communication from the War Department which I will give you a copy it is as follows

Commd Officer
Co A 25th V.V. Ind

Sir I have to inform you that Levi Thrailkill late a Private of Co A 25th Ind Vols. Inft. Died at Richmond Virginia while a Prisoner of War on the 29th Day of February 1864 of Disease————

This is all and the only word I have ever received of him since his capture. There is Pay Due him from the 30th Day of June 1863. I have forwarded his final Statements Descriptive List and all other Necessary Papers to the War Department and at some future Day you will hear from them

Very Respectfuly yours etc.

Geo. W. Ham Capt. Co. A

Reading, John had felt himself begin to tremble. The words had seemed to move on the paper. They made no sense. Not any at all. How could they make sense, for how in the world could Levi have died in the winter a year ago without anyone knowing of it in all this time? It was inconceivable to him, but his eyes still stung and he swore under his breath, and he understood, even as he fought against it, that he had to write to Caroline. He knew George Ham should have sent his notification directly in order to go by the book, but he was grateful that he hadn't. Perhaps he could ease into things, cushion the blow a little, let Caroline suspect what she would read before she read it.

He had a sleepless, very long night. In the morning, he all but tied himself to his chair and, with numerous false starts and crumpled sheets of paper, managed to write a letter that he thought would do. When he mailed it, though, it felt exactly like launching a cannon shell.

In the next days and weeks, the whole thing weighed heavily on John. The fact of Levi's death, which didn't always feel like fact—how could Levi possibly be dead?—insinuated itself entirely into his thoughts. It was there, no matter what he did. It was part of everything, and it was one more reason why he was perched less certainly on the fence he'd grown so aware of on his trips into Washington. Levi had died. He himself could die. He was twenty-nine, and both he and Levi had read *Don Juan* (and for more than its New Harmony reference). Did he really want to die as Levi had—as he was all but certain Levi had—without ever knowing firsthand what the sensual feeling actually was that had made Don Juan so ecstatic? It seemed a terrible idea—much more than terrible—and it seemed largely pointless.

It was even more on his mind since he'd gone up to Camp Stoneman on the other side of the Potomac from Alexandria and visited the Harmony boys in General Halleck's Corps—George Tretheway, Vic Miller, Harry Husband. When he finished riding them about how they could call polishing guns and cartridge boxes and bells and buttons real soldiering, he listened to Harry Husband talk about how he and Vic had gotten a pass to Washington, where they'd visited the public buildings and gone afterward to "the fancy jewelers' stores" where Harry had paid pretty dear, he said, for trying a "hair ring" on his finger. (There was much raillery, too, about a certain gentleman's sore finger.)

John was more than interested. The conversation stayed with him, although so did his ambivalence. Since early in his army days he'd made a sort of compromise with himself: he could have the fun of things, if not quite the pleasure. It was what he had decided on and he'd stuck to it this far, and it wasn't just thinking about Levi that made it more difficult now. He'd had another battle with himself over Ann Bradley. Jim Rippeto had finally gotten her to set a date and now she'd actually gone through with it. Ann had married Jim at the start of July.

John could have gone home for the wedding. He could have gone to the ceremony as an ordinary guest or to stand up and register his objections. His family had very much wanted him home for a Fourth of July to be celebrated like no other. But he hadn't gone. He'd made the excuse—which was real—that Captain Batty absolutely needed him, particularly now that they, too, had moved from the 9th Corps to Hancock's Corps at Camp Stoneman. There was nobody else who could do his paperwork. John had also written Harry Beal that, much as he'd like to be home, a fellow never knew what chances might arise to take advantage of, which was also a fact, and a reason not to be home yet.

But it was also the case that he both wanted to know every single bit about that wedding and yet couldn't stand the thought of seeing Ann Bradley as Mrs. Rippeto, which was the cause of his stormy self and the main reason why he didn't want to head back to Harmony now. In his dark moods, he wondered exactly what he was waiting for when it came to women if even Harry Beal could send such letters that John wrote back quickly, and with more seriousness than Harry might have imagined, that he would like to see those night attacks he spoke of, particularly if they made the fire fly as he'd seen it at Petersburg and if the resistance was truly as feeble as Harry said. He admitted his ignorance on the subject, but he wrote that he'd always been of the opinion that the charges and countercharges Harry spoke of would rival, if not excel, the charges made in the capture of Fort Mahone, though owing to the occupants being armed with shotguns (no bayonet) surely they were obliged to surrender to an antagonist with bayonet and fixed ammunition (balls).

The truth was that he was exasperated with himself. He thought he'd been drilled too long by priests not to feel he'd go to hell if he followed Harry Husband to the "jewelry shops," and it wasn't that he really believed it, but he didn't not believe it either. He thought too much. He knew he did. It was just as Father O'Gallagher had told him when he was a boy. And there was also the matter of his mother's ongoing rosaries meant to land him in the priesthood (at times, after all the carnage he'd seen, he thought they might work), to say nothing of the practical part that was his desire to have a normal life someday: to be a man with a wife and children and not a fellow gone skeletal and dying with the hideous, scabrous sores of a syphilitic. In the end, he didn't feel particularly good about what he was doing or not doing, but sticking within certain parameters, he did have his ways to enjoy himself.

The change to Hancock's Corps proved a hardship on more than one account. Before the move, John had been happy enough in Alexandria, though he did miss the Irish lads in the 208th. Except for a Maryland regiment, he and the captain had been with a brigade of real Yankees in Alexandria—men from Massachusetts and New Hampshire, from Maine and Vermont. John had liked the brigade staff at headquarters. He might have messed with them, but it cost two dollars a day, and it was far cheaper to mess with his assistant and buy what extra he needed beyond his army ration. But, really, he'd been pretty well fixed with the Yankees. He'd had a wall tent all to himself and, aside from a bad case of the chills that came on when he went into town and got as wet as the devil turning in surplus material that had been sent to the brigade, he had fared quite well. He'd even thought it likely that Alexandria would be his last base before he headed home.

Camp Stoneman, on the other hand, was entirely wretched. It was a hellhole, filthy and hot, and all of Hancock's Corps, who'd been stationed there, were being rapidly dispersed throughout the Union. John didn't think it would ever exist again as an organization. George Tretheway and the other boys of the 4th Regiment had already left, headed west to Columbus, Ohio, and, as far as John could tell, there was no mail delivery—or at least not for him. Ask as he might in his own letters, he'd not heard a word from Harry Beal about Ann's wedding or had a letter that said anything else.

Yet for all its deficiencies, before John's departure for Washington itself, which Captain Batty promised was their last stop before home (and where John knew he'd work hard and fast to finish the final papers since his salary couldn't pay the board), Camp Stoneman did give him a chance (and how he treasured it!) to write Harry his own fine story. The brigade's general had provided the opportunity by removing himself to the city and, in quite short order, a number of the more enterprising men took possession of his quarters, which were two large hospital tents that, for want of a better term, made a room.

"We're throwing a ball, Jack," they told him, laughing. "A very fancy ball."

John had his suspicions, but it took him the better part of a day in which he was frequently interrupted by men coming and going with stocks of food and liquor and the arrival of an omnibus loaded with flowers, before he had a certain idea of what was going on. Tapers had been placed the length of the general's room, and a wall tent was put up in the back. John had asked and was told that the tent was to serve as a dressing room and saloon. The wall tents of the staff officers were festooned with flowers and given their own tapers. John learned they were for sideshows, fifteen sideshows, he observed counting, and found himself wondering what his cousin James Mulhern would think of such a primitive use of math.

By late afternoon, he had lost any ability to concentrate on his work. The flowers had been placed so strategically around the tents and dancing room that their fragrance nearly covered the stench of the camp. The band had arrived. John listened to them practicing and thought they were nothing to rival George Warren, but certainly quite passable. He put his papers away. He walked out to the main road and stood with some of the other men, his arms crossed while he waited to see what ladies would arrive. When their carriages finally made the turn into camp, he watched them bouncing on the rutted road and knew that he was seeing the pièce de résistance of the entire occasion (or pieces, he thought). The band of fine-looking girls who waved out the windows was identified by a soldier standing next to him as being from Mrs. Maggie Walters' on 12th Street, a house reputed (in its ill-repute) to be the most fashionable in Washington. Whether it was or it wasn't, John knew from the papers that he'd seen at headquarters— and he'd actually looked at them quite thoroughly—Maggie Walters' house had the seal of the provost marshal's best rating.

The ladies who arrived were in splendid dress. The men surrounded the carriages and helped them down as if they were royalty. They were so done up in silk and jewelry that, with the low sun at their backs, John found them positively blinding, though he could still see they had a certain sway and saunter as they moved among the men. It seemed both vaguely demure and very provocative. Certainly, John thought, there had never been dancers in Harmony or the mountains of Donegal that were remotely like them. He'd never see such paint (nor anything like one particularly wanton mole). Whether the women effected a haughty aura or were giggly, they all proved to be great wine drinkers. There was no poteen or lemonade here. The women accepted the glasses they were offered quite eagerly. If they drank with a certain delicacy, and some of them did, although the wine was well spiked, that demeanor was very soon gone as the wine's effects began to appear. Steadily, the noise and mayhem grew. Officers and men alike looked feverish as they moved onto the dance floor. John thought he hadn't seen such heated faces since Colonel Grower had ordered the troops out to do the manual of arms in the Alabama sun.

There were various rituals played out. In general, men would dance with the women, having vied with each other for the right of a dance and the further chance to nuzzle the way down a plunging neckline. At some point, and usually sooner than later, they would hoist the women up, skirts toward the tent top, and carry them off to the wall tents amidst great hooting and catcalls. John, on his trips to the saloon, noticed that everyone was drinking a prodigious amount. The barkeeps had a virtually open spigot. The more men drank, the more raucous they became and the louder the musicians had to play to be heard, and the longer the lines grew in front of the wall tents. There were always a few women on the dance floor in various states of dress or undress, although they either pulled themselves together from time to time, or the dancers changed. John lost track.

Sometime well into the early-morning hours, when he and some other Irishmen had danced the jigs of a country-house hooley so many times that his leg, which had weathered the march after Lee, ached clear through the drink, he went out to relieve himself. With his head throbbing, he saw the candle-lit shadows that were thrown against the wall tents and then the herky-jerky of the shadows and of the tents themselves. He was uncertain if the tents were moving or his head swimming so it seemed that they were. He made his way to the front of the tents and with the tent flaps open and men gaping and giving their rough cheers, he had a good look for himself that provided the most remarkable pressure in his lower self though, with the drink in him, he kept thinking he was seeing a set tableau on the stage in Harmony's Union Hall.

This was his old compromise (or hypocrisy as he sometimes considered it): observe but don't really participate, and it was what he told Harry Beal he'd done after he wrote what a great time there had been and how it kept up until morning when the ladies went in ambulances back to the city "a little worse for the wine and the fatigue of dancing, etc." and with quite a difference in their looks and dress from the night before. Just as he knew Harry had believed him when he'd written in June how sorry he was to be the cause of marring the pleasure of those who were to have enjoyed themselves at his father's—that had he known his parents and the girls had planned a gathering, he would have waited a day longer before he wrote to Caroline Thrailkill (as he would have; he would have kept his pen well in his pocket and held the hope for Levi alive one more day)—when he wrote Harry this time that, as a matter of course he did not participate in any pleasures of the fancy ball except to look on, he knew that Harry would believe him. Harry might smile. He might even laugh and shrug but, friend and confidant that Harry was, John knew he would take him at his word.

New Harmony, Indiana
Fall 1865 and Early Winter 1866

27

Landscape paintings, fancy paintings, flower paintings, crayon drawings, pencil drawings, specimen of left-hand penmanship by a soldier who has lost the use of his right hand, penmanship, architectural drawings, ambrotypes and photographs, shell-work, bead-work, cone-work, hair flowers.

Amateur's List, *Catalogue of the Posey County Fair*

I t was a Saturday afternoon in mid-October, and Kate had dragged a ladder around the side of the house and climbed it to knock down the empty paper-wasp nest under the eaves above her parents' room. Since she had a broom in hand and her hair tucked up in a kerchief, she kept on working, cleaning off cobwebs and the leaves that were stuck in them. She was humming and even whistling as she worked, trying to remember the bugle calls John had taught her. She stretched each way as far as she could. Every few moments, she got down to move the ladder and planted it well, testing it before she climbed back up. She was making a circuit of the house, and she could feel the dampness at the small of her back and on her neck.

It was an absolutely perfect fall day, and the more she worked, the more invigorated she felt. And happy, too. Ever since the war had ended and John and so many of the other boys had finally returned for good, she'd felt remarkably content for she had the feeling that, after all the worry and bad times, things were going to turn out just fine. She had even gotten a dollar a week raise from Mr. Lichtenberger, which she felt she deserved for the family stayed more and more at

Mrs. Beal's since Mr. Beal's death, and she often had the work of two houses. And even though Alice and Mary now went to Terre Haute and St. Mary's for most of the year, there was endless sewing for them, and packages to ready that Mrs. Lichtenberger seemed intent on sending them nearly every week. Too, with her sisters gone, Eliza simply needed her more.

Kate moved the ladder again. She had great plans for the extra money. Already, she'd begun paying on a Tell City rocker at Fretageots' to give to her mother, just as she'd always wanted to do. She was also thinking quite seriously of making a trip. Her first choice was to accept the standing offer from her Aunt Mary to visit Chicago and the relatives there. She thought she might talk John into going with her. If she couldn't go to Chicago—if it was too long to leave the Lichtenbergers or if John, with his farm work and bookkeeping jobs, was too busy to make the trip—she hoped she and Margaret Mulhern might go up to Bridgeport in Illinois and visit their O'Donnell cousins. Not that she thought she could actually pry Margaret away, but she was considering the possibilities.

She had made her way almost completely around the house when a horse and wagon stopped in the street, and someone called to her. She held on to a ladder rung and looked around and, with a start of real pleasure, saw it was Harry Beal. She was surprised, for Harry was hardly ever in town since he'd gone to work at the mill in Grayville, which was up the Wabash on the Illinois side. She took one last swipe at the eaves and leaned her broom against the house as she went down the ladder. Then she started toward the wagon.

"Fix bayonets, is it?" Harry said, and Kate, who had started to put her hand out and then held it back when she saw that her sleeve was covered with strands of spider web, felt herself flush that Harry had heard her whistling bugle calls.

"You missed John," she said, thinking what she must look like. Harry, for his part, reached down to her kerchief and, with great concentration, his eyes focused on what he was doing, removed bits of bronzed oak leaves, and handed them to her, one by one. Kate flushed again, and then quickly pulled the kerchief off, which both undid the side of her hair—she could feel it loosen—and got pieces of leaf on Harry's shirt, which was a beautiful shirt. It was linen and bleached almost white.

"He's gone to Mount Vernon. He's gone to see Michael McShane," she said, trying to hold her hair up, and she had one little tremulous instant when she thought of poor Michael who'd come back from Andersonville completely toothless and with an ulcerated leg that seemed never to heal.

"I didn't come to see John," Harry answered, swinging down from the wagon. "Take off your apron, Kate. I thought we'd have a picnic."

"And who would we be?" Kate asked laughing, though it was an awkward kind of laugh since she didn't know the answer to her own question. She wondered if Harry meant that he'd gotten a group of their friends together and that she should see what her mother had in the larder to take along. Or if he meant just the two of them.

"That would be us. You and me. Kate and Harry," he said, looking at the wasp nest she'd left on the ground. "Unless your mother wants to send Charley along."

"Mother's not here," Kate answered, trying to think if the last time she'd been entirely alone with Harry Beal was the day she'd gone to his aunt's and barged in on the George Beals in Mr. Beal's workshop. "I'm covered with cobwebs," she said.

"Dust yourself off then. I'll wait." Harry took the ladder from her. "I'll put it away. And I've got a picnic basket in the wagon," he called after her as she went inside.

He was leaning against the wagon when she came back out. "That was fast," he said, helping her up, and Kate nodded and didn't say that she'd made herself wait by the back door a full two minutes so she wouldn't seem too eager.

"So where are we going?" she asked him as he flicked his whip above the horse's ears. She looked back at the wagon bed, which was empty except for a horse blanket behind the seat and a scattering of stray corn husks and a large basket covered with a fresh cloth. "Goodness, Harry, what trouble you've gone to," she said. "Did you hire the basket done? How is it you have an afternoon, anyway, when all the farmers are taking their corn to the mill?"

"Which question should I answer first?" Harry looked over at her, and Kate thought how brown he was from the whole summer of sun, and how blond and clean his hair was, and how his eyes were the light blue that was her favorite color of any eye color, for it seemed there was something very intelligent and engaged about them. You could see into them, she decided, with the slight cast in the right one that made you look again. There was something just wild and yet gentlemanly about Harry Beal that had always made him the most interesting of all John's friends. She thought it might be a way with Yorkshiremen, though she didn't know.

"You're a funny woman, Kate Given, who takes longer to answer a question than to change into her best dress, which is a very pretty dress, I might add."

"You could say where we're going." Kate smoothed the dress carefully across her knees. It was white with a thin blue stripe, and she and Margaret Mulhern had made it from the dress length Mrs. Lichtenberger had given her in the spring. It embarrassed her that Harry assumed she'd put on her best dress for him, though of course she had. She thought that the two of them might look romantic, she in her nice dress and Harry in his linen shirt, the sun dappled on them through a long stretch of brilliant leaves. The thought bothered her as soon as it came to her. It felt too girlish. It felt like Eliza making up stories for dolls. And, anyway, glorious as it was, she found autumn sad. Everything burst into flame and then disappeared. And it was so hard at first when winter came. It was hard until it felt like the everyday thing, and then hard again when it did.

"Where we're going is a place you haven't been, though you'll recognize it. And you'll like it, I think. When we get there, I'll feed you if you read to me."

"But I don't read aloud. It's not a thing that I do," she protested, not telling him that what she did do was recite well, though mostly in Gaelic.

"So that's a new thing I know about you. Or a thing I know your opinion about."

"You could read to me instead, Harry. What did you bring? I believe John reads poetry to a lady when he has the chance, but I'd like to hear the speeches in Congress with all the wrangling there's been, or something simple like the prices of muslin and mutton. Or the list of times when the mail packets run, though I'd settle for a note that tells when the passenger ships dock in New York."

"So a man only needs a newspaper to satisfy you and himself as well?"

Kate looked off across the golden field they were passing and then back at Harry.

"Did John ever tell you how the ship he and Mother and the children were on had to stay in port for a month before they were allowed off? I like hearing the practical things of life going on because so much of the time lately they haven't."

"They're going on now," Harry answered, and Kate thought, for an instant, that he was going to reach for her hand, though he didn't. "And since you wanted to know, I did the basket myself. A hospital orderly learns such things seeing what ladies bring to the men. You can judge how well it served me. And as for what I hired, it was a man to work at the mill. And as for where we're headed, we're going to the labyrinth."

"Except there's no lab— But, Harry, if I hadn't been home. Or if I hadn't been willing. Would you have asked some other girl? Is it your birthday, Harry?"

"It's not. And I wouldn't have. I would have hunted you down, Kate, or dumped my basket in the river if I'd hadn't found you."

Kate was quiet. She was pleased that he'd flattered her, but she had a lurking suspicion she couldn't quite conquer. She brooded over it a moment and then, in a rush, she let her doubts spill out. "There isn't any labyrinth. You know that, Harry. Not anymore. If we're to get lost, we'll have to do it somewhere else. It helps, I suppose, that Ann Bradley's Mrs. Rippeto now. Or helps when you're thinking of a girl to invite. And what is it that a fellow learns in the stockade? There now, I've been harsh when you've been kind. Harry, I'm sorry."

"Quills again and this time hurled straight from the porcupine. It's all right for, yes, I was in the stockade. What is there for you to be sorry about, Kate? I was the one sorry to be there. I was a very sorry fellow indeed."

They had come to a road south of town and, as they turned onto it, Kate thought they might have walked, although she liked riding on the wagon bench with the bright leaves close enough to touch and the light swaying of the wagon, which brought her shoulder next to Harry's now and again. "Are we going to the old cemetery? Is a place filled with dead people your idea of a labyrinth?" she asked, and then she thought, sighing, how right John was. That she didn't guard her tongue at all and that Harry would never guess that she quite liked the sight and smell of him and the look of his hands on the horse's reins. She knew, since John had told her, that besides having been shot above his ankle, Harry had awful veins in his legs. He'd been on a terrible march when his corps retreated to Louisville. His legs had turned black and swollen. They'd cramped so badly he could scarcely put his weight on them. Yet he limped no more now than John did and, to her, a man who limped from being in the army stood a great deal taller than one who didn't.

"So you think there isn't a labyrinth," Harry said.

"Well, of course the Rappites had one. And wasn't there a school nearby?—one we might have gone to if we'd been children here? I think Mr. Cannon told me there was, though maybe it was Mr. Bolton who went there. I've always liked it Father Rapp thought a labyrinth could represent the tortured life that leads to heaven. But there's no labyrinth now, Harry. Not unless you've a labyrinthian mind."

There. That was better Kate thought. It was playful, maybe even witty, and it didn't sound mean.

Harry slowed the wagon to a stop. "We'll see," he said, getting out and tying the horse to a tree branch. Kate waited for him to lift her down and, when he did, she wondered if her waist felt as small to him as she hoped it did.

They had passed the old cemetery, and the road had narrowed into a sort of lane with trees on either side. Where it ended, there were uncut cornfields beyond it. Kate couldn't think of a house anywhere near, and she watched Harry take the basket and the horse blanket out of the wagon bed and start up the lane. She wondered if he meant for her to follow him. "Are we going to picnic in a cornfield? What's the plan, Harry?" she asked, and he looked back and smiled at her.

"Wait here a minute," he said, and he went on, disappearing into the corn rows.

"If you've got the paper, you can read me the prices of corn," she called. "The yellow corn. Popcorn, too. Even white corn. Harry?"

There wasn't an answer back and Kate, listening, started to bite at her thumbnail. Then she put her hands at her sides. "Harry?" she called once more. She felt silly just standing there, and she wondered if maybe Harry was having fun with her. She walked over to the horse. She ran her finger up and down his nose just above his nostrils, pushing the fur back and then smoothing it down like the nap on velvet. A flock of crows flew up noisily overhead and Kate looked at them crossing the puffy bits of cloud in the sky and thought that Harry, whatever he was doing, must have flushed them out of the corn. Then she heard Harry whistling and it was a bugle call, the very one she'd been humming when he found her on the ladder. He walked back out of the corn with no picnic basket in sight.

"Miss Given?" he said, coming up to her and holding out his arm, and Kate slipped a hand around his elbow as though they were stepping onto a dance floor.

"You actually have, haven't you," she said, "planned a picnic in a cornfield? Is that really a holiday for a miller?"

"Shhh, Kate." Harry reached his hand over and covered her hand that lay inside his elbow. "Pay attention," he said, and she saw that the corn rows they'd entered weren't just any corn rows. They curved, and when they'd walked a few yards, the stalks rising green on both sides of them and taller than they both were, Harry pointed to a path cut into the row on the left.

"Should we turn here?" he asked. "You decide. It's your puzzle, Kate."

"My puzzle?" She took the path. It was narrower than the first path so that she and Harry had to walk closer together and, even with the breeze ruffling through the leafy stalks so that a rough green tip would suddenly touch her cheek or, for a second, seem to hold her dress, she was aware mostly of their game and of the way the two of them moved in and out of shade and light. Now there were two paths to choose from and, this time, she took the one on the right.

She looked up at Harry. "Of course," she said, "it is a labyrinth."

They went ahead without speaking, Kate making her choices and Harry walking beside her. As they kept on, Kate felt an odd but growing sense of peace. Whatever she'd said or should say or hadn't said no longer seemed to matter, for it was as though the many small wars inside her had simply stopped. She had walked into something like a moment of grace.

That sense of calm, of being exactly present, stayed with her when the last turn brought them to the center of the labyrinth. It was a grove of young cedar trees, most of them barely taller than the corn. The picnic basket was sitting on the ground.

"You didn't get lost," Harry said. "We didn't," and Kate nodded as he took his hand from her hand, unlocking her from his arm. "And what would you like?" he said, lifting the basket lid. He took out a root beer and offered it to her, and Kate laughed at how careful and proper he was being.

"In a moment. I hope, sir, you brought a beer for yourself. But how did you do it?" she asked. "All this." She turned around, tracing a quick circle that followed the line of the corn rows.

"In the spring. I planted it then, for I thought you would like it."

"In the spring you thought that?"

"It was late spring, but yes."

Kate felt a new suspicion crowding in on her lovely equilibrium. "And you thought I would like it?"

"And you do?"

"Very much. Yet, Harry, it seems that John wrote me you were thick with a Grayville girl in June—at least one—and did you really go to Ann Bradley's wedding without hoping she wouldn't back out? It's a lovely labyrinth, but—"

"Yes, it is. I've no claim to be perfect, Kate, but I've got something else growing if you need another witness."

Kate had started to take the plates from the picnic basket. She looked up. "More plantings?" She was all curiosity.

"Right here." Harry had gone to one of the trees and he was clearing the ground around it. Then he brushed at the trunk. "Would you read it to me?"

"That's the reading you wanted me to do?"

He waited. Kate put the plates on the cloth and went over and looked at the tree.

"The moss," he said, and Kate crouched down, and touching the deep moss, felt how it had been tended to grow into letters. She looked closely.

"Harry Beal wants Kate," she read aloud.

"It was supposed to say Harry Beal wants Kate Given to marry him. It said May 10, 1865, which is when I first made the letters, except that something ate the rest of them. You'll believe me, Kate? But don't believe me yet. I've something else to show you."

"I'll believe that you want me. But if I believe you want me to marry you, does it mean you're asking if I will?"

"You may not have thought it, but I've meant to ask since well before May. Years, actually. You helped your family. I went to war and I've saved enough money. There's nobody else I ever wanted to ask—"

Kate couldn't restrain herself. "Then do! Ask me right here in your labyrinth." She looked at Harry's eyes, at their wonderful, transparent blue.

"There's something else first. Have a little patience, Kate." Harry put his hand across her eyes, pressing her forward with his arm on her waist, and all Kate was thinking was that she wanted to say yes right now. She wanted to kiss Harry and feel the beautiful linen that stretched across his shoulder blades.

"Careful. There's a tree on your left. Another three steps. All right. Go ahead. You can look now."

They had come around two of the larger cedars and they were standing in front of a short hut, a cavelike thing made of woven saplings. "What is it?" Kate said. "Honestly, Harry. How do you even have time to mill?"

"It's a shelter. Some from the rain but more from the sun. You'll like it inside, Kate. I'll show you the sky. There's a whole patchwork of light."

"And we're Hansel and Gretel?" Kate had lowered her head to go in the entrance. She spotted the horse blanket spread out on the ground. For a moment, she hesitated.

Harry was at her shoulder. "Kate, it's all right. It's the best view if you lie down to look at the sky, but you can look alone if you want."

"And why would I want that?" Kate went ahead. She knelt on the blanket, eyeing the spindly diamonds of light that played on her dress. She tugged her skirt around so she could stretch out on her back. "You and your hideaways. It's very airy and peaceful. So show me the sky," she said, making room as Harry crawled in beside her.

They were silent a moment, lying there. Kate thought her heart would beat faster, and maybe it did, but they were both dutifully studying the sky through the snarl of feathery wood. Kate thought she knew what the first impressions of a hatchling bird must be.

"You like it?" Harry asked.

"Yes. Very much." Kate stared awhile longer. Then she pushed herself up on her elbow and looked at Harry instead. "It's loveliest because you're here. You're a lovely man, Harry Beal. And now have I had patience enough?" She picked up a small chip of wood and balanced it carefully on his nose. Then she flicked it aside and ran her finger across his lips.

Harry caught her hand. "Ah, Kate, you're making this difficult. I have a mission here. I meant to prove what a trustworthy fellow I am—to show you this place and then escort you out and propose to you properly with my feet on the ground—or my knees. I didn't want to do a thing that means your brother has to kill me."

Kate laughed. She let her arm collapse so she fell back flat on the ground. She stared up through the hut at a patch of green leaves and took a deep breath. Her heart really was beating faster now. Harry was so close. The scent of him. His skin. "Your shirt is so beautiful, Harry," she said, and she closed her eyes so she could feel every odd thing that was stirring inside her. It seemed her entire body, which for so long had seemed destined only to scrub floors and pull weeds and roll dough, wanted desperately to be touched.

"Will you, Kate? Marry me?" he said in her ear, and she nodded, her eyes still closed as he kissed her, the smooth skin of his lips pressing lightly against hers. His hands were touching her hair, her fingers finally climbing his back: the hard muscles, the wonderful shirt.

"Yes. I will, Harry," she said when they'd paused to look at each other. "There's nothing I want more." She slipped a hand out from under his arm and reached up to touch his face, amazed still that he was so near. A faint prickle had started through his perfect shave. "But, Harry, the girls I know claim men can do things that will stop just short of what requires the girls' brothers to shoot them. If that's what you mean . . ."

This time it was Harry who laughed, and Kate saw herself in his eyes. Then he grew serious. "Only if you're sure, Kate. John says you'd have worn bloomers with Fanny Wright. That your mind is an independent woman's. But only if you're sure."

Kate felt an unexpected flush of tears. It was a moment before she could talk, and then it was in a whisper as Harry stroked her eyelashes, that lovely, slight cast in his eye, the touch of his fingers seeming to run all the way through her. "I'm so grateful that you're here, Harry, that you're safe. I'm so happy the war and waiting are finally done. I love your shirt. I love your eyes. Yes, Harry. Yes, Harry, please."

28

State of Indiana, Posey County

This certifies that I joined in marriage as husband and wife Harry B. Beal and Catharine Given on the 25 day of January 1866.

Milton Fillingim, J. P.

The rest of the fall and early winter was a blur of color and excitement unlike anything Kate had ever experienced. She was amazingly happy. Nothing could shake her optimism. On the evening Harry asked her father for her hand, her father offered so many toasts that he and Harry both got quite drunk. To Kate's mild surprise, it only amused her, though she'd seen her mother's concern. Kate kissed her, but she felt no need to offer an apology. Instead she told her mother she needn't worry that Harry would drink like her father, that he'd only done it to be polite.

In general, she could see her mother's ambivalence. Her mother liked Harry and she was glad that Kate was getting married, but they had had a long, somber talk at the kitchen table—long because of all the silences from her mother. Kate had told her that she didn't plan to get married at St. Wendel's but to have Mr. Fillingim, the justice of the peace, perform the ceremony, and that it wasn't because of Harry, not to blame Harry, that Harry would do whatever she wanted.

"It won't be a marriage," her mother said, and Kate had told her that it would be, that the marriage lay in the vows she and Harry would make to each other. She was sorry to hurt her, sorrier than she could say, but it was what she felt and what she'd come to consider was true. She needed to start her marriage as her mother had started hers: on the solid ground of an honest belief.

"You've gone to the library too much," her mother said. "You've read too much about Fanny Wright and about Mr. Owen's hatred of marriage."

"But, Mother, I am getting married," Kate answered, and she squelched the slight touch of guilt she felt and didn't say more. She certainly didn't tell her mother that she'd already made a trip to the library to take a serious look at Robert Dale's *Moral Physiognomy* and its directions on how to avoid pregnancies. But gradually, as the days passed, her mother seemed to resign herself. Or at least she didn't talk of it again.

Mary and Margaret were excited for her. They both loved Harry, who'd always been great fun for them. Mary said that she'd known forever that Kate would marry him. Margaret said Mary had known no such thing, and they'd argued a minute but then both kissed her and said how happy they were. Denis was unimpressed. Charley was quiet for a time. Then he asked Kate if she would still seem like his sister, and she said that she would—that she was his sister no matter what. Of her friends and charges, Eliza Lichtenberger was the only disconsolate one for, though she agreed Kate should certainly marry, she said she'd meant to marry Harry herself, cousin or not, and that she needed Kate to stay her best companion.

Margaret Mulhern and John were bigger concerns. Kate and her mother had both noticed a coolness between Margaret and Charles Ward since he'd mustered out and come home in December and, though Kate had tried to find out why, she didn't know the reason. She did have the strong sense that a little door would close somewhere for Margaret if she got married before her. Yet in spite of that, Margaret showed not the slightest bit of jealousy but only the warmest affection when Kate went to tell her. Kate thought once again how good she was.

"If we'd not come here, I would never have met him," Kate said, "if we'd not left service in Donegal Town and come here with Father. Margaret, I've you to thank for how happy I am."

But it was John she was the most nervous about. Michael McShane was still far from well, and John had stayed visiting him for four days. Michael had all his Andersonville horror stories, and there'd been the dreadful accident to his friends—three dozen 10th Cavalry men and Aleck Twigg killed on the *Sultana*. It had exploded on their way home. And John hadn't seen Michael since the news of his wife's death. Michael had taken it much harder than Kate would have expected.

For four long days, she was anxious. She was aware that if someone could spoil her happiness it was John. Friends though he and Harry were, if John had any reservations about Harry, he would make his doubts known. Kate planned what she would say but, as it happened, John already knew her news when she saw him. What Harry told her, a long time later, was that John went to him first and asked him straight out if there was any reason—syphilitic or otherwise—that he shouldn't marry his sister. Harry had sworn that there wasn't, and so the John Kate met, when she was walking home from the Lichtenbergers', was absolutely jolly.

"What's better than this, my best sister and my best friend? He's a lucky devil, Kate. I'll not let him forget it," John said, and Kate had laughed with both pleasure and relief.

There were times when Kate wondered if it was fair to be so totally happy when her own happiness might bring distress or jealousy to others, and when so many people had lost so much in the war. Caroline Thrailkill, for instance, had been devastated when word came from John that Levi had died. She'd always believed—partly, Kate thought, to keep her parents from giving up hope—that Levi would return with the other captured men at the end of the war. The Thrailkill family was still in deep mourning, their house windows draped in black and a mourning wreath on the door.

And there were so many men like Levi who had died or been killed, and there were all the men who'd suffered injuries that would last a lifetime. Even Felix Edmonds, who'd snuck in and out of Harmony for nearly two years before turning himself in to a court-martial, had wound up with the Veteran 25th in South Carolina and gotten shot in the leg. John seemed to have little sympathy for him, but Kate, in her current frame of mind, had sympathy for everyone. She wished she had a magic wand to make everyone she knew as happy as she was.

Since they knew they'd be living in Grayville, the biggest thing she and Harry had to decide was when to get married. Harry was all for doing it right away. In some ways, Kate was, too, but she did want to savor their courtship awhile. She wanted to give herself a chance to get used to the idea that their meetings were no longer happenstance but something she could count on and anticipate, with Harry stopping for her with the wagon or having a place at their table right next to hers so she had only to move her fingers to touch his sleeve. She felt, too, that she had to give her parents, particularly her mother, time to absorb the idea that she was leaving to have her own home. There was also the work she had to finish for Mrs. Lichtenberger and the time Mrs. Lichtenberger would need to find and train a new girl though, as Harry's cousin (she was Caroline, even Caro to him), Mrs. Lichtenberger had seemed to regard Kate differently since their engagement. Kate couldn't quite put her finger on it except to think there was some new combination of surprise and respect in Mrs. Lichtenberger's attitude. She'd been very kind, of course. She had even offered Kate her parlor for the wedding ceremony, which might have tempted Kate if she hadn't already had Margaret Mulhern's proposal of the Sampsons' parlor and a meal to follow, a gesture that had moved Kate deeply. She knew that Margaret would never have asked such a favor of Mrs. Sampson for anyone else and that she'd only done so for Kate as a way of keeping the wedding a family wedding while sparing her mother the distress of having a daughter marry at home with no priest.

Harry had had his own suggestions. "We could marry at the mill," he said. "You'd be cold and I'd have to wrap you up, but there's a fine view of the river. Or we could go to my aunt's and get married in the workshop so we could just get right on with things."

Kate, who was snugged quite comfortably into his arm, had laughed, though she was still grateful that Harry, knowing the gathering had to be small, had left George Beal and Hectorina off the guest list. "I do love you, Harry," she'd said, tapping his knuckles with a fingertip.

Every day, it seemed, she had something new for her hope chest. Her mother and the girls were busy on her trousseau, and her friends were making linens with all sorts of fancy hemstitching and embroidery and finely scalloped edges. For her own part, Kate was busiest writing letters to all the family in Donegal and to her cousins in Bridgeport and to her aunts in Chicago. She knew there would be none of them who could come, for Bridgeport seemed far away even in the summer. It was an impossible distance in winter, and Chicago was as out of the question as Ireland. Yet she wanted very much to tell every single one of the people she cared for that she was to be married to Harry Beal on a Thursday in late January with Margaret Mulhern hosting a wedding meal, and that she and Harry, in their happiness, would think of them and drink a toast to them all. John, seeing her struggling, offered to write the letters for her but, though she queried him often about spelling and punctuation, she kept at it in her painstaking way. She was satisfied that, if her penmanship lacked ease and beauty, she was still writing the letters herself.

What she should wear was at least as much of an issue for her sisters as it was for her. More, she thought. Mary wanted very much for her to borrow something from Mrs. Lichtenberger and, in fact, had a pink satin dress in mind. Margaret thought she could find her a dress in the theater costumes at Union Hall and, being Margaret, add the bit of styling detail that would be perfect. Harry told her that no matter what she wore, he would think of her in the white dress that she'd worn to the labyrinth, and Kate herself was leaning toward wearing her black dress that was only two winters old. John weighed in, saying she might wear their father's nightshirt as she couldn't decide, but in the end she didn't have to make a choice at all for, on the Sunday a week before Christmas when she was writing the last of her letters, Caroline Thrailkill knocked at the window and then at the door. When Kate let her in out of a freezing drizzle, she came in carrying a large box.

"It's from Mother," Caroline said, pushing her hood back. "It's for you and it's to thank John for all his trouble over Levi. We might never have known . . . But open it, Kate."

Caroline stood waiting, and Kate, who had put the box down on the table, carefully took off the lid. "Oh, Caroline," she exclaimed then. She lifted out a heavy dress in deep red velvet with a broad skirt and with sleeves that puffed at the top and narrowed down to the wrists. She held it up, and moved back and forth to see herself in the mirror, thinking of the cost of the fabric (a great deal for the Thrailkills) and of the undeniable fact that Mrs. Thrailkill was as fine a seamstress as there was in Harmony. She fingered the skirt. "It's so lovely," she said. She looked back at Caroline. "I've never seen anything as beautiful."

Caroline nodded. "Mother thought it was your color, and it is, Kate. It sets off your dark eyes. She worried you'd think less of her for making such a dress while we're in mourning. I said that you wouldn't, and I did encourage her. She needs something to distract her. I've loved it, Kate, having something lovely to look at, and now I'll know what you'll look like when you and Harry get married."

Kate felt a choky little sensation in her chest. She hugged Caroline and put on the tea and, as they drank it, she thought maybe Caroline was hoping to see John, but he didn't come in.

By Christmas, Kate had tried on her dress so many times (stopping at the house after shopping for the Lichtenbergers) that her mother told her yes, it was very pretty but that marriage wasn't about vanity and that she hoped she was preparing herself in more serious ways for her new life. She didn't say more, but when Harry arrived and the family had eaten the turkey Denis had shot and her father had declared himself the new stuffed bird in the house, Kate was still feeling subdued. She and Harry took a long walk. They talked about the war, and Harry told her what a gruesome scene it had been arriving at Shiloh with Buell's army, that finding John in that wasteland of bodies had felt like encountering Lazarus. He said what a big part of their lives the war had taken and how he and Kate, who'd come to New Harmony just a year apart, were so lucky in being here now that they owed it to each other and to everyone they knew to have a good life. Then, because it was on her mind, Kate told him about the rocker she'd been buying for her mother, and she decided on the spot she would ask Mr. Fretageot for her money back to give herself a nest egg. Though it felt like a hard choice—she had so much wanted to surprise her mother—Kate knew it was what her mother would want.

Harry wasn't as sure. "We'll see, Kate," he said. "There's a bounty bill coming. We'll see."

At New Year's, she decided she'd picked the best time of the year to be married for, even if it was cold, it was still such a happy season. Nearly everyone who stopped in to give Mrs. Lichtenberger their greetings for the new year asked for her, too. So many people brought her their good wishes that she thought she'd wear a rut in the floor, going from the kitchen to the parlor and back. And the new year brought her mail as well. She had letters from cousins and aunts, and a sweet note from Alice and Mary, sent from St. Mary's, that told her they thought Harry was just as lucky as they knew she was.

Then, with what seemed to Kate like the speed of a sled flying down an icy hill, she was retired from service and her wedding day had arrived. She was dressing with her sisters for one last time up in their room. She carefully put on the velvet dress and waited while they did up the back. Then Margaret finished her hair with a twisting strand of loganberries that held it up from her face, except for the loose curls she'd done with an iron. Kate gave her and Mary the hair ornaments Eliza had helped her make from rain tree seeds.

"Mother may be O'Donnell royalty, but you're the first Given I've ever seen that looks it," Margaret said. Then John brought Mr. Wilsey's buggy to take their mother and the girls to the Sampsons' house. Kate rode with her father in Francis Cannon's old wagon, which she wanted to do, though she knew it and the dram of whiskey her father took would make him tear up.

Mrs. Beal was too ill to attend, but she sent her buggy for Harry to use. He and Mr. Fillingim were both in the kitchen at the Sampsons' when Kate arrived. She waited in the hallway with her father, still keeping her cloak on while the Lichtenbergers and then Robert and Emma Clarke came in and took their seats behind the other guests. At eleven o'clock, Martha Wilsey, who was Mrs. James Randolph now, started playing the piano, and Kate's father went to sit with her mother. Kate took her cloak off and left it on the hall table. Then Harry came and got her, and they walked in to the tall vases of winter wheat Margaret had tied with strings of cranberries, and Mr. Fillingim married them, with John and Margaret Mulhern signing as witnesses afterward.

"Let the party begin," her father said, kissing her after Harry did and after Harry whispered to her that she looked beautiful.

Kate could hardly talk from happiness, but she danced with Harry when Denis and Charley rolled up the rug. She danced with her father and John. All the girls helped Margaret Mulhern put out the food that she and Mary had made—Mary had done the cake all by herself—and it was a small group (not even Michael McShane), but a grand feast and dancing, with her father adding his fiddle to Martha's tunes. Kate wanted it all to last forever, really forever, except she knew that Margaret Mulhern needed the house back in order before the Sampsons returned, and Harry wanted daylight to start them on their buggy ride to Grayville. And, too, she was ready to be alone with her husband. Her very own husband. Her own Harry.

When it was time to go, John gave her a long hug and helped her into the buggy. He shook Harry's hand, and everyone gathered round while Harry tucked in the lap robes. Charley and Eliza banged loudly on pans until they were scolded. Denis stood up on the wheel and leaned in toward Harry, saying something Kate couldn't hear. Harry nodded and then started the buggy with the same quick snap of the whip above the horses' heads that Kate remembered from their first ride to the labyrinth. She had only a second to wave to everyone.

"What did Denis want?" she asked, watching Charley run ahead of them.

"Just to say he's delivered the chair."

Kate looked at him.

"The Tell City Rocker. For your mother. I didn't want you to start our marriage with any regrets, so she'll have your gift, Kate. She'll find it at home."

Kate, who had been resting her head on Harry's shoulder, sat up startled. They'd come to the Wabash and, as she watched the horses step onto the ice, she felt a quick, unexpected impulse to argue, to say that if it was to be her gift she would rather have known about it first. She was quiet for a moment, considering, for she knew Harry meant well. Not only that, but he'd been entirely generous so her mother would have the chair for her headaches and her back. Kate bit at her lip, and pulled the top lap robe tighter. Then she thought that this must be the deeper part of what her mother had meant about vanity, that there were times like this—it was so beautiful riding across the blue and frozen river—when she simply had to let it go, when she had to try patience and be much more like Margaret O'Donnell Given than Fanny Wright.

Still it nagged. She thanked Harry. The horse pulled them across the darkening ice, and she thanked him as sweetly as she possibly could, but it didn't go away until they'd gotten to Grayville—the one small thorn in the fall's months of happiness, the tiniest cloud just shadowing the bright new winter.

New Harmony, Indiana
February—September 1867

29

Our Fancy Basket–Supper–Ball is to come off on the 14th Inst. in com–memoration of the battle of Fort Donelson. If I am here I intend to go to that Ball and to the Children's Ball on the 15th as it will be so much pleasure to be able to shake that leg which I got crippled on that 15th of Feb. at Ft. Donelson.

John Given to Harry Beal, February 3rd, 1867

John was in Henry Schafer's barber chair in the tavern, his hair freshly cut and his face lathered and ready for the blade Henry was stropping. For months, Kate had been after him to have his picture taken, and he was having it done today before he was another year older, which he'd be at midnight. Mary had suggested he should look the part—his handsomest, she said.

He felt lazy, even dozy. He closed his eyes against the sun, which had glinted off the snow that was piled in the street and up against the window glass. He yawned and then tightened his jaw closed as he felt the razor slip down and below his cheek. Though everyone said Henry was ambidextrous enough to shave a man and pour a drink at the same time, and though John not only would trust him with his life but had, the very fact of having a man with a knife at his throat meant he wasn't really sleepy anymore. He kept his eyes closed anyway. He thought about his options for the coming weeks.

The G.A.R. boys had appointed him to the committee for their basket-supper-ball, which was to be on Valentine's Day, the fifth anniversary of the battle of Fort Donelson. John had declined because he didn't know if he was going to be in town. Ribeyre, the Frenchman who

460

was rapidly turning the Cut-off Island into his own little empire, had asked him to take his cattle to Memphis. John had told him he would if they were ready to go before it was time to burn logs with Denis and the hired hands. He had two preferences. He wanted Ribeyre's money and wouldn't mind seeing Memphis again; he also wanted to go the ball. There were bills up all over town advertising it, "Grand Army of the Republic" printed on a furled banner at the top.

"Did you hear about Mrs. Hernan?" Henry asked, wiping a bit of lather from behind John's ear and then cleaning the razor. "She did one of the smartest things on record in New Harmony. She went for the doctor in person and came home and gave birth to a daughter."

John laughed. "Very smart," he said. "And smart, too, to produce a playmate for John Clarey's new boys," he added, though Henry had turned away and John knew he didn't heard him. He looked at himself in the mirror. Then he left change on the counter and went out into the street, still considering the rapid ballooning of Harmony's baby population since the war. If the weather had been warm and the streets not clogged with snow, he thought he might have looked successfully on every corner for a young mother with her baby or, in Ann Armstrong's case—Ann Clarey's—two. There was no Rippeto baby, however. Whenever he spotted Ann, and he was grateful that was rare, it was very clear to him she'd not gained an ounce in nearly two years of marriage.

Of course there *was* a baby in Grayville now. Kate had been home for her confinement, attended by his mother and Mary. She'd had a fine boy in their parents' bed, and she and Harry had named him Clarence Barton Beal, which had sent John's father off in an angry mood to the tavern.

"So Harry's family's got Bartons in it. I can understand that. But what sort of a name is Clarence?" he asked when John had gone later to get him. "Has your sister, Mrs. Beal, forgotten where she come from?"

It had been noisy in the house with the baby squalling at any hour. His cries had startled John, for they began like the first pitch of a far-off artillery shell and, for a night or so, he felt he was back at the siege of Atlanta and had the nightmares to prove it. Then he either got used to it or the baby cried less and he was able to sleep again. The effect on the women seemed altogether positive, for Kate was pale but rapt, and Mary utterly smitten. Margaret, who'd married Andy Williams after he'd come back from Rough and Ready in California and lived in one of Ribeyre's houses on the Cut-off, came over to Harmony every chance she got. John didn't think he'd seen his mother as happy since Charley was a baby. She'd set up shop with her yarn basket and the rocker she'd gotten from Harry and Kate, and most of the time when Kate wasn't feeding Clarence or his aunts walking him, his grandmother was rocking him on her lap or nudging her foot against the cradle Denis had made.

Charley, for his part, seemed a little dazed. "I guess he's all right," he said. "But what's all the fuss about a baby?"

Much to Kate's satisfaction, their father, once he'd experimented with names (Bart and Barty, Clare and C. B., Larey), called Clarence Clarence and became a total convert to the baby's cause. He couldn't walk into the house without clucking at him or bringing some toy that he'd made to dangle over the cradle. The day Harry took Kate home, John half expected his parents to harness up the wagon and go right after them. The house and the whole town seemed quiet even to him. When the snow came, piling up faster and faster by the hour, John went out to cemetery hill, where men and girls were hurling snowballs at each other. Kate Marshal and Caroline Thrailkill, who had finally returned from her sister's in Galatia, told him they'd like Harry back. They said there was nobody who built a snow fort like he did, and John wanted to say that half the men in town could build forts in their sleep—any kind of fort—but the girls looked so ruddy cheeked and good natured that he agreed with them. He said he would write Harry how much they missed him. He thought Caroline looked as animated as he'd ever seen her with her bonnet pushed back and hanging from its strings and a snowball splattered on her skirt. He told her how well she was looking. He was thinking he might ask her to go to the ball with him, but he didn't know if he was actually going. There was also something aloof in her manner when Kate Marshal left them alone, and so, in the end, he didn't ask.

He was at Thrall and Mumford's now, where he'd come to have his picture made. He held on to the doorframe and knocked the snow from his boots, and then he went inside. He walked to the back of the store and, to his surprise, he found Caroline seated and posing perfectly still before the camera. John was eager to greet her, yet he didn't want to spoil her picture, and so he waited behind some boxes until he heard Eugene Thrall tell her she was done and could move. John wasn't sure she'd seen him, but a second later she peered around the boxes and said hello.

"It's for my sister," she told him. "She collects daguerreotypes and she's been after me for ages to have one done. I wouldn't have otherwise."

"And I'm here to get one for Kate," he answered, "and I wouldn't otherwise, so we've our sisters' wishes in common and our sisters to thank for our seeing each other."

Caroline busied herself in examining a tin with a painted bird on it. "I can understand Kate wanting a picture of her smart brother to brag about," she said, turning the tin in her hand, "but I find it morbid and odd of Ellen to want one of me. She's always telling me that if we had pictures of Amaline and Levi, they'd still seem alive, which isn't true at all. It makes me wonder if she thinks I'll die soon and that she'll have the comfort of hanging me up on her wall." Caroline laughed and put the tin back on the shelf where she'd found it. "But I've come to do it anyway and it's not for vanity, though it is vanity, I suppose, that I want you to know I'm doing it only because she asked."

"I can think of at least one man who would like such a picture," John said, feeling that he was taking her cue, and that they did have that old conversation to continue: *I think it quite likely my mind was woolgathering when I directed those letters—perhaps I was thinking of some young man.* But instead of flirting as he hoped she would, Caroline studied him for a quiet second and then, with that same touch of distance she'd shown at cemetery hill, she told him she had to go, that her mother was waiting for her at home.

John wanted to ask if she'd be at the dance, but her manner put him off. And, too, if he asked her and then had to take Ribeyre's cattle to Memphis, she could rightly feel slighted. And of course, he'd not seen her once at a ball since he'd been at home, and even considering the family mourning period and the time she'd been at her sister's, he thought he would have if she'd had any interest in going. Maybe it was a Methodist matter, he thought, a Methodist question for her or her mother. In any case, he said nothing of the dance or of anything else, for she left the store. He took his place in front of the camera and tried to hold still and not scratch his neck where it itched from the razor.

As it turned out, he needn't have worried about being gone. The snow melted and the sun dried the ground enough so they could burn logs, and Ribeyre held off on sending his cattle. There was no trip to Memphis, and John was headed to the ball with Mary and Alexander Porter, for his mother insisted on a chaperone, though Mary and Porter, who was from Cincinnati, had been engaged for a week.

"Why does she need a chaperone? He's an Irishman," John said, just to tease his mother.

"Precisely," she answered, and John knew she was thinking of her nieces Katie O'Donnell and Mary Mulhern. For himself, he was still wondering why it was that neither Margaret nor Mary had chosen a Harmony man. It would go hard on his mother, he thought, if they ever moved far away.

John walked behind Mary and Porter on the way up the street. As he heard them laughing and talking together, Mary walking along prettily in her bonnet that she'd trimmed in a Valentine red and Porter, who was more than a head taller than she was, carrying her basket, John felt a familiar wistfulness coming over him, a small sadness that things were changing, and a larger sadness that they hadn't yet changed for him. He'd talked with Harry about it, how it seemed that life should move forward but that, somehow, he had one foot left in a war that no longer existed.

"How did you get past it, Harry?" he'd asked him, and Harry had said all the right things about Kate, of course, but then he'd said, too, that it had been different for him since he'd followed his fighting soldier's life with hospital duty, with months in the brig and then working on fortifications.

"And I'm just happier than you, John," he added, "as a rule. Constitutionally happier. I circle things less."

John had felt he was right. But thinking about it now, he suddenly realized that, on this particular Valentine's Day—five years to the day since he and Felix Edmonds had found the beautiful, fair boy with the black hair and blue eyes, the boy who'd bled to death when they'd tried to lift him up from the snow—he wasn't willing to agree. He called out to Mary.

It was Porter who turned around, and John caught up to him and Mary, and then told Porter to consider himself chaperoned, that he'd be back soon.

"Where are you going?" Mary asked, but John didn't bother to answer. He took off on the double quick back up the street, never minding that it hurt his knee, and went all the blocks to the edge of town and knocked at the Thrailkills' door. It was a moment before John heard the sound of a boot against maybe a coal bucket, followed by steps coming to the door.

It was Mr. Thrailkill who opened it, and John thought, as he always did when he saw him, that Mr. Thrailkill looked the way Levi might have looked older except that Levi, in one crucial way, would have been like Caroline—more sure of himself. He thought, too, as he always did, of how Mr. Thrailkill had given him a perfect map to Shiloh so that he'd gotten there in plenty of time for the bloody thing that it was, which was still a bloody part of himself.

"Is Caroline in?" he asked, shaking Mr. Thrailkill's hand, but Caroline had come up behind her father. There was no need for Mr. Thrailkill to call her.

John waited, hoping Mr. Thrailkill would excuse himself. He didn't. In spite of feeling self-conscious, John went ahead and spoke to Caroline. "I've owed you a valentine for five years," he said. "I had your valentine at Fort Donelson. Or the one you helped Kate make, for I was certain it was your writing. And I had one the next year when the army and I were wandering somewhere in Tennessee. I'm late, but would you like to come out tonight for the Valentine ball? Mary has a basket."

John saw the doubt in Caroline's eyes and the quick way in which she turned toward her father as if to head him off, but Mr. Thrailkill had already called toward the kitchen. "Get her coat, Mother. She can go dancing if I say she can, and I do."

It was several minutes of bustling and whispered comments in the back room, and John offering remarks on the weather and news of Ribeyre's plans in response to Mr. Thrailkill's questions, before Caroline made another appearance. Her hurry to get ready had made the color rise in her cheeks. John found it particularly becoming. It didn't escape him that she was naturally graceful in her cloak, that she was tall and comely (taller than his sisters) and, though Margaret's age, very grown up and certainly more practical than Margaret had ever thought of being. But at the moment he was uncertain if she was coming out with him because she wanted to or because her father had insisted. He was eager to be out the door with her. Mrs. Thrailkill, however, made them wait while she put supper things in a basket.

"I was to chaperone Mary and Porter," John said when they were finally outside in the street. "If they've eloped, I'll be in exceedingly hot water."

"Not boiled in oil?" There was a slight dryness to her tone when Caroline asked the question.

"Possibly," John said. Then he found himself with little else in the way of small talk. They were the only ones in the street. They walked along beneath the bare rain trees, and Caroline kept her head bent toward the street as though she were deeply considering something.

"Are you doing the math tables?" John asked, reaching up to snap a twig from a tree. When Caroline glanced up, he smiled at her.

"If you are, I'd be happy to do them with you. You seem to be thinking very hard about something."

"I might be angry with you," she said quietly.

John rubbed the twig between his fingers. "And why would that be?" he asked, thinking that this might be a sort of progress.

Caroline didn't answer.

"Should I guess? You're offended that I waited so long to invite you to the ball or you're angry that I asked in such a manner that your father sent you off with me when you weren't at all sure you wanted to come. Or you feel I might have brought someone—say, Margaret Mulhern—to chaperone."

"I couldn't be angry with you. Not really. Not after Levi."

"But if it weren't about Levi? If it were just about the two of us? Or were you thinking, Caroline, of an old man as Andy Williams is to Margaret, which is what Kate says that he is?"

Caroline stopped walking and turned to face him. "John, what I was thinking is that you've not been to see me in all this time because you're carrying a torch still for your friend Mrs. Rippeto. And that's all I was thinking," she said, and as sharp as the actual words seemed, John realized with a sense of welcome surprise that Caroline had eased into the same tone of voice that Levi had always used when he was gentling animals, or maybe talking to his mother.

"I'm carrying your basket. I'm carrying nothing for her," he said. "And I assume Jim Rippeto carries what things there are that his wife might need carried."

"Make fun, John, but you know my meaning. A girl might feel slighted thinking her company had only been settled for."

"And a man might take insult that a girl would believe he might slight her so. You've been cool, Caroline. And I would be hot if I believed that those letters Ann read to others without my knowledge would not only make a fool of me but make me suspect for life. And your family was in mourning. You were gone to your sister's. When might I have called?"

"I shouldn't have said anything." Caroline started to walk again. "You're right, of course. I've sounded presumptuous and bungling, and we've really no ties. You were so good about Levi. You've been nothing but good."

"But I'm not good, Caroline, and it's I who've been bungling if you've thought these things." John wanted to turn her toward him. Instead he looked away, and what he was thinking of was Levi lying in the sour-smelling house full of wounded men at Fort Donelson, and of the two of them reading their valentines. He still knew Ann Bradley's verse ("Life is the flower for which love is the honey"), but he thought of Kate's riddle from Shakespeare more often. He wondered if Caroline remembered copying it.

"At Fort Donelson, when I found Levi wounded in a house they'd made a hospital" (*charnel* house, John thought though he didn't say it, wouldn't say it to Caroline), "mostly he was impatient to get to Margret Smith's card. But he knew the answer to the riddle you wrote out for Kate. Do you remember it?"

"I remember the answer was love."

"And the riddle?"

" 'What looks with mind and not the eyes / and therefore paints winged Cupid blind?' I told Kate it was best sent to a man, that a woman getting it would consider herself thought homely."

"Perhaps she would. And perhaps it was Kate calling me ugly, but it was the valentine I remembered, for it was in your hand."

"There was one like it for Levi."

"Yes."

They were quiet then—both, John thought, off in their own memories of Levi, though John knew he had the better of it, for Caroline was so much like Levi. She had the pretty woman's version of Levi's face, and Levi's wit and directness.

"It's that you remind me Levi is dead since you're here and he's not. It still feels hard and it's what makes me prickly and distant." Caroline looked at him and, even with the dark sky, John could see how bright her eyes had become. "It's not, though, what I feel in my heart. There. Like a hussy, I've said it."

"Like a hussy, you're not," he answered quickly. He went on. "There's another reason I'm tardy. Caroline, the war . . ." He swallowed, feeling a sudden need to compose himself. "It's just it's a thing written so deeply inside me. I don't know I'm good for much else."

Her eyes were still bright. "It's in me as well, John. Surely you know that." She paused a moment and then went on. "Isn't it a burden that's lighter with two to carry it?"

They had come to the corner of Main Street where they could cross to Union Hall. John reached to steer Caroline's elbow through the soft wool of the cloak. "I believe you're right. I know you are," he said, and he was thinking of all the things he wanted to tell her and—the wonder of it—that he didn't need to say any of them yet. There was plenty of time. There was the whole evening. There were all the nights to come.

"Inside, they'll make a big fuss," he told her. "Over the veterans. It will all be in fun, and you're not to think that it means they've forgotten Levi or the other boys who didn't come home. You'll dance, won't you?" he asked, and Caroline told him she would.

———

As courtships went, though John had limited firsthand experience, he didn't think there was anything else he might have asked for in the one that he and Caroline had embarked upon. The Caroline he had known since she was Levi's suddenly tall but calm and capable little sister had not changed in any intrinsic way. Yet, as his knowledge of her grew, John felt he had only known the surface of a character that, each day, showed itself to be ever more layered with remarkable stores of the human spirit. He had always been aware of how solicitous Caroline was of her parents. His own father had once remarked that she seemed, at times, almost to carry them. What John noticed now was that, while she was sometimes amused at them, she never showed the slightest trace of resentment for the ways in which her parents depended on her. She was kind to them. It was clearly her nature.

It was also like her to be inventive. She was helping with Mr. Felch's kindergartners again since she'd returned from her sister's and John, stopping on business with Mr. Felch, stood at the window and, seeing Caroline in the yard, noticed with approval that the children were busily digging for worms and hunting for insects under rocks. She was also totally natural with his own family. It was her suggestion that John's parents might keep their house in town but, for now, move over to Margaret's on the Cut-off. His father was working for Ribeyre, and it would save him the ferry trip back and forth every day, and it would also be easier for Kate when she visited. Caroline had offered the whole plan in such a simple, straightforward way that no one had thought it at all presumptuous. Later, John's mother had taken him aside and said what she liked best about Caroline was that she expected no other place than the one that was offered to her, which meant that that place would always be large and welcoming. John had found the endorsement remarkable, for he knew that his mother's first wish, after her wish that he would be a priest, was that he would marry a Catholic girl, and the Thrailkills were churchgoing Methodists.

The list of things that he admired and liked about Caroline seemed endless to John. While there was a part of her that he knew would always be sad at the loss of her sister and Levi—sometimes very sad—she often told stories about them. She said that she and Amaline had shared an Owen governess for a time in exchange for her mother's sewing and that Levi had always been first to find the most interesting books at the library. She laughed and said once he'd even brought home *Moral Physiognomy*, and her father had confiscated it, and then read it himself. In turn, John told her about Biddy. He found, though, that his most vivid memories were mostly of how small Biddy had been and then how very, very sick. It was not really a thing he could tell right. It was more like a feeling in his mind—one that Kate shared, but nobody else. Caroline had understood that, too.

For all the brimming excitement of their courtship, there was a calm at the heart of it that John found himself growing addicted to. They would go for a walk, or they would read to each other late into the evening until it was time for John to leave or for him to take Caroline home. On the days when he stayed on the Cut-off working late, if Caroline didn't come to visit with a friend, he would work until he was half asleep and, then, when he fell asleep, dream about her so it seemed she had still been part of his day. For the first time in his life, he knew what it meant to have a true companion of both mind and heart. He wanted to share everything with her—each idea and every observation, both his and hers. Nothing delighted him more than the times when they finished a sentence together as if they'd been headed the same place since its beginning. He liked it, too, that Caroline thought seriously about politics and religion but that she was not doctrinaire except in her strong feeling that a person's faith should not be interfered with since it lay at the center of who the person was. And she felt that, in the matter of opposing views, each person should let well enough alone unless one person's belief required participation from the other (as, for instance, in what manner of wedding a couple might have), but that such participation had always to be given freely.

John wrote to Harry in April that his hands were as big as bushel baskets and that he was as tired as blazes from rolling and chopping logs but that he was a hundred times happier than he'd been in the winter with nothing to do. What he thought of adding was that, with Caroline, he was a hundred times happier than he'd ever been, but it was only a passing temptation to write that, for he would not in any way trespass on their growing bond or make her the subject of light conversation with any man. Instead he complained to Harry about the wet weather that kept them from burning more logs and about the delays and confusion over the Bounty Bill, how the change in applications meant he was no further along than when he'd sent in his discharge papers to Indianapolis.

By July, when he wrote to Harry, which had become a form of writing to Kate that left him less exposed to Kate's ability to read between lines, he thought he was becoming two almost separate beings. There was the John Given who wrote like a soldier that he'd taken something like cholera morbus on Wednesday night that made him vomit his guts out and shit like a duck. John knew this sort of reporting came from his prosaic and public self, the John Given who was still used to a soldier's life and to a soldier's storytelling. It was accurately him: the fellow wanting to entertain and to be entertained when he could be. Yet there was another part of him now that reminded him most of himself when he'd felt deeply religious.

He'd told Caroline about some of those times—how at Easter Mass in Donegal Town when he was very young, he'd wandered forward toward the sound of the priest's singing before his mother had caught him and held him in her arms so the sound seemed wrapped around them both. There were other times that had had that same sort of mystery, particularly the early mornings in Navan when he and the other lads were rousted out of bed at St. Finian's and sent down the spiraling stairway of Power's Duck Egg, the subdeacon herding them to the river to practice the morning office. As first light brought up the image of their kneeling bodies in the dark mirror of the water, John had felt everything corporal seem to fall away.

He told Caroline about those mornings, that Navan had been the time when his mother had held the upper hand, that she'd had a cousin priest who found him a place at St. Finian's after the year at training college in Dublin his father had insisted on. John had never talked about it before, but Navan stood out to him now, not for the battle between his parents, but for those oddly sanctified mornings when he'd tried most earnestly to find the path of a mystic. It had seemed a wonderful calling to him, as alluring as it was elusive. Yet he'd pulled back from it finally—perhaps at the end at Navan or later at Letterkenny, where Bishop McGettigan, stressing the practical, had told him if he went to seminary at Maynooth, he could well be awarded Logic. It might even have been as late as at Trinity itself. Whenever it was, as he told Caroline, the crux of the matter was that he'd not understood how a quest for self-abnegation could not at its heart be about elevating the self. He'd been put off, unable or unwilling to pursue it.

He spoke quietly of the other times of extraordinary wonder. Once, in Dublin he'd stood inside the door of Dean Swift's St. Patrick's and, Church of Ireland though it was, felt himself soaring upward and upward with the flying buttresses. There was a morning, too, when the sea air that breathed across the *Fidelia*'s deck had swirled into a pale-coral and sulfurous fog that John thought could only exist in a dream. And the dawn at Fort Donelson when he'd left Levi sleeping with his valentines and gone outside with Felix Edmonds. He told Caroline it had felt a sort of resurrection—the bloody tracks they and the other men had made buried beneath a new inch of snow, the trees frozen in that clear and pockless ice, the light rising in the hills so that every branch had the sudden, dazzling shimmer of crystal. And he told her of Memphis and the extraordinary music he'd experienced like some new and weightless skin.

The ineffable strangeness for John in his new existence as the other John Given was that such moments of transport—of slipping free of what held him so firmly earthbound—came to him often now with Caroline. Mostly, it was something he felt, a sense of who they were together that was part calmness, part charged anticipation. Yet when he thought most deeply about it—when he tried to find words to tell him what it was—it seemed to him as if there were some Socratic ideal of the two of them—John and Caroline—which accompanied them as a sort of third presence. "It's our own sort of Holy Ghost," he said to her, trying to say it lightly.

Caroline had put it more simply, saying that the two of them together added up to a good deal more than the two of them apart. Whatever it was, John thought this added presence defined the moments they were together, whether it was Caroline accompanying his mother as she sang in the Wilseys' parlor while John listened, or John, bone-tired and his head in Caroline's lap, eating bites of the food she'd brought him across the Cut-off. Sometimes it was the particular nature of the two of them taking turns reading Shakespeare or Aeschylus, and John giving Caroline his translation of the lines he'd turned to for solace during the war: *And in our sleep, pain forgetting naught, falls drop by drop upon the heart until, in our despair and all unwilled, comes wisdom from the wondrous grace of God.* It was a feeling between them, which bound the past to the present and the present to the future and the future back to the past so they were poised, the two of them, in a timeless time in which their awareness of each other was an entirely willing enthrallment.

Yet the practical John Given did not leave the field. He made his plans as carefully as if he were quartering an army. They would marry—Caroline, in a moment of sweet tenderness, had agreed that they would—but they would not marry until the year's logs on the Cut-off were rolled and burned, and the wheat harvested on the old farm, and the grass put in to make the permanent meadow that Ribeyre had planned. John also felt a pressing need to see his parents well settled in their own Ribeyre house on the island with Denis and Charley, for Margaret and Andy were headed west—back to California and his sheep farm for Andy and, for Margaret, off on the kind of adventure she'd always dreamed about. And he wanted to take the wagon to Logansport with Caroline because his parents hadn't heard from Mary and Porter since they had moved there.

For the moment, John and his father decided to rent out the house in town for the summer, and John made his own arrangements to buy the Thrailkills' house, with a clause put in the contract that said the Thrailkills could live out their lives there. With nearly three years of savings, including money he'd earned clerking for Captain Batty and his current work farming and doing bookkeeping jobs, he thought he was prepared to handle what responsibilities he had and the others that would come his way. He had a new opportunity as well. Captain Boren was opening a store across from Fretageots', and he wanted John as his main clerk and had promised him a very good salary. John accepted, and the practical, regular John Given, with a house and savings and new job, sat down with Caroline so they could decide on a wedding date. The other John Given felt that his life was becoming everything he'd ever dreamed of and that even Harry Beal had nothing at all on him for happiness.

At the last moment, there was a small contretemps. He and Caroline had agreed that they would get married at St. Wendel's, just the two of them going in the wagon and coming back for a wedding supper with their families. His mother, grateful for an actual Catholic wedding instead of yet another ceremony conducted by Mr. Fillingim, seemed very well satisfied. Caroline's mother, on the other hand, was suddenly uncertain.

"Why would you have a priest marry you, Caroline?" she asked. "We know nothing of priests. And, anyway, I've heard that there're statues in that church."

John's mother, in her turn, was irate. "Your mother's going to swim the Wabash and have it out with Polly Thrailkill," his father said, lighting his pipe and laughing.

"Let her. And Mrs. Thrailkill can cancel her supper," John said. "I believe that it's Caroline and I who're getting married."

"Concede something now, John," his father told him. "It saves trouble later."

In the end, Caroline assured her mother that she would face away from any statues during her vows and, after the negotiation of other small points that John chose not to concern himself with, everything was smoothed over. He and Caroline rode to Mount Vernon to get their marriage license and, on the next day, John readied the wagon again to go to St. Wendel's and the ecstatic John Given was once more fully present and accounted for.

Later, as he thought of that day, it was like thinking of points on a circle. The first point was Caroline herself, beautifully calm in a light blue dress. When he drove up with the wagon, she was in the garden picking daisies and blue and purple asters. She wrapped the stems in a wet towel and then placed her bouquet in the wagon bed.

"When I was small, my grandmother told me that a bride should pick her own flowers, that she should bring all that is freshest in her life to her marriage," Caroline said when they'd settled next to each other on the wagon seat. She looked up at the sky and then at John. "And your mother told me that happy is the bride that the sun shines on."

John smiled and flicked the horse reins. "And you've a very fine day, Caroline, to bring you happiness," he said.

The second point was actually two points, for it was the road they passed both going to St. Wendel's and returning from it. John had always thought it was the most beautiful view in the whole area with its vista of fields opening on either side and falling away to woods at the southern horizon.

The church itself was the midpoint of the circle and the point of entrance, John thought, to the rest of his life. Caroline picked up her flowers and, as the two of them followed the priest down the aisle, John felt the silence around him. Briefly, he thought about what the difference would be if he were the priest leading a couple toward the sanctuary instead of a man accompanying the woman who was about to become his wife. It seemed an utterly impossible exchange. Whatever the priest might feel in exercising his powers (given to him by the church? by God?)—and John had certainly imagined the sense of transcendence that might come at the moment of the transubstantiation of bread into body and wine into blood—he could not conceive of anything more powerfully altering than the fact that he and Caroline were to formalize their closeness through vows that made them not just themselves, but each a part of the other.

There was no music in the church, yet for a puzzled moment, John thought that there was. He felt a steadily growing, thrummy hum. He pressed Caroline's hand, wondering if she heard the same sound, wondering if it came from the space of the church or from something behind his eyes that might expand until his head popped open like a split plum. He took a breath and another. Like a shell that had streaked past, the hum seemed to fade. Then it stopped. Caroline moved so her back was toward the crucifix, the wood of the church gleaming white where the sun struck it. The priest said his words, and John and Caroline answered with their own.

Afterward, the papers signed and the two of them on the trip back to New Harmony, John held the reins in one hand and Caroline's hand in his other. They went a long way in silence but, when they did talk, each word felt to John as if it stood for a hundred others that all meant contentment. He stopped the wagon at the road that dipped away south, and it occurred to him that it was the first time he had faced true south without the dark cloud of the war hovering, unvanquishable, over his spirit. Instead, he felt only the deepest sense of hope and good fortune.

At the Thrailkills', Mrs. Thrailkill put Caroline's flowers in a vase on the table, and all the family sat down to eat the wedding meal, with Kate's baby crawling around the chair legs. Later, there was a duet from John's mother and the woman Michael McShane had married at Thanksgiving almost a year ago, who was the widow of a man who'd been in the 10th Cav with Michael and a widow Michael, for a change, had been free to marry. John, as his father took his fiddle out, thought, with a sense of warm beneficence, how fine it was that so many of his family and friends had found a mate just as he had.

If the Thrailkills' house was the point on the day's circle that made it full—from Caroline in the garden in the morning to the family good-byes as they left in the evening for Denis to drive them to the ferry and Bailey, the ferryman, to carry them to the Cut-off Island—it was the walk from the Cut-off landing to his parents' house that made John begin to feel how entirely his life was arcing away into another sphere. Caroline was on his arm. The water slapped against the bank in the growing darkness. The air was the cool of early fall.

He'd made arrangements with his parents so that he and Caroline would have the house to themselves and he'd let it be known that he would not take kindly to a chivaree. His practical self felt briefly pleased as he pulled on the latchkey and led Caroline into the house where there were two places set at the table and Caroline's wedding quilt, which had been made by all the girls and their mothers, spread out on his parents' bed. That John Given, however, quickly gave way to the other John as soon as the door closed behind them. He lit the lamp and all of his skin felt as alive as if a layer of lightning-charged air was tracing his body.

Caroline had taken off her bonnet and the light shawl that, earlier, he'd draped around her shoulders. Watching her, for all the familiarity of the surroundings, he felt as odd as if he were on some faraway planet. He could hear the hum again, that odd vibration that had started in the church. Now it had returned with even more intensity, and he thought there was something about the blood rush in his body that had triggered his old battle deafness in which all sounds were a single sound that was trapped inside his skull. There was a part of him, too, that couldn't separate this moment from what he'd seen in the alleys of Dublin and the streets of Memphis and Washington and at the fancy ball at Camp Stoneman where the invited ladies went home in such disarray. He felt eager and skittish at the same time. With a wave of guilt, he realized his stray thoughts and general physical excitement were focused entirely on himself. It meant that, though he had stared at the gracefulness with which Caroline had poured water from a jug in the lamplight, in some real sense, he'd been ignoring her at the very time he should have been showing her the greatest tenderness.

"Would you like tea, John?" she asked him, her voice breaking the silence. He ran his fingers down the planed wood of the kitchen wall he'd helped his father nail in place, and thought how thirsty he'd been a moment ago, though he wasn't at all now.

"Whatever you'd like," he answered.

"Well I wouldn't. Want tea, that is. It was for a thing to do was all. I'm not used to being idle."

He opened the window. "We needn't be. Come look at the stars," he said.

"You can smell the river tonight," she said.

"Yes, but come look at the stars," he said again, holding his hand out, and this time Caroline crossed to the window. After he kissed her, she snuggled into his arm and they leaned back and eyed the sprinkle of stars and upside-down Cassiopeia and pentagonal Cepheus in the one patch of treeless sky at the window's top.

"When Amaline and I were small, we had starlight and moonlight in our window and we thought we turned blue at night."

"Shall I see?" John said. He drew his finger along her neck. "We've only the thinnest crescent moon, but should we see if you've turned blue again?" John used the gentlest voice he had, and the hum was there again, but now he knew what it was. It wasn't a battle sound. It wasn't a blood rush to his head. It was, instead, the sound of a violin that was caught in his memory from a time long ago. He'd been only a lad, a young, young lad, and he'd been walking home past a Ward house when he'd heard a violin being played, and it wasn't fiddle music. It was like nothing he'd ever heard before, but instead notes that were studied and drawn out and achingly pure as they coursed into the night air. He had listened spellbound. When the sound finally stopped, he had already stayed so long that he knew his mother would worry. But as he hurried his way home, he felt he'd heard something intensely private that spoke of a thing he might one day know but didn't yet.

"I wish I could play the violin and like a Ward man," he said. "Not one of the fiddler Wards, but one who makes a sound that's like nothing else. There'd be a long, slow note here." John moved his hand down Caroline's spine so she just shivered under his touch. "And a high note that's a little turn." He kissed her carefully along the jaw line. "And one that's like a long breath held underwater." He kissed her eyelids closed, and he wound his fingers in her hair, which was swirled and knotted and had intrigued him for the whole of the day.

Caroline opened her eyes. "A Ward man? Charles doesn't play."

"Not Charles. Donegal Ward men. I wouldn't talk of Charles now."

"Not if he's to cut out Margaret Mulhern and marry Flavinia Jones."

"I wouldn't talk of him anyway."

"Well, there's something we do need to talk of." Caroline turned away slightly, a little embarrassed, a little shy. "Mother made me a great many undergarments and she watched to see that I wore them all. Almost all." She laughed and pushed her face into his neck. "It's going to take a long time to undo me."

"We've time. We have lots of time," he said, and it felt to him like an extravagant thing (he who had often found time too short or too heavy on his hands).

Caroline twisted at a button on his shirt. "Then you don't hear its winged chariot at your back?"

"Not tonight. Not at all. Quote Mr. Marvell to me all you will. I'll turn his meaning and quote him back. Your beauty will last. Always, like morning dew, the youthful hue will sit upon your skin."

"I'm not a beauty, John."

"I've found no beauty I like better. Nor will I. If I could take you to Drimarone . . ." John was listening again to the high, pulled note of the violin as it grew steadily stronger, piercing the evening as it had the Donegal mists and calling up every single longing he'd ever had.

"We'll find our own way here, Caroline," he said. He led her toward his parents' room. In the corner where the lamplight shadow flickered on the wall, they began to undress, John folding his trousers over a chair arm. Then he helped her with the closings on her dress, undoing them so she could step from it and stand in her shift and whale-boned underbodice, her dress laid across the chair. Lifting her onto the bed, he felt her lightness.

"You'll find that, except for these bones of another animal and the layers of fabric, this is all me," she said. "I'm not like Mrs. Richard Owen that Mrs. Cawthorne pokes cotton down, front and back, until she has her figure ready to go out at noon."

John laughed. "They made you a very nice quilt," he said, and he felt the swelling hum of the violin—a good many violins, this time—and he lay his head near Caroline's heart, listening to it beat before he moved his hands down her arms and across the satin shift. He lifted his head. There was the faintest light of the moon on Caroline's face.

"Not blue," he said, stroking her cheek. "Will I find your stockings blue?"

Caroline smiled, and she put her arms around his neck. "Do we know what we're doing?" she asked. "And do you think that we'll like it?"

"So far, I like it very well." He lowered his head again and laughed against the poky whalebones until the laughter flashed tears in his eyes. "Already more than I can say. Caroline, there's a sound I hear. It's thrummy like a cricket chorus of violins, but very slow and pure. Here. I'll trace it on your skin. If I can keep that easy pace . . ."

"Not roll our strength and sweetness into a ball? Not tear our pleasures with rough strife?"

"We can do that, too. Whatever you like," he said, and what he didn't say was that he thought they could do it all, that he'd lived his whole life to arrive at just this moment when yes (to defy Andrew Marvell), they might make the sun stand still, and yes (to embrace Mr. Marvell), together make it race.

They did not talk more. They gazed at each other (how he loved the bemused look on Caroline's face); they kissed fervently and long. Gradually, all of Mrs. Thrailkill's carefully made underwear lay beside the bed. John felt the length of Caroline's body beside him and then beneath him—the firm skin, the perfect, beautiful breasts, the bone of clavicle, rib, and hip, the brush of hair that matched his own, the inner line of her arms and legs as he caressed them, the smooth inside curve of her cool feet. "I'll be careful," he whispered, and then he cautiously prized open the dark pink skin between her legs and, rubbing it damp, found his way inside her. He held her shoulders as his body moved, and then he dropped his head to kiss her and it was long and sudden both, the extraordinary and rapturous sensation that surpassed anything the practical John Given had ever known. Why had no one ever told him just this? Why had he never realized in thinking of life's transporting moments (or of a saint's feet bloodied by the rocky path he tread) that true ecstasy—spiritual or not—is so intensely of the body.

He thought he cried out then, though later he whispered. "Ask me for anything, Caroline. Truly, I'll give you anything I can."

New Harmony, Indiana
1868–1871

30

John Given Jr., Paid by Cash:
Lumber—$1.29, July 27, 1869
Chocolate—$1.51, November 24, 1869
Apples—$2.08, November 10, 1871

Account book of John B. Elliott, sawmill and farm

July, and it was as hot as hot could be. John had swept out the back storeroom and restocked the shelves, kerosene lamp in tow, before he'd taken the account books down to the cellar, where it was cooler for doing his figures and for writing the ad to go in the paper: *Bolt satinet—indigo blue, bolt satinet—common colors, bolt of Cassimere, doeskin, jeans, wool rolls, all-wool blankets, all-wool flannel, plain flannel, two-pound colored yarn, two-pound white yarn.* It all went under the heading of A. Boren and Company, Corner of Main and Church Streets: Dry Goods, Notions, Hardware, and Queensware. There were days when John's job did not seem so different to him from quartermastering if only the army had fitted itself out with finer and more frivolous things.

He looked at a spider crawling up its thread. He blew at it and the spider swayed. A puff of dust flew off the beam where its web was started. The dust stuck to John's shirt, which was soaked with perspiration, and it occurred to him he felt more like a soldier or farmer than a man who needed to present himself as someone closer to the merchant class, though he wasn't actually of the class or of the company in A. Boren and Company, but merely a clerk. Caroline, of course, would have a basin of water for him and a clean shirt when he got home, though he hoped she hadn't ironed in this heat. If she had, he would reprove her and remind her that she very much needed her rest and comfort now, even if it meant a strong-smelling husband. What he wished was that it was Saturday rather than Monday and that, instead of Caroline's sister and niece being here, her parents were in Galatia at her sister's. He and Caroline could fill the washtub in the kitchen, and he would watch the water playing over her body, which was still slim and firm if he looked past her distended breasts bobbing on the water, and past her swollen belly, which, of course, he wouldn't. He would smooth his hands along its roundness and wait for Caroline to laugh when a small foot kicked him. Then he'd wash her back and take his place in the water she'd gotten out of and feel himself soaking in her scent while she rubbed the washcloth over his skin.

He was farther into his daydream when he heard Charley calling him from upstairs. Then he saw Charley peering at him through the opening in the floor where the steps dropped down, not a man's extra pound on his new man's frame, his real weight, as Kate always said, in his thick head of hair. "They need you," Charley said. "Mrs. Thrailkill sent word Caroline's baby's started. She's asking for you."

John almost knocked his chair over in getting up. The spider swung down to his ledger page and he flicked it away. Quickly, he shut the book. He snatched up the ad and lantern, and he was up the stairs faster than he thought he could go. "You're not pulling my leg?" he asked, and Charley shook his head.

Outside in the street, the flags that still hung from the Fourth of July were limp along the storefronts and the sun so hot it seemed to have sucked up all of the air. "You didn't bring a wagon?" John asked, thoroughly agitated, for the seven blocks to home seemed suddenly a vast expanse of distance and a longer stretch of time. "Have they called the doctor yet? Charley, is the doctor there?"

"All I know is what I told you. I'll get you a wagon," Charley said, and he whistled a driver over to give John a ride.

John got into the wagon. "You come, too. I need you to go for the doctor," he said, and it was so hot, it might as well have been Alabama again with heatstroke rife among the troops. It could have been another of the hellish summer days at Camp Stoneman.

By the time the slow driver and slower horse Charley had commandeered got him home, John was even more beside himself. He pulled a coin out, but the man, who was hauling a load of bricks, waved him off. "If they don't have the doctor, if you could take my brother for him," John started, but Charley interrupted and said he could run or find his own horse. The man lumbered off in the wagon, and John hurried into the kitchen.

The curtains were closed against the sun, but it wasn't cool at all, and it was steamy from cloths boiling on the stove. "Is she all right?" John asked Caroline's niece, who was stirring a kettle. "Is the doctor here?"

"He's been. He'll be back." The girl wiped her face with her apron. "Mother and Grandma are with her. She's been asking for you."

There was a loud moan from the bedroom. It was punctuated by a scream, and John turned around and told Charley, who'd followed him inside that he should leave. Then he walked quickly through the parlor and stopped abruptly at the bedroom door.

The scene in front of him was like something he'd only heard or read about. Caroline was holding tight to the head of the bed, her face red and contorted. There was a bucket of bloody rags on the floor, and her mother and sister, Captain Barton's wife, were talking to her in low voices. They hadn't noticed John, and he didn't know if he needed permission to go into the room. For that matter, he wasn't sure if he really wanted to be there. It was like a field hospital with a single patient, but this patient was one he was responsible for putting there. The part of him that hadn't quavered as a soldier, quavered now. He stood still, wondering if he could edge his way back from the room and put a finger to his lips to Mary Ann in the kitchen and do the proper thing for a man—go wait on the neighbors' porch until he heard a baby cry or go to the tavern until someone came to tell him he was a father. Then he saw Caroline trying to sit forward on the bed, her mouth wide open as she cried out again, and he knew that she'd asked for him and that, if she was to bring their child into the world in such pain, it was pure cowardice of him to leave. Not that he didn't feel like a coward. He absolutely did, but he thought, too, that she'd seen him now. They all had, and it didn't seem they intended for him to go, though he knew that his mother, if she'd been here, would have shooed him out. He gathered himself to go over to the bed. Caroline, who always coped, seemed not to be coping at all.

"Oh dear God," she said, her voice hoarse, and she twisted on the bed as he tried to stroke her face, and then her eyes tightened and, instead of moaning or shrieking again, she bit hard on the bony part of his hand beneath his little finger.

"Shouldn't I get the doctor?" he asked her mother, trying not to wince, and he wondered if Caroline was delirious. He thought she'd recognized him, but he wasn't sure.

"Not now," her mother answered. Mrs. Barton called to the kitchen for more rags and told John to hold Caroline's leg open on his side of the bed while her mother held the other one. Both women were telling Caroline to push, which they'd been doing, he realized, ever since he'd arrived. John blinked hard while he held a leg with one hand and Caroline bit down on his hand again.

"Isn't the doctor coming?" he repeated. He thought there was a wild animal in the bed where Caroline lay.

"Again," her sister said, and her mother was speaking to her in a low voice, a kind of cooing. Caroline pushed once more. This time she didn't bite him but moaned with a short cry. Tears spurted into her eyes. John saw a slick of bloody hair touching Mrs. Barton's hands and, with extraordinary speed, a whole baby flying up into the air, its feet grasped in Mrs. Barton's hands as if she had performed the most astonishing magic trick. He stood looking up at the ceiling, mesmerized at this flying baby, and then it wasn't flying anymore. It was crying and handed off to Mrs. Thrailkill. It was secure in her arms.

Mrs. Barton was back working over Caroline, tending to her and the baby's cord. "You've a little girl, Caroline," she said. "Congratulations, John. You've a beautiful little girl. You can tell her you were drenched in sweat when she was born."

John couldn't think of a thing to say. He felt unreal and he looked uncertainly at Caroline and, then with relief, he saw that the wild beast was gone. Caroline was gazing over at the baby.

"May I have her, Mother?" she asked, and Mrs. Thrailkill, who had swaddled the baby lightly and cleaned its face, came around the bed. John looked at the baby with her mat of dark hair and a red hand pushing into her mouth.

"It's a girl?" he said, and the room seemed an alien place to him—alien and feminine, but as intense and bloody as any battlefield.

"John, your hand," Caroline said, looking up at him, and he shook his head and wiped his hand on a rag. Then he cleared his thoughts and leaned down to kiss her. He spooned some water into her mouth. He wished it was just the two of them—it had to be a hundred and ten in the room—or the three of them, he corrected himself as Mrs. Thrailkill gave Caroline the baby, though be knew it would have alarmed him if they really had been alone. He had no idea what the things were Mrs. Barton was still doing, and he didn't really want to know. What he needed was to be certain Caroline was all right. She looked happy but immensely tired, her face still heavily flushed from exertion and heat.

"Don't we need the doctor? Where is he, anyway?" he said, drawing the curtain back to look for a buggy in the street. The women seemed unruffled. Mrs. Thrailkill was busy showing Caroline how to feed the baby though, in John's opinion, it was the baby who needed instruction as she was rooting around in the folds of Caroline's nightgown. Caroline and her mother both laughed, Mrs. Thrailkill with the cooing sound still in her voice.

"We're naming her for you, Mother," Caroline told her, her voice still hoarse. "She's to be Mary like you, but Mollie instead of Polly so it's not confusing."

"But she's early, isn't she?" John asked suddenly, remembering that it was only the thirteenth of the month and they'd not expected her until early in August.

"She's fine," Mrs. Barton said from the end of the bed, and Mrs. Thrailkill reached over and touched the baby's wet hair.

It was a good deal later, days actually, before John realized how thrilled he was. With Caroline confined to bed and the other women so much in charge (even Mr. Thrailkill had left to visit his brother), their household felt out of sorts. John was still unhappy at having acquitted himself so poorly at the actual childbirth. He'd neither waited in the wings, appropriately nervous, nor been much comfort to Caroline when he was actually with her. Caroline, however, didn't seem to mind. Or rather, between her discomfort and her total absorption in the new baby, she didn't seem to have noticed. She was possibly even more besotted with Mollie than Kate had been with Clarence.

John tried keeping up his usual routine of work at the store and at home so it would seem he was now doing his part. He accepted congratulations for himself and good wishes for Caroline from all comers, but he still felt a good deal as an usher at a theater might feel who's there for every performance, yet really knows nothing of the show except the look of the patrons and the number of tickets he's taken. He was banished to sleep on hay bales and a feather tick in the shed for Caroline wasn't to be disturbed, and her niece had the daybed in the corner of the kitchen. Though he glanced in on Caroline from time to time, she was generally sleeping or feeding the baby and he didn't think he was supposed to stay.

Things began to change, however, when he got home early from work on Friday. It had been slow at the store, and Captain Boren had let him go as soon as the accounts were done. When he arrived at the house, quite aware that his daughter was already four days old as he'd just done the math again, he found the two Bartons and Mrs. Thrailkill picking beans in the garden and the baby asleep in her cradle. Caroline was quietly crying. John was alarmed, but he still hesitated, not sure he should sit on the bed. He reached over to pull up a chair and then carefully began to stroke her arm.

"What's wrong?" he asked, and Caroline seemed to startle at the sound of his voice as if she hadn't recognized his step or even his touch. He stood up uneasily, uncertain, and he thought of going for her mother, but Caroline looked up with her tear-stained face and reached for his hand.

"Oh, John, you're not leaving again, are you?" she said.

John shook his head. This time he sat on the bed. He told her that he wasn't going, that he hadn't known that he shouldn't, that it was the very last thing that he wanted to do.

"She's so tiny, John. Is that why you're afraid of her?" Caroline wiped her nightgown sleeve across her eyes. "And is that why you're afraid of me?"

"Am I?" he said. "I'm maybe afraid of your sister. It does seem that she knows all the rules."

"Well I certainly don't. Nor do I want to if it means going on like this. How can we raise a happy child, John, if her parents aren't happy—if her mother isn't sure she's doing things right and if her father has never even touched her?"

"Haven't I?" John said, genuinely surprised but convinced, as soon as Caroline said it, that it must be true.

Caroline wasn't done. "And, John, if the doctor, when he was here, told you that you weren't to be with me now—to know me or whatever he said—he certainly must have meant it in the biblical sense and not that you were to go into hiding."

John stifled a laugh, covering it awkwardly with a cough. "I haven't been hiding," he said, and he squeezed Caroline's hand and then he looked at the baby. "She's eavesdropping. She's got her eyes wide open, haven't you, Mollie?" he said, trying her name. He moved closer to the cradle and made little clicking noises that made Mollie stare. "Do you know how to smile?" he said. Then he lifted back the eyelet coverlet, which Kate had sent over with Bailey, and picked up his very tiny daughter. He watched as she grasped at his finger.

Caroline had pushed up on her elbow to look at them. She lay back down then, but kept her eyes on Mollie. "I've never worried about the children at school and it didn't worry me when I helped Ellen with her girls when they were small but, John, Mollie is all ours and it seems such a huge responsibility. What happens when Ellen goes home or if Mother gets sick or if my milk dries up? What happens if I spoil her somehow so she'll be unpleasant and nobody likes her? What if she has no sense of humor? She seems very earnest."

John was watching Mollie try to work his finger toward her mouth, but he stopped for a second to lean over and kiss Caroline. He kept himself from laughing again. "Not this lady," he said, turning back to Mollie, and he loved her feather weight on his arm and how squirmy and little her body was. He was feeling very smitten. "Tell your mother not to worry, Mollie," he said. "Everybody's sure to love you. And you'll be exactly like her. Everyone will laugh at your jokes."

Mollie stretched and then yawned.

Gradually—though not instantly—John found the household returning to normal. Caroline was growing stronger and the Bartons had retreated to Galatia. Mr. Thrailkill was back from his trip to Tennessee and, if he was disappointed at having yet another granddaughter, he certainly didn't show it. He was good company for Caroline while John was at work. The house was happy again. Mollie reigned, and John, particularly, was pleased to let her.

August passed. By the end of September, when he bought anniversary chocolates for Caroline, he thought what a fine year he'd had as a married man. In fact, he was sure he had the life that he'd dreamed of in all those miserable nights on whatever skirmish line: a good job and a perfect, small family. He liked nothing more than the times when he and Caroline lay in bed with Mollie. She cooed. They babbled, and it wasn't just that they exclaimed over how wonderful and beautiful she was, although they did. It was more that they realized the importance of shaping this small new life together. It was a serious joy. That was how Caroline put it, and John agreed with her entirely.

He liked it, too, that she had cousins, as he'd had, and that she would certainly have more. The Given baby mill was in full swing. Kate and Harry, who were living in a house on the Cut-off now, had had a second son, called George, and John had found himself quickly disabused of the notion he was named for George Beal, Harry's cousin. Kate had told him emphatically that Harry's father and grandfather were both George. Mary had given birth to a new little Maggie in Logansport, and Margaret Mulhern had surprised them all by going the whole way to help. When she got home, she reported the baby to be long and sturdy like Porter, and claimed she was already a force to be contended with.

If the heart of his small family felt absolutely solid and if it wasn't long before Mollie was toddling and Caroline was carrying another child, there were a number of things that caused real distress. Mrs. Thrailkill, whom John had grown quite fond of and even revered for raising such a wonderful daughter, became ill over the winter and, when spring came, she didn't get better. Two days after Mollie's first birthday, she died in a seizure of bloody coughing.

Of the sad things that happened, that was the most immediate. John's mother, however, was more upset with news from Margaret in California that her sickly baby had died. She and Margaret Mulhern were busy with their rosaries, his mother fretting that her dreamy-eyed child was so far away with no family to help her.

"She's got Andy's brother's wife," Kate said. "Did you tell her that, John? There's family, even if it isn't ours."

In the same conversation, Kate told him what Margaret Mulhern had confided about Charles Ward. John had always assumed that, when it came down to it, Margaret was one of those women who was too pious ever to decide on a connection with a man that involved more than a handshake. Kate reported something else. "She was afraid she was too old and would leave him childless. She never told him that, but simply asked to be released from her promise when he came home from the war."

"That's like her," John said, "to be selfless. But she has her own streak of vanity. Are you sure she wasn't just afraid to tell Charles how old she actually is?"

"John," Kate said, and so he added that it made him sorrier than he could say that Margaret, who'd given their family so much, would not have a husband or family of her own.

The oddest bad news was that Jim Rippeto had died, though it was mostly odd to John when he saw Ann and her baby and heard people saying she was marriageable again. It crossed his mind that, if he hadn't discovered Caroline, he might have missed out on his wonderful life and now been in the line of suitors certain to find Ann's door again. It was a dismal thought, and he went immediately home to Caroline, who was laughing at Mollie trying to eat grapes. He clasped his arms around her hard belly and held her tight until Mollie tossed a grape from her chair that hit him square in the forehead.

With all these matters causing concern in varying degrees, the biggest nagging worry for John was that Mrs. Boren was in poor health and that Captain Boren was talking of moving his family to California in hopes that the climate would help her. "He might sell the store, or sell off the goods and close it altogether," John told Caroline, although whenever he mentioned it, he always hastened to tell her that he could find another job clerking in Harmony or farm for Ribeyre once more until he got a big enough stake to buy land of their own.

"Will you be happy just farming again?" Caroline asked, and John told her that he would and then added that, if times became difficult, they could always move to Bridgeport in Illinois. He could work in Menomen's packing plant.

"I don't see you a pork packer," she said, squinting at the baby gown she was sewing. "Would you do his accounts?"

John watched her making the tiny stitches. "Maybe Mrs. Boren will get better," he said.

When the new baby arrived in February, he was a fine boy. John's only worry was that his father would be miffed that his first name wasn't John, but Charles. His parents were staying at the house in town, and when John went to look for his father, he found him in the shed wearing a coat covered with wood shavings. John plunged straight ahead. "His middle name is William—like yours and after Grandpa Given— and he's to be Charles William," he said, though he kept it to himself that he was honoring what his Grandpa Given had told him a long time ago: *You know and I know I'm your best friend. Your best grandpa. But you'll owe your learning to your Uncle Charley O'Donnell. To Charley O'Donnell's purse. Whether your father likes it or not, John, see you remember it."*

His father eyed the hog hurdle he was building and then took a swing at it with his hammer. "For Charley O'Donnell?"

John nodded. "And for Charley."

"It's better than Clarence," was all his father said.

With the Borens gone to California, John was working for Ribeyre full-time again. Part of his work was handling supplies for the families on the Cut-off, for Ribeyre had made an arrangement with Fretageots' to buy goods for them. John was often in the fields, too, and in charge of loading Ribeyre's corn boats that went downriver to market. All in all, he was satisfied. He had excellent prospects again, which was what a man wanted and lived through a war for, and he was working hard to take advantage of them. And if sometimes he had to listen to his mother's worry that Denis seemed aimless, and that Charley seemed too fond of dancing with the crowd on the Cut-off Island (she thought they were wild like the boys and girls of Drimarone who drank poteen up in the Blue Stacks), and that his father himself had grown too fond of his bottle again, John knew he could make her feel better. He had simply to reassure her and, even if he couldn't really change a thing, it would somehow seem that he had. At the moment, it was as if he had a magic touch. When it occurred to him that such a thought might have scared him but didn't, he decided he'd banished whatever Irish superstitions he'd ever had.

It was Kate who asked him first—almost casually—if Caroline was getting thinner. She'd put it tactfully for Kate, asking if perhaps the baby was eating more than his share.

John had brushed it aside. "She's had a cold," he said. "And the children keep her busy."

His mother was the next person to say something, and this time John paid more attention. "She looks worn down to me, John," she said. "And how long has she had that cough?"

Yet even his mother's concern had not seemed like an alarm bell, for Caroline was always her calm and fresh self when he came home at night. She was quite ready to bring him up to date on what they'd dubbed Mollie Given's Strange and Inspiring Adventures with the English Language, or to tell him of some small punishment Mollie had received (and how prettily she had said she was sorry when Caroline, after a moment, fetched her from her chair in the corner), or of how close Charley had come to taking a step. John thought she seemed tired at times, but Harry had told him how worn out Kate often was, running after their boys. "We can think what we did to our mothers," Harry said. "Rest me mum's soul."

John, looking for signs of health in Caroline, decided her cheeks were rosier. By the night Charley toddled three steps into his arms, he'd nearly forgotten his concern. "He's walking!" he and Mollie exclaimed together. He turned to Caroline and saw her quick whisk of a bloodied handkerchief into the pocket beneath her apron. It was the action of a lone instant: those first tottering baby steps, his and Mollie's single exclamation, and Caroline's cough and quick, concealing gesture.

He did not speak to her about it until the children were in bed. He did not want to speak about it at all. He wanted to believe instead that he'd imagined what he saw. He was ready to think that Caroline had coughed into an old handkerchief stained from canning berries, or that some stray image from a battlefield had pasted itself, ghostlike, into the secure world of his family hearth. When he finally sat down with her, he was still hoping—believing really—that she'd have a simple explanation that would make his new uneasiness fade quickly into relief.

"Is there anything wrong?" was what he said, and instead of asking him what he meant or laughing and saying it was very wrong that Charley had walked first for him, in the most un-Caroline way, she burst into tears. She covered her face with her apron and then, as if locked into place, swayed back and forth, crying and crying so that it seemed to him she might not ever be consoled again.

He had the story from her finally in fits and hiccoughs—that she, too, had thought she had only a nagging cold, that when she'd first seen the blood—really, she thought it was only a week or two ago, though maybe a month—she'd assumed it was simply the dry winter air irritating her throat. She knew now that it was something more. It had come to her in a flood of certainty, that it was her mother's illness, and she was so immensely tired. She had not known she could be so tired and there was nothing for it but to get her niece, to have Mary Ann to care for the children until she had her strength back, until the time she could care for her own babies, who would need their mother just as John needed his wife and her father his daughter.

John comforted her as he could. When she was finally asleep, streaks of tears still on her face, he stood a long, anguished time at the window and stared into the bleak January night and the plumes of black smoke that rose above New Harmony. He might as well be suffocating from that very smoke, he thought. He was full of dread, filled with a sense that he had stepped through a trapdoor, that he was falling and falling into some infinite and airless darkness.

Yet throughout the whole course of her illness, there were so many times when he felt unbounded hope—times when the two of them put aside the specter of her weakness and resumed the regular flow of their lives as if nothing at all had happened. The doctors came and went. John's mother and Margaret Mulhern arrived and set to work fumigating the entire house, which his mother reminded him was what had been done in New York with the cholera epidemic and might work with another disease. "And forget Polly Thrailkill's old worry about drafts," she told him in a low voice. "Keep a window open. Keep fresh air in your house. It's what saved the rest of you after Biddy."

John had nodded. As Caroline stayed more and more on the day-bed, he heaped her with quilts and kept the fire going, and he did as his mother said, always keeping a window open, if only a crack on the bitterest nights. He and Caroline kept up their habit, too, of reading together and concerned themselves even more with the education of the children. John taught Mollie the "Hail Mary" and "Our Father." Caroline taught her a bedtime prayer and helped her with the words as she knelt to say it. As familiar as his own prayers were, it was the baby prayer that utterly charmed John and that always brought a smile to Caroline's eyes before he picked Mollie up and carried her to the trundle bed next to Charley's cradle.

There were days when John thought Caroline was stronger. On those days they considered various plans, both those that were almost possible and ones that were entirely fanciful. "We could go to California like the Borens did," he said. "Margaret Mulhern says Mrs. Boren is doing much better. We could go to Andy and Margaret, and I could work on his brother's sheep farm. I know sheep. I knew sheep before I knew cattle and hogs. We could go a long way by train if I raised the fare."

"And how much money and how many more miles by wagon?" Caroline asked in a thin voice. John was quiet, imagining the beautiful but arduous trail Margaret had described in a long letter home.

Another time, he told Caroline what he'd read in a book at the library. "In Europe, there are sanatoriums where the sick go. They have a proper diet and lots of rest and a regular regimen. Their lung patients often recover completely."

"Then take me to Europe," Caroline said. "What about Switzerland? Or perhaps Germany. My mother's family came from the Palatine. Further back. Yes, take me to Europe, John, as long as we take Mollie and Charley and fit them out like little European travelers. Don't you think Mollie might have a parasol?"

In Galatia, there had been a long discussion in the parlor when John went to see the Bartons, for Mrs. Barton and the captain were reluctant to send Mary Ann to care for the children. In the end, they called her into the room and she made the decision herself. "Aunt Caroline took care of Grandma Thrailkill," she said. "It would be unfeeling, even unchristian not to help her when she has Mollie and Charley to see to. And anyway, I want to go. I love the children. I love New Harmony."

Her parents had been silent, but as John was getting the wagon ready in the morning, Captain Barton, whose arm was withered from the war, asked him to bring out Mary Ann's trunk. John did, putting it in back, and the captain looked at him with his fine black whiskers and sharp blue eyes and said, "She's twenty, John. Find her a good beau. In the end, that's what will make her mother happy."

When summer came, Caroline seemed suddenly better and John, afraid to believe it at first, began to let himself hope ever so slightly that she might recover. She was well enough for them to go out for occasional short walks, her light weight heavy against him and her gait slow, though she didn't complain. She seemed happiest when they encountered friends who stopped to greet her and wish her well, though she was still his Caroline and after one walk remarked dryly that she had not known how many friends a serious illness could make.

John had laughed as he helped her back into bed. "Constance Fauntleroy came to visit when I was shot," he said. "Or her aunt did. Kate said Constance waited outside the door."

There were even evenings when the family came and Caroline felt strong enough to play a short game of charades, or half charades as she called it since she lay propped upright in bed. The house felt happy on those nights. Mary Ann would set off excitedly with Denis or Charley for a ball or a play, while John's father and Michael McShane, if he and his wife had come from Mount Vernon, played with the children. Then Kate bundled her two in with Mollie and baby Charley, and the adults played cards while Caroline dozed.

"It didn't tire you too much?" John would ask when everyone left, and Caroline held his hand without talking—contented, it seemed, at life going on.

On a slow stroll beneath the rain trees early one evening, the two of them encountered Ann Rippeto. She was no longer in her widow's weeds, and she was walking with her young daughter. John had been telling Caroline of a new plan he'd thought of—that he could visit Menomen and borrow money with their house for security. They could leave the children with Kate and his mother and take the train east to catch a steamer. He would book an actual cabin of the kind Menomen had had when he'd gone back to Drimarone and toured Europe before the war. They'd sail to Bremen. They'd take a train to Switzerland and go to a sanatorium where Caroline would be entirely cured. "You could rest the whole way. I'd read to you," he was finishing when Ann and her small Maria were suddenly right in their path.

Ann extended a gloved hand for John to shake. "How lovely to see you looking so well, Caroline," she said. She leaned down to her daughter. "Say hello to Mrs. Given and to Mr. Given," she told her, and the child did so politely but not, John thought, with the charm that Mollie would have shown though, to be fair, Mollie was older. Aware then that Caroline was seriously flagging, he called to Louis Pelham, who'd come out of Fretageots' store, and asked him to give them a ride home.

Caroline was unusually quiet when they got there. The house was quiet, too, for Mary Ann and Mr. Thrailkill had taken the children on a picnic and left them a cold supper.

"No, I'm not hungry, John," Caroline said when he brought her a plate. He stuck a fork in a bit of spiced apple, trying to persuade her, but she shook him off and reached for her handkerchief in that movement that always made his throat clutch. Then she broke into a fit of coughing that turned the cloth a muddy red. When her attack had finally subsided, she looked up and managed a weak smile.

"If you'd married Ann," she said, "you couldn't have had a finer-looking wife. But Mollie is as pretty as Maria and a good deal sweeter." There was one more long cough here. "And we've Charley besides. John, could we have a sunnier boy?"

It took John a long moment before he was able to answer, but finally he did. "Never even think about it, Caroline. It's not even a question. If ever a man was given complete happiness, I am that man."

It was senseless, he knew, to blame Ann for the fact that Caroline took a turn for the worse from that evening on. Yet, for a while, John did. It was the proximity of it all: Ann greeting them, and Caroline bringing up his old attachment for the very first time since that Valentine's Ball when he'd carried the basket her mother gave them, and then Caroline's relapse.

Eventually, though, he let go of the idea. "It was bound to happen," Dr. Rawlings told him on a visit as he closed up his case. "Be thankful she had those stronger days. I've seen it before. The weather changes, and it's like a false spring. Just be thankful for it, John."

He tried. He tried to fix his mind on the image of Caroline walking beside him under the curving bow of rain trees and listening to him as he'd sketched out his plan of escape and rescue. Yet each week, even each day, she seemed farther away—weaker and less able to rouse herself to smile at the children's antics. In his worst moments, John thought she had already ceded the children to his mother and Kate and Mary Ann. It felt to him as if his world was shrinking and his head closing inside a vise with a constant sound of swarming bees.

It was not that he stopped doing all that he had to do. He did his work for Ribeyre. He applied for a pension in hopes that the extra money might buy a treatment that would make Caroline better. He went to the WMI and G.A.R. meetings when he could, as he felt he needed to be on good terms with the men he knew in case opportunities arose, something that could be helpful to his family. Whenever there was gossip at the post office, he laughed with his friends. He never broke down but instead developed a certain way of inhaling and then tightening his eyes so that everything he was feeling when he thought of Caroline stayed right there at the top of his head. He didn't think it was a soldier's trick. He didn't remember ever doing it before. It was something specific to Caroline and a physical thing that let him keep going.

The rest of the family was praying, or at least the women were—even Kate—but he'd found he was unable to. It was partly his old sense that God didn't intervene but simply set things in motion and let them play out. But it was something else, too, a part of that same tightness he felt in his eyes that told him if he could stay on an even keel and not really recognize that the world was shifting about him, some ballast might remain.

There were moments, too—most often when Caroline's fever made her talkative—when a flash of new hope would come over him. He would touch her cheek and listen to the almost lucid things she had to say. "I'm teaching Mollie French," she might say, and he would nod and press her hand.

"I don't mind that you're sick," he told her, not even knowing if she actually heard him. "Just as long as you're here. I do need to know that you're here."

Fall came. Then November and December. The thermometer dropped, and the week before Christmas John, coming home from work, heard that boys had skated out on the river and that one had fallen in and had been pulled out half frozen and half drowned. When he got home, ready to tell the story, Mary Ann met him at the door and told him that the doctor was there, that she'd sent a boy for John, and the boy was still out looking for him. She held his arm as he turned toward the bedroom. Then she let it go, and that was how he knew in the silent house with the children gone to his parents' that he had come too late. The doctor had already put his coat on. Mr. Thrailkill was slumped in a chair. Caroline, whose eyes had not yet been closed, lay staring at the ceiling as the beautiful boy at Donelson had stared at the sky, her gaze fixed on nothing.

"Leave," John said, his voice filled with harshness. "Leave me with my wife." When the door was closed, he flung himself on the bed and touched Caroline's icy, skeletal hands. He sobbed with the harsh sound of a barking dog, and it was the sound that stayed with him for days whether he was stony silent or chipping away at the frozen ground on Maple Hill to dig Caroline's grave. He heard it listening to the hymn sung at the graveside. He heard it again when he was raging by himself, running and crying in the cold, a man cut in half and trying to race out of his grief, though it kept catching him and swallowing him up in its black desolation. Finally, he stopped running his long circuit of the graveyard hill and fell still on the ground, hugging Caroline's new gravestone.

Kate and Harry found him there. Kate huddled him against her shoulder and rocked him like a baby.

"She won't be there. She won't be at home," he said, despairing, and he wondered how it could be that the heart of his life had been given only a single chapter.

"You'll catch cold, John," Kate said. "We all will."

Harry brought their wagon up. He and Kate took him home. His mother was there, and Mollie in her linsey-woolsey nightgown and Charley in his baby one were waiting for him, their faces pressed against the window glass.

New Harmony, Indiana
February 2, 1880

31

Harry was up and moving around in the half darkness. He'd buttoned his shirt and pulled up his braces, but Kate was still dozy in bed when a thought presented itself to her with a grave certainty. She would talk to John. Tonight, when Harry came back from the G.A.R. meeting, she would go to John's and finally confront him. It was high time that she made her case, though it was the first time she'd considered it in just this way.

"Are you getting up?" Harry asked, reaching for her toes through the comforter as he went by the bed, and Kate yawned a yes. She steeled herself against the cold air. By the time she'd gone to the corner basin and splashed water on her face, she'd already begun to think of what she would say. She mumbled into the towel as she rubbed her face dry. She practiced to herself while she fixed Harry's breakfast. When the boys were ready for school and she'd bundled up Maggie (for all Kate's love of her rapscallion sons, her sweet Maggie had made her prize motherhood all over again), she was still hunting for words for John. She stared so intently at a ray of morning light that Maggie, her chin quivering, asked her if she'd seen a bat.

Kate laughed. "Not in the winter." She planted a quick kiss on Maggie's cheek and handed her her schoolbag. "Only in August when it's hot in the attic. And hardly ever then. Don't worry, pet," she said, nudging her out into the chilly day and calling for her brothers to wait for her.

As she did the morning work, which she thought for the thousandth time she could certainly do blindfolded, Kate considered further just what it was she would say to John. The more she thought about it, the less certain she felt of the right approach. As close as she was to Margaret Mulhern, it wasn't a matter Margaret could help her with any more than her mother could have if she were still alive, which she hadn't been for almost a year, a blow that still felt very recent to Kate. The person she really needed was her father, she thought. She needed his bluntness or she needed him to be the messenger, which he almost certainly would have been except that he, too, was gone. He'd died on the Cut-off the month before Maggie was born. Kate, putting the broom away and, for a moment, pitying her orphaned self, took out paper and pen and sat down at Harry's desk.

The year had been hard. John had seen to their mother's estate but, as the oldest daughter, and with her sisters a long trip and an impossible trip away from New Harmony, it had fallen to Kate to take care of her mother's things. She'd dispensed them as fairly as she could or made the harder choices of what to throw away. Often, she'd agonized over it, worrying out loud to Harry, who'd been practical, suggesting that she do what they'd done in his hospital days at Louisville: have a yes group (things or soldiers to save), a no group (soldiers or items beyond saving), and a last group for maybes. It helped some, but she still wasn't finished.

She had written only a doodle and a *John, dear, please understand* before she put her pen down and went into the bedroom. When her father had died—too ill to be moved into town from the house on the Cut-off—her mother had held his hand for the longest time before she placed it carefully on his chest and said, "The good die young and the Givens die young. Even if it's not the same thing, it's still true he was good in his heart. And such a bonny, lovely boy he was."

Kate had thought it a touching eulogy—even if she was the only one to hear it—but it had only been after her father's death that she'd realized how very much he'd gentled her mother. It had surprised her, but it clearly was true. Her father had teased her mother's anxiousness away. He made her smile, and it helped her to be more tolerant. Without him, she seemed nervous and afraid, and she defended herself by becoming more rigid. Kate knew it was partly age and failing health that had altered her disposition, but she still thought her father's death had been the real key. It was why things had grown difficult, particularly with her mother and Charley.

Well, certainly with her mother and Charley.

Kate touched a warm patch of sunlight on the wall. The Charley matter was something that always upset her, that upset her now. To his credit—and she'd always pointed this out to John—Charley was honest about things from the start. He'd told their mother he'd gone to a dance on the Cut-off and, looking through the window, spotted Cynthia, who was so laughing and beautiful with her dark hair swinging as she moved about the dance floor, that he'd made up his mind on the spot to marry her. Kate thought it was the most romantic of all their family love stories (though Harry still got private points for his labyrinth). Without an instant's hesitation, Charlie had vowed to marry Cynthia even if she was already married, which it turned out she had been. She was divorced and Protestant and as in love with Charley as he was with her. Their mother told him marriage was out of the question, that she'd seen her children drift from their faith far enough. She drew the line at a divorcée.

Of course it hadn't stopped Charley. He had married Cynthia anyway, but even when Ulla was born and they gave him the middle name Denis—which was such an O'Donnell name—their mother still didn't budge. "Tell him he's put an awful curse on that child, and I can't bear to look at it," she said. Then she'd kept her word, which was horrible for Charley. He stormed about it to Kate and John. Kate thought John could have been more sympathetic—if anyone could have intervened, he might have—but their mother had died, and the house and lot in town went to John and Denis. Charley was cut out and, though Kate was sure John had given him money to build a house on the lot, Charley—unforgiven—was unforgiving himself. It had all been dreadful and Kate felt that it still blighted the memories of their happy family life. And it was part of why she felt she had to speak to John—not about Charley, but to help avert another disaster when she'd stood by for the first one. And there was this other odd thing: it seemed her role now, for better or worse and even if it didn't quite fit her, to be the family's conscience just as her mother had been.

The cat had followed her into the bedroom and, feeling it bump back and forth against her skirt, Kate reached down to scratch it. At the moment, although she missed her mother and father, it was the absence of Margaret and Mary's sisterly counsel that she felt more keenly. In fact, it was the reason she'd come into the bedroom. She nudged the cat away and got down on the floor. She looked under the bed for the box with both her own letters from Margaret and the ones Margaret had written to their parents. They were in her keeping now—forever, she supposed—unless, of course, she sent them back to California. The first box she could see had John's letters from the war, and she was tempted, but she nudged it out of the way. She stretched on her side and, when she'd reached Margaret's box, she pushed at the corner, angling it toward her until, finally, she had it in her grip. She pulled it out. She blew off the dust and then, leaning against the bed, she took out a packet and set it on her lap. Carefully, she slipped a letter from an envelope and, as the cat strolled over her knees, she began to read.

It was a long while before the clock in the parlor struck the hour. By the time it had struck the hour again, there were letters scattered across the floor beside her, and Kate had read through much of what they'd learned of Margaret's life in the dozen-plus years since she and Andy had headed west. It seemed such a distance, farther even than Donegal, though John would say that it was only that she could imagine Donegal, having walked the bogs and the Blue Stacks and breathed in the moist, peaty air, while all that they knew of California was something they could conjure up from words and pictures they borrowed from their memories of other things.

"When I think of California—not the desert but where Margaret is," John had told her, "it's like the hills in Tennessee but with an ocean and with rocks like the cliffs above Bunglas."

Kate was trying to imagine such a scene when she felt the current of air from the front door opening, and then heard Maggie, home from school, bumping her bag across the floor. "In here," Kate called, still holding a letter. When Maggie came in, Kate stretched her arm out and hugged her around her knees, feeling the cold stiffness of her coat. She smiled up at her, at the small face with Harry's blue eyes and the blonde curls escaping beneath the bonnet.

"What are those little ribbons for?" Maggie asked, looking at the two letters that were tied with black bows.

Kate was quiet, following her stare. She could tell Maggie about Margaret's babies who'd died of a horrible fever, and they could add those babies to the list of cousins that Maggie liked to recite. Kate knew she would never have thought of leaving Biddy out of her own family, but the fact was she'd not known Margaret's children, and she did know Maggie. She didn't want her waking at night frightened that something might happen to her or her brothers.

"Grandma put them on the letters Aunt Margaret wrote when she was sad," she said. "California is so far away. She missed New Harmony."

"And what is California like?" Maggie asked, not for the first time, and Kate, happy for the change of subject, tried to remember all of the parts of Margaret's story that Maggie liked the best.

"It's a very big place," she said, unbuttoning Maggie's coat and untying her bonnet. "In some places they've found gold. I knew someone once, or knew her a little, who worked teaching gold miners to read. There's an ocean, of course—the Pacific Ocean—and it's bigger even than the ocean Mama and Grandpa and Cousin Margaret crossed coming from Ireland."

"Grandpa died a month before I was born."

"He did," Kate said, "and he would have loved you very much. California is so large that it has whole deserts and real mountains and great stretches of farms like the sheep farm Uncle Andy runs."

"The sheep's wool is a fine mer-*eeen*!-o," Maggie interrupted, and Kate laughed while Maggie went on. "And Aunt Margaret sent Grandma a beautiful shawl."

"It's what she wore when she was sick and needed to be warmer."

"And you have the shawl now."

"I do."

"And you won't get sick if you wear it."

"I won't."

"And we have Grandma's Tell City rocker that you gave her."

"That Papa did, and she rocked you in it just as I do."

"And it's all very pretty in California. There're Indians and men from China but hardly any women at all."

Kate laughed once more. "Are you hungry? You really know this story, little minx," she said, standing up, and she thought, as she often did, how very much she liked having a daughter who was eager to learn so much of what she herself knew. And there was this other feeling she had—one that was more complicated. She wanted Maggie to have something of the spirit of Fanny Wright. She didn't mean the tendency toward ill-planned schemes or odd arrangements with men (Harry had asked Kate if it was her doing that his cousin Eliza was still unmarried and at home with her mother), though Kate didn't think she'd necessarily object to such things. What she wanted for Maggie was something hard to define. A sense of independence, certainly, and of inquiry—a feeling that a woman might think about the world as broadly as a man. Or more so. More broadly and deeply than a man. And, too, though it was nothing specific, she wanted more freedom for

Maggie than she'd had herself, although Harry might argue she was free enough when he'd irked her or when she thought he'd had too much to drink. She knew she had more than she'd ever hoped to have. She was Mrs. Beal, wife of an Englishman with a collateral relationship to the town's old luminaries. She was the sister to Mr. Given, an Irishman, yes, but through his knowledge and hard work and his service in the war, known as a man of worth. Yet, selfish or not, Kate often thought these things weren't really about her. For Maggie, she wanted more.

"What are you writing, Mama?" Maggie asked, stopping at the desk on their way to the kitchen, and Kate didn't answer, but picked up her doodled paper and drew a funny face on another sheet for Maggie.

When Harry got home from the mill, and the boys had come in from a football game, Kate was glad she'd made soup in the morning. She and Maggie had taken over the entire kitchen with bowls of flour glue and Maggie's paints. They were working on foolscap laid out on the table.

"What's all this?" Harry asked, kissing Kate and then dangling Maggie squealing over his shoulder before putting her right side up in her chair.

"We've got the whole family. All the Givens," Maggie told him when she'd swallowed her last giggle and caught her breath. "We haven't put the names in yet. But we're going to. And the ages all my cousins are."

"Your American cousins. Tell me who's who." Harry sat down and looked at the whole population spread out on the foolscap, the girls with bows and the boys with shaggy topknots made out of yarn. He listened to Maggie's recitation and then pulled her onto his knee. "A man could get lost in all these Maggies and Mollies and Kates. And in the Charleys and fellows named Denis. Clarence, you hear that? Be glad you've got a name of your own. Who's this?" he asked Maggie, pointing at a single drawing.

"Mama's sister Bridget who died. There aren't any cousins for her," Maggie said, and Kate saw she looked stricken.

"And this is your Uncle John?"

Maggie nodded. "And Mollie and Charley and Miss Barton."

"The last time I looked, Miss Barton wasn't your aunt. She certainly isn't your cousin." Harry looked over at Kate.

"But I like having her at Uncle John's house," Maggie answered, and she slipped off his lap. She carefully lifted up the foolscap, and carried it walking tiptoe to put it on her orange crate as Kate had told her to do.

Harry stood up stretching. "Mouths of babes," he said, and Kate nodded, getting the spoons.

"If you could come home after the meeting instead of stopping for a pint with John, I've an errand to run. And it's to see John, so I'll need him to be there. If you could tell him," she said, and she stood at the stove, worrying her words for John again as if they were rosary beads in Margaret Mulhern's fingers.

———

Union Hall was brightly lit. Seeing it as she walked up Tavern Street and wondering if the girls of the town had begun decorating for Valentine's Day, Kate thought her evening errand had actually started three years ago. She closed her eyes a second. Yes, it was three. It had been the fifteenth anniversary of the battle of Fort Donelson, and they'd all convinced John to attend the ball for the first time since Caroline's death. Kate knew he hadn't wanted to go, but Eugene Owen had made it very plain to him that he and George Tretheway and Robert Clarke were to be honored again for their battle wounds. Reluctant as John clearly was, he couldn't say no. He and Harry had gone to the tavern with the other veterans before the ball started and, when Kate arrived at the hall, Church Street had been filled with buggies and with ladies dressed in their best gowns, supper baskets in tow. Harry and John were walking up the street with Robert Clarke. Along with Robert, John was dressed in his uniform and, thanks to their mother's mending and the few pounds he'd gained, Kate thought it looked far better than when he'd returned from the war.

Inside that evening, it had been clear the town girls had outdone themselves. The hall was illuminated with white tapers in red, heart-shaped shades, and the walls were lined with various booths. There was a kissing booth and a booth to buy fancy valentines, both of them meant to raise money for disabled veterans. There was a booth displaying memorabilia of the Fort Donelson battle and of the men who had died there. Kate had been interested in all of it, and she was interested in what Harry had to say. While they danced, he told her about the conversation at the tavern. It had gotten hot about the election, he said. The electoral college was ready to vote, and most of the men thought Hayes would win over Tilden, that in the end there would be a compromise to appease the South by withdrawing Federal troops. Captain Boren, back from California and working as a commercial traveler, was beside himself, insisting that if the troops left, the country could just as well forget the slaves had ever been emancipated.

"I told him I spent enough life and leg on the goddam South. I don't care anymore," Harry said, and Kate had shushed him, for the band had stopped and Colonel Owen had started his remarks. When it was John's turn to be acknowledged, he spoke simply, thanking everyone for their kindness and saying a ball was a far better way to spend Valentine's Day than the way he and George and Robert had spent it fifteen years ago. Then he'd offered a salute to the men whose hearts had stopped on that bloody field—those men and all their brothers who hadn't come home. When he finished, there were quiet *hear hear*s around the hall.

Harry had started talking again, but Kate was distracted by a small drama that had begun across the room. The 25th's battle flag was on display at Eliza Lichtenberger's table among the regimental artifacts. There was also a drawing of Levi Thrailkill that Kate thought Mary Ann Barton, in town from Galatia to play duets with Eliza, must have brought from home. Mary Ann was helping Eliza, and John had crossed the room and stopped at the table to talk with her. Kate watched the two of them over Harry's shoulder. The candlelight flickered on John's face, while the starched silk of Mary Ann's gown shimmered so beautifully that Kate found herself nearly mesmerized. John, however, was moving away. A second later, Kate pinched Harry to look. John had turned back, and Mary Ann was standing up to dance with him.

It was really because of that moment—because of Mary Ann and John beginning their dance three years ago—that Kate was out tonight.

A bright moon reflected off the snow and, turning from Brewery up Steam Mill Street, Kate thought she was finally ready with her speech. By the time she had knocked at John's door, all that had changed. She was nervous. She was very nervous. She knocked once more, and then again. When there was still no answer, she slipped inside. She called out. She stood in the curtained dark of her parents' parlor, which was John's parlor now, and she could scarcely remember a word. She was unsure she could even stay on her feet, and she was entirely aggravated with herself. It wasn't like her. Harry would be astonished at her; Harry would be speechless. Yet the stakes, as she considered them, seemed so very high.

Hearing the back door open and John stomping his way inside, her breath quickened. "I'm here," she called. "It's Kate. Are the children still in Galatia?"

"They are," John said, coming in. "What are you up to? It's not like you, Kate, to be in the dark about something." He put down the load of wood he was carrying and planted a quick kiss on her cheek. He lit a single lamp. "What brings you out at this hour?"

Kate swung her gloves in a looping, nervous motion around her wrist. She watched John put a log on the fire. "I've wanted to talk to you," she said. She backed into the chair that stood where her mother's used to be and, putting her gloves on her knees, she felt more Mrs. Beal than Kate. She wished they were in the kitchen. "Since Mary Ann's birthday," she said. "Well, before that. Since before Christmas. For a long time I've meant to talk to you. I'm certain of this. John, you should marry her."

She had placed her sword shakily, but now that she'd finally done it, Kate felt more energy than nerves. She could feel John waiting as she went on. "It's the right thing to do. I know it sits hard, what the priest thinks. But it's a foolish rule and a church with no heart that asks it. It's a bond of paper not blood. You're no actual relation. She was Caroline's niece, not yours. And you love her, John. I know it. If you didn't, would you have spent this time a widower? There are women enough who would have you—even Ann Rippeto before she married Gilbert Schnee and moved out to Kansas. Why should Mary Ann wait longer? A woman wants children. She's thirty, John. There's no war to wait on. This time there's nothing."

Kate felt an errant heartbeat catch her last syllable and she wondered if John noticed, but she kept on. "For my whole life I've thought you the decentest person on earth, but you change my mind if you leave Mary Ann hanging like this. You're a free man, John. I don't deny God, but I do deny any man who would tell you you're not free to choose for yourself what is right."

There. She had said it all, the whole thing, with only the part left out she'd decided against. She would spare John the picture of Mary Ann crying in the Lichtenbergers' pantry on her birthday.

Now, though, Kate felt drained. She didn't know what John would say. Perhaps he was surprised, perhaps angry. She had no idea. She had not really thought about this part, and her back ached from his hard chair, and she wanted very much to be on her way. She wanted to be home with Harry and checking on the boys. She wanted to be settling the comforter on Maggie once more.

"John?" she said. He had turned down the lamp and walked to the piano he'd bought for their mother. He struck a chord and then one more. Kate leaned against a knob of the chair back looking at him. Even in the dim light, as he bent over the piano she could see the muscled line of his back through his shirt. It moved her. She hardly knew a man with a weak back, and yet the sight of a strong one always surprised her.

"Play for me, Kate?" he said. He struck another chord, and

Kate didn't want to, but she crossed the room anyway and sat on the piano bench. "And what will you have butchered, John, from a woman who learned so late?" She set her fingers on the keys and felt the smoothness of the ivories, the tiny pit in middle C. "The songs Mother taught us?" She laughed then. "I'm sure I can play at least one."

"Yes. Those songs. Her songs. Who do you think first sang them to her, Kate? Or did she learn them herself?" John sat down the wrong way on the bench, his shoulder next to hers, and Kate decided the single, low lamp and the firelight were enough to see by. And if they weren't, she still liked the way the keys seemed to glow with a dulled phosphorescence. Carefully, she began to play, leaving out the notes in the bass she wasn't sure of. Since it was just the two of them, she knew John would sing, his baritone stretching to reach the Irish tenor. She played "The Minstrel Boy" and "The Harp That Once Thro' Tara's Halls," and the song about a hue most rare that their mother had made her own melody for.

"What about the Spenser?" John asked, and Kate reached for the soft pedal in the dark and found F minor, the key that seemed right for the darkness.

. . . I from thenceforth have learned to love more deare.

Kate played very softly, listening to John sing, his voice shading the flatted third.

When the song was done, she set her hands in her lap. "You sound like an Irishman, John Given, even if you're an Irishman transplanted for good. Could you marry her now that Mother is gone? If it was Mother as much as the Church . . . Mother fearing you'd be excommunicated."

"Hush, Kate. You've had your say. I can tell you this. Caroline died and I died. Whenever it was I found out I could live once more, it was Mary Ann who was there and that thought has hardly left me—and I'd thank you not to mention Ann Bradley—Mrs. Rippeto—Mrs. Schnee—in my house. But a man has things to decide, and I won't talk of it more now."

Kate, her interest piqued, felt her energy returning. "Don't brush me off, John. Don't act as if what I think is less important than what you do. It's your decision, of course, but I know, as well, that the honorable thing is to make it soon. In fact, shouldn't you make it now?"

"And you would expect to know before Mary Ann herself?"

Kate gave herself a long instant before she answered. "You mean you've decided?"

"I didn't say that I have. Do you know the row her mother would make? That our mother would have?"

"But think of the calendar, John. Is there a day there that strikes you?"

Kate waited for him to make the mental picture himself, but it took him no time. "The twenty-first. It's a year then since she died—since Mother died."

"Yes."

"And you think that if Mary Ann will talk to her parents and take me on and—Kate, is there any secret I can keep from you?—I should marry her the very next day."

"Have you already thought that? If you have, I've intruded and made a fool and a pest of myself." Kate began to stand up, but John shook his head.

"You've been Kate," he said, "and whatever feelings I had that I couldn't wound Mother in just this way—especially after Charley—nor violate the time of mourning for her, and whatever light concern I might still have that I'll fry in hell, excommunicated as I'll be—though this fool priest as I've argued with him knows nothing of canon law—I like your certainty. If it's right with you, Kate, good heart that you are, it ought to be right with me."

"But it's not yet?"

"I don't know. The fact is my mind tells me one thing and my heart two. It's a faith that's hard to abandon when you've felt it so keenly at times. And there was the comfort of it, too, after Caroline's death."

"The Hamlet of Harmony," Kate said, feeling both mischievous and brave.

For a moment, John looked taken aback. Then he laughed. "Yes. It does seem grandiose when you put it that way."

"Well I have," Kate answered, and she put on her cloak and gloves and said her good night.

———

There were two codas to the evening that, for Kate, remained perpetually linked to what she had said. She hadn't the gift or curse of foreknowledge (or even a belief in such a thing) and, leaving John's house, neither eventuality was something she knew or could even consider beyond certain general thoughts about a wedding and family for Mary Ann. She was pleased at her success. She was happy and even triumphant. She was the hurrying Kate of old, covering the blocks home through the frosty evening to check that her sons were asleep and to count Maggie safe once again before she went in to Harry, and woke him to tell him what she had done.

The codas were what she knew later. There was the joyous one when John stopped for her and Harry, taking them with him to Galatia for his wedding to Mary Ann (Mrs. Barton happy for the party, but not the occasion), and in January of the next year, she and Maggie adding a new baby, John Barton Given, to the list of cousins.

The other coda functioned as terrible subtraction. It was one that Kate would have erased forever from her story. She would have bargained with the devil to blot it away, for less than two months from the day she and Maggie had printed his name on the foolscap, the baby had died, and four weeks later Kate herself was devastated. She was utterly desolate and wondering if she'd jinxed the earth, the whole planet—why had she ever pushed John to defy a priest, any priest?—for her precious, precious Maggie was gone, her small body wasted in spite of everything that Kate and the doctors and Margaret Mulhern could do, her face wearing the same scarlet mask that Biddy's had.

New Harmony, Indiana
January 1, 1898

32

NAME OF WITNESS AND REPUTATION:
ACHILLES H. FRETAGEOT—EXCELLENT
A. H. Fretageot, Deposition H, is the leading merchant of the town and is a first class man.

NAME OF WITNESS AND REPUTATION:
JOHN GIVEN—GOOD/EXCELLENT
John Given, Deposition B, is an educated man and stands high for truth and veracity in the historic town of New Harmony, Indiana which has since its foundation been noted for the superior character of its people. . . . The deponent's family were very fearful that I would unduly excite the soldier and it is very doubtful if he will recover. Deponent says he has been sick with pneumonia for two months and in bed since January 10th.

D. E. Buckingham, special examiner, widow's pension claim of Charlotte M. Boren, March 4, 1898

I t was New Year's Day and mild for the season. John was sitting on the porch swing at Kate's house, a letter from Menomen he'd just been reading open on his knee. The house wasn't actually Kate's any longer, but Margaret Mulhern's, Margaret who lived there with Kate's bachelor son, George. John hadn't gotten used to it yet. He had the new family landscape in his head. Denis and Charley were living in Illinois, as he and Mary Ann had done off and on for a decade. Charley was on a homestead and Denis on Bull Island, which he and John had bought together to farm when John owned land in Bugtown on the way to Poseyville. A year ago—a little more—Margaret had died in California (John always wondered if Margaret's life had been happy, if she'd found some of the excitement she'd dreamed of or if, instead, everything had been hard). Mary and Porter had kept moving west until they'd wound up in Durango, Colorado, where Mary's oldest girl and her husband ran a hotel.

And Kate was gone. John still had a hard time accepting it. Even believing it. Without ever really thinking about it, he'd always counted on Kate to be there, but she wasn't any longer. She'd died a few months before Margaret. He'd looked at her in the black shroud Margaret Mulhern had chosen—still with her smooth Given features and skin, but thinner from her final bouts of illness. In death, she looked so peaceful that he'd had to turn away. He realized that Mary Ann was right: for all her spirit, Kate, his eager and always striving sister, had never truly recovered from her little girl's death. The loss of Harry (his old soldier's heart giving out) and then Clarence, who'd died of consumption at twenty-six, had finished the injury. John had understood it when he saw that the strain had left her face. In death, Kate, who had always imagined a more ambitious and deeper life than she had been given, and who had tried in vain for the dream at the heart of New Harmony, was finally serene.

On this New Year's Day, he had brought his seven-year-old Louise out in her very new dress to make New Year's visits (yes, *Kate, my sweet child from late age, from experience a workman's finest work; yes, Kate, Mary Ann and Mollie spoil her still: fifty! children at her birthday party*). They had saved their last call for Margaret Mulhern. Margaret had asked him in, but John had declined for he knew she and Louise liked their own private tea ceremony with Margaret's New Year's treats, and the Catholic trinkets and pictures that Louise found intriguing. She'd asked John once if she could be a Catholic, too, for Mollie was Catholic and Mollie, in fact, had been Margaret's charge in moral matters. Mary Ann, however, was raising the children as Methodists with John's tacit consent.

He had been glad to stay on the porch. He had his letter from Menomen to read again, and he was enjoying the weather, which was a bit damp he noticed with a sneeze, but still almost springlike in its warmth. It was nearly sunset, and the sky was pinking up and the sun, as Kate had often noted, hung like a lollipop on the turret of David Dale's laboratory.

John stretched his good leg out and got more comfortable in the swing. He was feeling quite contented. At home, there was a New Year's supper of wild turkey and oyster stuffing cooking, and in all the things that he could do anything about, his life felt orderly and good. It seemed a small miracle to him. With Caroline, he had known such joy that he had not thought he could survive the loss of it, and he and Mary Ann had suffered their own sorrow. Their baby boy lay in the cemetery under the rough stone lamb John had carved. A decade ago they'd buried sweet, two-year-old Ella. Yet the deepest losses in his life had gradually, if imperfectly, been covered over and here he was: father to Mollie and Charley. Father to Will and Louise. Husband to Mary Ann. He was fortunate, though it saddened him more than he could say that in the end, just as in the beginning, he'd been luckier than Kate.

John watched a dancy, small sparrow peck at the ground where the snow had melted. He glanced across the alley at the laughing young people leaving Dr. Rawlings's house and then pushed himself back in the swing. Earlier, walking with Louise, he had waved at Robert Clarke, who was riding by in his buggy with Emma, and he'd thought that for every old soldier like Robert and him who were still out visiting this New Year's Day, there were so many more who were gone. Harry. Michael McShane. The long list of men from the old 25th. Levi. Of course, Levi. From G.A.R. meetings, he knew that the men, for whatever reason—maybe a bullet lodged near a bone or the memory of a time when life had been heightened—still looked back at the war as the central fact of their lives.

If the men had all been Menomen—in Vincennes now and growing old in his white beard—it would have made more sense. The letter, which Menomen had sent after Christmas, was full of his own family news and of word about the families still in Drimarone. But the real news of the letter was that he had received a singular award. All these years later, for gallantry at Vicksburg and Fort DeRussy in Louisiana, he'd been given the Congressional Medal of Honor. John was pleased; he was puffed up about it. He knew Menomen deserved it and he'd tell him so, though he already knew he would kid him, too. When he wrote back, he would say it was good the medal was only decades late, and not posthumous.

It was a funny thing really. Menomen had every reason to be proud, but John thought it likely he'd taken a quick look at himself in the mirror and calmly noted the warrior was gone. Yet other men, with far less right to be thought heroes, kept their soldiering life front and center. Their war memories hid the more mundane facts of their lives. Even Harry, when he was still alive, seemed destined to end up a general in his stories when he'd had enough to drink. The hyperbole was widespread. It was distasteful to John, and never more so than when he indulged in it himself, for he'd never been as fervent and clear about why he'd fought as he thought he should have been. And what it meant was that, if the war was central in his own life, his life had missed a clear and defining belief.

He wondered if it did. Really, he still wondered. Sometimes at night—the moonlight falling on the comforter and on the caned bottom of a chair that shaped a dim crosshatch on the floor—Mary Ann slept, and he tried to understand it all. Generally, he would start from this point: it was not that the war itself had lacked a great issue. The opposite was true. And yet, for him, the enormous sin that lay behind it was something he'd always looked at with an immigrant's eye. What, after all, had he known of the politics of America when he arrived at twenty-one? When had he ever owned a slave? How was he accountable for an institution he could never have imagined, let alone have fostered? And for that matter, when he had finally begun to know a black man in Hamilton the clerk, hadn't he acknowledged to himself that he didn't feel his superior? He had simply never been able to do what Abraham Lincoln had done at the last: believe that the terrible bloodshed of both North and South was a necessary redemption for a country shaped with slavery at its heart. He understood the concept and the anguish that it came from. What he hadn't understood was all the blood.

John brought the swing to a halt and held it still with the heel of his boot. He wasn't blameless. Since he'd gone to war from New Harmony, it might have given him a certain awareness, he thought. He might have considered that a hoped-for utopia would wear the name oddly with people excluded on the basis of who they'd been from birth and that, by extension, the same would hold true for democracy. The fact was that, for all his idealism and certainty, Robert Owen had kept blacks out of his societies, and John thought this contradiction in principle meant that he and Owen had made the same blunder of sensibility. They had both experienced America as strangers. They had both been baffled by its variety.

Yet Robert Dale Owen and Kate had both seemed to find a more open view, Robert Dale writing letters to Lincoln encouraging emancipation, and Kate so fascinated by Nashoba and Fanny Wright's boldness. Perhaps, John thought, it was just him. Perhaps it was the particular way he'd been an immigrant (Robert Owen, after all, had barely even lived in America). Certainly, if he'd never left Ireland, he would have been a Parnell man and gotten that part right. And yet his life was in New Harmony—in America—and he still had never made the full emotional equation: Englishman is to Irishman as white is to black. He hadn't done it, and he saw it now as waffling and a lack in himself.

The sparrow had hopped onto the porch, and John called to it with a chirping sound. He looked at it as it flew up to a tree branch. It settled for a moment. Then it flew away and he watched until he couldn't see it any longer. He glanced at the letter once more and then folded it away in his pocket.

He sighed a deep sigh. Would he ever be done thinking about the war—about the war and all it had meant? Would there always be a letter like Menomen's? Would there always be a story? And would his mind always circle it, the gyre gradually widening and widening so that his thoughts mirrored the wartime ellipse that an eagle could have flown. Banking. Lightening its wings over river ports and the deep-river country to the south and east of St. Louis. Sailing on to Cairo (Little Egypt where Mary had lived). Flying to Memphis and Nashville, to Knoxville and Louisville.

The older he grew, the more present the war seemed to feel. Yet it had been only four years of his life. Four.

At times, he was caught up short, thinking that his keenest memories should revolve more around his family and the other years and places that had made his life what it was. In some ways they did, though he could not think straight on about Caroline and the lost children, but only of that reflected sheen that almost covered his sadness. Still, he remembered Drumboarty and Tullynaha, and the other towns of Drimarone so vivid with fog and gorse and small pink wildflowers and the perennial scent of burning peat and, in Montcharles the post town, the gray stone buildings that climbed the streets. In these memories, he was a boy again, and his body so sound and able that anything was possible.

Sometimes he traced his oddly looping arc toward the priesthood that had begun after hedge school in Tullynaha. The training college in Dublin substituted for school with the Christian Brothers. The minor seminary at St. Finian's in Navan where, in retrospect, he'd come closest to finding a vocation on those morning climbs up and down from the quarters in Power's Duck Egg. Letterkenny and the Port Road school on the days when Bishop McGettigan came to prepare the students from his seaside lodgings at Rathmelton. And finally, the rooms back in Dublin and the remarkable tangent that reading with William Reeves had become. In all that time, there had been nothing that could make him more than a man, even if it made him a priest, and so, as a man, he had turned from taking Orders and, with a sense of both failure and relief, had come with his family to America.

John lifted his foot from the porch and let the swing carry him slowly backward and forward again. He nudged a loose clapboard in place with his heel and made a mental note to fix it. It was, of course, another legacy of the war, but when he thought about America, he could not imagine it as undivided. Seeing the bitterness of the South and the way that Negroes, who had seemed on the verge of something new, had struggled and then slipped largely from sight, he sometimes wondered if it might not have been better if the South had simply gone its own way, gradually relinquishing its myths and sorting out its racial household in its own time (if it could). How much suffering and blood would have been spared. Whatever the political lines of the continent might have become, there would not be the South as it was now—vanquished but, in some real way, undefeated and gripping the North in its vise like a dog with its jaw clamped tight on another dog's flank.

And, too, if the war, in its deepest sense, had been about race, what a distant shadow it had left outside the South. In New Harmony, its peaceful heart the flat grid and tree-lined streets and Rappite buildings (and the Angel's Rock, both real and ghostly, still in the yard at Church and Main), there were so many people who had migrated or immigrated and so many people who had come from the South, but not a single black person in the whole town. John hardly knew a man who had fought as a real abolitionist, though he knew there were some, and others who'd said they were abolitionists later. He'd even heard Louise, who'd read her precocious way through *Uncle Tom's Cabin*, telling her teacher that her father had fought and been wounded so Uncle Tom's friends could be free.

John had been surprised when he heard her, but when he thought about why he'd really been fighting, he couldn't come up with a better answer even if there was the truer one that he thought the war was inescapable. It was like the fights his younger boy Willie got in at school when he ran out of words and gave in to frustration. He always had plenty of people to goad and to cheer him on, just as the North and South had had, though at times John thought the rivalry was as strong between the North and West as North and South. When he'd read General Grant's *Memoirs*, he'd agreed it was best that the Army of the Potomac had beaten Lee on their own ground instead of having Sherman and his western troops finish the job. In Washington, the tension between the armies had been palpable. The Grand Review itself had been split in two, East and West, to avoid conflict.

He knew it because he had been there. Though he was done being a soldier who passed in review, he had watched the Army of the Potomac—his last real billet—as they marched through the streets of Washington. They were still well drilled and full of pride that their army under General Grant had finally lived up to its promise. And then, though he'd assumed he'd be a spectator again on the second day and watch Sherman's men, ragged and bronzed from their march through the South, he'd been an actual participant.

John took out his handkerchief and wiped at his eyes. He blew his nose. He thought he might be catching a cold, but he knew, as well, that this particular memory had always flooded him with emotion, and it was no different now. He had gone to the 25th's encampment the evening before they marched, and his sole purpose was to make sure he'd be there to see them as they entered the march at dawn. But George Ham had ordered the men to cobble together a uniform for him and find him a musket so he could march for all the Harmony men of the 25th who'd mustered in at Camp Vanderburg and hadn't lived to see such a glorious day. John had considered arguing with him, but there was no real argument to make if he was to march, not for himself, but for the ghosts of men like Captain Saltzman and Al Norcross. He'd polished his boots and put on the uniform and, when he stepped into the line of march in the morning, he felt the old ache in his leg and the burning in his stomach that never quite went away. His musket barrel flashed in the morning light, and he had a scrap of feather for his cap that he pinched in with a sprig of green like all the Irish lads were wearing.

In Drimarone, he thought, they wouldn't have known him. His hair was long with streaks of blond burned into it from his weeks of marching around in Virginia. His beard was full. He could see the blue of his eyes in his musket barrel, and his face was as brown as it had been in the heat of Alabama. His skin felt sealed to his bones, his borrowed uniform faded from blue to dust.

He came to attention then. In front of the company, the battle flag would not unfurl but collapsed back on itself, the breeze pushing through its worn riddle of familiar bullet holes. The color bearer John had seen the evening before, cleaning mud from his boots and oiling the last of their leather, finally got it to stay open, the brass buttons the company had scavenged together gleaming at his cuffs.

John felt a stirring in his chest. The men stretched before him farther than he could see. The lines had no rear. Sherman's soldiers—200,000 and more men of the western army—were emptying out of their camps, falling in with bloodied stretchers at their backs to cross the Potomac. They'd begun their war on parade, men like him and Harry Beal and Levi Thrailkill—God save the Union and hang Jeff Davis—who had started as play soldiers drilling in Owen's pasture in front of the Harmony cows. The men who were left were ending their war as real soldiers (or in his case, almost real) on parade in front of General Grant and a president who'd not gotten warm in the job. The mourning bunting was down, and the flags flew at full staff, but it wasn't six weeks since Abraham Lincoln had died.

Dust hung in the air. The black men who trailed the forward division moved their families and mules into the line. John heard a scurry, a squawking of turkeys and squealing of pigs. Laughter rolled through the troops. A black boy had battled two turkeys apart and held one firmly in his arms and ducked his head away from its beak.

A young boy. A boy like the shy one who had held John's berry pail the day before when he'd gone out looking for early huckleberries. John watched him and the turkey in his grasp. He knew that he'd not gone to war for such a boy. He had gone for honor, for Union, for a sense of belonging and for some idea of manhood that had long since drifted away. He had gone as a son, but not for this boy. Yet somewhere along the way, they'd become inseparable—the boy with the pail, the boy with the turkey, and young John Given in Donegal: an Irish lad layering the peat from the bogs in even-cut rows and then resting against his shovel to stare at the moody sky. Yearning. Always yearning.

John felt the pulse of the men. He saw the lines thrust forward and, anchoring the musket on his shoulder, he squared himself in the ranks as the company swung into file and, with the sun glancing into their eyes, all stepped forward in a single motion.

He could still feel that movement, feel the sunshine of that morning even as the sun moved down behind David Dale's laboratory and the Harmony day fell away.

He felt a drip from the roof on his hand. Then, sighing on its hinges, the door opened, and he turned to see Margaret Mulhern, still slim and erect, ushering Louise outside. John stood up stiffly. The light from the lamp Margaret had lit in the parlor just caught her grayed hair, and she had a napkin for him that he knew covered a small loaf of fruitcake. He thanked her. He kissed her and wished her Happy New Year once more and then, coughing for a moment—there was a real frog in his throat—he leaned down to Louise and asked her what she was guarding so closely in her hand.

"Should I show him before Mama?" Louise asked, looking up at Margaret, and Margaret laughed her still lovely laugh, and nodded.

"Yes, of course, Louise. Go ahead," she answered, and Louise opened her hand, and she worked carefully at the drawstring on a thin, flannel pouch and then pushed out a teaspoon. She held it up for John.

"See? It says *Louise*. And it's silver," she told him, excitement ringing in her voice.

John made a nodding appraisal and told her to thank Cousin Margaret again. When she'd slipped the spoon back into its pouch, they set off on their walk home, Louise chattering as they went, and holding his hand with her free one. John, who was feeling a slight chill, checked the top button of his coat and of Louise's as well. They went down West Street. They walked past Ribeyre's house where Louise always asked him about the porch trim with the half paddle wheels on each end or about the reflection in the window that sometimes looked like a ghost and that tonight made her hold his hand tighter. Always, when they walked, he answered her questions. He made up stories for her, too, or reached far into the past to tell her the things his father and grandfather had told him.

But the stories he couldn't tell her on this night or on any night were stories he would never know, though he might have told them if he could have. *Scraps of things.* Margaret's California children with a Williams cousin who drove a team of four belled horses that looked and sounded like silver. Denis's daughter, arriving from her Montreal home in a chauffeured car and smelling of whiskey. Mary's daughter planting a Colorado yucca plant in front of her grandparents' tombs on a visit to New Harmony. On Charley's farm, grasshopper-shaped oilwells punctuating the days and the nights. Among James Mulhern's talented grandchildren, the spoiled priest turned scholar, the mathematician who made an accounting system for the United States Navy, beautiful Maud, who was offered a place at the Abbey Theatre in Dublin (but not allowed to take it), and Nan, a doctor who went to South Africa and left press clippings at her death that said she'd "rid the diamond fields of typhoid." There was James himself, who was tight with a farthing but built his daughters houses in the valley in Drimarone and spent his money and Margaret Mulhern's to educate priests. As a very old man, he was caught by the Black and Tans standing lookout and giving a signal.

Bits of other stories. Descendants of Rose and Ellen laced throughout Chicago's Irish neighborhoods, their names in all the parish registers, and one of Ellen's great-granddaughters (related on her father's side to a notorious Hogarty gangster) looking out at the rooftops and saying how beautiful it must have all been once, and her father answering, "No, Baby, it was always a slum." John's Aunt Mary Gleason laid out in the McAuliffe parlor. Her great-niece, whose teetotaler mother had died in childbirth and, at the last, asked for a beer (the one with a ribbon on it), made to sit with Aunt Mary, terrified the whole time that the cat would pull the sheet off her face. The jarring illumination of two world wars where other men of the family wore the uniform of their country as John had. The family stories went everywhere so that a whole host of people, whether they knew it or not, had their roots in Drimarone and had something unmistakable in their blood that meant they loved a good story and the scent of a moist morning, and often a drink and sometimes a fight, and always to dance and to sing.

For John, in the gathering evening of that New Year's Day, these stories and the rest of the history, both happy and star-crossed, of a family that had spilled out into the world, were nothing he could tell or foresee. Nor could he envision his final day when Louise, her face floating toward him in his bed—black eyes on a white bowl (was it Louise?)—would bring him the last of the day lilies and whisper, "It's me, Papa. Anna Louise. Your cricket Louise. I put the day lily on your bureau, and I rubbed the vase dry like Grandma Barton does so it won't leave a ring." Nor did he know that one day Louise's granddaughter would pore over the letters that Kate had saved and piece out his story.

Yet, as he and Louise crossed the street at the corner of Tavern and Brewery where three Rappite houses still stood and he sneezed once more ("Bless you, Papa," Louise said when he dropped her hand and sneezed yet again), and Louise, remembering the spoon, began to run the last blocks home to show it to her mother, John felt the pull of the hovering, invisible future where she was heading. Her curls were bobbing (her hair so dark like her mother's), and her coat swinging against her white cotton stockings and—as if to recall that long ago Valentine's Day when he'd held her swirling mother in his arms (black slippers skimming the floor, a whisper of silk gown touching his trouser leg)—her heels blurred in a flash of patent leather shoes.

That perfect moment.

That airy, rushing-onward motion of their quick and shining flight.

Epilogue

T he death of our esteemed comrade, John Given, removes another veteran from the fast disappearing ranks of the heroes of the Civil War, and takes from the social and civil life of our community a man of sterling worth and useful qualities. His voice is forever still in the council room of our municipal government and in the Grand Army Hall of our fraternal order, and in each will be missed his faithful guidance in the respective affairs of town and lodge.

Horace Pestalozzi Owen, Julian Dale Owen, Morris Ford
September 4, 1898

AUTHOR'S NOTE

Bridget (Biddy) Given is an assumed character, her existence based on the ages of the Given children, the Irish tradition of naming the second daughter after the paternal grandmother, and the toll of the Irish Potato Famine in County Donegal. Of the named characters in the book, only Hamilton the clerk is entirely fictional. He was created to help explore John Given's evolution on the subject of race.

ACKNOWLEDGMENTS

I am grateful for an individual artist's fellowship from the National Endowment for the Arts that opened countless doors and helped to finance the research on this book, and for earlier support from the Loft Literary Center and the Minnesota State Arts Board. Many institutions and their personnel were crucial to my research. My thanks to the staff of the Indiana State Library, Genealogy and Newspaper section; to Stephen Towne of the Indiana Archives for sharing his knowledge of Indiana soldiers in the Civil War; and to the Indiana Historical Society, where I found the account book of John B. Elliott and the Thomas and Sarah Pears papers. Other important Indiana resources included the Workingmen's Institute in New Harmony, Indiana, whose archives hold the diaries of Achilles H. Fretageot and the 1865 catalogue of the Posey County Fair, and its librarians, including Owen descendant Sherry Graves and Frank Smith, who was particularly generous in his help; the Alexandrian Library in Mt. Vernon, Indiana, and June Dunning of its Area Research Center; the Willard Library in Evansville, Indiana, and its staff, including Sue Hebbeler; the workers at the Posey County Courthouse and Recorder's Office in Mt. Vernon, Indiana; Wanda Griess and the Posey County Historical Society;

Historic New Harmony; Jean Lee of New Harmony, State Historic Site; Gina Walker, who gave assistance with the Blair Collection at the University of Southern Indiana; and David C. Rice, president emeritus of Southern Indiana University, who provided a fascinating tour of New Harmony's Granary.

My main American institutional resource outside Indiana was the National Archives in Washington, D.C., where I made repeated trips and received particularly welcome assistance from Michael Pilgrim. I also received help from John Hoffman of the Illinois Historical Survey at the University of Illinois; Douglas L. Wilson of the Lincoln Studies Center at Knox College; John Dougan, Shelby County, Tennessee, archivist, who was a whirlwind of energy and information; Patrick Schroeder, the historian at Appomattox Court House; the librarians of the Memphis and Louisville Public Libraries and Atlanta History Center; the U.S. Park Service at various battlefields and other Civil War locations; and the staff of the U.S. Army Quartermaster Museum in Fort Lee, Virginia, and Pamplin Historical Park in Petersburg, Virginia.

Numerous private researchers were invaluable for this work. They include Darlene McConnell of Mt. Vernon, who so willingly added many of my searches to her own; Gloria Cox, who offered suggestions and whose work with her husband preserved so much of the history of Posey County; Don Blair, who shared his keen interest in New Harmony with me in the early 1980s; Josephine Elliott, who exchanged letters with me and gave me a rare interview that drew on her remarkable work archiving New Harmony records; Deborah Burdick for stories about New Harmony and the Cut-off Island; L. Eugene Smith and his son for information and a tour of the Cut-off Island; Tish Mumford for access to family archives relating to New Harmony; John Heuring, who helped me with family documents on the Reverend Frederick Heuring; Jill Kinkade for aid in taking notes on the journals of Achilles Fretageot; Robert von Lunz, who used his expertise to assist me with Pennsylvania regiments; Bill Corl for information on Alfred Corl, his great-great-grandfather; H. Popowski for first putting together the history of the 25th Indiana for me; the mysterious and effective Hartslog Society, who found and copied many Indiana service records and pension files; Gene Russell, whose love and knowledge of Glenn County, California history and sleuth's instinct opened a gold mine of family knowledge; Peggy Tuck Sinko, professional genealogist and the best possible guide to unlocking Chicago's past; my father's friend, Donald Bateman, who allowed me to copy his great-grandfather's manuscript from his teaching days at Kildare Place in Dublin; Don Pitzer and Don Jantzen for their insights on "intentional" communities; Kristy Armstong White for sharing her unpublished thesis on Union encampments; Terry Johnston, whose doctoral research on the Irish in the Civil War added new insights; Lincoln scholar Allen C. Guelzo for his clarifying comments on Robert Dale Owen and Lincoln. My special thanks go to Lucy Jayne Kamau, anthropologist, generous source on New Harmony history, and entertaining e-mail pal; to Bill Emmick, historian of the 25th Indiana, who willingly swapped stories and research with me; and to Jim Stinson of the Old Rooming House in New Harmony—host, supplier of leads, and friend.

My research trips to Ireland were part love affair, part daunting challenge. I received aid from numerous institutional sources, including the National Library of Ireland, whose Colette O'Flaherty made special microfilm arrangements; the staffs of the Valuations Office of Ireland, the National Archives of Ireland, and Donegal County Library in Letterkenny; Kathleen Gallagher and the staff of Donegal Ancestry in Ramelton; and Fiona Fitzsimons and her assistants at Eneclann Ltd. in Dublin. Other helpful individuals were Valerie Coghlan, Church of Ireland librarian for the College of Education at Rathmines, and genealogist Mairead Gregory, who expanded on my searches in Dublin; Rena Lohan, College Archivist of University College Dublin, who searched in training college records, and John Looby, S. J., who checked on Clongowes Wood College records; Stephen McCarran, who provided information on St. Finian's National School; and Jane Maxwell of the Manuscript Department of the Old Library in Trinity College, who hunted in records and offered research ideas. I will also never forget amazing Sylvia McMullen at the Guild Hall in Londonderry, who pieced the O'Donnells and Mulherns together in fifteen minutes from newly created public cemetery databases, when I'd been puzzling over the connection for years. In addition, I received information from Sinead Devey on the Glen of Glenties and from Godfrey Duffy on the Conyngham Estate lands and from Father John Silke, archivist of the Diocese of Raphoe in County Donegal, who provided ideas both by mail and in person on the education of Irish priests in the nineteenth century. Eamon Harvey offered hospitality, a tour of Drimarone, and insight into Irish education, which he shared in stories and through his thesis in peace studies. My thanks also to James McGroarty for his knowledge of Drimarone and the road to Ardara; to Joe Boyle, who wrote to me about the national school lists for Drumboarty; to Kathleen Espy on Inver Bay for hospitality and assistance in locating Maire Nic Suibhne; and especially to cousins Charley Sweeney, Paddy Sweeney, Ronnie Regan, and Maire Nic Suibhne, who helped fill in the Irish blank spaces and knowledge of the Mulherns.

Johnny Reb and other Civil War forum members such as Keith Young and Brian Swisher often clarified things for me by answering my many questions, and they were only a few of the people who offered help on the Internet. I also received tremendous assistance from the fine family researchers on GenForum and other genealogy sites in piecing together the farflung Given family and their connections. My thanks to Julia M. Case of Missing Links, who helped me cast the net wider for my own missing links; and to other researchers, including Mamie Betterton Carter and Mike Linville for information on Martha Jane Linville, Denis Given's wife; Chris McShane, Linda Redden, and Dan Kelleher for McShane information; KayLeen Munsel, Pat Youngberg, and Tom Murphy for their knowledge of Menomen O'Donnell, and Robert Collins on possible links to Menomen; Robert and Pat Solon Todd and Merril Bourne for help with the McAuliffes; Fred Biddy for the Thrailkill family tree and Neysa Dennis for other Thrailkill information; Mary Cummins on the Thrailkills and Bartons; Charles Dawkins for information on Michael McShane from the pension file of Van Buren Jolley; Cynthia Braun for assistance with the Rippetos; Rose Correa-Young on the Hurley-Given connection; and the Northern California Rootsweb participants. In addition, Kathleen Moran, clerk of court of Colusa County, California, located Margaret Given Williams's descendants; Hattie Gillaspie shared memories of Andrew Williams's nephews; and Marilyn Holzwarth of the Kansas Historical Society helped trace Mary Given Porter's family west.

I reserve a special place for Elaine Doty Dooley, who made the quest for her Doty cousins' Given family relatives her own, and for all my wonderful American cousins with their stories and documents and pictures, particularly Sharon Brandt, Adelaide (Babe) Hogarty Butler, Wanda Given Cusack, Mary Ellen Dudek, Margaret Dunn, Craig Hurley, Karen Given, Ron Given, Wayne Given, Pamela Williams Greer, Gail Van Syoc, Dorothy Given Williams, and Rebecca Given Wilson. I owe particular thanks to my cousin Connie Baker, whose genealogical skills helped me with information on the Thrailkills and Bartons and the California branch of the Given family. My thanks, too, to Frank Price, for his warm enthusiasm about John Given's story even though John isn't the Civil War great-grandfather we share; and to Sigrid Nunez, Christina Ward, and Loretta Barrett for early encouragement (and to Loretta for careful editorial suggestions); of my friends and fellow writers, great thanks to Mary Coolidge Cost, Marianne Herrmann, and Patricia Zontelli for their buoying encouragement, to Paulette Bates Alden and Eileen Hunter for their unwavering support and editorial ideas, and to Janet Holmes for sharing her publishing knowledge; and my gratitude to the team behind Sky Spinner Press, who helped bring this project to fruition, especially Mary Byers, Jeenee Lee, Richard Molby, and Birgitta Nybeck. If I have missed any of the many people who contributed to the research for this book or made its path easier, the oversight is unintentional; you have my sincere appreciation.

Finally, I am beyond grateful to my parents for who they were and to my mother for leaving John Given's letters to me and my father for introducing me to genealogical research; to my daughter, Whitney, for her reader's ear and support in this sometimes quixotic pursuit; and to my son, Adam, for his interest and useful ideas, a place to stay on various research trips, and his accompanying me to sites in the eastern theater. My very special thanks go to my husband, Bob, who was my always welcome companion on so many of the highways and byways of this book.

I will end these acknowledgments with this: the vast majority of the characters, places, and events in *Suite Harmonic* are real, not fictional, but the subtitle of the book—*A Civil War Novel of Rediscovery*—is as true as anything it contains. Starting with John Given's handwritten letters, my first goal was to reconstruct his world with as much fidelity as possible. My second and equal goal was to internalize the facts of that world in order to make the shimmering story implicit in them emerge with all the force of imagined life. To write this book, I needed access to each of the places I traveled as well as the help of all the people who made my quest their own. John Given's story belongs to them, too.